A CENTURY OF
LESBIAN
EROTICA

A CENTURY OF
LESBIAN
EROTICA

Credits continue on page 472

First Edition 1998
First Printing January 1998
ISBN 0-7858-00891-4

Distributed by Castle Books
A Division of Book Sales, Inc.
114 Northfield Avenue
Edison, NJ 08837

Manufactured in the United States of America
Published by Masquerade Books, Inc.
801 Second Avenue
New York, N.Y. 10017

A CENTURY OF LESBIAN EROTICA

BELLA'S SECRET GARDEN
Antonia Paris

One of my favorite things about staying in a hotel is the maid service. I can't tell you how luxurious it is to know that I won't have to pick up after myself, won't be required to fold the towels and place them on the rack when I'm through. But my girlfriend cannot get the hang of hotel life. She actually cleans our room before the maid arrives.

"I don't want her to think we're slobs," she says.

"That's her job," I tell her.

"To think we're slobs?" (An intentional misread. I want to smack her for it.)

"To clean up," I say through clenched teeth.

Amber shrugs, then makes the bed. When she's finished, she writes a note to the maid, places it with a five-dollar bill on the dresser, and gets ready to go. I watch her but don't say anything. There's no point.

When we return from sightseeing, our maid has left us a note of her own. It says, "Thank you very much for the tip. You don't need to make the bed since I change the sheets every day." She's signed it "Bella." I show the note to Amber who announces in her haughtiest tone that she doesn't care. She'll make the bed anyway.

The next day it's raining and we stay in. Part of our vacation is just relaxing, which means we don't have to sightsee each and every day. Part of *my* vacation, that is. Amber takes her camera— in the rain—and leaves. I snooze until the maid knocks on the door. I stumble to the latch and open it. Bella stands in the hall-way. She's a pert and perfectly adorable blonde with short, curly hair and clear blue eyes. She takes one look at me and says, "You're not the one making the bed each day, are you?"

I shake my head and invite her in. Something in my look must let her know what I want, and she obliges. She's easy in my arms, a sweet 115 pounds with a lithe, athletic body. I kiss her mouth, then her freckled cheeks, then nibble on her earlobes. I move her with me into the bathroom and we take a shower together, getting warm and wet and soapy. Laughingly we dry each other off.

We leave the towels in a soggy heap on the floor and make it halfway to the bed before I grab her and throw her down on the plush crimson carpeting that Amber has picked lint off on her hands and knees. I climb on top of Bella in a still-damp sixty-nine. She knows how to use her tongue, probes me expertly with it while stroking my ass and lower back, rubbing in small circles, dragging her nails against my skin.

I follow her lead, running my short nails the length of her inner thighs while keeping my mouth busy on her cunt. I like the way she tastes—clean from the shower, of course, but musky beneath it. Earthy and real and delicious to my taste buds. Her fragrance is rich and heady and entirely unlike the antiseptic flavor of Amber's well-douched vagina. Amber doesn't really like it when we sixty-nine. She can eat me for hours, but she doesn't like me to go down on her.

I lap away at Bella with no thought of what she's doing to my own cunt. I am lost within the walls of her pussy, drinking in each drop of her nectar. Finally I pull away from her, lying flat on the floor between her legs, and concentrate totally on giving her plea sure. She wraps her thighs around me and lets me work, whispering what she wants, how she likes it. "Harder," when she needs it that way. "Faster, ohhh, please, faster." I make spiraling little circles as quickly as I can until she thrusts her hips forward and drenches my lips with the juices of her climax. The taste is pure sweetness.

By the time Amber arrives, Bella and I are on our third beer. Amber doesn't know what to make of the scene, so I tell her. "You're doing Bella's job. Cleaning. Folding. Running around. I invited her to do yours—kick back, relax, and make love."

Amber leaves with her very neatly packed suitcase. Bella and I have another beer, then climb beneath the untucked sheets.

BLOOD AND SILVER
Pat Califia

Once upon a time (and still), there was a young woman named Sylvia Rufina who was very tired of being treated like a little girl. Like most female persons in her predicament, the only avenue of rebellion available was for her to pretend to obey the commandments of others while protecting a secret world within which she was both empress and impresario. Having frequently been told, "Go out and play," more and more, that was what she did. Her family lived in a small farmhouse which felt smaller still because of the vast wilderness which surrounded it. She was at home in this untamed and complex landscape, if only because there was nothing false or sentimental about it.

One of the games she played was "holding still." This was a game learned under confusing and painful circumstances at home. But hidden within a stand of birches or scrub oak, she was not molested. Instead, if she learned to let her thoughts turn green and her breath slow to the pace of sap, she became privy to an endless variety of fascinating things: how beavers felled trees, how mice raised their children, the way a fox twitched its nose when it spotted a vole.

One day, when she was studying the spots on a fawn that dozed in a copse just a few dozen yards from where she held her breath, the wolf appeared. He (for there was no mistaking the meaning of his big face, thick shoulders, and long legs, even if she had not espied his genitals) was an amazing silver color, with dark black at the root of his stippled fur. His teeth were as white as the moon, and his eyes were an intelligent and fearless brown. They studied each other for long minutes, wolf and woman, until he lost interest in her silence and relaxed limbs, and went away.

The next time he came, he walked right up to her and put his nose up, making it clear that he expected a greeting of some sort. So she carefully, slowly, bonelessly lowered her body and allowed him to examine her face and breasts. His breath was very hot, perhaps because it was autumn, and the day was chilly. His fur smelled of earth and the snow that was to come, and the air he expelled was slightly rank, an aroma she finally identified as blood.

Satisfied with her obeisance, he went away again, tail wagging a little, as if he were pleased with himself. This was the only undignified thing she had seen him do, but it did not make her think less of him. She appreciated the fact that the wolf did not caper, bow down, yelp, or slaver on her, in the slavish and inconsiderate way of dogs. The wolf was no whore for man's approval. He fed himself.

She did not see the wolf again for nearly a week. But when he returned, he brought the others: two males and three females, one of them his mate. This female was nearly as large as her man, and dark as he was metallic. Some instinct told Sylvia Rufina that she must greet them on all fours, and then roll over upon her back. This seemed to excite everyone no end. She was nosed a good deal, fairly hard, licked three or four times, and nipped once. The surprisingly painful little bite came from the leader of the pack, who was letting her know it was time to get up and come away with them. It was later in the day than she usually stayed out-of-doors, and as she fled, lights came on in the little house, dimming the prettier lights that came out in the deep black sky.

Racing with the wolves was like a dream, or perhaps it was normal life that was a dream, for the long run with the wolf pack was a flight through sensations that made everything that had happened to her indoors seem drained of color and meaning. She never questioned her ability to keep up with them, any more than she questioned the new shape she seemed to wear. Her legs were tireless; running was a joy. Even hunger was a song in her belly. And when the group cut off and cornered a deer, she knew her place in the attack as if she had read and memorized a part in a play.

After they ate, most of them slept, yawning from the effort it took to digest that much raw red meat. Unaccustomed to so much exercise and the rich diet, she slept also.

And woke up miles from home, alone, in harsh daylight. Every muscle in her body hurt, and her clothing was ripped, her hair full of twigs, leaves, and burrs. Her shoes were gone and her stockings a ruin. Somehow she made her way home, hobbling painfully, trying to think of a story that would excuse her absence without triggering a proscription against hikes in the mountains.

There was no need for an alibi. Her family had already decided what must have happened to her. She had followed a butterfly, or a bluejay, or a white hart, and gotten lost in the woods. When she crossed the threshold and heard inklings of this story, she saw that each of her family members had picked a role, just as the wolves had memorized their dance of death with one another.

And she gave herself up, too exhausted to fight back, letting them exclaim over and handle and hurt her with their stupidity and melodrama. Though a part of her sputtered indignantly, silently: Lost! In the woods! Where I've roamed for three-and-twenty years? I'm more likely to get lost on my way to the privy!

Unfortunately, when she had gone missing, they had called upon the Hunter and asked him to search for her. He was someone she avoided. His barn was covered with the nailed-up, tanning hides of animals and thatched with the antlers of deer he had slain. Sylvia Rufina thought it grotesque. Her father had taught her to recognize certain signals of an unhealthy interest. After having finally grown old enough no longer to be doted upon by him, she could not tolerate a stranger whose appetites felt revoltingly familiar. When the Hunter lit his pipe, waved his hand, and put a stop to the whining voices so glad of their opportunity to rein her in, she gaped at him, hoping against her own judgment that he would have something sensible to say.

He had brought something that would solve the problem. No need to restrict the young woman's love of nature, her little hobbies. No doubt it gave her much pleasure to add new leaves and ferns to her collection. (In fact, she did not have such a collection; but she was aware that many proper young ladies did, and so she bit her tongue, thinking it would make a good excuse for future rambling.) The Hunter shook out a red garment and handed it to her.

It was a scarlet leather cloak with a hood, heavy enough to keep her warm well into winter. The lining was a slippery fabric that made her slightly sick to touch. He had kept hold of the garment as he handed it to her, so their hands touched when she took it from him, and her eyes involuntarily met his. The predatory desire she saw there made her bow her head, as if in modesty, but in fact to hide her rage. Even during a killing strike, the wolves knew nothing as shameful and destructive as the Hunter's desire. She knew, then, that he had bought this red-hooded cloak for her some time ago, and often sat studying it, dreaming of how she would look laid down upon it. If she wore it in the forest, she would be visible for miles. It would be easy for a hunter, this Hunter, to target and track her then.

She was poked and prodded and prompted to say thank you, but would not. Instead she feigned sleep, or a faint. And so she was borne up to bed, feeling the Hunter's scowl following her supine body up the stairs like an oft-refused man on his wedding night.

It was weeks before she was deemed well enough to be let out of the house. The red cloak hung in her closet in the meantime, its shout of color reducing all her other clothes to drab rags. It would snow soon, and she did not think she would survive being stranded behind the pack, in human form, to find her way back home in a winter storm. But she must encounter them again, if only to prove to herself that the entire adventure had not been a fevered dream.

Her chance finally came: a neighbor nobody liked much, a widowed old woman with much knowledge about the right way to do everything, was in bed with a broken leg. This was on the same afternoon that other neighbors, a prosperous married couple, were hosting a dance with an orchestra. People were to come early to an afternoon supper, dance in the evening, and perhaps spend the night. The young woman made up a basket of victuals, picking things she herself was especially fond of because she knew anything she brought would be found unpalatable by the injured woman, and kissed her mothers and her sisters as they went off, consciences relieved, to the dance. She set off in the red cloak and kept the hateful thing on until she had gone over a rise and down the other side and was out of her family's sight.

Then she took off the cloak, bundled it up as small as she could, and put it inside a hollow tree, heartily hoping that birds and squirrels would find it, rip it to shreds, and use it to make their winter nests. At the foot of this tree she sat, snug in the nut-brown cloak she had worn underneath the hunter's gift, and ate every single thing she had packed into the basket. By the time she finished her feast, it was nearly dark. Cheerful beyond measure to be free at last from human society, she went rambling in quest of her soulmates, the four-footed brothers and sisters of the wind.

Faster and faster she went, as her need for them became more desperate, and the world streamed by in a blur of gaudy fall color. The cold air cut her lungs like a knife, and she found herself pressing the little scar the wolf had left on her collarbone, using that pang to keep herself moving forward. The sun plunged below the hills, and she ran on four legs now, chasing hints among the delicious odors that flooded her nose and mouth. At last she found a place where they had been, a trail that led to their present where-abouts, and the reunion was a glad occasion. There was a happy but orderly circle of obeisances and blessings—smelling, licking, and tail-wagging—and favorite sticks and bones were tossed into the air and tugged back and forth.

Then they hunted, and all was right with the world. She was happy to be the least among them, the anchor of their hierarchy. Despite her status as a novice, she knew a thing or two that could be of value to the pack. The crotchety neighbor would never be in pain again, nor have occasion to complain about the disrespect of young folk or the indecency of current ladies' fashions.

But this time, forewarned that dawn would put an end to her four-footed guise, the young woman took precautions. While everyone else turned in the direction of the den, where they could doze, meat-drunk, she bid them farewell with heartbroken nudges of her nose, and retraced her footsteps back to the hollow tree. She slept a little, until dawn forced her to put on the hateful red cloak again and return home. She was lucky this time and arrived well before her hungover, overfed, and overheated relations.

She thought perhaps with what she now knew, she could endure the rest of her life. She would have two lives, one within this cottage, and the other in the rest of the world. Knowing herself to be dangerous, she could perhaps tolerate infantilization. And so she made herself agreeable to her mother and her sisters, helped them divest themselves of their ballroom finery, and put out a cold lunch for them. She herself was not hungry. The smell of cooked meat made her nauseous.

She had not planned to go out again that night. She knew that if her excursions became too frequent, she would risk being discovered missing from her bed. But when the moon came up, it was as if a fever possessed her. She could not stay indoors. But she pined for the soothing sensation of earth beneath clawed toes, the gallop after game, the sweet smell of her pack-mates as they acknowledged her place among them. And so she slipped out, knowing it was unwise. The only concession she made to human notions of decorum was to take the hated red cloak with her.

And that was how he found her, in the full moon, catching her just before she took off the red leather garment. "Quite the little woodsman, aren't you?" he drawled, toying with his knife.

She would not answer him.

"Cat got your tongue? Or is it perhaps a wolf that has it, I wonder? Damn your cold looks. I have something that will melt your ice, you arrogant and unnatural bitch." He took her by the wrist and forced her, struggling, to go with him along the path that led to his house. She could have slipped his grasp if she had taken her wolf form, but something told her she must keep her human wits to deal with what he had to show her.

There was something new nailed up to his barn, a huge pelt that shone in the full moonlight like a well-polished curse. It was the skin of her master, the lord of her nighttime world, the blessed creature whose nip had transformed her into something that could not be contained by human expectations. The Hunter was sneering and gloating, telling her about the murder, how easy she had made it for him to find their den, and he was promising to return and take another wolf's life for every night she refused him. His lewd fantasies about her wolfish activities showed, she thought, considerable ignorance of both wolves and women.

"Refuse you?" she cried, finding her voice at last. "Why, all you had to do was ask me. It never occurred to me that such a clever and handsome man would take an interest in someone as inexperienced and plain as me." Where this nonsense came from, she did not know, but he lifted his hands from his belt to wrap his arms around her, and that was when she yanked his knife from his belt and buried it to the hilt in the middle of his back.

He died astonished, dribbling blood. She thought it was a small enough penance that he made for the many lives he had taken in his manly pride and hatred of the feral. She took back the knife, planning to keep it, and let him fall.

She dragged him back by his heels into his own house. Then she took the hide of her beloved down from the wall, shivering as she did so. It fell into her arms like a lover, and she wept to catch traces of his scent, which lingered still upon his lifeless fur. It was easy to saddle the Hunter's horse, take food and money from his house, and then set fire to what remained. The horse did not like her mounting up with a wolf's skin clasped to her bosom, but with knees and heels she made it mind and turned it toward the city.

Since a human male had taken what was dearest to her, she determined the rest of the Hunter's kind now owed her reparations. She would no longer suffer under a mother's dictates about propriety and virtue. She would no longer keep silence and let a man, too sure of his strength, back her into a corner. The wolves had taught her much about wildness, hunters and prey, power and pursuit. One human or a thousand, she hated them all equally, so she would go where they clustered together, in fear of the forest, and take them for all they were worth.

In the city, the hunter's coins obtained lodging in a once-fashionable quarter of town. Down the street, she had the red cloak made into a whip, cuffs, and a close-fitting hood. For herself, she had fashioned tall red boots and a corset. The next day, she placed an advertisement for riding lessons in the daily newspaper. Soon, a man rang her bell to see if she had anything to teach him. He wore a gray suit instead of the Hunter's doeskin and fur, but he had the same aura of barely controlled fury.

Since he despised the animal within himself, she forced him to manifest it: stripped of anything but his own hide, on all fours, forbidden to utter anything other than a wordless howl. He could not be trusted to govern himself, beast that he was, so she fettered him. And because he believed the animal was inferior to the man, made to be used violently, she beat him the way a drunkard who has lost at cards will beat his own dog. He forgot her injunction against speech when it became clear how the "riding lesson" was to proceed, but she had no mercy. Like most men, he thought a woman a sort of animal, so if he wanted to experience servitude and degradation, he would have to experience sexual violation as well as bondage and the lash. In the end, he proved her judgment of his character was correct—he knelt, swore allegiance to her, and tried to lick her, like a servile mutt who wants a table scrap. She took his money and kicked him out with a warning to avoid attempts to sully her in the future.

Soon her sitting room was occupied by a series of men who arrived full of lust and shame and left poorer but wiser about their own natures. But their pain was no balm for the wounds the Red

Mistress, as she came to be called, carried in her psyche. Her self-styled slaves might prate about worship and call her a goddess, but the only thing they worshipped was their own pleasure. She knew, even as she crushed their balls, that they remained the real masters of the world.

Her consolations were private: the occasional meal of raw meat, and nightly slumber beneath a blanket of silver fur. For one whole year, she tolerated the overcrowding, bad smells, and disgusting, scorched food of the city. Her fame spread, and gossip about her imperious beauty and cruelty brought her paying customers from as far away as other countries. The notion that one could buy a little freedom, pay for only a limited amount of wildness, bored and amused the Red Mistress. But she kept her thoughts to herself and kept her money in an iron-bound chest.

Fortunately, in the spring, a companion came to her. This girl wore the scanty and scandalous garments of a streetwalker, and her tousled blonde hair looked like a wrathful storm. "Men pretend to serve you," she told the Red Mistress. "But I will serve you in truth. In word and in deed."

The Red Mistress was at first angry that someone had breached her solitude. And so she put her suitor to the severest of tests. Rather than imprisoning her with irons or cordage, Sylvia Rufina bade the blonde postulant pick up her own skirts, assume a vulnerable position bent well over, and keep it until she was ordered to rise. With birch, tawse, and cane, she meted out the harshest treatment possible, unwilling to believe the golden one's fealty until it was written in welts upon her body. The severest blows were accepted without a murmur, with no response other than silent weeping. When her rage was vented, Sylvia Rufina made the girl kiss the scarlet proof of her ambition that lingered upon the cane. And the two of them wept together, until they were empty of grief and could feel only the quiet reassurance of the other's presence.

That night, the maid, who had been put to sleep upon the floor, crept into the bed and under the wolf hide that covered the Red Mistress, and made love to her so slowly and carefully that she never fully awoke until her moment of ultimate pleasure.

They became mates, a pack of two, hunter and prey with one another, paired predators with the customers who were prepared to pay extra. With the assistance of her lovely submissive maid, the Red Mistress's income doubled, and by the time another year had gone by, she had enough money to proceed with her plan.

On a day in the autumn, a month or so before the fall of snow was certain, she locked up her house for the last time, leaving everything behind except the trunk full of coins and gems, the maid, and warm clothing for their journey. They went off in a coach, with a large silver fur thrown across their knees, headed toward the mountains, and no one in the city ever saw them again. On the way out of the city, they stopped to take a few things with them: a raven that had been chained to a post in front of an inn; a bear that was caged when it was not dancing, muzzled, for a band of gypsies; a pair of otters that were about to be made into a ladies' fur stole.

Sylvia Rufina had purchased wild and mountainous country, land no sane person would ever have a use for, and so it was very cheap. There was plenty of money left over to mark the boundaries of her territory, warning hunters away.

They gave the horses and carriage away to the last farmstead they found before crossing the boundaries of her land. There would be a cabin there, suitable for primitive living. They walked the last few miles, carrying the things they would need to set up minimal housekeeping for their human selves.

And that night, amid the trees, with a crescent moon to keep their secrets, Sylvia Rufina took the form she had longed for during two impossible years of bondage to human society, and bit the girl she loved, to set her wild (and wise) self free as well.

Then they were off, to meet the ambassadors of their own kind. If you go walking in dark places, you may meet them yourself. If they ask you a question, be sure you tell them the truth. And do not make the mistake of assuming that the wolf is more dangerous than the woman.

STREET FIGHTER
Red Jordan Arobateau

W

oody felt renewed.

Her clock ticked inside its crate; luminescent green sticker proclaiming DYKE POWER! gleamed from a blue wall.

Woody trudged down the long narrow hall to the toilet; when she returned, stepped quietly on stocking feet to the mattress; stared down at the girl. She's naked, knees apart, big tits, pink nipples hard; face smiles up at Woody.

Anticipation of the sex she was going to have with her. The butch stood strong. Could see the need in Marcy, too.

Knelt down, and Marcy closed her eyes. Stroked her butch hands over Marcy's milky shoulders. The girl opens her eyes, now sees Woody's eyes are closed; & she returns the caress.

To get herself horny, Woody used the fantasy that the girl was a stranger. Woody looked at her with contempt. "All you are is a bitch to be fucked."

And Marcy enjoyed it that way.

"I'm only a slut. My only desire is to please you."

"You're a slut to put it into. My slut."

Woody smelled Marcy's sweet body perfume left from the night at the club, and their morning of amorous heat & cum.

"Open it up, bitch, and put it on." Woody growls painfully thru her mouth, and tosses her a condom.

Then Marcy got an eyeful. Woody's cock, unwrapped from the towel, 9". Thick. It pulsated as the butch strapped it on using a black leather harness over her lean hips. The femme tore the condom packet open with her teeth. It smelled like a balloon.

When the butch took her woman that night, she did it with the pride of ownership. Marcy was hers for the remainder of the evening, if never again. She fucked her with authority.

Marcy's cunt was sore from being well-fucked by fingers and being fisted hours ago; yet Marcy's clit felt rushes of urgent lust. Her pussy opened up inside, wanting more pleasure.

As Woody knelt on the mattress, big dick bobbing in front of her thighs, she talks. "Let me fill you and give you all you need tonight."

"Oh, yes, baby!" Marcy hisses with a sharp intake of air. Lay back on the mattress and spread her legs.

Woody fantasized she was a man with a dick ramming it in her. "You want my dick in your cunt?"

"Oh, yes, honey, please!" Marcy encircled her slim hips and pulled Woody down into her. The butch held the lifelike dick expertly, stroking its tip over Marcy's swollen clit, up and down in the pink flower of her sopping pussylips. Her pubic hair was wet and soft on her cunt. Woody pushed the tip into her hole. Hard, the cock sank down into the woman easy—she was wet, ready & big. Hungry for love.

Woody began to drive it into her.

"You like my dick, baby?" They began the rough ride. "You like my dick in you?" Fucking her with hard, short thrusts, in rapid fire, which went on for a long time.

Sweat pours off Woody's shoulders. The she pulls out, sits back on her heels, kneeling, and commands: "Turn over, slut."

Obedient, Marcy rolls over. Her white body lies on its stomach a moment, glistening with a film of sweat. Then she rises up on all fours, head bowed, to receive the tool in her cunt from the rear.

Woody jams it in, and pulls almost out, then pushes in deep; her thighs smacking against Marcy's buttocks. With a frantic motion of one hand, Marcy masturbates her clit while Woody's fucking her. "OHH! BABY! OHH!" Marcy moans in uneven tones as her body jolts up and down with each of Woody's cock thrusts.

The butch's clit is hard in her swollen cunt & ready. Firmly, she turns Marcy over on her back to finish.

Marcy holds herself open for Woody to drive it into her. Orgasm is cumming. Moves hips and body in rhythmical motion. Soon it will lead to fireworks.

Woody's on top; bruised arms hold herself up on the mattress, hips going bam bam bam, filling her woman with cock. The cock's base has worked her clit almost to climax; she grinds in deep, going up and down. "Oh, baby, oohhhh!..." The mattress bumps against the floor as the two women rut in ecstatic heat.

Marcy receives Woody's hot lust of lightning thrusts that make her vagina muscles contract and lubricate still more. Still wetter. Arms hug Woody tight. "Oh, God! OH! OH! OH!"

"OH, YEAH! AHHHHHHHHHHHH!" They orgasm together, seconds going on and on and on into a minute of pure delightful ecstatic fire.

Lay in each other's arms.

In a while, time's passage counted off by the clock inside a red crate, Woody says, stern, "Suck my cock, slut!"

Marcy obeys. Woody stands up, bare feet planted on the mattress on either side of Marcy, who kneels between her legs. 'Shit, I might not be able to make it again,' Woody doubts, privately. But as Marcy carefully slides her fingertips under the leather harness to rub Woody's hot, distended clit & over, and with the other hand holds Woody's cock firmly so she can place her mouth over the tip, the sight was so erotic that Woody feels lust power shoot up thru her clit into the erogenous reaches of her body.

Marcy's lips go up and down the cockshaft. Swallowing, then withdrawing. The condom is slick, transparent, and glistens with Marcy's own pussyjuice and spit. Her fingers work under the harness in rhythm that builds the fires of cum. She licks with her tongue and sucks deep. As she kneels there working, Marcy opens her eyes to observe the expression on the butch's face. She's in seventh heaven. Ecstasy. Felt Woody's lean hips thrust up to meet her face, steady, then faster, faster, then losing control until she's thrusting involuntarily. And the butch's own eyes flicker open, gaze down to watch; mind in a fantasy that she's a man with a big cock, as this slut sucks it off. Red fingernails—three of them cut short—rub over her clit, over & over. Hot and powerful, Woody thrusts her hips fast, devouring with her total body the freakish sight of the slut doing this for her. Every so often, their gazes meet. Marcy looks up into the butch's brown eyes filled with under-standing, & an impish delight; then her head bends back down to her work, lips around the cockshaft, pushing into her mouth again, while her small fingers strum Woody's clit like an instrument.

"Suck my cock, woman!" Woody hollers. Her hips thrust up. Her body twists from left to right, up and down losing herself in orgasm. "OHHHHHHHHHHH!"

Maybe that's what Marcy wanted to see, her butch weakening and cumming.... It was worth the effort.

It had been cold, no emotions. Just sex.

Now, liquid brown eyes, and warm blue eyes fluttered open. They lay in each other's embrace.

"You're so good, Marcy."

Full of each other's cum & saliva.

They spent that night & the rest of the weekend together in bed. The fleeting promise of a Sunday job that the butch had wanted so bad earlier that week was now forgotten & she didn't call.

The two women did everything. Finger-fuck, fist, dildos—put her rod into her long and hard. And talk. And Marcy informs Woody she'd be happy for the day a butch would play a role reversal. When a butch would tire of venting her passion in a masculine way—when she had had her fill of taking her woman as a butch does; and would roll over on her back & let Marcy strap it on and take her turn and do it to her.

"Just once in a blue moon, honey!"

All day and all night they made love.

They were full of Chinese food. Woody hungrily devoured the noodles, meat and vegetables in the remaining cartons. Felt she'd eaten the best meal in her life.

Marcy lay back on the mattress, stares at the ceiling while she listens to the butch ramble on and on about her life. '…As far as I'm concerned, she's passed the exam. She likes me for her girl— a femme—a lady and not another butch.

'She can fuck.

'She's got a job & don't mind working & expects to work steady on thru the rest of her life, like a good workhorse, and not try to be lazy and live off her woman!

'She's sincere.

'She is respectful; yet, when we play, is an erotic, nasty master who can treat me like a slut.

'Yes, she can fuck.'

* * *

Marcy lay in one of Woody's plaid shirts and the rest nude. Black curly hair of her pubic mound visible, pretty, underneath. Had, in secret, reapplied her makeup to look beautiful even tho they were still in bed.

'She don't want to run off to Europe somewhere and leave her lover without a boyfriend—Woody made that quite clear. And she don't seem popular enough to worry about other femmes stealing her away from me. She don't have another woman, or kids. And she's completely straight—gay.'

Woody was EZ. Just let her talk and pretend to listen, interject a few words of encouragement when the conversation grows thin.... She is talking now. Listen!

"I was hurting all the time. These girls. These porno photos where I lived downtown. You see naked girls' pictures, and it drives me wild. And it's all for some man."

"You got a girl now," Marcy says quietly.

CHEATING TIME
Jasmine Hall

When Sheryl cheated on me, I thought I could forgive her and forget about it. I thought I was a bigger person than I turned out to be. I didn't mean to get even—didn't know I was considering it. But I guess Sheryl knew. I guess she knew me better than I knew myself.

Lauren and I were assigned to work together on a project, a major ad campaign our company had recently landed. It was mandatory for us to spend a huge amount of time together. Working, you know. Late nights. Early mornings. A few overnighters. A few weekends. We ended up crashing at the office, knowing we'd have to get up and work in a few hours anyway. It was meant only to be a time-saver.

But one of the mornings when I woke up on my leather sofa in the office, I found Lauren curled in my arms. And I knew it was going to happen. I guess I could have stopped it then. That's what an outsider might say. But an outsider can't see it from my perspective: her chestnut-brown hair spread over me. Her peaceful, lovely face relaxed in sleep. I pulled her closer and shut my eyes, joining her in dreamland, deciding then and there that we would make love…and soon.

What I didn't expect was how soon. Or how soon we'd be caught. Sheryl must have sensed it in my behavior before I did. Maybe her own guilty conscience recognized mine. She hired a private eye immediately, a woman so good at her job that she caught us on film the very first time. Lauren splayed out on my drawing table, her cunt held open with two of those heavy-duty clips used for capturing sheaves of paper, her nipples pinched between clothespins I'd snagged from the film-developing room. I'd tied her wrists with her own hair ribbons, turning her into a present I couldn't wait to unwrap. She was beautiful bound up, exactly as I'd fantasized. Exactly as I'd known she'd be. Willing, humble, subservient. I paddled her ass gently with a wooden ruler I'd had in my top desk drawer for ages, punished the backs of her thighs playfully with a thin cardboard mailing tube that made a delicious smacking sound when it connected with her naked skin.

The pictures came out well. I'm sure Sheryl got wet looking at them before confronting me with the evidence of my sins. The photos were black-and-white glossies of Lauren's face contorted in agony and ecstasy. Pictures of her striped ass, her parted thighs marked with the legal lines of my ruler. The images of me were all in motion, my hand pulled back to spank that gorgeous ass, my hips rotating as I thrust my cock into her willing mouth.

Those pictures are framed now, hanging in our bedroom. Lauren's bedroom and mine. I don't feel as bad about cheating as I thought I would. In fact, I feel satisfied. I only hope Sheryl has her own copies to look at during her long, lonely nights.

And I hope they make her happy.

DARK ROOM
Alison Tyler

The four days went by slowly, achingly. Four days, hours blurring with hours, minutes with minutes. I did very little work. I ate very little food. I walked as slowly as always, though now I found myself pacing back and forth through my living room. I even had a nifty little route: to the coffee table, around to the left, by the rocking chair, to the sofa, and then a quick turn and back again. As I was walking, I spoke to myself, saying, among other things, this: "I do not pace."

I am in control of all things in my world. But not Kate. Not yet. Perhaps that was my problem, I decided, reaching for it. Perhaps I needed to own her, to control her, to pin her down, to take her picture. Maybe then I would find peace. Or maybe I was no longer allowed peace. Maybe I had moved on to the next stage...whatever that might be.

On Wednesday night, I dressed meticulously, choosing from my two-toned wardrobe with extra care. I wore a long straight black skirt, black silk turtleneck, and high laced boots. I swept my hair back and pinned it with a tortoiseshell barrette. I stared at my reflection without recognition, concerned only with how she would see me. I wondered whether I had read her correctly—I was sure that I had—and then I wondered whether I would suit her needs as perfectly as I sensed that she suited mine.

It had been a while since I'd last been in a serious relationship. I hadn't given up, per se, but I had stopped looking actively. Still, I knew the routine—you never forget the basics—and I set out a bottle of Bordeaux, two glasses, and a bowl of fruit. I did this for custom's sake—not because I thought there was actually a chance we would eat. Unless I fed her. Then I paced some more, and I waited.

At five to eleven, the doorbell rang. Very prompt, I noted, pleased, giving her mental bonus points. I buzzed her up, and she arrived, instant color in my monochrome world. Her cheeks were flushed with a fever-blush, her eyes glowed dark and hot and liquid. Her mouth was full and ready to be bitten. She was a meal to a vampire. She was a human to my alien-coldness. She was touchable and bitable and spankable and she responded in excess to each of these. When I stroked her tangled curls away from her forehead, she sighed and leaned back, regarding me with a hungry look under half-closed lids. When I pulled her toward me, biting hard on her bottom lip, she moaned aloud and snuggled forward, wanting more. And when I grabbed her by the wrist and dragged her down the hall, hissing to her how she would be punished for knocking my world on its side, she went easily, complacently, and ultimately was bound without a word of protest.

"I have thought about you over the past few days." I pulled her into my room and then closed the door behind us. "Did you bring your recorder?"

She nodded, her eyes opened wide, showing me both fright and anticipation.

"Give it to me." I extended my hand and then waited while she dug nervously through her satchel until she found the tiny tape recorder and handed it over.

"Now strip."

She stared, for one beat too long, and I set down the recorder on my antique dresser and reached for her velvet jacket. "I said, 'Strip.' I warned you in the gallery. You knew this would be expected of you."

And she nodded, eyes still wide as I tore off her black jacket, unbuttoned her dress, and ripped it roughly over her head. "Yes," she said, more of a sigh than actual words. "Yes, I knew...." Now she was standing before me in a satin bra, garter belt, panties, stockings, and boots. "I knew, but I didn't believe."

"Strip," I said again, giving her one last chance.

Eyes on mine, she unhooked the bra, removed it, and folded it neatly. She lay it on the top of the wood dresser, and I noted her hands shaking as she set it down. She took her boots off next and placed them side by side on the floor by the bed. Just as carefully, she unfastened her stockings from her garter belt and slipped them off, rolling them tightly and placing them with her bra. The black satin garter belt came next, her matching panties last.

I stood back and inspected her. Beautiful. I had known she'd be lovely beneath the costume of her clothes, but I hadn't known that she was perfect. I motioned for her to turn around, and she did, gracefully, pivoting before me as if she were on a moving pedestal. My princess. My goddess.

"Oh!" I sighed. "You are exquisite. You will let me photograph you, won't you?" (Last chance to turn back. Last chance to flee.)

"Yes." She was faced away from me, and I came up close behind her, lifting those silky curls up from the nape of her neck and bringing my lips in close. I kissed her gently at first, and then nipped at the tender skin there, making her start forward. She caught herself quickly, holding still while I brought my mouth down her spine, kissing her, tickling her with the tip of my tongue, stopping only when I reached the dimples above her ass. Now I went on my knees and began a more thorough inspection, telling her first that I wanted her to watch in the mirror, to keep her eyes opened and watch her own face while I probed her.

"Yes…" she said, a whisper. "Yes, anything you say."

Anything. I liked that.

She was slender, my Kate, with her fine-boned body; long-limbed and athletic, agile as a gymnast. She had a gentle waist, subtle curves at her hips, and a firm, round ass. I parted her asscheeks and tickled her between them, moving my tongue in and out of her puckering hole, teasing her, taunting. I squeezed the globes of her ass while I tickled her, letting her grow accustomed to the feel of my touch. Then, still on my knees, I lowered my head and darted my tongue in between those sloping thighs, lapping at the juices that waited for me, glistening dewdrops of nectar.

"Good girl," I told her, my voice lost against the pure skin of her thighs. "Good girl for standing so still." She was frozen, holding herself carefully, reigning in that wildly beating heart. I could feel her pulse in her cunt, that throbbing staccato beat, and I loved her for it. I knew just from the taste of her what she would look like when she came. Unleashed, ragged, sparkling. I knew. I could visualize it in my head, developing slowly as if it were one of my pictures. Kate, with her body curved in one long arch, fists clenched, teeth biting into her lower lip, hands wrapped in my hair, screaming, screaming, screaming.

I knew, and I knew that I would make that vision happen soon. But not yet.

"On the bed, young lady," I told her, liking the depth in my voice, the frosty quality. Just having her in my grasp had restored my power. "On the bed, on your stomach, hands over your head."

She followed my order instantly, and I stood back and watched, liking the subtle tremble of her body, the slight shudder from fear. Good, I thought. She *should* be afraid, and the fact that she knew enough to fear me let me know I wasn't working with a novice, a virgin. I love to teach, but I like to know that my playthings are at least experienced enough to understand the ground rules, the basics.

"Safe word?" I asked, moving close enough to her that she could feel my breath on her skin. "Tell me now."

"Sin," she said, her voice soft, her eyes shut. "Sin."

I nodded—of course, it suited her—then reached for her tape recorder and pressed the "record" and "play" buttons together to turn it on. I set the machine on the table by my bed and then picked up my cuffs.

"I told you that I'd grant you an interview if you showed up. So you may start asking me questions."

While she was still processing the information, I slid the fur-lined leather cuffs on her wrists and buckled them tightly, fastening them to the hook over my bed. Then just as carefully, I tied her ankles with silk ribbons and bound them firmly to the wood posts at the foot of my bed.

"I..." Her face was flushed. She did not know how to be professional in this position.

"It's the only chance you'll have," I told her. "This is a one-time interview—I will not grant you a second."

"How long have you been taking pictures?" It came out in a rush. Her voice was still low, but she seemed more focused. Until I brought out my crop and lay it inches away from her face on the pillow.

"Since I was eight." I removed the lens cap from my favorite camera and moved around her on the bed.

"Who gave you your first camera?"

"My father."

There was a pause while she bit her lip, worrying it between her teeth as I set the flash on my camera and prepared for the first shot.

"When did you sell your first picture?"

"In high school."

I moved in tight on her face and shot. She swallowed hard, forcing her eyes to stay open, though they desperately wanted to shut from the bright flash of light. She was seeing blue spots dancing in front of her. I knew it, and I was gratified to see her fight the desire to close her eyes.

She trembled slightly, working to get her mouth to formulate the words.

"What was it a picture of?"

I rolled back the film, stood a few feet away from her, and shot again.

"A woman," I told her, tilting my head to see what was wrong with the picture, then coming close to her and lifting her hair away from her face. Her cheeks were warm, her eyes on fire.

"A woman I knew, a neighbor. She was getting married, and I took a picture of her in her wedding gown. I sold it to a brides' magazine that spring. I think it was because of the way she had her hair, all pinned up with a few tendrils falling loose, wild violets woven throughout her curls. It was a fluke, I suppose, but it was my first professional clip."

Now I came in again, framing her beautiful heart-shaped face as tightly as I could, and I whispered, this time under my breath: "You're perfect, do you know that? Tied to my bed. You are a masterpiece." And then, with her eyes glowing at me, I took the picture. That would be worth keeping—I could feel it. That would be worth framing.

Setting down the camera for a moment and lifting the crop, I began to talk, filling in the answers to questions she had not yet thought to ask.

"I've taken pictures of nudes only for a few years. I choose women alone, often bound like you, and I sell to the top magazines. The art 'zines, not the smut, men's rags. I like women bound because their eyes change. I'm sure you know this. I'm sure you understand. You can quote me on this; I don't mind. And although photographing is like foreplay for me, I never shoot long-term lovers. Nor friends. Only models. I am making an exception this once. Just this once."

I slapped the crop against my open palm and watched her body tense. Then, liking the new attitude that inhabited her frightened figure, I exchanged the crop for the camera.

There was a silence while I moved in closer, focusing, aiming, choosing to replicate her image, the double image in the mirror above my bed. I have an expensive antique mirror in a carved wooden frame, one that I would not have above my bed if I lived on the West Coast—for fear of earthquakes. But in New York, where only the subway rumbles, it's safe enough. And I kept it there, liking the many advantages it gave me as a photographer. I kept it there until Kate died, and then I replaced it with the solitary image of her headstone.

I continued: "I film nudes because I usurp their power with my lens. How do you feel, Kate? Do you feel powerful in that position?"

There was a moment of silence while she contemplated her answer, realizing somewhere deep inside herself that at some point she would be playing back this tape—even if she were the only audience ever to hear it—and that she would have to reconcile herself with the answer she gave me. She would have to steel herself for the words she spoke. Both she and I knew that they would be true. When bound, so helpless, to a stranger's bed, most people find it very difficult to lie. Test yourself if you dare. You may discover the same phenomenon. How can you possibly sink any lower? How can you possibly sully the scenario by not telling the truth?

Kate thought about it, and I could tell that she was weighing her words by the way her forehead wrinkled. Then she said: "No. You have all the power, don't you?"

I laughed darkly, setting my camera on the table next to her tape recorder and positioning myself on the bed at her side. Slowly I stroked her alabaster skin, noting the absence of tan lines, the fine quality of her beautiful covering. I could suddenly foretell the future, knowing that I would weave a tapestry on that pure skin. I would decorate her with lines and welts, with bruises, with fingerprints, with bite marks. I would paint her with pain. I laughed and said: "Wrong answer, Kate. You have all the power. One word from your lips, and the games end. Don't you realize that? You are calling all the shots."

More silence.

"All the power, my darling. I am simply acting out a role that you wish to have played. I am speaking words that you long to hear. I am giving you things that you think about at night, that you concoct in your fantasy realm. You are the scriptwriter. I am merely an actor in your play."

If you live in this world, you'll understand what I meant. If you play by these rules, you'll understand my words to be true. Because it's scarier for submissives when they realize that they do have a choice. It's easy to give into a dominant, to say, "Okay. I have no say in the matter. Do with me what you will." But when you admit to yourself that there is a finish line in sight, a way out —that there is a light at the end of the tunnel—then you also have to admit that you are choosing to submit. You are choosing to be bound and tied.

Giving over your power is a frightening thing. It means the end of all decisions. Or, to be more precise, it means the beginning of the end.

"Do you understand me?" I asked, standing so close to her, still stroking her skin, testing the response when I pressed my fingers firmly—visualizing the sculptures of Michelangelo, the way the fingers of his subjects left indentations pressed deeply into the marble skin of those they embraced. What a master he was at working with marble. Would that I were that masterful with my camera, with my bare hand, with my belt. I do not dare compare myself to someone so skilled. Not yet.

"Yes," she finally said, her voice almost lost in the stillness of my bedroom. "Yes, I understand." Another pause. "But I don't agree."

The crop came up into my hands then, like a magician's trick, and before she could tense, before she could process what was going to happen to her, I brought it down hard on the slope between her ass and her thighs.

"Now," I said, ignoring the harsh dry sob that had escaped from her lips. "Now," I repeated. "If you want me to stop, you only have to tell me your safe word. You only have to whisper the word 'sin' and I will let you up. Then you will be free to go. I won't see you again—ever—but it will have been your choice. You have the power. You can unlock those handcuffs without the use of a key." A laugh. I knew that she wouldn't leave. "How powerful is that?"

She blinked her soft doe eyes at me, trying to focus, still concentrating solely on the pain.

"I don't want to get free." The hurt in her voice was transparent. "I don't want to," she repeated when she could formulate the words. "I don't want you to untie me."

"No." I shook my head. "Of course you don't. But you do understand that it is your choice. That you hold the power. You understand that better now, don't you?"

This may be the hardest thing for a true submissive to admit. It is almost the equivalent of the religiously fervent who flog themselves. How much control does it take to be able to hit yourself hard enough to hurt? Not pulling back at the last moment, but following through.

"Yes," she finally said, nodding slightly, her breathing ragged, near tears not from the pain, but from the image of herself I was forcing her to confront. "Yes, I understand."

"Good." Now to explain the rest. "At some point, we will go beyond this. My favorite part of any relationship is the power structure, the slip-slide, up-down of it all. And someday, Kate, you will lose your power. I know that is what you long for, the day when I will take it all away and leave you, broken and sobbing, finally at peace. It's what we are all hoping for, isn't it? Peace. You will not be able to comprehend this all now. I know that. I understand. But at some point, you will look up at me from a similar position in my bed, but you won't be tied, and you will take everything I have to dish out without any bindings but those in your own heart to hold you in place. And then, humbly, you will ask for more. And there will be no more 'sin' to free you. I know that you don't get it now, Kate, but before we are through, you will give me your safe word."

I was telling her too much to comprehend all at once, especially with that one lone line of pain coloring the crescent under her asscheeks. I was telling her too much, but to be true to myself I had to spell it out for her. I had to be as clear as possible. She would remember it later. She might not thank me for it. She might even curse me for it. But she would remember it.

I continued to stare at the welt I'd given her. I liked the look of it there, and I picked up my camera and shot from behind her, catching the rise of her ass, the line of the blow, the curls flowing past her shoulders. I wouldn't be able to sell it to the good magazines, not unless any of them did a feature on SM…it was a bit too hard-core, but I liked it anyway, and I took another, then grabbed the crop again and moved forward, ready to go to work.

"You have the power," I hissed at her. "Remember that."

A nod.

I slapped her for it.

"Yes, I will."

I didn't expect to hear the word "sin" from her that night. And I didn't. A good Top knows the limits of a submissive, even from the first time, from the first encounter. One knows. One knows. One knows. I can't emphasize this enough. The rhythm of the breathing, the way the muscles tense. It's like being a good doctor or a palm reader or in any profession in which deciphering signals comes into play.

There are louder cries in the wire-line of a muscle, louder screams in the way a submissive tosses her hair, louder sighs in a fist clenching and unclenching than in any scream.

I used the crop on the backs of her thighs, only down to her knees, in case she wanted to wear short skirts. I let her cry—I could tell that she needed to—but I did not make her sob. There is a difference, and it is not a subtle one. Sobbing is wrenching, uncontrollable. Crying is close to the surface. I'll let you guess which one I prefer. But at the start, I am always gentle on my submissives. I might have worked Kate a little hard that night— a little harder than usual—but I knew that in order to keep her, I had to surpass anything she'd experienced previously. I wanted to win her over from the first time, and I did.

I demolished her. You can bank on that. I whipped her steadily, without a break, without a moment to let the pain sink in com- pletely. She cruised on the pain, riding the waves of it, without comprehending each individual blow. I wanted her to feel it for days. I wanted her to feel it when she sat at her desk and transcribed the interview. I wanted her to think of me, and miss me, and hope that I would truly fulfill all I promised.

I wasn't really concerned, of course. I had years of experience on her. And I will tell you this: when I want something, I get it. Always. When I want a particular shot, I get it. When I've wanted a woman in the past, I have never failed to own her.

I want Kate now, and I am having a fucking difficult time comprehending the fact that I can't have her.

Hades had Persephone six months out of the year.

Cupid and Psyche were reunited.

Prince Charming brought Snow White back to life with a kiss.

Why can't I make a deal with the gods? I am willing. I am so willing. My soul is here; my heart is ready. Take what you will, but leave me Kate.

FIRST TIME
Lizbeth Dusseau

B y the Tuesday following my ravaging, I was again a bundle of fear, caught in a dilemma I had no way to solve, at least to my mind. The instruction to seduce and make love to Joanna reached far beyond the simple conversations about the club we'd had. For those, Joanna remained an uninvolved observer. This new instruction, while it touched my lust for female flesh, was still beyond the concept I had of my sexuality, not to mention its threat to that sweet friendship I had with Joanna.

Even so, Tuesday's fear led to a trembling dinner invitation to Joanna. As we were leaving the office, I suggested we have dinner together. She turned the invitation around and asked me to her house instead, saying she had lots of food in the fridge and a burning need to cook. I willingly consented to be at her house at seven, and all too soon I found myself on her doorstep with my heart in my throat. When she invited me, little did she know what I had in mind.

While she continued to prepare dinner, I walked about her newly redecorated townhouse. It was quite different than I remembered it, in black and white, with black lacquered furniture and two white overstuffed sofas. A splash of red stood out from the stark paintings on the wall. For all its seemingly bold, cool style, there was still a soft warmth from the art deco lamps that glowed on either side of the living room. I drank in the simple beauty that, like Joanna, was softly sensuous. And like her steady and certain manner, the room calmed my fears of what might happen later.

After a luscious salad and homemade bread and a bottle of wine, I still had no idea how to begin my seduction. I was afraid I'd be going home without completing the instructions—there seemed no way to bridge the space of sexual convention that kept us "straight."

But I had to try. I wanted to try.

We sat together on her couch. I hugged a pillow in my lap, she casually sipped her wine, innocent of the instructions that consumed my mind. She was wearing jeans that looked as if they were painted on, they were so tight. I could see them rise in her crotch, defining her cunt beneath. On top she wore a cream-colored sweater, knit with a loose weave that showed her black bra underneath. The neckline was so broad that the sweater fell off one shoulder at an angle, and as she moved, it dipped lower and lower, so I found myself staring as her black-laced tit came into view. Her body invited me with every move she made, with each subtle, seductive gesture.

I sipped my wine, hoping it would give me more courage, then spoke. "Joanna," I said carefully, "do you ever fantasize about women?" I paused. "I mean, sexually?"

She looked at me calmly, not at all surprised, as if it were just another question. "Yes," she answered with a hint of interest in her voice.

"I do, too, more often than I'd like," I admitted.

"What do you mean, 'more often'?"

"Oh, sometimes I wonder if I wouldn't prefer women to men...sometimes," I added.

"Well I definitely prefer women to men on occasion. There is a tremendous difference."

"You mean, you've made love to a woman?" I asked, astonished.

She smiled warmly. "Yes, I have." Her voice, like a sultry breeze, caressed the air around us.

I felt like something was altering in me. The knowledge of that fact was like sudden inspiration, made me view her differently, gave my task that night a different meaning. More than anything, it took the instructions out of fantasy, into the realm of possibility. My loins and heart pounded simultaneously as I continued to gaze intently at her sensuous form.

"Have you had more than one?" I asked, hoping I would not tread too deeply, but I was terribly curious.

"I've had many women over the past four years, some just once, others have been lovers between my affairs with men."

She sat there calmly revealing a fact that seemed so easy for her to tell about herself. Obviously she was quite at peace with the varied sex life she'd chosen. It answered questions about her occasional aloofness, her vague answers to casual inquiries about her time away from work. It told me much about her reluctance to talk about her "friends." I should not have been surprised by the truth.

"You know since our vacation in Florida, I look at you sometimes with the strangest feelings inside," I admitted.

"You mean lust?" she probed gently, as if she were controlling the conversation, not me. "Is it really different than your feelings for men?"

Until she asked, I'd not allowed myself to think about it that way. It had a different guise than lust for men, a gentler feeling, but it was sexual lust the same.

"This is so hard for me to take in!" I exclaimed. I squirmed in my seat, not sure where to go with the conversation that, to my delight and fear had landed me in the center of my assigned task.

But Joanna accommodated me further by moving the subject forward. "You must have brought it up for a reason," she said. Curiosity was written all over her face.

I could never let her know the reason why. The club must not be mentioned. "I guess the drink has made me bold. I've been haunted by it for months." That was quite true. And strangely, it seemed once again the club knew just what was in my mind; it had climbed deep down and caught a truth that I had been afraid of recognizing.

"You remember what I said before?" she reminded me. "If it excites you, why not?" There was an enchanting gleam in her eyes. "You could pretend it excites you and see what happens."

I'd lusted after her all night, as I had on so many occasions. But, in a new light, I viewed her as an object to fondle and touch and kiss and excite to orgasm. Letting myself set free those thoughts, I saw her as the one I wanted to take to bed with me that night. Everything about her, her dress and manner, was inviting me, and now, with her own words, the invitation lay before me waiting for my acceptance. I wondered who was seducing whom?

My body begged for me to reach out to touch her. All the desire for her I'd suppressed was surfacing: the days in Florida, the time in the dressing room, and the many times before and since when I'd been fascinated by her exquisite female treasures and had relished her attentions to mine.

The wine acted like a tonic to remove my inhibitions and I reached for her thigh, which was just inches from me. My hand felt the smoothness of her leg beneath the denim, and it slowly followed the tender line from the knee to her thighs.

I was on my knees between her legs before I realized what I was doing. My hands stroked her legs, though I wanted her flesh, not the jeans that clothed it. Sensing this, Joanna responded and unbuttoned the fly so she could pull the jeans off her hips. I took them the rest of the way off and threw them aside, my lust set on the naked flesh before me.

Her skin was so soft to my touch, smooth and tender, I could have caressed it for hours. But I couldn't stop with just the touch. I began to kiss her between her legs, my lips fondling her skin just as my hands were. I began at mid-thigh and then, moving slowly, I made my way to the patch of hair between her legs.

But I stopped short, not yet ready for the moist skin and the soft hair of that place. I moved higher, to her belly, where I carefully pulled up the sweater that separated me from her luscious breasts. She looked down at me with a blissful smile.

Not once did she balk. Instead, her hands reached down and clutched my shoulders, bringing my lips to the two twin tits that faced me. I pushed away the delicate lace to view the more delicate skin, soft as any skin I'd ever touched. I kissed them; they were deliciously warm. My mouth opened on them as they would a cock, although smaller than the male organ. I darted easily between them, planting little kisses and pecks all over them. Burying my face between them, I couldn't kiss them enough.

She lay back as I continued. She gasped. Her hips, like mine so often did, pushed up at me. I wanted to feel her pussy against my naked flesh, so I pulled off my sweater and the bra beneath and let my undulating breasts fall out against the soft hair at her crotch. My hands massaged her tits with endless interest as I continued to move upward with my kisses.

Her lips seemed tiny in comparison to male lips, small and

delicate. I showered them with little kisses and she kissed me back, our mouths and tongues open and playing with each other, exploring the places inside that ignited our loins below.

My lust for her body was like nothing I could remember; all my held-back desires flowed into her and she welcomed them with a smile of peace and supreme delight and mounting urgency that begged me to continue.

As my lips played with her soft mouth, my hands moved between her legs. I had never done this to another woman, but my instincts, my vast experience with my own body guided me to the moist flesh and the sensitive points that responded savagely to any touch. She jerked as I toyed with her, and I relished the way she responded to my play. I finally moved my head back down between her pulsing thighs and let my tongue enjoy the sweetness that my hands had known.

Like a piece of luscious chocolate, she was sweet. But more than that she was hot! She smelled fresh at her thighs and musty in the wet spots. I licked with an instinctive artistry, lapping at her clit and the folds to each side with earnest attention and a growing fierceness that responded to her small cries. I stayed there with my mouth fully attending her sex, knowing her orgasm was close.

Two fingers poked her vagina, and with a rapid motion, pumped in and out of that hole. I felt even lower for the deep cleft that hid her anus and planted one finger against that hole, too. She bucked hard against my fingers and I moved with her rhythmically.

"Oooh...ahhhhh!" she gasped. She jerked and jerked again, stretching back as far as she could and tightening firmly against my hands. I continued to massage all those fine places with my fingers and mouth so her pleasure would continue on and on and on.

She went limp when it was over, but she didn't want me to leave. She reached down and caressed my hair, the energy that flowed through her fingers arousing my body, the forbidden desires seeming the most natural thing in the world.

Moving off the sofa, Joanna pulled me from the floor and helped me to the soft cushions where she could have full access to my pulsing body. I was ready for anything she wanted to give me.

She kneeled by my side and began with my lips, kissing them tenderly. Then, removing the rest of my clothes, she proceeded rapidly to knead and prod at every place my body desired touch. She knew every hot spot, like I'd known hers.

Her hands and mouth devoured my tits. They were larger than hers, and she dove into them with relishing zeal. She pushed them together and pinched the hardening nipples, then delicately tongued the buds until they stood out like bright cherries from the surrounding flesh. She gave them little stinging slaps that sent my fire shooting unmercifully through me. She slapped them harder, and I could see redness rising on the flesh. I jerked my hips against the couch and begged for more.

And when I could hardly stand myself and the mounting flames, she buried her head and mouth between my legs and began to play ardently with my clit in a way I'd never experienced before. She nibbled at it, and I jerked more. She tongued it, and waves of sensation shot through me. She pushed her tongue against the sensitive flesh around it and brought my body to the edge.

And, as I had done, but more vigorously, she pushed her fingers inside both the fiery holes that awaited their pleasure; and as she tongued my clit, I peaked.

"Ah! Gaaaawd!" I gasped as I strained against the couch, my back arched, sensations of pleasure washing over me. It was the first time I'd come at the hands of a woman, the first time that such careful attention had been paid to me, and a curious satisfaction overwhelmed me. I nearly cried with delight!

But I was not finished. She didn't back away. Unlike other

lovers, she kept going, taking charge of my body so I was forced to go beyond the simple come I'd just enjoyed. She pushed me further, drawing me to another edge that needed breaking. She sucked my clit with fervor, working my body with an experience that could have only come from other times. She made my clit and cunt and ass respond when they were used to stopping, and I found myself going beyond the usual control to another climax.

"Aah!... Aah!" I whimpered. Her hands had kneaded me. "Aah!... Aaaaahhhhh!" The wildest sensation burst through me. I thought I was going to melt away, disappear into nothing.

She continued to caress me, even as the orgasm was dying quietly away. I backed off into a heaven of the senses, and of rich love I'd not expected from this source.

"You *have* done this before," I murmured.

"Many times," she whispered as she leaned over to kiss my lips. Both our fires melted away into those tiny kisses and the gentle play of our tongues. Such tenderness brought me back to the warm room that surrounded me. "You are very special, dear Kate."

Gratitude swept over me for the club's once-threatening instructions. How perfect it had been!

We pulled ourselves up on the couch, back in the corners where we'd begun. We donned only our sweaters in order to cut the chill while still allowing us to see each other's cunts between our crossed legs.

A cool breeze from the open window played delicately with my moist pussy. I took a large gulp of the wine still in my glass.

"I'm reeling," I said truthfully. I was so relaxed, it would have been easy to drift off into a pleasant sleep.

"I've wanted you for years," Joanna said. "But I know it takes some time to cross the line, when you no longer care about the shape or size or sex of the body you want. It seems silly to live with rigid rules for our natural desires."

I understood. I swam in the thought for a long, drawn-out moment.

"That's why you've changed so much in the past few years," I said. It seemed that Joanna's blossoming was now becoming clear, just as my own was evolving in a curiously odd way.

That loving, knowing, almost mentor smile crossed her glowing face.

We didn't talk about the club, or about anything much else. We'd said enough and done enough to keep us both content.

THE BAD GIRL
Chea Villanueva

What's taking them so long? I know they're up to something."

"You think they're lezzies?" Sal took another long sip from the can of beer she was holding. Suddenly she felt sick. Her head started to spin as the thoughts formulated in her mind. How many other times did Nadine and Jess disappear for hours with no explanation? Why was it when other girls were dating, Nadine and Jess made up some excuse about homework? And Jess—everyone at school was talking about her short hair. It wasn't the fact that it was so short, but the way she combed it back from her face, kinda like all the guys did. And she was so tough. Nothing feminine about Jess at all. Sal tried to think of something—anything—that would redeem Jess's femininity, but her mind kept drawing a blank. Not like Nadine. Nadine was so pretty and could have any guy she wanted, but somehow had escaped all the boys' advances. When most of the girls from their gang had a date for the senior prom, Nadine made an excuse about helping her mother out with the kids, and Jess—well, none of the guys wanted to go with Jess.

Sal made a decision. "C'mon, Carla, let's find out. If they are lezzies, I don't want to hang out with them anymore!"

While the dancers swayed to the beat of the music one floor below them, Jess and Nadine were locked in their own erotic dance. Nadine was backed up against the bathroom door, her panties in a bunch around her ankles while Jess's hand disappeared inside her cunt. Jess cushioned Nadine's back with her right arm while her hand cradled Nadine's neck. Her arms were strong from lifting weights, and she liked to show off by holding Nadine until she was captive in her grip and Nadine's struggles got her nowhere but closer to Jess's body. Jess ground her pelvis in time to Nadine's rhythm. By now, the white stain on the crotch of her new jeans was spreading with Nadine's wetness. Nadine liked the feeling of Jess's strength. She felt protected and knew Jess loved her. She flashed back to the time they were kids....

Jess was thirteen, a few months older than Nadine. But Jess had lost a mother and just gotten out of reform school, so she seemed much older then what she actually was. It was the day Nadine's father had gotten drunk and went into a violent rampage. Jess had spent the night there, and the three of them were alone in the house. That was the day Nadine fell in love with Jess. The day Jess led her by the hand and ran with her, protecting her from her father's fists. Five years ago....

The knock on the door brought Nadine back to the present danger.

"What's going on in there? C'mon, you two, we know you're in there! Open up this door right now!"

Nadine hurried to straighten her dress and pull up her panties while Jess struggled with soap and water, trying to erase the stain on her jeans.

Nadine tried to sound sick as she flushed the toilet. "We'll be right out!"

She whispered, "Hurry, Jess, before they break the door down!"

Jess kept her own thoughts private. She knew this was it. When all their friends and all the world would finally know that she and Nadine were lovers. There would be no mistaking the damp marks on her clothes or the smeared makeup on her T-shirt. And Nadine— Nadine looked like a woman who had just gotten it good. Jess pulled the bathroom door open, and in tumbled Carla and Sal.

"What the hell's going on in here? What was taking you so long?" Carla ignored Jess and turned her attention to Nadine, who was busy splashing water on her face. "I told you I got sick. I needed to throw up."

Sal wasn't easily fooled, not like Carla. "And I guess Jess had to throw up, too. What happened to your clothes, Jess? And how did all that makeup get on your shirt? I didn't know you were finally turning into a girl!"

"Shut up, Sal! Nadine was gettin' sick and needed help up the steps."

"Oh, yeah, right! Looks like you helped her real good, Jess. Nobody could get in this bathroom for almost an hour. So what were you really doing in here? Is it what I'm thinking? 'Cause if it is, I think it's disgusting."

Sal was angry and needed to know. She hoped they'd deny the rumors that had been going on about them all night, but deep down she knew the truth.

"Yeah, you two turning lezzie on us, or what?" Carla giggled.

Nadine kept her back turned. She was getting red in the face and wanted to cry. She planned on one day coming out to Sal, who was her best friend. But now she was forced to admit it in front of everybody, and she knew the scene was going to get out of hand.

By this time, a few boys had come up and tried to get into the conversation. "Hey baby, you wanna ride home?" Tony Lee put his hand on Nadine's shoulder.

"Take your fuckin' hands off her!" Now that the truth was out, Jess felt comfortable telling Tony how she felt. She was sick of him always calling her lover "baby," and it pissed her off that he was always trying to get Nadine alone and cop a feel.

"Hey! What's up with this fuckin' chick? Tony turned to Sal for understanding.

"I'll tell you what's up!" Sal screamed. "Nadine and Jess are fuckin' lesbians!"

Neither Jess nor Nadine went to school on Monday. By Tuesday, carloads of boys drove past Jess's house and screamed obscenities.

"C'mon out, you titless bitch! Are you a boy or a girl? Let's pull her pants down and find out!"

Nadine was followed home from the grocery store by a bunch of boys that hung out on the corner. "Yo, Nadine! You put out for guys, too, or just for dykes? Lemme show you what a real man feels like. I'll bet I can suck your pussy better than Jess can!"

They spent the rest of the week huddled in Nadine's old playhouse until Jess's father left for work and then spent the remainder of the day in Jess's room with the shades drawn, not daring to move for fear the floorboards would creak and the neighbor who lived in the next row house would alert Jess's father that someone was creeping around his house. Nadine forged sick notes to school, while Jess planned their future together. Final exams were coming and classes would be over in a few weeks. They would deny the rumors, graduate, and then they'd be free! After graduation, Jess wanted to enlist in the Army, she said, so she'd have a steady job and could take care of Nadine. After boot camp she reasoned, she'd move off the base and they'd get their own apartment. It was a good opportunity and a chance to travel all over the world! Who else would hire a kid from the projects with no job history and a reform-school record? And besides, Jess could keep her hair as short as she wanted and wear an Army uniform. She would get a free college education, and after four years, she could leave the military....

"That's fine, Jess, but where will I be living while you're away? I can't stand living in my house anymore or this neighborhood! I'm afraid, Jess! What am I gonna do?"

Jess took Nadine in her arms and rocked her as she reached frantically for the right words to calm her lover's tears.

Nadine was right. Neither of them had any money or even a car. Jess thought about stealing one—but no, with her reputation, Jess would be the one they'd point the finger at. After the scene at the party last week, she didn't have any friends left. Most of them would love to see Jess sent to jail. Everybody was saying it was all Jess's fault that Nadine was acting different. There was only one option. She would steal the money from her father. Her hard-working father who drank to escape the pain of his wife's death. Jess felt guilty taking the money, but she'd pay it back as soon as she could, and besides, the loss of the money would prevent her father from drinking too much. Jess's father was a gentle man. He never raised his voice, and except for one time, Jess never remembered him whipping her.

Not like Nadine's father. He beat Nadine, her mother, and her sisters every chance he could get. Jess's dad was a loving father and husband; but after her mother's death, he withdrew from the routine of his daily life by drinking and crying himself to sleep night after night. He missed her so much that he didn't know how to live anymore. Jess would leave him a note and leave enough cash in his wallet so he'd have bus fare and money for food. She only hoped he'd be strong enough so his heart wouldn't break a second time.

"Nadine, honey, please don't cry. This is what we're gonna do.... As soon as we graduate, I'm takin' you away from here. I'll get the money, and you can stay at the motel outside of the base. I'll send you my paycheck, and when boot camp's finished, you'll go wherever I go. I promise I'll never leave you; only for a little while, and then we'll be together forever."

"You promise, Jess?"

"I promise."

Nadine dried her tears on Jess's shirt and for the very first time looked forward to a new life. Her and Jess forever....

"Lezzie! Lezzie!"

Nadine and Jess were greeted with that on their first day back to school. They both tried hard to be brave for each other. Nadine took her seat beside Sal for the first few classes she didn't share with Jess. She held her head high and tried to act as if it were idle gossip; but toward the end of the day, Sal slipped her the note that set her nerves on edge. "This is all Jess's fault that you don't have a boyfriend. Walk with me after school and the guys will take care of her."

Nadine knew too well how the guys would take care of Jess. They'd follow close behind her and then drag her into the alley where the Dumpster was kept. A girl was raped there last year. Jess would get it worse. They'd brutalize her and leave her broken, bleeding body in the trash heap. Tony Lee, whose jealousy was sickening, would be the first one to do it; and in his angry need for Nadine, he might even kill Jess. She had to get to Jess now....

Jess was indifferent to the stares and whispers. She walked the halls alone, careful to keep her hand in the pocket of her leather jacket clutching the razor-sharp switchblade. She sat by herself in the back of the classroom. The walls protected her back from anything that might be thrown at her. She was used to being a loner and not a stranger to the gossip. Hadn't she spent a whole year avoiding the bathroom and wearing her gym suit under her clothes so she didn't have to use the girls' locker room? She knew the talk: Jess wanted to watch the girls undress. Jess thought she was a boy. Yes, they were right, but wrong about one thing. Jess had never wanted or lusted after anyone but Nadine. She had nothing in common with other girls. Hadn't she always hung out with the boys from the time she learned how to walk? And now she was their enemy, with their prize possession. Nadine....

"Oh, Jess, I was so scared for you. You can't ever go back to school now." Nadine showed Jess the crumpled note that Sal had given her.

They had made it home safe from school with no incidents. Somehow they had sensed at the same time that their lives were in danger. As Jess bolted from her classroom, Nadine was already at the door to meet her. They ran the thirteen city blocks, not daring to wait for a bus until they got to Nadine's house. They were still sitting on the bed when the door to the room crashed open, sending splinters of wood everywhere.

"What's this talk all over the neighborhood? You little slut! I don't pay the bills around here to have you layin' up in the bed with this dyke!" Nadine's father made a move to push Jess, but she was too fast. Nadine was not so lucky. As Jess rolled off the bed, she heard the slap that sent Nadine crashing into the wall.

"Bitch, I'll kill you!" He had his hands around Nadine's neck when Jess jumped on his back, pulling him to the floor.

"You little fuck! Get your hands off me or I'm callin' the cops. I'll have you arrested if you ever come in here again. Get outta my house! You hear me, dyke? There's a place where they lock up queers like you!"

Jess knew too well what he was talking about. She was still getting over the nightmares from her year in reform school. The year that so brutalized her, she still had emotional scars that might never heal....

"Jess! Get out before he kills you!" Nadine's scream broke through the split-second silence in the room, as Jess took the full force of the punch that ripped through her lip, tearing a tooth from her jaw. She took another punch to the head before Nadine's mother rushed into the room, pushing Nadine away and moving Jess away from the madman who was her husband.

"Marvin! Stop it! You'll kill these kids! She wailed like a woman on fire. "Marvin, please stop!" She cowered as the man's kicks and slaps pummeled her body.

Jess was at a loss what to do. Should she protect Nadine's mother or run with Nadine?

Nadine made up her mind for both of them. "Jess!" she screamed. "Just go. You're making it worse for all of us! Go on! Get outta here!"

Queer. It was worse than a slap to the face the way he made it sound—like the filthiest, lowest person in the world. A person not entitled to any kind of love or friendship.... Jess hurried around the corner. She was ready to face the showdown with her father now. She'd show everybody how tough she was. "Let them all turn against me!" she thought.

* * *

"You have to go, Chulo. They don't want you in this neighborhood anymore. I got a call from the school, and they don't want you back there either."

Jess cried for the first time since her mother's death. She didn't want to leave her father. He was the only family she had left.

"How do you know all this?"

"I know. I know everything from the time you were a little girl. You were always different, and I didn't care because I wanted a son, and you were always like my boy to me. You're a good kid, but you have a lotta trouble and I can't help you. You have to go now before it gets too dangerous for you. If you don't go, the state will take you away from me, and they'll put you away for good."

Jess hugged her father tighter, but it was no use.

"Here. Take this. I have this money saved up for you so you could buy a car when you get out of school. Put some clothes in a bag. Hurry, these people in this neighborhood are bad."

Jess followed her father into the kitchen and watched as he prepared a few sandwiches for her journey.

"You call me so I know you're alright."

Jess felt like the little boy who was her father's son as she left the house she grew up in.

"'Bye, Daddy, I love you."

She stood for a long time, watching the door that was now locked to her.

As the rain poured down in a torrent, Jess poured her tears out inside Nadine's old wooden playhouse. This is where it all began...where they played as kids, where Jess kissed Nadine for the first time, and in the summer, when they turned fifteen, the place where Jess took Nadine and made her Jess's woman. Now the place was Jess's refuge until the morning came and Jess would have to run for her life with Nadine.

Daylight. Jess fought the sleep dragging her down into its abyss. She had to be fully awake to catch Nadine on her way to school. Warn Nadine...

It was too late. Jess blanked out as the sun shed its first rays. As morning turned into noon, the heat was unmerciful. It baked the house and its occupant, sending Jess into a sleepy stupor.

Nadine walked for hours. The heat from the sun made the throbbing in her head unbearable. She wanted to lie down and die to escape the pain and blot out the memory of last night. To lie down in green grass surrounded by trees with limbs as large as the sky itself—protecting her in their brown embrace. Protecting her in their strong...in their strong...arms. Like Jess... Jess's arms were strong and would protect her. Where was Jess now? Nadine realized she was lost, that she had been walking around like a blind woman in the dark. Oh, where was Jess?

"Jess! Jess!"

Jess must be dreaming. She dreamt Nadine was there beside her calling her name over and over. While Jess dreamed of stone walls with barred windows, Nadine poured cool water on her lover's lips and smoothed back her hair with a damp cloth.

"Jess, wake up. There's no more stone walls anymore. It's just you and me. Jess...Jess..."

Nadine's soft voice chased the ghosts from the past away until Jess finally opened her eyes.

"I was dreaming...."

"I know, Jess. I know all your dreams...."

There was no more need for words as they walked into the house and climbed the stairs to Nadine's bedroom.

They were sleeping; exhausted from lovemaking and the day's ordeal, when they thought they had lost the way to each other. That's how Marvin found them. Tangled in each other's bodies—the sweet smile of desire still on their faces, caught up in the sleep of innocence. His belt rained down violence, breaking the first peacefulness they had felt in days.

"You fuckin' dyke! I told you to stay outta my house. You turned my daughter into a goddamn lesbian!"

The belt ripped into Jess's and Nadine's flesh as they struggled into their clothes.

"Don't bother gettin' dressed, bulldagger. I'm gonna fuck you like I fucked Nadine! I'll teach you both a lesson and then kill you with my bare hands...."

The words registered in Jess's brain as Marvin tore at the zipper on his pants. "...fucked Nadine." She took Nadine's hand and ran from the room, swearing that Marvin would never touch her again. The thought sickened her as the knowledge crept in—that while she hid like a coward in the playhouse, her own lover was being raped just ten feet away. She'd kill him!

Jess grabbed a long butcher knife from the kitchen. She and Nadine would hide in the hall closet, behind the long coats, until Marvin left the house. Hadn't they always hid in there when they were small—when Marvin beat his wife? Her screams were so terrible that Jess would come running, taking Nadine with her to the closet, closing her own hands over Nadine's ears until the screams grew into moans as Marvin took his wife to the bedroom and proved his manhood.

They shut the door as Marvin took the last step down the staircase. Chairs overturned and dishes broke. Pictures were ripped off the walls and smashed as Marvin made his way through the house. Jess couldn't remember feeling so big behind the coats. Their small hiding place felt smaller as the doorknob turned and Marvin reached in with his large hands, shoving the coats aside. Nadine was sitting behind her as Jess plunged the knife through Marvin's chest. He would never touch Nadine again. Never beat her, rape her, or use his threats. They sat there numbed, watching Marvin die outside of the closet. It took him a while. Just enough time for Nadine to tell Jess what happened that night....

They found Jess in the playhouse. Nadine's mother came home after spending the night at her sister's house. She had run from Marvin's rage and taken the small kids with her, leaving Nadine alone in the house with her drunken father. She didn't think he'd hurt her....

She found Marvin's bloodless body and called the police.

The trial lasted only a few days. Jess was convicted of first-degree premeditated murder. Her sentence was forty years to life, with chance of an early parole, but Jess knew her chance of getting out before those forty years was slim.

Nadine wept at the sentencing. It was harsh, but the comments from her friends were chilling. "She got just what she deserved, Nadine. She killed your father and deserves to go to prison."

Her mother's words were just as unkind. She had expected more compassion from this woman who endured the same cruelty that Nadine faced every day of her life. "Maybe now you'll get back to normal. She's a sick girl, you're not."

Nadine had never hated anyone as much as she hated Carla, Sal, and her mother that day. She vowed in her head that she'd never love anyone but Jess, and never feel anyone's arms hold her like Jess's had. People said Jess was bad, but only Nadine knew the hurts Jess had suffered, and from that sadness a gentleness was born. Her lover's touch was softer and warmer than summer raindrops. Only Nadine knew the sweetness of Jess's poems tucked under her pillow or under a rose she'd picked for Nadine. No, Jess wasn't bad, only misunderstood....

Nadine saw the tears well up in Jess's eyes and knew the dam in Jess's mind would soon stop the flow. She knew Jess had to be strong for both of them. If Jess broke down, Nadine would break down, and the handcuffs at Jess's side would prevent her from holding Nadine in that comforting way that only Jess knew how to do. Nadine did what she knew only Jess would understand. She stood up straight and glared defiantly at the onlookers. A look that dared anyone to separate her love for Jess. Her lover was going to prison. Her punishment for killing a man who hurt Nadine so badly with belts, sticks, and anything else he held in his hands. How many times as children did Jess try to protect her from his punches and kicks—only to be pulled from the man's back and thrown roughly against a wall until her face bled, and the man who was Nadine's father became so exhausted he collapsed on the floor until Nadine's mother found him and then the fight would start again? No, Jess was not a criminal. Nadine would defend her lover's honor by waiting diligently in her mother's house, and seeing the court-appointed psychiatrist for an illness she didn't know she had. She'd never lay with a man or give her kisses away. Only to Jess—and Jess's touch was magic and would carry her through all the years of waiting.

Nadine left the courtroom alone after locking her eyes with Jess and mouthing a whisper: "I love you, Jess. I'll wait for you."

The year they took Jess away passed into two. Nadine was denied visits and her letters were sent back open, in a large manila envelope, and stamped unacceptable. For Jess's twentieth birthday, she baked a cake and rode the bus out to the prison, leaving it outside the confines of the gate.

The nights took on new meaning. Sleep was not just an escape from the daily pain of living, but Nadine found Jess in her dreams and together they knocked down the walls that held them apart. Their love had finally found a way to break through all the years of waiting.

Jess's touch was still magic, and when the morning came, Nadine's body still felt the imprint of her lover's hands.

Soon after Jess's birthday, Nadine heard her name called. Before waking, she had a vision of Jess climbing over the wall, and she hurried to meet her. She parked the car that had once belonged to her father at the far side of the prison. All at once the sirens went off and bright lights lit up the sky. She ran to the concrete barrier as Jess scaled the top.

The gunshots from the tower covered Jess's body in a hail of bullets. As Jess fell, a single bullet entered her body, pierced her heart, and entered Nadine's body. They died at the foot of the prison wall, entangled together, Jess's body covering Nadine's. At peace at last, together again, their souls rose as shadows in the moonlit sky. All was silent but for the whisper: "Nothing can ever separate us again."

INSOMNIAC
Serina Jurgens

I'm ghostly as I putter around the house, walking through the moonlit rooms, running my fingers along the edges of the furniture to help guide my way. I don't want to disturb Karen, and I should just park myself in a chair and read until I'm sleepy, but I can't. I need to move. When I feel this way, I always need to move.

As usual, I find myself on our second-story balcony, looking down the Hollywood hills to the city below. This balcony is the reason I bought the house. You can see everything from here. You can lose yourself in the lights of the city, truly the jewels of L.A. You can lose yourself in forever.

I don't know how long I spend watching the twinkling red and gold dots, standing outside in my blue flannel robe, not noticing the chill creeping beneath it and next to my skin. I am unaware of the time, of the sound of her feet behind me, of anything until her hands steal around my body and gently pull me to her.

She's taller than I am. I fit against all the grooves and swells of her body. I have always taken comfort in how well we align ourselves together. She unties my robe from behind and removes it. I am naked underneath. When she wraps me in her arms again, I feel that she is naked, too. Suddenly the air is cooler to me, but her body saves me, protects me. She bends and kisses along my shoulders and each kiss is followed by a breath of iced air that makes me shiver.

She doesn't speak as she kisses lower, following the line of my spine to its base, doesn't seem to mind the cold stones as she settles on her knees to continue. She probes my ass with her tongue. She pushes me forward until I am leaning on the railing, offering myself to her, my legs parted, my hips back. This has always been her favorite position in which to take me, to dine on me. I stare out at the lights as they mock me with their firefly quality. One twinkles and goes out. I fix on another as it does the same. Shimmering bits of fairy dust strewn over the dirt of our city.

Karen is more insistent now, her tongue joined by her hands. One hand snakes in front of me and begins to play my clit the way a musician might strum a guitar. The two sensations, her hard, forceful mouth against my ass, her soft fluttering fingers on my clit, drive me mad. My legs grow weak, but I grip onto the railing even tighter and beg her silently not to stop.

She won't. Not yet. She'll continue, as always, digging her naughty tongue deep inside my asshole, rubbing my clit between her thumb and forefinger. She'll continue until I am as close to coming as a person can possibly get.

And then daylight will arrive and bathe my naked body with its first rays of warmth. And the lights of the city will fade, one by one, until all but the stoplights are extinguished. And Karen's touch will lift from my body like the gossamer stroke of a silken sheet billowing in the wind.

And when I turn to catch a glimpse of my one true love, she'll be gone.

Because I'm the insomniac, but Karen's the ghost.

SLIPPING
Diva Davies

A silvery ringing fills my head, and I close my eyes. The ringing stops abruptly and her sweet, husky voice replaces the bells. "Yeah?"

"Lisa?" I waver. "It's Sam. Are you busy?"

"No, baby, what's up?"

I hesitate, bringing my finger near the "disconnect" button. *What am I doing? What in the hell am I doing?*

"Nothing much," I lie. "Just wanted to talk to you."

"How're you and what's-her-name getting along?"

"Fine." I swallow. "Well, okay, I guess."

"Sounds great, kid," she responds, her voice filled with sarcasm. I hear the sound of a match as she lights a cigarette. I imagine sitting across from her in her dark studio, watching her blow smoke rings toward the red-glossed ceiling. I imagine....

She inhales and asks, "If everything's fine, why are you calling me?"

Embarrassed silence on my end. My mind hissing, *Everything's wrong. Everything's wrong. Everything….*

"Never mind," she purrs, her voice assuringly soft, but insistent. "What's on your mind?"

Her studio is in Hollywood, and the neon light from the clubs fills her apartment. When I lie naked on her floor, the red neon flickers over my body, illuminating my pale skin with a slide show from hell.

"We're steady," I say. "I mean, she thinks we are. But when we're in bed. When we're, you know, in bed. You…"

"You think about me?"

"It's the only way that I…"

"Can get excited." Not a question.

"Yeah."

"What do you need me to do? What do you dream about?"

I swallow hard, admitting something I'm ashamed to even think about. "We do it in the dark, with all the lights off. She brushes her teeth before…and after. She's so clean." You'd have thought I'd said a bad word. Clean.

"And you need it rough and raw and dirty. You need the lights on to see the filth. You thought if you went with a nice girl, it would rub off on you, didn't you?"

I nod. Can you believe it? That's what I thought. But it didn't work. And instead of getting cleaner, I am making Rebecca dirty by being with me. I am marking her with the deviousness of my thoughts, with the impurity of my desires.

"Have you been bad, baby girl?" Lisa's voice crawls through my head, into my blood. Her voice beats in my heart. "Should I put you over my knee and spank you? Have you been a naughty girl?"

Just calling is naughty. Just admitting it is bad. "Lisa," I am starting to say it, starting to beg. "If you're good, I might take out my crop."

It makes me so wet when she talks to me. My own private 900 number. My own dirty fix. I want to be on the floor, looking up at her. I want to feel the point of her stiletto heel on my shoulder, pushing me back down. I want the neon glare to blind me.

"If you're really good, I might use my cane. That's what you want, isn't it? That's what you need."

I nod, but she can't see me. I roll onto my stomach and stare at my reflection in the mirror on the back of our closet door. I see someone not all there, hazy, fading, slipping away.

"I want what we had," I find myself saying.

"Can't go back." She sounds smug.

There's the sound of Rebecca's key in the lock. Opening the door. Pulling me back to reality while driving me farther away. I say softly, "I have to see you," but the connection's dead and Lisa's gone and Rebecca's walking down the hall toward our bedroom.

I hang up the phone. I look at the window.

I see the doorknob start to turn.

But I'm no longer there.

CHOCOLATE CAKE
K. T. Butler

I love chocolate. Anything chocolate—M&Ms (my favorite candy), chocolate-covered cherry cordials (I like milk, but dark's my fave), chocolate mousse, chocolate fudge ice cream... well, you get it now. Especially chocolate cake. The more chocolate, the more dark, the better!

So where was I? Oh yes, I love chocolate. Now what does this have to do with anything, you're asking? Well, there's always a story....

I recently had the occasion to take myself out to dinner. Not so special, really, but when you're used to eating with your lover every night and all of a sudden you're eating by yourself, it's a bit of a shock to the system. She had to go out—without me!—for a business dinner meeting, and I was left to my own devices. I was given some money and told, "Now make sure you eat something, even if it's Burger King."

Well, I'm proud to say I did better than some fast-food grease pit. I decided to go into Philadelphia to a restaurant I'd heard a lot about and have myself a real honest-to-goodness gourmet dinner. Soup to nuts. I don't eat much as it is, but I was a real gastro-glutton this night. I had Caesar salad for one, bread and butter, and shrimp scampi on rice with garlic wine sauce. I was in the middle of sucking on a shrimp when I happened to glance up from my gluttony and notice this woman sitting two tables in front of me. She was staring right at me. At first I thought she was staring at me, that is, but then I realized she was staring at my food.

She got up and walked towards me. She was taller than I am, which isn't saying much (I'm 5'2"), but she had to be at least 5'8". And when you're my height, everyone looks six feet tall. What a gorgeous woman! Dark brown shoulder-length hair that looked like, well, a river of chocolate. And what a bod... Anyway, she came toward me, pulled out the empty chair at my table, sat down, and in this unearthly, gorgeously Lauren Bacall-ish husky tone said, "I'm dying to know—what is that you're eating? It looks like shrimp scampi, but I couldn't tell from my table." What an intro-duction. I politely dabbed at my mouth with my napkin. How I managed to remember manners I will never know. And I replied, "It *is* scampi. You're very perceptive. Would you like a taste?"

Well, of course she did want some. Isn't that how all fantasies go? So I scooped up a nice fat forkful of shrimp and gathered up a heaping gob of rice with my spoon. I was going to put the contents on her plate and, I hoped, just sit back and watch her eat. She was gorgeous. I could pretend I was one of the shrimp. I began maneuvering both fork and spoon towards her plate. I am not very big and consequently am cursed with short arms, so I could not reach her plate without standing up and leaning across the table. When I leaned over, my concentration was broken by the view I had of her breasts. A partial view, true, but it was enough. I could see the roundness, the beginning of nipple, but I needed a better vantage point. Maybe if I moved in closer. I tried to stretch myself across the table even more. Being the extreme klutz I am, what else would have happened but that my fork full of shrimp fell out of my hand, clattering to the floor. I heard someone from the next table over remark, "How disgusting." Well yeah, honey, I hadn't planned on spilling it either. "Oh my God, I am sorry. What a klutz," I heard myself say. It was the end of my scampi. There was no more to give her, only my wimpy, wilted steamed broccoli. Yuk. Well I could place another order for scampi. Hold on! It's $15.95 and I only had $30.00 to begin with. I hadn't even had dessert yet, which I cannot do without. Ahh, dessert. Salvation, maybe?

She must have been reading my mind, because she said, "It's okay. It's time for dessert and coffee. What do you think we should have for dessert? You choose."

So, what do I do? I'm here alone in this great restaurant with a wonderful woman who wants me to order dessert and coffee for her. I hoped she liked chocolate. She had to. Chocolate…it has a rich sensuality, an allure. Most people I know avoid it because of diets, or the caffeine, or whatever. It's the ultimate, the forbidden, the one thing everyone dreams about when they think of eating dessert. How many times have we all been at the office, listening to a late 40ish, almost menopausal, very much overweight woman complain, "Oh, I'm on a diet, I couldn't possibly eat any chocolate," and then she takes a piece, saying, "Well, just a small piece. I am on a diet, after all."

I can eat as much as I want of it because I never seem to gain weight. Working out like an Olympic hopeful five days a week helps. But it pays off because I get to have my chocolate. Well, back to the story. I regained my senses and looked back at this gorgeous thing at my table and said, "I'm going to have a look at the dessert tray, and then I can make up my mind about what to have. Would you also like some cappuccino?"

"Absolutely."

I called the waiter over and asked to see the dessert tray. He brought it over immediately, it seemed, and I had the feast of the world before my eyes. German Chocolate (hmm), Black Forest (oohh), Chocolate Cheesecake (yuk), Chocolate Mousse Pie (possibility), and then there was Chocolate Chip Supreme—it was a dark devils' food cake with almost black chocolate icing inside and outside and semi-sweet dark chocolate chips embedded within. A winner. I told the waiter we'd have two servings, but my new friend said, "Just one serving. We'll share."

Our order was served. I got the cake and she got an empty plate. I said to her, "Mind if I try it first?" She shook her head of marvelous hair which I took as a "yes" and I dug in. It was absolutely delicious, the chocolate, and I could feel the instantaneous rush through my body, I suppose much as a vampire feels the rush of the blood from his victim. It was exhilarating, addicting. No wonder people felt so strongly about chocolate. I sat back in my chair and sighed. Ahh, it was sinful. I closed my eyes for a moment and began imagining all kinds of things. But I had to share. I dug my fork in and carved out a nice big chunk of cake. I again tried to lean across the table, mindful this time of my previous unsuccessful effort, and I held the fork out and said something stupid: "Open wide, here comes your ecstasy." Ooooh. I have got to get better lines.

She opened her mouth, so wide that I could see she didn't have much dental work. But she was so beautiful I couldn't focus on her teeth. Again, I had the pleasure of viewing her cleavage, but from a much better position. But my innate clumsiness failed me again. I was so close to her, I looked down again and saw her nipples, soft and brown, and I saw both breasts, the roundness and shadows descending below. As I strained forward to see better, it happened again. I lost my balance! I could feel myself falling, and I tried not to fall onto the table. I succeeded and managed to fall onto the floor next to the table where I had previously heard, "How disgusting." This wasn't pretty. I was sprawled on my back on the floor with a forkful of cake in one hand and the other clutching the chair I had managed to drag with me. I was so embarrassed. I wasn't hurt—though I wished my pride had not made me do this stupid thing. I thought about turning over and crawling away on my hands and knees when all of a sudden she was there, leaning over me and offering me her hand, saying, "Are you all right? Let me help you up." I accepted her hand, and she said, "Let's get the dessert wrapped and go." So I paid the check, got my cake in the customary Styrofoam box and started for the door. I didn't even get to drink my cappuccino. And I had paid $3.75 for it, plus $4.75 for the cake, tax and tip. I didn't have much money left.

I was positive she wasn't coming. I knew a little coffee shop where I could get my cappuccino cheap, so I started out towards the lobby with my little Styrofoam prize tucked under my arm. I heard the sound of heels clicking against the marble of the lobby floor and I heard her calling, "Wait! Don't go!" I kept going, trying to lose her voice and knowing that if I heard her once again I would stop and there was no telling what would happen next. After all, I had a lover. I was committed, though not trying very hard to continue to be so. Selfishly, I decided that I wanted to eat my cake by myself. I marched on, my cake securely tucked in between my hand and hip.

What happened next was totally unexpected. She ran up, planted herself in front of me and said, "I have a room. Let's go upstairs and have the cake and I'll order some cappuccino from room service." I tried to walk around her, but she placed a hand on my shoulder and said, "Let's go. Now." She was definitely the dominatrix type. I was playing the victim well, I suppose. I guessed I could just go up, let her eat some cake and then go. Let her eat cake. Although it didn't work for Marie Antoinette, maybe it would work for me. It was good cake.

We stepped into the elevator and rode up to the 35th floor. We'd have a very nice view of the city. Walking down the hall to her room, I again felt a twinge of guilt. What was I doing here? My lover was out having dinner with a bunch of stuffy old business people and here I was contemplating adultery with a stunning accomplice. It wasn't fair. We continued down the hall and she slid the keycard into the door, opened and beckoned, "Come in."

I followed her inside and my eyes feasted on the lavish surroundings: mirrored walls, plush carpeting. I peeked around and noticed the bath had a Jacuzzi. I vaguely heard her talking on the phone. She had a very nice situation for me to fall into. I walked over to the couch, sat down, and she slid beside me. "Well, let's have that cake. I've ordered cappuccino and ice cream from room service."

I fumbled with the lid and managed to retrieve the cake from the container. She took the cake from my hands, broke off a chunk and brought it to my lips. I devoured the cake and sucked on her fingers, licking every last drop of chocolate. There was a knock on the door. She got up and I heard her thanking the bellboy, and the door closed. "It's the ice cream and cappuccino," she said, and she reappeared with a container of Chocolate Cherry Cordial, a tray with two cups of cappuccino, whipped cream, a bowl of chocolate shavings and a very large spoon. She set the tray on top of the small dining table. "Let's eat."

She sat down on the couch next to me and proceeded to unbutton her shirt (no bra!). She removed her shirt and began to coat her torso with ice cream and cake. I was mesmerized by this sensual attempt at fresco (Michelangelo never had it so good), and I was so moved I buried my face in her chocolate-covered breasts, and began to lick and eat until the chocolate was gone and there was only nipple. The nipple had some chocolate left so I sucked on the nipple until the chocolate was gone while she moaned and writhed. Then she stood up and reached for the silver tray. "We need the cappuccino."

After she sat back down, she took off her remaining clothes. She sat down next to me, naked, and she took my hand in hers and said, "Make me cappuccino." I started to pick up the coffee cup, and her hand grabbed mine and she said more forcefully, "Make me feel cappuccino." Her hand gripping mine moved down between her legs. I felt the softness of her hair, her wetness. "Make me cappuccino—with whipped cream and chocolate," she said. I leaned down toward her legs when all of a sudden she jerked my head up, pulling my hair, which hurt tremendously. "No! Make me cappuccino, but tell me about it. Describe it. I want to imagine it."

I removed my hand from between her legs, and I took a spoon from the coffee tray and began to spoon whipped cream into my cup. "As I take this cream, I'm taking you. I move my lips against yours, I move my lips down your face, I feel your neck. I kiss your neck, your shoulders, and then I move toward your breasts." As I said these words, she sighed and moved toward me. "And now I'm at your breasts." I took a deep sip of the cappuccino. "I'm licking your breasts, pulling on your nipples with my teeth, biting you just a little, not enough to hurt but enough to make the liquid flow between your legs."

She moves on the couch, arching her back so that her breasts stand up firmly. I am ready now. I move in toward her and her hand stops me. "No. Tell me." I stop, dumbfounded. What else can I tell her? Just tell her as if it's happening. So I do.

"I suck on your nipples, I take my hand and put it between

your legs and feel the softness, the wetness. You open your legs and I can see your cunt. Waiting for me."

"Take the cream," she says. "Spread it on me."

I take the cream, spreading it between her legs, on top of her rich mound of hair. I sprinkle the chocolate shavings on top of the cream, and I bend down to eat. Licking the cream, I taste the chocolate, and finally I begin to taste her. "Now pour the coffee on top of my cunt," she says.

"Pour the coffee? But won't it burn?"

"Do as I say." I reach up and grab the silver container, twisting the lid, and then I gingerly pour a small stream onto her. She winces a bit, and she grabs my hair, hurting me a bit, and says, "Here's your cappuccino." I dive in, licking the coffee mixed with cream mixed with chocolate mixed with her come (and she is coming in a big way), and I can't get enough. I pour more hot coffee, she screams a bit, and I spoon more whipped cream and chocolate and I keep licking. And licking and licking. I can feel her move into me, her cunt in my face, and I cannot stop myself: I grab her legs and hold her to myself, bringing her cunt into my face. I go completely crazy on her, licking and sucking. She is dripping wet, coming all over my face, liquid running down my chin, and I sit up, exclaiming, "Something's missing!"

I lean over her naked and beautiful body, reaching for the remnants of the ice cream (now sadly melted) and the leftover cake. I sit down and smear the cake and a handful of ice cream on her cunt and dive in.

Never had I tasted anything so good. Chocolate come. How divine. I kept going, going until all of her limbs spasmed, and she shook as though having a fit and said no more and I knew it was no more. She was spent, completely exhausted. I had never made anyone come like that. She sat up, looked at her watch. It was the only thing she had on. Then she said, "It's time for you to go."

Time? Who could think about time? I started to protest, as I was incredibly turned on and was hoping she'd reciprocate the cappuccino-making (we could have more cake and leave out the coffee—I have a low pain threshold), but she gently pushed me away and said, "You have to go. I'm expecting my husband at any moment."

"Will I see you again?"

"You'll know where to find me—I love chocolate cake and cappuccino."

So I left, bewildered, bewitched, bedazzled and a little bit sad. After all, this had been a most incredible experience. I started thinking about how I would explain this to my lover—I hadn't washed up and I probably had chocolate stains on my shirt, for godsakes! What had been an evening of astounding highs was quickly becoming one major depression for me.

I entered the cab, gave the driver my address and we were off. It seemed like we flew to my little row house and still I had not thought of a plausible lie to tell my lover. I paid the cabby with my last $2 including tip and I put my key in the deadbolt. As I opened the door, my lover walked into the dining room from the kitchen. She was putting wine glasses back into the china cupboard and though she knew I was there she wasn't looking at me.

"How was dinner? Where did you go?"

"I went to the Bellevue."

"The Bellevue! Well, I'm proud of you. What did you have for dinner?"

"Shrimp scampi."

"And for dessert?"

"Chocolate Chip Supreme."

"I might have known." As she walked into the living room to embrace me, she stopped dead, looked at me and said, "What the hell happened to you?" Looking down at myself, my worst fears were realized. I had chocolate on my shirt, chocolate on my hands. I raised my hands and ran my fingers around my mouth and discovered sticky chocolate smears all around my lips. Plus I probably smelled like cunt to boot. I thought I'd have a heart attack. Well, better to tell the truth since I couldn't think of a believable enough lie. "Well, there was this woman and she made me go back to her room and eat chocolate cake with her and she took off all her clothes and spread the cake all over her and I ate it off her and made her come."

She put her hands on her hips, tilted her head in that funny way that I love so much and started to laugh. "That's the best one yet. I swear you come up with the best stories. I know you too well, my little klutz. You're just too embarrassed to tell me you tripped and fell into the dessert table." I laughed, probably a little too much, and I shifted my feet. "You'd better go upstairs and get those clothes into some cold water in the sink. And wash up. I'm not going near you until you do."

After I regained my sense of feeling in my legs, I started for the stairs and said, "You know me too well."

She smiled and said, "I just made some coffee. Want some?"

UNDERGROUND
Agathe Godot

China hadn't memorized the metro system yet. On the map, she knew to choose the lines by following the colored tracery of underground veins to their final course. But sometimes, when she reached her destination, she would learn of a shorter route, one that involved fewer transfers, fewer long walks beneath the city of Paris.

Still, she didn't really care. If it took her twice as long to get to the museum of her choice, that simply meant she would have more time to observe her fellow passengers.

On nearly every metro ride, a musician would join the car and play the accordion, or strum a guitar, or even sing while shaking a tambourine. It was an exciting prospect, wondering which type of entertainment she'd have the pleasure of hearing. The locals were interesting, the way they wore staid, serious expressions;

but all—even the most unsmiling—would pay for the musicians when they passed around a hat.

When China arrived at her day's destination, she would set up her easel and her drawing pad and charcoal. Soon, tourists would come and stand behind her, watching the careful strokes of the black against the white. They bought her pictures. They always bought her pictures. This was because she was talented, something she knew but didn't think too hard on. Talent is a birthright. What you do with it is your choice. She was choosing to use it to fund her travels. She had no set plans, and she liked it that way.

After riding the metro for almost two months, she began to recognize the faces of the passengers who shared the same lines. One girl in particular caught her attention. China would pretend to be staring into space, but she was really focused on the girl's curly blonde hair, on her suntanned cheeks, brown eyes, full lips.

At night, in her tiny one-room studio, China sketched the girl. She filled pages in her sketchbook, posting the pictures around her room when they were complete. Everywhere she turned, the woman looked back at her. She liked that, liked the feeling of being watched by those wistful brown eyes.

China found herself memorizing the names of the lines the girl rode on, the times she most often saw her. China would set her own route to match the girl's, until, finally, she followed the girl out the metro doors and up to the streets of Paris, deciding that she would get the nerve up to approach her, to speak to her. But she didn't. China simply followed the brilliant blonde until the girl entered the doors to a bank. Then, not able to follow, China returned to her apartment.

The next day, armed with her portfolio, China followed the girl again. This time, when the girl went into the bank, China set up her artwork, posting the pictures on the wrought iron fence across from the front doors of the bank. When the girl left the building at lunch time, she started to walk past China's display. Then she stopped.

Each picture was of herself. Each one capturing a slightly different expression, a different look in her soft brown eyes. She tried to find the artist, but China had gone. Slowly, the girl took down the pictures. Just as slowly, she walked back into her office.

The next morning, on the metro, the girl sat at China's side. She didn't speak, which China was glad for. Instead, the girl placed her hand on China's and squeezed it. When it was time for the girl to get off the metro, she shook her head at China, indicating that she wanted to stay. As the metro began to empty of the morning's commuters, the girl rubbed her hand slowly along China's thigh. Gentle strokes, like the lines of a charcoal pencil, back and forth, creating a commotion in China so strong that she thought she wouldn't be able to take it.

The girl rose at the last stop and pulled China off the train. They walked into the bright sunlight and to a small park directly opposite the metro stop. In the park, hidden by drooping trees, the girl came easily into China's arms. She kissed the artist, kissed her mouth for a long time, kissed her until China's lips felt bruised with the force. Then the girl moved lower, kissing China's neck, the hollow in her neck where her pulse beat rapidly. The girl moved lower still, kissing China's collarbones, kissing along the buttons that ran up China's blouse. Then even lower, bending on the park bench to place her lips against the crotch of China's faded black jeans.

China looked around, but the park was empty. She put her hands in the girl's hair, then brought the girl back to a sitting position. This time China did the kissing, ravaging her model's mouth. Biting the girl's lower lip. Kissing the girl's eyelids, the rise of her cheekbones, her dainty earlobes.

The scent of the flowers in the park surrounded the lovers and made them dizzy. There was a smooth part of grass behind the bench, and China led the girl to it, spread her coat upon it, undressed the girl, and laid her out. They made love beneath the rustling leaves, beneath the pure blue sky, with the scent of the roses, with the scent of Paris, around them.

And when it was time to go, they found their way back to the metro and returned to the mysterious, magical world of the underground.

STEAM
Deborah Kelly

I don't visit my gym regularly, although I did purchase a year-long membership in a burst of guilt last New Year's. I guess I thought that buying it would assuage my guilt at not being in better shape. In L.A., everyone is in better shape. Better shape than me, than my friends, than the airbrushed beauties in the smut magazines.

L.A. is filled with gorgeous people. All of them go to my gym.

Wrapped in sweats from head to toe, I walk with my eyes down to the treadmill. I could walk outside, I know. I could forgo this humiliating experience of striding through a room of thong-wearing, spandex-clad Barbie dolls. But then I'd probably end up at the doughnut store and cancel out the effects of exercise. This way, at least I'll be forced to sweat. To pay for my latest chocolate spree.

I don't look at anyone while I jog in place. I look at a spot directly in front of the machine, fixate on it until I am almost meditating. This is why I don't notice the woman at my side waiting impatiently for me to finish. It's not until she says, rather rudely, "You've been on that for over thirty minutes. That's the max when someone's waiting." I turn to look at her, nearly losing my balance in the process.

She is my age, early thirties. She has straw-colored hair swept from her lovely face in a ponytail, and she looks like an actress I've seen on one of the soaps. I look closer as I press the Stop button on my machine. She is the actress I've seen. Of course she is. All of the actresses you've seen have memberships at my gym.

I murmur an apology for keeping her waiting, then shuffle to one of the racks of weights and start lifting. Again I lose myself, but this time I am meditating on her, visualizing myself as I peel off her red spandex tights, cut through her black spandex thong, wrap the spandex strips around her wrists to capture her.

I have her tied and tormented before I realize that she's staring at me in the mirror. I look at my own reflection rather than meeting her gaze. I am wearing black sweats in a sea of colored spandex. My Medusa ringlets are free and curling more wildly than ever because I'm hot and sweaty. My normally pale cheeks have circles of color in their centers—"apples of color" my grandmother would say.

I'm not overweight. I'm not even untoned. I simply do not look like the Malibu girls who grace the Stairmaster machines. I do not have a swishy ponytail, nor a face you've seen on TV. I work behind the camera.

When I'm done with my self-scrutiny, I realize she's still watching me. Whatever, I think, mimicking my hairdresser who accentuates the statement by making a little *w* with his fingers and thumbs. Then, because I am uncomfortable, I head to the showers, and then to the steam room.

That's where she finds me. She comes in, wearing only a towel, but holding her leotard in one hand. She says, "You were looking at me in the oddest way"—exactly what I want to say to her. She says, "I don't think we'll be interrupted. There's a step class going on, and all the women are in there, sweating."

I say, "But we're in here, sweating." She drops her towel and lets me ogle her beautiful form for a moment before coming toward me and offering me that twisted rope of red Lycra. I don't hesitate. I let her lie down on the white towel on top of the wooden boards while I wrap her leotard around her wrists. I don't have the rest of the accouterments to trick out my envisioned torture chamber, but I like the way she looks as is. Bound, semi-helpless, her muscular thighs spread, her body arched and ready.

I climb up next to her on the wooden bench, and I part those sturdy thighs and go instantly to work. She's wet from her post-workout shower, but she's also wet from want. The subtle flavor of her cunt envelopes me in the same manner as the steam does. It goes to my head, but it's too tasty to pull away from. I lose myself in her cunt. I would climb inside her if I could. I know I should practice a bit of foreplay, let her see what a dutiful and passionate lover I can be. Instead, I go for the prize in the box of Cracker Jacks, fastening my lips in a circle around her clitoris and sucking on it as if it were a piece of hard candy, an everlasting gobstopper that gets sweeter as it melts in your mouth.

She moans and tries to use her hands to push me down on her, but they're tied and helpless. That spurs me on. I lift her thighs up over my shoulders and impale her asshole with my fingers, never moving my lips from her cunt. She's still as I probe her insides. She's completely still, as if I might stop if she moves. I can see how much she likes it, likes the feeling of intrusion there, and that makes me wish I had a dildo to impale her with, instead of only my fingers.

We're both sweating wildly now, but she's close to coming. I bring her to the very peak with fingers, tongue, mouth, the palm of my free hand on her ass, the dig of my nails into her skin. I know the step class must be nearly over, that I need to finish this up. I penetrate her cunt, keeping my busy fingers in her ass, my hungry mouth sealed to her pussy. Her orgasm is an explosion of juices all over my face and lips and sticky fingers. We're both wrecked as we hear the door open, and we hide quickly beneath our towels, her with her bound wrists hidden.

We share secret smiles on the way back to the showers, and she says, "I'm glad I skipped step workout today."

I cock my head at her and bite my tongue, thinking to myself, "Heck, if it burns up the calories, who's to complain?"

SALES QUOTA
Susan Lakow

Everyone knows the reason why Camile Adler sells so much product. It isn't that her line is better than that of other companies. It isn't because she wears cowboy boots with her suits, or has a mane of ginger-colored hair that seems to glint beneath the fluorescent office lights. It's because she takes her job seriously. Her job isn't really to sell her product—anyone could do that—her job is to sell herself. And Camile Adler is very good at her job.

I'm not one for idle gossip. I don't hang out around the water cooler during my coffee break. I don't listen when the other ladies discuss who is sleeping with whom or who broke up with whom. I really don't care.

But when I hear the name "Camile," my attention holds. I continue typing, eavesdropping on the conversation going on outside my office, picking up any information I can. Knowing that Cam has slept her way through the various sales departments in our industry should make her unattractive to me, but it doesn't.

You'd think with all I know about her that I'd be immune. I'm not immune at all. I'm human. And Camile knows all the tricks, all the buttons. She arrives with her sample case and whisks me out to lunch. She orders wine for us, discusses trips she's been on, strokes my hand between courses, strokes my thighs under the table, doesn't talk about business at all.

And I buy her product. I always buy from Camile. Her items are more expensive, but I tell myself, and my bosses, that they are of higher quality. I don't tell them that Camile's ginger hair has marmalade tones in it. That when candlelight casts a glow around our booth, Cam's hair seems to shine with an inner fire. I don't tell them that Camile doesn't wear shirts under her blazers, she wears lacy camisoles you can see when she leans forward, the edge of the lace peeking through, just a little tease of it.

Camile called me recently and asked if I could meet her for dinner instead of lunch. "Above and beyond the call of duty," she said. I could tell she was smiling as she spoke, her perfect teeth glinting against her red-slicked lips. She said, "I know it's after hours, and I won't be offended if you say—"

"Yes," I said quickly, before I could be a good girl and talk myself out of it. "Of course."

She chose a new place, a fancier place. Once we were ensconced in our private booth, she said, "I've been promoted. I'm in charge of a whole sales team now."

"How wonderful," I told her, feeling the tips of her fingers brush against my knees.

"It means someone new will be taking over my territory. Someone else will be calling on you."

I felt cold, and then suddenly hot. I'd grown accustomed to

our lunches, our flirtations, my fantasies. The fingers on my knee worked their way up to my thigh, under my skirt, almost to my panties.

"But I don't want to stop seeing you," Camile said. "I don't think you know how fond I am of you."

"Fond…" I echoed, disliking the word.

"Attracted," she corrected herself. Before the main course came, we were out of the restaurant, Camile paying for an uneaten meal quickly with her corporate card. Camile leading me to a hotel room paid for by her company. Camile bedding me with the skill and finesse of a pro, starting slowly and thoughtfully, undressing me as if I were a very fragile work of art. Keeping one light on in the room so we could see each other's expressions change, but draping the lamp with her scarf so the room glowed gold and pink and made our silhouettes loom large on the wall.

She undid her hair and spread it over my body, covering me with the mane of hair I had so longed to run my fingers through. She stood above me on the bed when she took off her panties and I looked up at her, up the line of her thighs to the delta between them. I asked her to part her lips and she did, moving over my head, letting me lean upward and lap at her like a deer lapping up dew from a fragrant plant. She was agile with her body, first straddling me so that we could kiss, then switching so that she was kissing me down there, kissing the outer lips of my cunt, squeezing them together with her fingers so that my juices were forced to burst through, to coat my lips with a thin, shining gloss.

Camile never tired. She seemed to revive after each climax with more energy than she'd had before. She said that she loved my breasts and suckled from them for long minutes at a time, like a baby, looking up at me with her wide eyes, simultaneously so innocent, so knowing.

When we finally slept, she covered my body with hers, giving me warmth from herself. And in the morning, when we awoke, she insisted on another session. This time with more force behind it, a passionate romp from behind, her with a strap-on brought out of her briefcase, me with my ass in the air and my head in the pillow.

When we checked out, she shook my hand and promised to be in touch. And then, as she walked toward a waiting cab, she called out, "Your new sales representative is Carrie Steinberg. I hope you treat her the same way you've treated me!" And I could only blush.

CONFESSIONS OF A TEENAGE LESBIAN
Susie Bright

It took me six years of fucking women before I was absolutely, positively, certain that I was a dyke. Some lesbians are born; but I was made, slowly and thoroughly, in my own crockpot of sexual adventures.

Now don't get the idea that I ever called myself straight. I received a powerful omen as a teenager that convinced me that I was bisexual.

At fifteen I was extremely unhappy that I had never been kissed. Never held hands, never been on a date, never had an invitation to even one lousy boy-girl party. Not only that, but it was 1974, and virginity was passé in Los Angeles. I was convinced that I was among the handful of girls in my ninth-grade class who hadn't gotten laid yet.

I had certainly been doing my homework for the big occasion. I read all the sexual literature that I could find. I became an expert at finding the sex scene in an otherwise-plodding novel. I practiced kissing with my pillow and was anxiety-ridden over my changing teenage figure.

Like many dykes, I was strictly femme from the word go. No tomboy background for me. I despised sports so much, I ran the wrong way around the bases. Dolls and dresses were where it was at. I was in tears at my first communion because I was the only girl who didn't have a frilly lace outfit to make my historic appointment with Jesus.

When I finally took an interest in boys, it was completely sexual, since I certainly hadn't been able to find any other use for them. I threw my Ken doll away and gave his clothes to Barbie, who had better things to do than make conversation with a dumb boy. Barbie and I were both getting dressed up—and psyched up —for the ultimate date, where the date himself was faceless, but the appointment was definitely for s-e-x.

Probably the best thing I did to get ready for sex was to masturbate, plus all the fantasies that went along with it. Unfortunately, at age eight I had no idea what I was doing. I was pretty sure that the devil had invaded my body, and only a long, dutiful session at church would cleanse me. My duty, however, did not extend to speaking to the parish priest about it. After my first terrific orgasm, I knew I was never going to confession again. How on earth would I explain to the priest what I had done? Before or after my penance for not doing the dishes?

I had to wait until I was twelve before I ever saw a definition for masturbation. Little girls sure didn't talk about it. I never connected jerking off to what I would eventually do in bed with a lover. I made my baby-sitter tell me what "fuck" meant, but I didn't know what a lesbian was, except a nasty thing to call somebody. I remember finding a petition in my desk in the sixth grade, signed by virtually everyone in class, that said "Susie Bright is a faggot." When you're a kid, you don't need to know what a word means to know that you've been scorned.

The summer before I entered high school, I met Christine, my first lover. She was French and lived up the street with a bohemian grandmother and an absentee father. Christine had witchy blonde hair, brown eyes, and a tight, brown, square body. Always barefoot in jeans that clung like sweat, she looked like a tramp and would knock people out with how literate, uninhibited, and reckless she was. I was wildly attracted to her fearlessness, but I was the one to hold the reins. If we were going to drop acid, I had to call up my dad and tell him about it. If we were going to have an orgy in her room, I felt obliged at least to sit down and have supper with her granny beforehand.

Christine was the one who suggested we skinny-dip in the next-door neighbors' pool while they were on vacation. Even though the family was away, they had recently rented their basement apartment to an unemployed soap-opera actor, a Hollywood hunk about to turn thirty.

In what must have been the biggest tease of all time, Dennis the Movie Star, as we called him, would come out with his mirror shades on to watch us play naked in the pool. We upped the ante by coming up to him, still unclothed, and pestering him with personal questions. The scenario moved inside when Christine suggested that he pay us to clean his apartment.

Pretty soon we were at Dennis's every day, mostly talking about sex, scripts, and his health-food fads. He lied terribly about his age, so we stole and hid his driver's license to teach him a lesson. He retaliated by talking about our puberty-struck bodies and what lay ahead in our sexual futures. This sort of scene would inevitably end in pillow fights and wrestling. We all knew what was coming, and Christine and I were not about to let Dennis's guilt get in the way of us losing our virginity.

It finally happened during the World Series. Dennis had the TV on, and we were all lying on his bed as usual, with our legs and arms entwined. I forget what triggered it; maybe the Orioles got a home run. Dennis squeezed the two of us together and said, "Oh, I give up. Let's get on with it."

We buried ourselves in a group hug and, when I looked up, Christine's fresh face was right in front of my eyes. She was the first one I kissed. I wonder whether this first kiss was so fantastic because it was my first kiss or my first woman. I remember that Dennis's lips did not give me the same electric shock. But I really wanted him for one thing: our deflowering. I was ecstatic to be finally doing it. I wanted to do everything I'd ever read about, all in one hour. I was sublimely gratified when Dennis remarked that he couldn't believe this was the first time I'd ever sucked cock.

Our threesome was quite conventional, as a ménage à trois goes. Christine and I put all of our efforts into our shared male animal. We kissed each other and touched breasts but, curiously, we never went below the waist. Maybe if I had read something about how lesbians do it, I could have included it in my homework. But, like the most innocent homophobe, I really had no idea of what two women could do together. I had been so hyped up about the ultimate union of cock and cunt that it was hard to imagine anything else. It was sort of disappointing to discover that the old in-and-out didn't get me off. I didn't play with my clit as I normally did while masturbating, and I would have been embarrassed if Mr. Movie Star had made any mention of it.

Christine and I made a good fucking team. Our experience with Dennis made us very bold and enterprising to meet other men in the same way. Picking up a stranger might have been intimidating all alone, but the two of us could storm the available field. We insisted that the two of us come together with every sexual encounter. Most men were delighted; it was their fantasy come true.

And Christine and I were the stuff men's lesbian fantasies are made of—young, soft, and eager to please, just like the spreads you see in men's magazines, except that I wore glasses, and both of us wore flip-flops instead of high heels.

The first time Christine and I did it for ourselves was at the end of a long day of psychedelics. We decided to jump into a shower together and wash off all the bad vibes. Something about the euphoria of all the hot water and steam suddenly made our below-the-waist barrier melt away. I moved from washing her back to sudsing up her pubic hair. There is nothing like a soapy, slippery, bubbly cunt in your hands. I started licking rivulets of water off her neck, and she continued the same on my breasts and stomach. I felt this hunger in my gut to take all of her into me, to do anything for her. This was beyond "eagerness to please"—I needed it for myself. "I have to tell you something. I haven't been able to before—" she began.

I couldn't wait. I just knew she was going to tell me that she loved me, and I was going to return her love with all my—

"I can't stand the way you kiss; you don't know how to kiss at all!"

Christine didn't pull any punches. She proceeded to give me a kissing lesson. Even though I was offended, even though the intensity from the shower was dissolving, I was shocked by her criticism and took her lessons to heart. She let me practice a bit on her precious French mouth, and then it was over.

Christine never found out whether my lovemaking techniques improved. Something about that night drew us apart, rather than closer. Christine started hanging out with bikers in Topanga Canyon and ripped off my motorcycle helmet as a farewell gesture. Meanwhile, I discovered the women's liberation movement.

You know, some teenagers get into Bible-study groups, some go off into athletics, and a few, like me, get involved with radical politics.

I got initiated into the local women's movement because a group on my campus organized an event-filled Women's Week to counteract the traditional Girls' Week. Girls' Week was planned by the dean of women to include powder-puff football, a mother-daughter fashion show, and the prerequisite bake sale. But Women's Week was a different matter. The students proposed panel discussions on birth control, rape prevention, and sexuality, including an appearance by a real live lesbian. After months of protesting and fighting, we got what we wanted, with the stipulation of a parental-permission slip.

The Lesbian Sex Panel was packed to the rafters with students who had produced authentic or forged permission slips. I didn't realize it at the time, but the school's entire gay faculty, including the school's damned closet-case dean of women, was in the audience.

This was my seventies-style introduction to the gay community. I knew nothing about gay bar life, and I didn't look old enough even to try. I came to think that lesbianism was a righteous response to sexism, a noble commitment that I identified with intellectually. I didn't connect the lesbians in meetings with the hunger I had felt with Christine in the shower.

Just as I missed the connections between masturbating and making love with a partner, I once again completely missed the boat when it came to putting lesbian politics together with lesbian sex. Maybe I'll blame some of this on the first lesbians I ever met. They never talked about sex.

I passed feverish notes to my dyke classmate Sherry, but they were all about "women making coffee instead of policy" and only rarely about getting it on. Sherry once confided to me that her girlfriend Yvonne, of whom I was envious enough already, was multi-orgasmic.

"She comes if you even look at her," Sherry complained. "I can't come at all."

I didn't understand that; and since I didn't get into bed with Sherry for another two years, I forgot about it.

Immediately after my fling with Christine, I began to have affairs with all my girlfriends. They were "liberated" and willing, and I was the happy initiator. My friend Beth will always be memorable. We used to make out in her bedroom while her parents were just down the hall, and laugh ourselves silly because they would never suspect what we were up to.

Beth and I were shy with one another in bed, and it set the tone for my relationships with women for many years. We didn't play with each other's breasts too much because perhaps that might seem like some awful man-type thing to do. We didn't penetrate each other because that must obviously be "male-identified." These hang-ups, which we thought were so politically correct, succeeded only in casting aside practically everything one could do in bed as the private turf of "heterosexuals only." We might as well have gone to the pope for advice. Oral sex was fine, of course, but since none of the women I seduced had ever even looked at their own cunts, it was sometimes difficult to jump into muff-diving.

Beth and I were getting into some pretty sophisticated lovemaking with our male lovers, but somehow it wasn't ladylike to share this behavior with each other. Thank God what we lacked in boldness we made up in goofy creativity. One time we covered our pussies with salami and avocado and ate each other out. In bed with Beth, I spent more time laughing than coming, but that still beat a lot of other bedtime stories I could tell.

Two years later, at a large social function, Beth came up to me and exclaimed at the top of her lungs how happy she was that I had made her into a lesbian. I was somewhat taken aback since, as I said, we were not the most sexual couple; but I accepted the compliment anyway. Beth is now married to a man and working as a deputy district attorney in a large West Coast city, which goes to show that just because you come out of the closet doesn't mean you can't change your mind.

I continued my career of fucking older, kinkier men and at the same time seducing my naïve straight girlfriends. As I learned more about what I liked in heterosexual sex, I grew increasingly frustrated with the inhibitions in my affairs with women.

By now I knew that I like getting fucked if I could play with my clit. I liked fantasizing and telling stories while I made love. I liked anal sex. I liked the rubbing and humping that came before screwing. I was also learning more subtle things, like how even though my nipples weren't very sensitive, I loved my breasts to be desired and caressed. Or how I never got a physical kick out of sucking cock, but I sure liked the feeling of power it gave me.

With women I was now in the position of being the veteran dyke: "Susie Bright's Coming-Out School for Young Ladies." Though at first I liked the thrill of turning on another woman for her first time, the novice response got to be predictable. Either she wouldn't stop gushing about how perfect gay life was going to be, or she couldn't look me in the eye the next morning. I could understand why some lesbians thought bisexuality was a pain in the ass.

Still, I had always been scared of "real" dykes, and I had yet to go to bed with one. The "real dykes" were the ones who seemed masculine. Female masculinity was weird to me. I had never considered that my fearful fascination might be an attraction. All my girlfriends were very fluffy and feminine; they made me seem butch by comparison.

Butch. The first time I heard that word was the fateful night I finally got my old high-school dyke friend Sherry between the sheets. I figured that if I was going to take the plunge with a genuine lezzie, Sherry would be the perfect initiator. Was I ever wrong.

"Don't try to make me come, 'cause I won't," she warned me before we even got our tops off. She started giggling like mad. "Don't you know? I'm butch!" she said, as if butchness were an automatic qualifier for not coming. And with that she sank her sharp little teeth into my neck.

Who knows what would have happened next if her ex-old lady hadn't picked that exact moment to knock on the door. Sherry hid in the bathroom, locked the door, and left me in bed with a Spinners record blaring "For the Love of You." The visitor banged and yelled at the door for fifteen minutes. When she finally quit and left, Sherry packed me up and out of there before you could say "disaster area." Once again, my lesbian love life had been nipped in the bud.

I came out of Sherry's wondering whether being butch meant that you couldn't come or that you had a thing for hickeys. I could hardly believe a super-political dyke like Sherry would use that word. I thought butches and femmes were from the bad old days of gay life, when everyone thought they were sick or twisted. The gals who were butch felt that they should have been born men, and heaven knows how femmes fit in. No one ever bothered to explain femmes.

Many people think that a woman who is feminine couldn't possibly be a dedicated dyke. The truth is, a femme like me never appreciated my feminine possibilities until I hooked up with another woman. Butch women are my biggest turn-on, and it's a very gay feeling to me. I wish that masculinity and femininity were erotic opportunities for people to express themselves, instead of some predestined roles in which they feel enslaved.

Heterosexuals have always been the most uptight about sex roles, but a lot of lesbians react in the opposite extreme. I have lesbian acquaintances who think that if I'm a femme, I must have to wash the dishes all the time; and that if I'm a good girl, maybe my butch will fuck me in the missionary position. Give me a break! Gender-fuck scenes like butch-femme are self-conscious sexual decisions about what turns us on, and that's a special freedom I'll always treasure.

At twenty-one, I was finally old enough to go barhopping. This was my first nonpolitical introduction to gay life. It was a blast. I met gay men for the first time. Gender was an entirely sexual passion to them, a hot fantasy; not a reason to get married, have kids, and grit your teeth. By talking to men who loved to suck cock, I realized that I didn't. Certainly there are straight women who love cocksucking just as much, but they don't get much support for talking about it.

Women don't get much of an opportunity at all to talk about what turns us on, and the result is that we have a limited vocabulary. Case in point: when I finally got out onto a mere dance floor with one of those butch women who scared me so, my body started sending up signals that my mouth couldn't interpret. I didn't want a real man, I wanted a real bulldyke.

"Come on, let's cool off outside," was my clever line. I dragged the butch off without waiting for an answer. We stood outside this bar located in the middle of a warehouse district—all alleys and dark shadows and railroad yards. There was only one thing to do, and that was to lie down on the tracks. She pushed my legs open with her knee, and I thought I was going to come right then and there. She leaned my head deeper into the gravel and slipped her fingers into my mouth. Next time you see an airbrushed lesbian fantasy of two ingenues licking each other's wrists, think of me being finger-fucked in my mouth while I rode this lucky butch's knee until the denim tore.

My disco-side encounter didn't last long, but it gave me an idea about how things could be different. I started looking for a different kind of woman. I told my boyfriend that I was going butch or bust.

For a while, it was just plain bust. That's how I discovered vibrators. I went vibrator shopping for the common reason that I didn't have a lover, and I wanted to spice up my solo sex life. I had been masturbating in the exact same style and position since I was eight, and it was about to break my arm.

The vibrator, with its humming round head, was irresistible whether I was lying on my back or standing on my head. At first it was a gas to see how fast I could come—under two minutes. But then I changed the game to see how long I could make it last, how long I could hold myself in the exquisite place of almost-coming-but-not-quite. Not having to worry about my arm pooping out opened me up to a lot of possibilities.

I tried sticking the tip of my hairbrush into my cunt while I vibrated. That was so wonderful that I started scavenging through the fridge to see if there were any other delights that could be used in the same manner. I found a summer squash that I could have settled down and had a family with. Actually, my whole approach to my new toys was just that: like a kid who's has never even had a wooden spool to play with. How unfortunate that I had waited to be single before I picked up a few of these items.

I waited a spell before I had the nerve to show my dildos and vibrator to a new lover—of course it helped that the lover I chose was an ex-vibrator saleswoman herself. My self-consciousness reminded me of how nervous I'd been to touch my clit in front of Dennis or Christine so long ago.

Showing someone what turns me on seems like a secret, and a

shameful one at that. I made a tragic pact with the devil when I was a God-fearing little girl, to keep quiet about masturbation. I was afraid of where my orgasms might lead me—hell was my best guess. Part of Satan's deal was to keep your mouth shut and don't let others see your sinful pleasure. That's the only way you'll get to keep it to yourself. Funny how an eight-year-old can come up with a rationale like that, but I had the whole history of the church's and state's values bearing down on me.

My American Catholic experience made me a little slow to realize my predilections: bisexuality, butch women, gay society, Hitachi magic wands. But once I'd seen the light, I started talking —and writing—in all the velvet and wet tongues I know how.

SATAN'S BEST
Red Jordan Arobateau

Afternoon light lifts into the window. Angel had noticed that just like herself, Crystal was a real blond. Curly near-platinum blonde hair grew out from the roots. It grew out of her eyebrows & her pussy.

Crystal humped on the bed. Flat belly tight with effort, she pushed her fuzzy cunt into Angel's mouth. All the while kept her blue eyes fixed on Angel's face lapping & sucking her pungent cunt. And the butch was so hot, her hands squeezing Crystal, feeling her tits, her warm body; she just wanted to crawl up the bed over Crystal, get on top & fuck her. She wanted her so bad!

"Wanna fuck, Angel?"

"Yeah," Angel said softly.

Crystal wriggled up the bed by the pillow to lay back, naked, eyes riveted tenderly on the butch. But Angel reached the pillow first, fumbled under it, then pulled out her gun, and put it on the nightstand shyly.

Sheepishly, Crystal bounced off the side of the bed, went to retrieve her pink leather jacket which lay on the floor, zipped open a pocket, got her own gun, & put it on the nightstand next to Angel's. Then threw her jacket into the chair.

Angel saw the marks. Scab healing, traces of the whip welts; what Hawk had done to her days ago, & was mad. Thought about the warlord's blood she had shed at the fight & was glad. 'It makes up for this.' Then, a second, powerful thought: how she wanted to make up for the pain even more, with love. They both lay together. Arms embracing. The world had left its marks, hard, on them.

The two lesbians lay on the bed, on top of the covers. Angel admired Crystal's nails, saw her toes & fingers were painted the same color. And her ears were pierced with tiny gold earrings under the fluff of hair.

The cozy hotel room was silent. Daylight muted thru venetian blinds, dusty. —It had seen many transient couples at play. Boy/girl, boy/boy, & even girl/girl, before.

Painfully aware that her feet stank, —from having worn no socks in her boots, Angel was sorry now she hadn't taken better care of her hygiene. But the young woman didn't seem to mind.

"Excuse me a minute."

Went into the bathroom, pulled off her stinking pajamas gingerly, over the cuts and bruises. The pile of her leather clothes from last night;—pissed-in pants, torn jacket sat in a pile. Threw the pajamas on top of it. Got a bar of soap, muscular body downed with blonde hair, stood, lathering her armpits & between her legs; and washed her feet quickly. Washed off the old body smell from the fight, from the road.

Now she was clean. The fresh butch limped back to the bed,

stood naked before Crystal. Square shoulders, medium-size breasts with pink nipples. Beautiful breasts. A flat belly covered with blond down. Long sculptured white legs, muscled. Stood, feet planted firm, before the pretty femme, arms dangling at her sides. She wanted to say something,—what she'd been wondering: 'Is she here because she really wants me, or because the warlords made her come?' Then shrugged & kept silent.

The femme was eager for her, arms open wide. They lay beside each other, pressed together, hot; stomach to stomach, tits smashed together; horny cunts waiting to receive each other's love.

For the first time, Crystal saw the butch's body completely nude. The tattoos, the scars. Her dragon & hearts stenciled into flesh. And the permanent record. —Those long scars across her lower ribs from the incision where they'd put her internal organs back together were evidence of her brush with death.

Crystal traced a scar with her finger. Gradually it turned into the green stem of a rose. "Let me look at you, baby! OHHH! I've never seen you with your shirt off!" Crystal admired the entire rose tattoo, blue, red & green on Angel's left shoulder twining over her back, with the green stem curling around near the 2nd rib. "OHHH!" The blonde cooed, eyes shut a moment, feeling what Angel was patiently doing to her; stroking, sucking her tits, & beginning to work her long, sturdy fingers down into the wet slit between her legs. "Ohhh, you're so nice, Angel.... Whoever had you all these years, they had a prize. Ohhh, Baby!" And the femme leaned down & kissed her neck softly.

Angel stroked Crystal gently. Massaged her firm young flesh. Angel winced—so did Crystal—trying not to hurt each other's scrapes & sores & cuts as they made love. Soon the hungry adult aroma of their bodies filled the room.

Lay in bed, caressing. Crystal wondered how it would be. 'With Hawk, sometimes I had to wait all night. Lay there waiting for her to take me, for her to make her move. *God,* I hope Angel *is* a butch. She *seems* like one. She *walks* like one. She *fights* like one. But she's soft... Sometimes Hawk she goes for my tits first, or my cunt first with her fingers, & I have to beg her to take off her rings.'

'I want to do everything at once,' Angel thought.

'Unless she's sick with cramps...or high on crank... then she won't do anything,' Crystal thought.

The sturdy blonde butch caressed the sweet vision steadily, massaged her lovingly. Took time, & aroused herself & Crystal simultaneously.

'What will it be today?' Crystal mused, as sexual heat began to sweep up from her groin & shoot through her body. 'With Hawk I could either spread my legs & draw my knees up so she get her cunt to my pussy; or fight. —And the fight might last 5 minutes, if Hawk decided to throw & break the last dishes she had in her house.'

"My sweet, sweet broad..." The sound of Angel moaning in her ear brought Crystal back to reality. Angel was whispering lovetalk. "My sweet, sweet broad!" Angel moaned.

Finally the blonde butch couldn't stand it. She had to stop and ask, "You came here 'cause I won the fight, I guess... Outlaw Code?"

"*Nobody sent me!*" Crystal's eyes flashed, mad. Paused a moment, then explained, "I came because I wanna see how good you can make love to me! I never got the chance before! *Remember?*"

"Oh..." Angel was sheepish, & returned to her work, placing her hot mouth over the nipple of Crystal's full breast as she kneaded the round orb with one hand. Sucked & licked the pert pink nipple.

Crystal smiled down at the head sucking at her tits like a greedy baby.

Crystal saw Angel's womanly body & masculinity—both. Knew she wanted to make love to the butch, too. Pink bodies, blonde pubic hair. Secretly she compared their bodies together.

Crystal was sleazy, nasty; & it was consensual.

Angel had progressed from licking the soft warm cleavage of Crystal's full bosom, to sucking her clit nested in wet flesh inside her pussylips and pubic hair. Soon Crystal's thighs were wet with saliva & discharge. And Crystal moaned, lifted up the big butch's head & shoulders, and turned around the opposite way, scooted down the bed to put her head between Angel's thighs, to lick her sex as well; in the 69 position. Both women were burning with lust; felt they could suck, lick, & penetrate each other's pussies all night long.

They were a bride & her groom in marriage.

There's always something special about undressing a woman for the first time; to see how she moves; what she can do for you; how she makes your pussy feel.

Angel's big hands—one with the Born to Raise Hell tattoo—pushed Crystal back on the pillow, taking charge. Got the other pillow and slid it under her ass. She mounted her. Crystal spread her thighs wide, legs up in the air. Angel was between them, her clit mashed into the curly blonde femme's wet cunt, taking a long, leisurely screw. Around and around, up and down, working her hips till beads of sweat glistened on their backs.

Angel thought privately: 'God, her pussy *is* nice! Just like Hawk said! She's built right so I can get to it easy. Big cunt lips to roll my clit around in; and nice & wet. FUCK!'

The butch could almost hear a crackling fire in the stone fireplace of the castle. Because now she was Lord of the Manor. Having dined on a sumptuous feast of pheasant under glass, and goblets of the finest wine, feet up on a polished mahogany table, & now the evening was culminating in the sexual favors of her favorite wench—Lady Crystal.

Getting It. Tension in her muscles grew strong. Clit was hard. Her knees pressed into the sheets, one hand on each side of Crystal's body, bracing herself up as her hips drove in & out, pressing her pussy down so they were clit to clit, pubic hairs mixing together; her fucking driving Crystal's ass into the mattress. The unfamiliar scent of two new lovers. Hips moving, rocking, rolling as the slow circular motion becomes rapid…. As each had learned to do with different partners thru time & loving before.

Outside the window, past the iron city, was the music of the sun. Blare of traffic below. —So far removed that its noise did not touch these dwellers on the hotel's higher floors.

She had took so long because she wanted to enjoy lovemaking before she had an orgasm. —The path leading up to it was so splendid.

Her hot throbbing pulse.

Sex between women.

BANG BANG! The peak hit her. Angel's body writhed in ecstasy between Crystal's legs.

The femme was very excited but still hadn't cum. Angel had a solution for this, but Crystal wanted to do something first. She asked the blonde butch a very pertinent question to which she got this response. "I'm not just a butch!" Angel said. "I'm a dike who is a woman and who loves women!"

"Oh good, honey! Let me touch you! —A lot of butch women won't."

And she did.

One of her manicured hands touched Angel's tit. Fingers spread over it like a starfish. Squeezed. Lifted its weight in the palm of her hand while squeezing the nipple. Generating a rush of sexual heat. Put her mouth to the butch's breast & sucked.

A while later, a shy voice asks, "Can I go inside you?"

"Yeah," Angel sez. A smile spreads over her broad face. Pushes aside her blonde hair, lay back on the pillows and studiously watched the femme bend over her carefully, with her fingers parting her wispy blonde pubic hair.

Crystal's bare fingers slid in Angel's clear mucus and cum, and pushed inside her vagina.

Put her mouth back to Angel's breast & began to suck the nipple. Courses of desire began to run thru the butch anew at the expert treatment she was receiving. Fingers went in & out of her. Now she saw why Crystal kept her nails so short.

The femme's wet lipsticked mouth covered Angel's in a long tongue-probing kiss. Their tongues swirled around & around each other's mouths, mixing their saliva. Angel felt chills of lust with each thrust of those fingers pounding her cunt.

A femme's sweet fingers in a butch's cunt, wet, bare, its needs so hot. Rejoicing in the feel of a lover inside her.

Butch cunt; dripping hot hole opening up, wanting to be fucked.

Crystal slid down so her curly head was near Angel's pubic curls; blonde curls mixing as her tongue sought Angel's clit. Her hand continued to pound hard and fast, thrusting her shapely fingers; the butch felt it all thru her body. Was so excited. Her lips quivered involuntarily. Lipstick was smeared all over her thighs.

Soon the butch threw back her head, hollered, as her hips pumped in a climax, giving herself up to it with total abandon.

In a while, Angel had enough. Rose up, encircling the femme in strong arms.

She stroked Crystal's thighs, and pressed her face to the hot wet crotch. Crystal held her shoulders & squeezed as the sexual tension grew. The butch sucked her off, pink tongue darting over & over the pearl of Crystal's clit, as her full lips sucked at the same time. Crystal's hips went up & down as she rode Angel's mouth, faster, faster, until she, too, hollered, *AAAAAAHHHHH-AAAAA-OOOOOOOUUHHHHH!*" It was so good; a giant thorough climax.

Angel smiled up at her. Then buried her face in Crystal's fuzzy cup once more. Gently planted a full lip kiss on her labia.

Then they lay side by side.

About thirty minutes later, after they had rested from multiple orgasms, the blonde Angel swung her sturdy bruised legs out of bed. Shoulders flexed as she got up and went to her music system on top of the dresser & put on some hot sounds with a pounding beat; so to make love in time to the rhythm with synchronized hip thrusts.

Back on the sheets, sitting up on her knees; as Crystal lovingly slipped the silver-studded black harness around her thighs and waist, then lay back on the pillow to admire it.

Satiny black leather; silver buckles that held an 8" cock in place. —One of many from the dresser drawer. Its rubbery substance, flesh color protruded out of the harness, ending in a lifelike tip. Its base rested against Angel's swollen clit.

Crystal grinned. Lipstick had worn off her full lips, which remained faint pink; blue eyes twinkled. She slid her hand up and down Angel's muscular thighs. Expressionless, the butch reached between her legs, pulling the rubber cock & pointing it at Crystal. "Want some sugar, Crystal? Want some honey from your Daddy?"

And came to her again as the femme spread her legs willingly, moaning under her, caressing her back passionately with both hands; moving her hips, opening her thighs, as Angel entered her with the cock.

As she put her long, hard female rod down in her, Crystal felt ecstasy.

She took her strong.

Angel supported herself up on her hands, one on either side; hips going *bang bang bang* fucking hard.

Pushed the tool in and out of her femme's cunt.

First she fucked her deep and slow.

Crystal moaned and groaned, turning her head side to side; knees open brought up to her chest. Ringed fingers clenched the flesh of Angel's butt, gripped it, and drew her ass closer; swallowing the thrusting cock deeper inside herself.

Since she'd already cum two times, it was harder to make it for the third. Angel lasted a lot longer fucking. White ass going up and down on Crystal. Crystal's butt raising up and slapping back down onto the sheets in a rhythm that matched. And the beat of the pounding music drove them into higher thrills of lust. The two women steamed up Angel's room.

Angel. She rode her women like she rode her bike. —Hard.

Crystal felt the long tool in her cunt. Felt the thrusts draw out, then plunge in deep. In/out. In/out. Drew her knees up & spread wider, eyes squinted as she strained to reach the pinnacle, lips opened, issuing a long series of moans of pleasure.

Two blondes. Angel's arms taut on each side of Crystal. Muscles flexed with effort & the sweat of their bodies mixed as they humped together. Crystal's grip tightening on her butt; now Angel caught the wings of sexual tension, felt her crotch rise in power; the woman was bucking up underneath, her stomach hard, body taut, humping bare hips in short jabs to match her own.

And Crystal came, rising up so beautifully beneath her. Crystal clawed Angel's shoulders. "DON'T STOP, BUTCH BUTCH! DON'T STOP! UH UH UH OH OH OH *OHOOOOHHH! BUTCHY BUTCH! ANGEL! UHHHH!*" Crystal hollered. Angel's white cheeks were red with effort beneath her scars; blue eyes serious watching the girl under her as she fucked; hot sex lust growing wild out of control like wild horses between her legs.

Crystal had her orgasm first: "*OOOHHH AAAHHH AHHHH UHHHH OOOOHHH!*"

A serious look on Angel's face; "*UH UH UH!*" Made a sound with each thrust. Then Angel came. She melted into a malleable substance. Female ejaculation dripped down their thighs from her release; body kept going like a bucking bronco a long time, up/down, up/down, writhing between the femme's legs, using every last ounce of lust, cumming and cumming till her clit was drained dry. And wrapped her arms around Crystal, mightily, in a hug, as if for an eternity.

Stars flashed in their eyes.

The equipment was hot. —Unbuckled it and threw the rubbery toy aside. It had worked their clits well.

Flopped down next to her sleeping mate.

They awoke soon.

Crystal couldn't keep her mouth off Angel's fuzzy blonde cunt.

Told Crystal after, "My body gushes when I cum. It ain't piss, it's a female ejaculation. It's sort of a water spray & it tastes like sugar. —So I been told."

"I'm proud of you. You went on and on for *minutes*."

"It tastes sweet. That's what my jail wife told me. That's where I got time to practice it & learned how. I use to do it before just sometimes, when I'd been fucking a long time. Women would think I was pissing on them—it was embarrassing."

The couple lay back on the sheets of the double bed. The blonde butch's lacerations began to hurt once more, now that passion had subsided.

Angel breathed a deep sigh, resounding out of her guts. She had been thoroughly serviced by an Outlaw biker chick. Cunt, clit, & tits. 'So I'm a member of the Outlaws now.... It's been decided for me.' Angel thought. Arms around the girl. Inside the cozy room. —Within the warm animal needs of each other.

The two had done some hard fucking. Now they were covered with each other's sweat and cum and juices.

Lay as if in the hand of God. Two dikes in completeness. Felt that motion like the sea rock thru them, in an echo of their screwing.

BLACK MAGIC WOMAN
Anastasia Philips

J anina had always been into the occult. She'd worn witch costumes each Halloween from first grade on. She painted the walls of her bedroom black and replaced all of the normal light bulbs with red ones. Her parents, a musician and an artist, encouraged her to explore and, when talking among themselves in bed at night, assured each other that she'd grow out of her witchy ways. But she didn't.

Instead, she grew into looks that confused her parents continually. Her mother took down the family photo album and paged through it, trying to find the ancestor responsible for Janina's eyes. Her eyes, a normal green at birth, turned gradually as she grew older, becoming a fiery emerald with purple rims and huge liquid irises. Janina's mother looked for the relative who had bestowed ebony hair upon her daughter, hair that had been brown when she was born. Janina's father was a sandy blonde. Her mother dyed her gray hair the same shade of brown it had always been. But during her thirteenth year, Janina, with no assistance from dye, sprouted thick black hair that grew quickly, until she had a coil of it she could unwrap and let hang to the ground.

By the time Janina left home for college, her friends (referred to behind their backs as "the coven"), had studied enough of the occult to be able to perform minor spells. Actually, the girls studied, but only Janina could make the spells work. She was particularly good at love spells and love potions and, at one point or another, all of the girls had availed themselves of her services. However, Janina had never used a love spell herself. Not until she graduated from college and got her first job, one with the avant-garde 'zine *Soiree*.

Here she felt truly at home for the first time. The other women at the 'zine didn't comment on her clothes or appearance. In fact, many of them dressed in similarly unconventional ways. And it was here, at the 'zine, that Janina met Audrey, *Soiree*'s editor-in-chief.

Audrey had hair that was black on one side and pure white on the other. Audrey's eyes were like two sapphire balls. Even in dim light, they shone. When Janina and Audrey shook hands for the first time, an energy crackled between them strong enough to send tiny bursts of light flickering from the tips of Janina's midnight hair. That made Audrey laugh and lead Janina to the safety of her mammoth cavelike office.

"You're new," Audrey said, once both women were seated in her plush, zebra-lined chairs. Janina nodded. She could feel the heat and power radiating from her new boss, and she could also feel something else, an undercurrent of sexual desire. She'd always been able to cast love spells for her friends. Now she wondered if she could cast one for herself. She stared long and hard into Audrey's eyes.

Audrey laughed again, this time so loudly that the black marble walls of her office shook and their white veins shifted their designs. "You're trying to cast a spell on me?" Audrey asked, still laughing. "You...?" While Janina searched for an answer, Audrey winked. Suddenly Janina was naked. Audrey spread her arms wide apart, and Janina found herself standing, pirouetting before her boss, under no power of her own. Her pussylips were spread apart by invisible hands, her insides were probed and prodded, then filled, as if with a thick, living cock, but no lover could be seen.

Audrey enjoyed the spectacle without moving from her chair. Through her commands, Janina was stretched out in midair, arms and legs apart, head back, long hair undone and floating like a dark halo around her.

Janina didn't dare speak, could not compete with a power as strong as Audrey's. Instead, she let herself enjoy the sensations... Now her asscheeks were parted and a new member inserted into her asshole. These probing cocks felt almost snakelike, wiggling into her, touching all of her secret places. The invisible dildos throbbed and pulsed, changed temperature as if responding to her inner desires, glowing warm in her cunt and cool in her ass, then changing. Janina closed her eyes and basked in the feeling of being so well-filled. She opened her mouth, obeying a command in her head, and a third probing, pulsing toy filled this orifice.

Audrey clapped her hands at the spectacle, then rotated her fingers. The members inside Janina began to spin, their vibrations welling up inside her until she began to come. She opened her eyes and could see her cuntjuices dropping to the floor below her. Each droplet created a rainbow of lights when it hit the floor. The effect was too powerful. She felt herself swoon. She woke, dressed again, being rocked against Audrey's breast.

"Never try to outspell a more powerful witch," Audrey whispered.

Janina nodded and lowered her mouth onto the smooth, cool skin of Audrey's nipple, suckling gently, until she was rewarded with a honey-sweet nectar. Audrey stroked Janina's hair softly and sighed with the pleasure of finding her one true love.

DINNER FOR SIX
Carole Few

Valentine fluttered about the apartment waiting for her guests to arrive. Candles lit, table set, flowers arranged...everything was in perfect order. The musical chimes sounded and she raced to the door.

"Damn! Where'd I put the dildo?"

The bells rang again and she spun wildly, then stared at herself in the hall mirror, brushing a wisp of hair from her eyes. Ah...

The bullet-shaped silver toy lay on the antique dresser behind her. She slipped it into the top drawer, then ran her hands down her thighs, smoothing her red silk dress. Finally, as the bell sang out for the third annoying time, she whisked open the front door.

Ella and Simone breezed into the foyer in a flurry of air kisses and high-pitched twitters. They each shed the expensive fox furs draped artfully over their shoulders to reveal matching tuxedos.

Ella and Simone lived on the edge. Valentine had gone over it.

As she ushered her first guests into the living room, the bell rang again. The rest of her guests, Max, Samantha, and Tess, had driven together. The three friends were all in black, and Tess had a becoming leather collar around her neck. The trio greeted Valentine and followed her into the living room, where Ella and Simone were already in a sixty-nine, sprawled on top of their furs. Ella's golden body was astride Simone's. She looked up, her mouth glossy with Simone's heavenly come, and then motioned for the others to join in.

Valentine, immensely pleased that her party was already in full swing, hurried into the kitchen for the champagne. By the time she had it open and on a tray along with six glasses, the party of two on the living-room floor had become a party of five.

Tess, now wearing a leash attached to her collar, sat on her haunches, licking Maxine's asshole like a good girl. Samantha, wielding a crop that Valentine had left out for just this purpose, stood ready to punish Tess if she stopped or failed in her duty. Maxine, on hands and knees, was busy licking Ella's own exposed rosebud. The group was so beautiful that Valentine had to get a photo. She set down the tray and rushed to the study for her camera.

But when she returned, the women had switched positions. Now Tess was over Maxine's lap, being punished for touching her own cunt while servicing Max. Ella regarded the discipline session lazily while Simone lapped busily between Ella's legs, sucking hungrily on Ella's clit.

Samantha still held the crop. She decided to put it to new use, thrusting the handle of it into her pussy and rocking on it. She was so enjoying this fucking that Valentine wanted to give her an even better one, rushing away again, this time for her dildo and strap-on. She returned, stripped of her red silk dress, and wearing the silver toy in a harness.

But now, as if to mock their host, the women had maneuvered into a chain of tongues to cunts. Maxine had her head between Simone's legs. Ella had her mouth sealed to Max's cunt. Tess, her poor hot bottom up in the air, was taking care of Ella. Sam, who had relinquished the dripping crop, was servicing Tess. And Simone, the breathless brunette beauty, was making nice to Samantha's lovely pussy.

Valentine sighed and sat down on the edge of the sofa. Her guests were enjoying each other most obviously. Things were going well for her. Dinner parties usually made her so nervous. Now, watching the glorious chain of lovemaking, she removed the dildo from the harness and turned it around, inserting it into her own cunt. She fucked herself while watching the women, finding the rhythm she liked the best, rocking her hips on her velvet couch and watching, watching....

Above her fireplace mantel was a framed print of Klimt's *The Virgin*, below it the women were all lapping and overlapping each other's bodies beneath a multicolored blanket. As Valentine looked back and forth between the picture and the women, she had the feeling of watching art in motion, art come to life.

CLEO
Isabelle Nathe

C leo tied and untied the snakelike silk belt around her wrists. It belonged to the gold Oriental robe tossed casually over her shoulders. Jamie was watching television, not paying attention to Cleo at all. There was a basketball game on—the Lakers, Jamie's most-beloved team. Cleo would have to wait, as always.

Sighing, Cleo returned to their bedroom and lay down on the brocade, canopied bed. She stared at the heavy fabric above her, still tying and untying the belt around her wrists. She pretended that she was tied down, unable to get free. She imagined that Jamie came into the room and took advantage of her bound form. What would she do? What would happen? Jamie might undress Cleo slowly, sliding her nightgown up her thighs, revealing the porcelain-pale skin of her belly. Jamie might nuzzle her face

between Cleo's legs, giving upon her that most enchanting pleasure. She might even make her come slowly, sweetly, with her
tongue alone. That kind of climax made Cleo soak the sheets.
Then, when Jamie entered her, she was wet and open, her body
receptive to Jamie's huge synthetic cock.

Cleo could hear the cheering from the other room. The Lakers
had scored. She tied and untied the belt around her wrists again,
doing it tighter this time. She closed her eyes. What if Jamie
caught her? What if Jamie came in and took the ends of the belt
and tied them for real? She wouldn't be able to move her hands
then. Jamie might tease her, might not give her the pleasure she
longed for. Instead, Jamie might take Cleo her own way. Turning
her lover over, face down, thrusting her cock inside Cleo's pussy
and forcing her way in.

The thought made Cleo very wet. She could imagine being
face down in the pillow—not really screaming, but close. She
liked the thought of being taken, of being play-raped, her wrists
tied, Jamie's firm hand on the back of her head. The image made
her so wet that she considered relieving the throbbing need
between her legs, untying herself and rubbing her clit between her
fingers until she came.

Another cheer from the study. Jamie's dark, sultry voice gone
suddenly deeper with excitement. Cleo untied her wrists and then
brought the belt between her legs, pulling on the loose ends so that
the coil of gold fabric pressed firmly against her cunt, dividing her
pussylips and digging into her clit. She felt weak for a moment,
then pulled on the ends of the belt even harder, rocking her hips
against the wedge of material, imagining a machine that might do
this for her. A machine in which she were captive, bound to a wall
firmly by her wrists. A machine with a snakelike attachment that
went between her legs, a coil of thick, soft fabric that was pulled,
in the same manner that she was pulling on the belt now. She

would beg for mercy. She would plead. But the nasty thing would keep rubbing until its pressure made her come.

She liked that thought, removed the belt and brought it to her lips, tasting her own juices that had soaked through the gold fabric. She inhaled deeply to smell her rich fragrance. She wondered how Jamie would act if she confessed her deepest fantasies, her desire to be bound and made love to.

She tied the belt around her wrists, then untied it. In the other room, the television shut off. Jamie's voice called out, "Cleo? You awake?" And then the footsteps sounded down the hall and the bedroom door opened.

Cleo lay with the belt between her lips—it was a gag, placed there by the queen. She must not undo it. In Cleo's fantasy, the queen was now servicing Cleo herself. But Jamie couldn't see it.

Cleo opened her eyes and removed the belt from her mouth. Slowly, she tied it and untied it around her wrists. Her eyes locked on Jamie's, as she wondered, wondered....

What would Jamie do?

THE EXHIBIT
Mathilda Van Ness

Everyone was talking about Anne Marshal. She of the signature red lips and the avant-garde way of looking down at you, as if she were standing up on a pedestal and you were a tiny ant, crawling on the floor below. Artists in the spotlight can behave like Anne. And art enthusiasts, patrons willing to fork over hundreds of times what a piece of art is worth, seem to like being treated badly by the artists.

Don't ask me why this is. I don't know. I can only assume it follows the same rule that people will think something is more valuable if it is more expensive. Most of us know that this is not always the case. But if you take the same two sweaters, price one at $300 and the other at $30, there is a group of women who will buy the $300 and give you reason after reason why it is better quality than its identical, cheaper counterpart.

Anne's artwork fell into this category. Her pieces were average. You could find her match at any local art college. But someone, some doddering patron, had decided that Anne was an up-and-coming somebody. And this person single-handedly got Anne a showing where other patrons, like those characters who watched in breathless awe as the emperor paraded in his new clothes, walked around the gallery oohing and ahhing and writing out multi-thousand-dollar checks.

At the show, the buzz of the crowd centered on the fact that Anne's work was different. Unique. That she had created her paintings in an altogether previously-unheard-of manner. That piqued my interest and, as critic for one of the country's most respected papers (I won't toot my own horn by telling you which one), I accepted the invitation and attended the show.

I'd met Anne before, and she was just as uninteresting to me in person as she'd been in the gossip. But, as I walked around the gallery, studying the paintings, I tried to figure out what it was about them that made them so…well, different. I was startled to find myself falling into the same category of fawning art lovers that I so detest. And yet, there was something—something that had not shown up in the reproductions I had seen—that had not been captured by the photographs.

I moved closer, until my nose was nearly against one of the paintings. Just then, I felt a body next to mine. Anne had moved stealthily into my personal space. She had pressed her ruby-glossed lips to my ear, and she was whispering, "I have a secret…should I share it?"

Then her hand was in my own, leading me to the back of the gallery, to the gallery owner's private office. She locked the door behind her and moved into my space again, so close that I had to keep myself from stepping back.

She said, "I mix something special with my paints. A pure ingredient."

I squinted at her. There was something so peculiar about the girl. Her golden hair shined oddly beneath the lights. Her face had a slight patina of age, as if she might crack like an old painting and flake away. Then her lips, in that bizarre shade of red, turned upward in her bewitching smile, transforming her face into one of ethereal beauty. While I watched in stunned silence, she removed her dress, then her undergarments, spread herself out on the floor, and began to masturbate. She continued to speak to me as she worked herself, her fingers disappearing into the slit between her legs, her hips rising and falling on the cool marble floor.

She said, "I mix this special, secret substance with my paints. And somehow, for some reason, people think my paintings are remarkably beautiful, almost addictive to look at. They have a magical shine to them...."

And all the while she was talking, those slender hips of hers were bucking against the floor. From my vantage point, I could see her shaved pussylips, their pale pink skin richer and darker on the inside. Her fingers moved rapidly. She was using two together to impale herself. Her thumb joined the act, rubbing around and around in quick, darting circles over what must have been her clit. I couldn't see it because her thumb shielded it from view.

"You've told people this?" I asked softly, for some unknown reason, not wanting her to stop. She was angelic there, on the floor, her breathing coming faster now. I could see that she was growing closer to her peak because her cheeks had a warm pink glow and her lips were parted. It was more difficult for her to meet my eyes when she spoke. In fact, she could barely keep them focused on me.

"No..." she said breathlessly. A third finger joined the first two inside her, and I could guess that she was squeezing these fingers with her inner muscles. "No... people don't know about it. But you"—she took a deep breath—"you're a critic. You would have guessed...."

I shook my head, then bent at her side and began to run my fingers over her body, tracing her ribs, the flat, smooth line of her belly, using my own fingers to part her pussylips and look inside at the true work of art: the gradations of color so mysterious, dark, deep pink, a fabulously rich hue.

"Can you imagine...?" she whispered, "Can you imagine dipping a paintbrush into your cunt...and then sweeping it across a finished work, creating this mystical glossy shine?"

I shook my head. But as she spoke, I could see her doing exactly what she said.

She arched her back and shuddered, coming, I could tell, because I was helping her. Artists always need an audience.

"Will you reveal it?" she said next, trying to collect herself, but obviously still cresting from her climax. "Will you reveal me?"

I shook my head, somewhat dazed from this show, this display. But then, as she dressed herself, as we returned to the main part of the gallery, I grabbed her by the shoulders and pulled her close. This time, pressing my ears to her lips, I whispered, "I would like to buy one of your paintings."

Her face lit with a smile.

"But I would like you to do a portrait of me."

Now her smile broadened, and she nodded. "A special painting," Anne whispered back. "One that you can exhibit only privately."

THE HAVEN
Valentina Cilescu

Ros pushed open the door of the women-only singles bar and blinked in the twilit, smoky atmosphere. She didn't normally make a habit of frequenting these places, but tonight she needed a drink, and she needed some company real bad.

She walked down the dozen or so steps into the basement of the Club Jacinthe and crossed the floor of the club to the bar. A few couples were dancing together, but they didn't take any notice of Ros as she sat down on a bar stool and ordered a double gin and tonic.

Ros drank the first drink in a single draught, and made up her mind to ease off. She didn't want to get drunk, just drown her sorrows. She put the glass down and looked around. Everyone looked so laid-back, so normal. That couple over there—the tall brunette and the redhead in the short skirt, dancing so close they were almost making love—it was obvious they were crazy about each other. They couldn't keep their hands off each other's bodies. Ros felt a surge of pain as she watched the redhead fondling her lover's backside with a slow-motion eroticism that reminded Ros of the days when she and Annie had been like that. They'd spent entire lazy days in bed together, just kissing and fondling each other, getting to know every nook and cranny of each other's nakedness.

That seemed a very long time ago now. Ros sipped at her drink, and its cold bitterness seemed painfully appropriate. It was exactly the way she felt. All Annie cared about these days was getting between the sheets with J, and Ros couldn't help feeling that in some small way it was all her fault. If it hadn't been for her own stupid weakness, all those years ago at school, J would never have come looking for her.

Come to think of it, why had J come looking for her? How many years had it been since Ros had heard from her? Eight years? Nine? And how had she tracked her down? It must have taken quite some effort. So why bother? Intrigued and suspicious, Ros sipped her drink thoughtfully. J often acted on a whim, but there was always some dark purpose behind it. She surely wouldn't have surfaced after all this time without a reason....

Suddenly an unseen presence jogged her arm, and there was gin and tonic all over the polished bar top.

"Oh, sorry! Let me buy you another one."

Ros looked around, meaning to snap out a curt response, but the stranger was really beautiful—a breathtaking girl with porcelain skin, and eyes as dark as her glossy black waist-length hair.

"It was very clumsy of me," the girl went on, ordering a fresh gin and tonic and a glass of champagne for herself. "But I've had a terrible day, and I'm all thumbs."

Ros felt a warmth wash over her. This girl was utterly stunning. Suddenly she felt like a kid again. What should she say or do?

"Tell you what," Ros began. Her mouth was dry with tension, and the blue haze of cigarette smoke that caught at the back of her throat. "Why don't I buy us both a drink?"

The girl smiled. "That'd be great. My name's Joanne, by the way. What's yours?"

"Ros. I teach math—and a little psychology."

"Really?" Joanne sipped her champagne and smiled. "So you're a people watcher, are you?"

"I take an interest in other people, yes." She looked at Joanne's long sweep of ebony hair and the delicious way her tight Lycra minidress molded every smooth curve of her perfect body. Lust gave her courage. "Leastways, I always take an interest when I see something I really want."

"Oh, yes?" Joanne lowered her eyelids modestly, but Ros could see her dark eyes glittering playfully under the silky black lashes. "And when you see something you want—do you get it?"

Ros swallowed. This girl, with her butter-wouldn't-melt smile and her air of fragile innocence, was clearly a far more experienced player in the game than she had imagined. Far more experienced than Ros was, certainly. Was Joanne calling her bluff? Time to act now, if she didn't want to let fortune slip away.

Did she really want to do this? Get off with some femme she'd met in a bar, do it with her solely out of spite, because Annie had stolen her self-respect and given the favors of her cunt to a leather dyke with a cruel smile and hands that couldn't tell pain from pleasure?

She hesitated for a moment. Joanne was looking at her now, her dark eyes bright and questioning, her lips moist with strawberry lip-gel and her own sweet saliva.

Thoughts teemed in her overcrowded head. What the hell did

she need from Annie? A warm bed and a roof over her head? She could get both elsewhere, anywhere she chose. She'd been independent long before she met Annie, and if Annie chose to ignore her warnings and give herself to J as a slave…well, that was Annie's choice. Love? What was love, anyway? There was a dull ache in her heart, but she forced herself to ignore it. Whatever she felt for Annie, whatever she had ever felt, she couldn't afford to let it be love. That would mean that Annie had a power over her, and right now, in this dimly lit singles bar, Ros needed to feel that she was the one calling the shots, the one in control.

Joanne repeated the question. It echoed in Ros's head.

"When you see something you really want, what do you do? Do you go for it?"

Ros looked down over the brink of the cliff face, then dived into empty space. She drained her drink in a single long sip.

"Always, Joanne. I always go for what I want. Life's too short for hesitations and regrets."

Joanne's handsome face was transformed by a slow, sensual smile. "Oh, good. I'm so glad. For a moment there, I thought you were going to give me the brush-off. You see, I always go for what I want, too. And I want you, Ros. I want you to want me."

"I want you, Joanne. You'd better believe it."

Ros took hold of Joanne's hand and guided it to her thigh, their entwined fingers pushing up the fabric of her dress and skating over the sheer nylon of her stockings.

"Feel my desire, Joanne. Feel how much I want you."

Leaning back a little on the bar stool, Ros parted her thighs and pressed Joanne's hand against the hot, moist gusset of her panties. The wetness and the fragrance surprised Ros as much as they delighted Joanne. Up till now it had all been just talk, but in these few seconds since she had taken the plunge, Ros's body had taken over. Her desires were now in the driver's seat, not her reason or her common sense. It was a novel experience, not one she'd had for a very, very long time.

She freed Joanne's hand and waited to see what the girl would do. Joanne's eyes closed and her fingers explored the scented garden between Ros's thighs.

"You feel wonderful," she whispered. "Soft and hot and wet. I bet you've got the most beautiful pussy."

Instinctively, Ros glanced around her, certain that someone would be watching and listening, maybe even getting off on the intimacies going on at the bar. But nobody gave a damn what two horny women were getting up to. Their lust was their own affair. All around the club, women were getting acquainted. Right in the middle of the dance floor, the brunette and the redhead were trying out a whole new choreography routine, the bodices of their sequined evening dresses pulled down to their waists, revealing twin globes of flesh tinged red, green blue and white in the disco light-show. In darkened alcoves around the dance floor, those with a less exhibitionist outlook were discreetly getting to know each other's bodies, getting it on to the accompaniment of a hypnotic, thumping disco beat.

Ros gave a little groan of pleasure as Joanne's fingers plucked aside the sodden fabric of her panty gusset and slid slickly inside. Every tiny movement of those butterfly fingers felt like heaven, and she could feel the honey-dew of her cunt trickling out of her and down onto the warm plastic seat of the bar stool.

"I just knew you'd have a beautiful pussy," Joanne sighed bliss-fully. "Won't you let me kiss it?"

"What…here?"

Ros felt her heart leap in her chest. She felt dizzy, disorientated, and there was a rushing sound in her ears that she knew must be the blood pumping through her arteries.

"Doesn't have to be right here—though I wouldn't mind, and neither would Kath."

"Kath?"

"Oh, she's the owner of the bar. She's used to all her regulars and their little games. Her being on the local police committee means the club never gets raided. It's quite safe to do whatever you feel. Kath won't mind, and I don't mind either."

"Where else could we…?"

Joanne slid off her bar stool and held out her hand to Ros.

"Come with me, sweetie. I know just the place."

Ros shook her hand free of Joanne's. She didn't want the scene to be played like that, with Joanne as the mistress and herself as the innocent little foil. J had made sure that she'd had quite enough of those games to last her a lifetime. She nodded.

"Okay, take me there." Her hand rested for a moment on Joanne's shoulder, establishing the ground rules of ownership. "And maybe I'll let you get inside my pants."

Joanne led the way across the dance floor, through a door marked Cloakroom and down a narrow corridor. At the end they turned right into a small, marble-tiled room with three toilet cubicles and a few sinks.

"Here?" Ros hoped the doubt didn't betray itself too clearly in her voice. "In a public toilet?"

Joanne shook her head.

"I've done it here a few times, but it's a bit cramped. Go through the curtain at the far end."

At the far end of the room was a green velvet curtain that Ros had assumed was just there for decoration. Joanne pushed it aside a little way, and Ros saw that there was a further small room behind, partitioned off from the rest of the cloakroom just by the curtain.

In the room, perhaps six feet square, was an old bench-seat in dark brown velveteen, and Joanne smiled again, pulling the curtain back to its original position and screening them off from the prying eyes of anyone who might pay a visit to the cloakroom.

"Why don't you just take a seat, honey, and we can get to know each other better?"

Gratefully, Ros sank onto the scratchy old velveteen. Her legs felt wobbly with excitement and too much alcohol.

"Come and lick me out, you outrageous little tease," she demanded, clutching at Joanne's blouse. Willingly, Joanne submitted to having all her blouse buttons undone, one by one, until her bobbing breasts were exposed. Ros could barely choose. Should she suck Joanne's blossoming nipples, or should she simply spread her legs and let Joanne lick her out—to the undoubted pleasure of both of them?

Enough light filtered in under the hem of the green velvet curtain to illuminate the dingy cubbyhole, throwing surreal shadows on Joanne's face. Ros felt suddenly very weird indeed, as though she had just woken up and found herself on the wrong planet. Here she was, in something little bigger than a cupboard, with a girl she'd never seen before in her life. The drink had gone to her head more than she'd thought, and to her own surprise she let out an involuntary giggle.

Joanne silenced her with a kiss. "Hush, Ros. We need to be very discreet in here—you understand? Sometimes some of the straights come in here from the conference room upstairs. You wouldn't want them to hear us, would you?"

Right on cue, the sound of voices and footsteps filled the cloakroom as three or four women came in to use the lavatories and freshen up a bit. Suddenly Ros felt a pang of real doubt. She could always get up and just push the curtain aside, walk boldly through the cloakroom, and leave; but that would mean uncomfortable explanations. Besides, Joanne was now on her knees in front of the couch, and Ros could feel her whole body begging her to surrender.

This really was an unreal situation. It felt as if they were getting it on in a boutique dressing room, knowing that at any moment some officious saleswoman might whisk back the curtain and reveal their shame to an entire, horror-struck shopful of gaping customers.

The women were talking and laughing as they put on their makeup, excited about some company function in the rooms upstairs. What would they think if they knew that, only a few feet away, a girl with innocent eyes and glossy black hair was darting her eager tongue-tip between the moist pussy-lips of a lover who scarcely knew her name?

What the hell! Danger added a sweet spice to pleasure, and Ros was only just beginning to realize how much. How good it felt to have this lascivious young woman sucking on her inner cunt-lips as her wicked little tongue played a symphony with variations on the engorged stalk of her clitoris.

Orgasm was so, so close. Ros fought hard to control her breathing. Mustn't give them away with a stray gasp or moan of unrestrained enjoyment. No one must know about the drama that was being enacted behind the green velvet curtain. Joanne must suffer, too; must suffer for the indescribable pleasure she was inflicting on this stranger who had fallen into the sweet honey-trap of her dark eyes and bobbing breasts.

Ros reached down and began twisting Joanne's nipples between finger and thumb. She gasped, her face contorting into a mask of tormented arousal. Good. Very good. Joanne, too, must know the meaning of pleasure that never ends until it has reached the very limits of endurance.

When Joanne's index finger slid into the depths of her cunt, Ros knew she could hold out no longer. The first spasms twitched and jerked her whole body, a great warmth spreading out from her clitoris and belly to encompass her whole lust-weary, aching body.

Ros was in a turmoil of exquisite pleasure. She gave up trying to fight it and let herself float away on the spring tide of her desire. How could she ever have been stupid enough to imagine that Joanne was a guileless innocent? Joanne had more sensual knowledge in her fingertips and tongue than Ros had ever dreamed of. Why, the little minx had probably even contrived the little scene with the spilled drink!

Was she, then, the victim and Joanne the pleasure-mistress, just as Ros had been with J? No, no; that thought was too painful to contemplate. But as Joanne brought her to orgasm, it was Annie's face that Ros saw, and J's mocking laughter she heard in the dark night of her blackest, most secret thoughts.

Joanne sank to the floor, her own orgasm overwhelming her as she realized the supreme bliss of tasting Ros's cum on her lascivious tongue. Only through the pleasure of her lovers could Joanne come to her own climax of enjoyment.

Ros got to her feet, unsteady, head spinning. She didn't pay any attention to Joanne, though the girl was clutching at her legs and moaning softly, "Again, Ros. Let me do it again."

Gently, she pried Joanne's fingers from the hem of her skirt. Her cunt felt wet and empty, but her mind had found a new direction. She knew now what she had to do. Running away from her problems wouldn't solve them, and she wasn't going to find any answers either at the bottom of a glass or between the lips of a dark-eyed temptress.

Yes, it was about time she got a grip on herself. Not caring who the hell saw her, she pulled across the curtain and blinked in the sudden light. Two women were standing by the sinks. As Ros emerged from behind the green velvet curtain they turned to stare, but they weren't staring at Ros. They were staring at Joanne, still sprawled on the floor behind the curtain and mouthing her litany of lust:

"Your pussy, Ros, your sweet pussy. Let me lick your pussy out again."

With determination in her heart, Ros summoned up all her dignity and walked through the cloakroom, down the corridor, and up the stairs that led back to the street.

The night air was cool, fresh, and clean after the stuffy atmosphere of the club. Ros breathed it in deeply, cleansing herself of all her cowardice and her follies.

Time to do battle. Time to tell J just exactly where she got off and take possession of what was rightfully hers.

PRICE TO PAY
Estelle Reiter

When I want something, I get it. If I can't buy it, I'll steal it. If I can't find it, I'll have it made for me. I was born rich, and I have turned my birthright into a fortune that would have impressed my father, an unimpressionable man.

When I saw Elaine up on that stage at The Pussycat, holding onto the metal pole and swinging her slender body around it, I wanted her. She has that kind of a body that takes hours of toning daily, corded thighs, a flat, taut stomach, an ass you could cup in your hands. Her face was smooth and impassive, her eyes a dark, unwavering blue. I could tell she was wearing a wig—no one's hair is so highly glossed except Barbie's. I wanted to know what her real hair color was.

I requested a lap dance, paid for it, requested another, paid for that, and then asked her out.

She said, "I don't date the clientele."

I said, "You ought to just say yes now and save yourself the trouble." She questioned me with her cobalt eyes. "I always get what I want," I informed her matter-of-factly.

She smiled at me, if you could call it that. Her eyes were unresponsive, the smile only on her lips. She said, "You must have a nice life." One long beat. "I'm not for sale."

"Everyone has a price," I said confidently. "Everyone."

She tilted her head, her eyes never wavering from mine. "You can't afford me." Then she stood and walked to the stage door.

I was there the next night. And the next. She would give me lap dances, would tease me with her body, with her eyes that never changed. I bought her gifts: sapphire earrings, an emerald bracelet, and finally a thin black collar with diamond studs. That caught her eye and I smiled to myself, realizing I'd overplayed my hand. Realizing that the answer was so easy I hadn't even caught on. I walked to the back room, where the strippers change between shows, pushing past the bouncer who halfheartedly told me I wasn't allowed. As Tom Waits says, $100 makes the talk inside. I handed over a bill and stalked after Elaine.

She was seated in front of a mirror, her hair up, her real hair, a finely spun golden mane, and she had the collar in her hands, fingering it. I met her eyes in the mirror, took the collar from her and fastened it around her neck. Then, without speaking, I lifted her into my arms and carried her out the back way, to the parking lot. I had my convertible with me, and I set her in the backseat and peeled off her clothes, devouring her nipples, her flat stomach, her cunt. I had been restrained longer than I like, and I let her know it, ravaging her body with my tongue, fingers, fist. She moaned, grabbed my hair, let loose with a stream of foul language that made me even hotter. "Fuck me, oh, please, fuck me. With your hand…harder! Harder!"

"Whore!" I spat, liking the way her eyes grew darker when I said it. At least I'd made them change. "You'll be my whore. You said you didn't have a price. I didn't realize that meant I could take you for free." I slipped two fingers under her collar and tugged, so she could feel the bite of it. Then I went back down to her pussy and let her feel my bite there, on her cuntlips, on her clit, digging at her, lapping at her. It was so easy, making her feel it, breaking open that iced exterior and bringing her molten core to the surface. I swam in her, dined on her, ruined her for another.

Then I wrapped her in my coat, brought her into the front seat, and drove her home, telling her of my plans. "You'll wear silk," I told her, "or satin, or leather, or vinyl. Or nothing. You'll have jewels and bathe in champagne, and anything you ask for will be yours." She turned her head on the seat and looked at me. "But you'll be mine," I said. "Mine," repeating the word and watching the way her eyes seemed to get softer, more willing. "And you'll do what I say."

"Yes," she murmured, agreeing. "Whatever you say."

I grinned, thinking about what I wanted, what I desired. "Part your legs," I told her. "Make yourself come while we drive." She set her feet on the dashboard, spread her thighs, and placed her fingers against her clit, rubbing at it while the cool night air washed over her body. She closed her eyes and rocked her hips against the leather seat.

I tried to keep my eyes on the road, but I stole silent glances, memorizing the look of ecstasy on her face, promising myself I would bring it to her often. And forever.

THE LIZARD QUEEN
Julia Richards

I'm not a ghoul. I don't usually hang out in cemeteries. But on our trip to Paris, my lover insisted on visiting Jim Morrison's grave at Père Lachaise. "Can't we just say we went?" I was not excited about spending a day with the dead. "No one will know."

"What's your problem?" She shot me a look. "It's only a cemetery."

We went, of course. We do whatever Laura says we're going to do. Always. As we made our way into the place, the gatekeeper told us that they were almost ready to close. "We'll be quick," Laura promised in French. I was glad for that. The days were shorter, and a cool wind had begun to blow, stirring the leaves around us.

As we made our way through the graves, Laura grabbed me by the hand and pulled me toward one of the mausoleums that had a broken entrance. I shook my head and tried to stop her. But there really is no stopping Laura. When she says "jump," I bounce like a fucking bunny.

Inside the mausoleum, she crouched down, pulling me with her. "We'll wait until the keeper locks up for the night," she said, "and then we'll go find the Lizard King." I was against it, but we don't have a democracy. The last rays of sunlight hit the stained glass window, bathing us in shimmering blues and reds. The light fell on Laura's face, on her eyes. They glowed, a green fire burning wickedly within them.

While we were waiting, we ended up kissing, and that's always good. I had my shirt off and my bra undone. Laura warmed my nipples with her mouth before clamping them with the ridged clips she always carries with her. The clips have a chain hanging between them, and the weight of it makes my pussy ache with want.

"Please!" I pushed against her, begging with my body and with my words until she undid my jeans and prodded me with her fingers, rubbing my clit until I thought it would burst, treating me to a few of the soft caresses and pinches I crave. She knows how to make me come, but she didn't. She kept me on edge, fucking me, fucking with me, making me stand so that she could bite my shaved cuntlips until I was marked by her pointed teeth, nearly out of my skin from wanting to come so bad. She wouldn't let me, though. She never makes it easy for me.

It was dark by then, and we were cramped in the small quarters, so Laura pulled me out of the mausoleum after her, insisting that I leave my top and jeans in a heap. I wandered naked behind her, feeling the cool bite of the fall air on my pale, smooth skin, nearly glowing beneath the moonlight. Finally we found the grave, and Laura sat on the headstone.

"Come here!" she ordered.

I got on my knees on top of the grave and waited.

I don't know when the music started, the haunting few bars of "The End." All I know is that Laura was there, and then she wasn't. And I was lying on Jim's grave watching him get into leather jeans and toss his hair out of his eyes.

"Pamela's going to love you," he said, reaching for my hand. I looked down, at the velvet dress that shimmered above my skin, at the red roses he held out to me. Then I took his hand and followed him into the night.

WITHOUT HER
Jasmine Hall

I never would have planned it to happen the way it did. I mean, you hear people say stuff like that all the time, and you shrug to yourself, "If you didn't want it to happen, you could have stopped it." But now I'm on the other side of things, and I see life from a new perspective.

I take pictures of cheating couples for a living. That's what I do. I'm a private eye. Give people the evidence they need to confirm suspicions they already have. It never works the other way. I never prove innocence; I only confirm guilt.

I guess I'd have to say I always felt above it all. Knowing I'd never bend that low, cheat on someone I loved, make them feel the kind of pain I'd seen so many times in a woman's eyes. Why would I do that? I'd simply break off the relationship, sever the ties, and then plunge the filly that needed plunging.

Innocent thoughts. I never will be that innocent again.

Julianne and I had been together for eight months, a record for me. I'm a bit of a slut—you may have guessed that from my attitude. I don't like to be reined in. I don't cheat—or I didn't cheat—but my relationships rarely have lasted longer than a month. But Julie was special, pretty and smart and giving. By our third date, she had me ensconced in her apartment. (I never told her I kept my own place, paying rent on an empty room as a backup in case things didn't work out.)

I was on a job, snapping pictures of a couple from an office building across the way. I had my telephoto lens and had everything I needed. But as I took each shot, as I stared at the lovers entwined, I felt something new. A desire I'd never felt before. The two lovers were both women. The one on top was your average dyke, heavyset, attractive. The sub was something special, though, something worthwhile. She had a mane of dark hair and a face like an angel. I wanted her. I needed her.

I approached her with the pictures—something I'd never done before. "Your girlfriend hired me," I said. "I don't have to give her these...but I will."

She looked at me with angelic blue eyes, then swallowed hard and invited me into her office. She took the pictures from me and placed them in her top dresser drawer. Then she stared at me, begging with her eyes and then her mouth, "Please"—just what I wanted to hear—"I'll do anything."

She sucked my cock. She offered me her ass. She called me Daddy, let me do things to her. Anything I wanted to. I tied her up. Took pictures of her with my cock in her ass, a dildo in her cunt, and a third, massive toy in her mouth. She looked glamorous when she was wallowing in the filth. But there was something even more than that. Other girls will let you do stuff to them. And if you can't find the right ones for free, you can always pay.

But this girl was magical. There was something about her, something transcendent. Her smell, her face, the way she batted her eyes.

The way she said, "I love you! Oh, how I love you!"

I can't describe that. Can't believe I fell for it.

I had her any way I wanted her. Fulfilled every fucking fantasy I'd ever even thought about. Every image that had ever flickered through my twisted mind.

And when she went to Julianne and told her everything, I can't describe that, either. But I sit here alone in this empty room and I wait for the phone to ring, wait for Lauren to call. And I wonder what it was I saw through that telephoto lens of mine. Something angelic? Something of the devil? I don't know.

I only hope she'll call.

STALKING

J. A. *Silver*

It had been two years since my last love affair, six months since my last orgasm, and I was getting desperate. Truly desperate. Usually, I can control my desire. I handle my sexuality the way I handle a thermostat. I turn it off or on when I want to.

But now something had happened. During my morning bus commute, I'd seen a woman I couldn't get out of my head. And no amount of masturbation could control the images of what I wanted to do with her. Nor could I get myself off. I rubbed until I was raw—but couldn't climax. This was new to me. I'd never experienced this before. In all aspects of my life, I am cool and contained.

She'd ruined me.

I decided I would find her. I rode the bus until the driver seemed suspicious of me. This isn't entirely unreasonable, even when I'm not stalking someone. I cut a fairly startling picture.

I'm six feet tall, slender to the point of emaciation, and I wear my bleached blonde hair razor cut. After my fourth daylong journey on our local transportation system, she got on. She was wearing leather, as she had been before, and her long blue hair was plaited in two tight braids.

I moved to the free seat at her side. "Are you taken?" I asked.

She looked at me. "Is this seat taken?" she repeated, correcting me. I shook my head. She blushed and lowered her eyes and I knew I had her, but I waited until she said, "No," in a low, semi-scared voice.

"Good!" I grabbed her wrist and traced her pulse with my thumb. I took her hand and placed it against the bulge in my pants. Her eyes grew wide and moist with want. She stroked my cock, then unzipped me and reached her hand inside to feel it. She sighed when she made the connection, running her fingers over it, brushing against the skin of my belly as she did. Her touch sent a shiver through me. I used my own hand to explore the crotch of her leather pants, not caring about the horrified stares of the other passengers, not caring about anything until the bus driver screamed for us to leave, to get off. I was quick to oblige.

I pulled her through the doors after me, dragging her to one of my favorite alleys.

She knew what to do. She put her hands flat against the brick wall in front of her and let me undress her from behind. I pulled her leather jeans down her slender thighs and began pawing at her ass. I made her crack wet with my spit before introducing her to my cock. She didn't moan as it went in, she simply steeled herself, flexing her body like one long, hard muscle.

I pressed my lips against the back of her neck and said, "It's been two years since I fucked someone."

"Make it last." For someone in her position, her voice sounded tough. Instead of making it last, I made it count, rocking my eight inches in and out of her ass like a piston, getting it all dirty and foul for her to clean with her mouth. I worked her until she couldn't handle the wait, until she took one hand away from the bricks and brought it between her legs, teasing her clit, tugging on it. I liked that. I let her almost come before I made her get down on her knees to finish me off. I liked the hurt look in her eyes as she took my toy down her throat and got it nice and clean.

She kept her hand working between her legs, and I felt myself build to climax, one half of the double-headed cock sliding around inside me as she sucked on the other. As I shuddered and started to moan, she let herself go with me. We came together in a rush. It was quick, but it was necessary. It did the job. I couldn't wait to do it again, slower, but I wanted to be in my own place for the sequel.

We didn't bother with the bus this time. We took a cab.

EXECUTIVE PRODUCER
Pamela Morrow

I was standing in line at the grocery store, my nearly empty basket containing only a can of tomato juice and a small container of cottage cheese. I'd left my shades at home, so I was squinting, trying to cut the glare from those ever-friendly fluorescent lights. The woman in line behind me emptied her cart onto the turntable. I could sense her movements, could sense that she was staring at me. Finally, I turned to look at her.

I recognized her from the trades: a new executive at one of the studios. She was about forty, on the tall side, her short silver-flecked dark hair slicked back. I met her eyes. They were a pale green with dark rims. She was striking, handsome, my type exactly. But I wasn't in the mood. It had been a long night for me, and I was fighting the killerest hangover of my life. All I wanted to do was get home and climb into bed.

The woman moved closer to me in line, invading my space. She brought her lips to my ear and whispered, "You have a look...."

It's a Hollywood line, apropos to give budding young starlets hoping to break in. You're never supposed to be rude in L.A., on the assumption that you don't know who you're being rude to. It could be the next casting director you try out for, the next producer you hope to assist. I didn't feel well enough to care. I said, "A look? Hmmm...the hungover, slept-in-my-clothes, dumped-by-my-girlfriend look?"

I thought it would make her back off. Instead, she grinned, her teeth gleamingly bright under those hideous lights, and told me to wait in the parking lot for her.

"I've got a cab," I said.

"I'll drive you where you need to go."

I stumbled into the lot and paid off my driver. Then I waited. She emerged with a small bag of groceries and led me to her Jaguar. Inside, she looked me over again. "There's something"— she muttered to herself, shrugging, then louder—"you remind me of someone."

I leaned over the seat toward her and kissed her hard. I cupped her chin with one hand and wrapped my other arm around her slender body, pulling her to me. When she didn't struggle, I moved aside to unbutton her crisp white blouse, and I began to kiss and nibble at her collarbones, her breasts beneath their underwire lace cups, her flat, toned stomach. I would have continued, but she said, "Wait," put the car in drive, and shuttled us to a nearby alley. Then she lay back again, ready for me to do my duty. Instead, I opened the car door and got out, staring at her through the windshield until she followed me.

We were behind some of the biggest mansions in Beverly Hills. The alley was wider than many streets. I pressed her hands against the stucco wall of the nearest chateau, breathing in as I did to catch the fragrant wisteria drooping above us. Then I stripped her, leaving each article of her clothing on the hood of her car. She didn't protest. I liked that.

I freed my cock—I always pack—and got it wet with my own spit. I needn't have bothered. Her cunt was nice and liquid for me, as fragrant as the pale purple blossoms that dropped on us from above. I slid my tool between her thighs from behind. I like going at it like that, in that animal way. I rocked it in deep, then grabbed her around the waist and used her body against mine, moving her forward and back, setting the pace with the rhythm of my heart-beat.

She was silent as we fucked, much different than my recent ex-lover whose faux screams had caused our neighbors to alert 911 on more than one occasion. This lady was self-contained, but I could sense when she neared her peak. Her body grew still in my hands. Her muscles tightened. Her skin seemed to glow beneath the warm California sunlight.

I liked the way her naked body looked against my black-clad form. I liked how wet she was making my slacks when she pressed back against me.

I liked her not knowing who I was. She would when she saw the trades in the morning.

When she came, violent shudderings filled her and then subsided slowly, leaving her breathless and her green eyes shining. She got dressed quietly, those stunning eyes focused on me. I opened the door of her car, grabbed my package, and headed down the alley.

"I'll drive you home," she called after me.

I pulled my keys from my pocket and unlocked the back gate to my house. "No problem," I said grandly. "I'm already here."

SURPRISE PARTY
Belinda Evans

I didn't want a party. I told Eliza that, repeatedly. I don't even like to mention my age anymore, despise seeing it in print, refuse to acknowledge it when census-takers call. The thought of my closest friends shouting it out to me was less than appealing.

Eliza didn't listen, though. I walked into our house after a very long day at work to find all my dearest friends shouting, "Happy fortieth birthday, Celine!"

I shot Eliza a mean look, then spent the next hour with a false smile plastered on my face. After the third champagne toast, I relaxed a little, enough so that when Eliza came up to me with a red silk scarf and asked to fasten it over my eyes, I let her.

What happened next was bizarre. I felt myself being lifted and moved, carried down our hall to our bedroom. I knew it was our bedroom because of the water bed I was set down on. Hands—many hands—undid my suit and removed every article of my clothing. Voices—many voices—hushed me when I asked what was going on. Eliza's recognizable voice, in my ear told me to be quiet if I didn't want to be gagged.

At that point, I decided to roll with it. And soon I was doing exactly that, rolling, or being rolled, on my side with one synthetic cock in my cunt, another in my mouth, a third probing my back door. I sucked the cock that teased my lips. I reveled in the feeling of being filled, of being probed, and in the knowledge that there were so many others around me, watching.

I didn't have too much time to think, but I flashed on the picture I'd shown Eliza in a recent issue of *Masquerade: An Erotic Journal*, the one of the woman masturbating for a crowd, a piece of performance art from the sixties that I adored. I'd told Eliza that it was my personal fantasy to take the woman's place. And now, for the ultimate gift, Eliza was making a version of that fantasy—a more perverse one, of course—come true.

Soon, there were more bodies around me, pressed against me, and I could hear different sounds, moans and sighs, the unmistakable smacks of a spanking occurring right next to me. Our water bed jostled and bounced, and cocks entered and exited me, different sizes, different girths. Suddenly I recognized Eliza's, finding my smeared cuntlips, parting them, and I heard her shoo away the others. In an instant, we were the only ones on the bed, and I was rocking with the familiar feel of her fucking style, jouncing along with it on my way to an unreal orgasm.

A hand tugged at my blindfold, moving it. I stared into my lover's eyes as she came, her pretty mouth slack, her eyes half-closed, her body trembling. I love it when she comes on me, on top of me, because I can watch her face change as I feel the spasms in her cunt subside.

There was a sudden burst of applause, and I looked around, at our friends, as they cheered us on. Suddenly I realized that the lights in the room were candles. "Forty," Eliza whispered as she climbed off me, showing her beautiful ass before she slid into a robe. "Forty candles. Forty friends. Forty cocks fucking you. Not a bad way to enter a new phase in your life, is it?"

I shook my head, my face flushed, my heart racing. "No," I said, "not such a bad way, after all."

She leaned over to kiss me, to murmur into my ear, "Surprise, baby. Surprise."

BLIND DATE
Eleanor Chang

Jasmine said the girl was perfect for me. Exactly what I was looking for.

"How do you know what I'm looking for?" I asked.

"Trust me." She winked. "I know." Then she smiled and added, "Sometimes blind dates are the best kinds."

I took a deep breath, considering it. I hadn't been on a date in a while. Not a real date, anyway. I'd been slumming, hitting the bar scene maybe too heavily, winding up in strange beds and slinking home before the owners of those beds awoke and started doing a postmortem on the previous evening's activities.

"One night," Jasmine urged, running her fingers through her curly dark hair. "What's one night out of your whole life?"

"Fine," I said, more to quiet her than anything else. When Jasmine gets hold of an idea, she doesn't let up easily. But that Saturday night, as I got ready, I actually found myself excited. Nervous, butterfly-excited.

I spent an extra long time with my makeup, outlining my eyes with the new gold liquid liner I'd bought on a whim. It made my brown eyes look Cleopatra-like, which I thought was rather sexy. I brushed my thick black hair until it gleamed with a tempered blue halo.

Standing in my black lace lingerie, I agonized over my outfits before choosing a berry red dress, one I'd never worn but had mocked me from the back of my closet for too long. I wore the matching red heels I'd bought to go with it.

The doorbell rang while I was dabbing perfume at my pulse points, Liz Claiborne's new Curve. I smiled at my reflection in the hallway mirror before opening the door. It was my blind date.

"Jasmine." I didn't immediately get it. "What's up?"

"Ready?" She moved past me into the living room, her arms filled with flowers, her slender, boyish body sleek and lean in leather pants and a leather vest. I followed her and stood as she made herself comfortable on my sofa. She'd sat there often in the past, but somehow she looked like a stranger this time.

"Who'd you expect?" she asked, making me feel like an idiot.

"Oh…" I stammered. "You, of course, you. I knew it was you all along." Maybe because I continued to prattle, Jasmine stood and grabbed me around the waist, silencing me with her lips on mine. Regardless of the reason for her actions, the kiss did the trick, hushing me, making my body come alive in her arms while clamming up my vocal cords.

She moved away and said, "You know I'm right for you. Think about it while I take off your dress." I stood absolutely still as she unzipped me, undid my bra, unhooked my garters. I thought of all the fun we have together, the way we can finish each other's sentences like an old married couple. Then I stopped thinking as she bent me over my sofa and undid her leather slacks, letting me feel the skin of her outfit against my naked skin before diving inside me with her pink plastic cock.

I gripped onto the sofa pillows to steady myself, but Jasmine would have none of it, obviously trying to keep me continually off guard. She grabbed my wrists and pulled them behind my back, anchoring both in one of her hands. I didn't struggle too hard, not even when I felt the cuffs slip over them and click shut. She'd come prepared.

"Take it," she said. "You deserve this...for all the times you've spent telling me about your whorish ways. For all the times you made me listen, rather than letting me do what we both know should have been done a long, long time ago."

Captured like that, I didn't have much of a choice. But I didn't want much of a choice. I felt her slam into me, felt it in the depth of my being, and I relished it. Each stroke was perfection.

"You don't have to slink home anymore," she said.

I shuddered, unable to answer.

"You just have to face me, every morning, in our bed."

She knew exactly how I wanted to be touched, her hard palm coming down and connecting firmly with my ass. Repeatedly, accentuating the way she was fucking me.

Jasmine's right about a lot of things. It's why she's my prize confidant. She was right about us, too. How well we fit together. Our bodies, our desires. She rode me, pressing me against the sofa, making it hurt while she made me come. Sublime.

After, basking in that warm golden glow, she repeated her words of wisdom. "Sometimes blind dates are the best kind."

And, knowing she was right this time, I just smiled.

CHARLOTTE AND ROBIN
Lindsay Welsh

"Open it," Charlotte said.

The box wrapping was almost too pretty to ruin, and Robin admired the cunningly twisted bow and silver paper a moment longer before she unwrapped it. Inside was yet another box, this one long and narrow, and its shape reminded her of something; she caught her breath, hoping that she might be right. She was, and she let out a coo of delight when she saw the object nestled in paper inside the box, seemingly waiting for a touch to bring it to glorious life.

"I thought we could have some fun with it," Charlotte told her, and Robin kissed her before she went back to examining the gift.

"That's an understatement," Robin said, taking her birthday gift out of its box. It was a vibrator, almost a foot in length, delightfully thick, made of a soft rubber that felt almost humanly warm in Robin's hands. She ran her fingers over it, her pussy stirring just from the sight of it. "How did you know I wanted one?"

"Because woman doesn't live by hard plastic alone," Charlotte said. "Everyone needs a few luxuries in life." Her fingers were straying to her lover's thighs, tracing patterns on the stockings and moving slowly up to the hem of her skirt. Once she reached it, Robin spread her legs apart, and Charlotte kissed her deeply while her hand strayed up to the hot area in between. Robin wasn't wearing any underwear and she could feel Charlotte's fingers brush her wiry pubic hair and then tickle at her swollen pussy lips. She moaned softly and begged to try the vibrator out right away.

"Oh, no," Charlotte smiled. "We have dinner reservations, remember?"

"Then you should have given me this when we got home!"

"I will," Charlotte promised. "Only now look what we have to come home to. This way, you can spend the next few hours just thinking about what we'll do when we come back."

Reluctantly, Robin put the vibrator back in its box and got up to get her coat. As she stepped back from the closet, Charlotte came up behind her and pressed hard against her. Robin let herself go limp and leaned back into her lover; she could feel the swell of Charlotte's firm breasts against her spine and imagined she could even feel the heat of her pussy through both their skirts. She could definitely feel Charlotte's hands making their way to her tits, to fondle and massage and ignite the fire between her legs.

Charlotte was hot herself, and she wouldn't have been surprised if the heat of her cunt was strong enough to be felt. She loved to touch Robin, loved to see the contrast of her pale skin against Robin's muscular dark body. She loved Robin's small, hard tits and the impossibly ruby red hue of her sweet pussy. She reached down to pull up the hem of Robin's skirt and groaned aloud when her fingers came away wet from the object of her desire. She moved them about as she kissed Robin's neck, listening for the quick intake of breath and the long, soft moan that told her she had hit her mark. She found Robin's huge clit and pressed it back and forth with a fingertip, while another finger gained just the slightest entry into that sweet, deep tunnel.

Robin's body was no longer limp; she was hard, on edge, delighting in the quivers that ran through her body from between her thighs. Her eyes were tightly closed, but her mouth was parted halfway, her breath coming in sharply, escaping in groans of desire and delight. Her hips were now moving, seemingly independent of her, matching the rhythm of the hand that gave her such pleasure. Charlotte was an expert at this, and she could draw feelings out of flesh with an ease that never failed to amaze her lover. But that was unimportant now; the only thing that mattered was her finger on Robin's clit, now wet with nectar, rubbing and trying to coax an orgasm out of her burning cunt.

"You're going to make me come," Robin gasped, her eyes squeezed tightly closed. "It's hot, so hot...ooooh!" She trembled all over at this sweetest release, and when it finally passed completely through her, she was left gasping, once again weak and limp.

Immediately, Charlotte stood up straight and gave Robin a gentle slap on her behind. "Hurry up, we're going to be late," she said, and got her own coat. It was a game she loved to play often; when Robin least expected it, she would hold her, quickly make her come, and then act as if absolutely nothing had happened. Robin laughed and took a moment to calm her breathing before she put on her jacket as well.

The restaurant was Charleston's, Robin's favorite, and one where the two women often met after work for a drink in the dark, richly paneled lounge. The maître d' greeted them warmly and they requested a cocktail before their table was readied. Within moments, they were beside each other in the lounge, sunk into one of the overstuffed couches, watching the hypnotic flames in the fireplace. The hour was still early and they had the room to themselves as they lifted their champagne to toast the occasion.

The wine was like silk, and Robin sat back and admired its color through the glass. "All I can think about is my present," she said quietly. It was the opening Charlotte was waiting for. "All I can think about is how good it's going to look on your sweet pussy," she said. She had deliberately selected a vibrator finished in a light-colored rubber, so that she would be better able to enjoy the contrast between the device and Robin's skin. There was no doubt: this was a present chosen for both of them.

"I can see what will happen when we get home," she continued. "I want to be the one that holds it first. I want to put it on your cunt and make you come. Maybe you'll have on a pair of panties."

"The red ones?" Robin was getting into the game herself, smiling mischievously, sipping at her champagne.

"The red ones will be perfect," Charlotte said. She knew the red panties well; they were silk, cut in a roomy tap-pant style, so that Charlotte could rub the silk on Robin's cunt, or slip them aside effortlessly for a finger or tongue to gain access to the hot flower underneath them. "First, I'll rub the tip of it all over your lips, just to get you wet."

"I'll be soaked," Robin said.

"Soaked through," Charlotte agreed. "Then I'll turn the vibrator on, just a bit, just enough to tease you. You'll beg me to turn it up, but it won't do any good. You'll just have to wait for that."

"It'll feel so good there," Robin said.

"It will look good, too. I'll rub it all up and down your pussy, right through the panties. I'll move it beside your clit and go right down to your ass just as if it were my finger. After a long time, I'll take those panties aside and put it right on you, and I know you'll moan like you always do when I touch you."

"Tell me more," Robin coached.

"I want to put it inside you," Charlotte said. "I want to spread your pussylips with my fingers and put the very tip of that vibrator inside you and then turn it on. I want to hear it buzz up against your sweet pussylips, and I want to see it inside you. That pink rubber will look so nice against your cunt. You know how much I love to see my fingers in there, and this will be just the same."

By this time, Robin was obviously excited, and Charlotte looked around quickly. The maître d' and the sommelier were engaged in a quiet discussion, and the waiter was looking the other way. Assured that she was not seen, Charlotte let her hand stray to her companion. As she had expected, the thick hair around Robin's pussy was as damp as a light mist of dew on a morning meadow.

They finished their champagne and were escorted to their table. The restaurant wasn't very crowded and the closest diners were several tables away. They knew their dinner conversation wouldn't be revolving around the food or their day at work.

They ordered and then sat back with the wine that had been brought for them. Charlotte wasn't letting her lover relax for a moment. "It has a variable speed dial," she said, almost clinically. "I made sure of that, and I made sure to get a spare set of batteries. Do you know what that means?"

"No," Robin whispered, almost dizzy with anticipation.

"I'll be able to drive you crazy with it," Charlotte promised. "I can turn it down and just tickle it across your clit. Then I can turn it to medium and get you all excited. I can just see your hips moving when I have it on your cunt. Then I'll turn it up high, and you'll be at my mercy. I'll make you come again and again. And when the batteries get a little low, I can just pop in a fresh set and send you off again. So what do you think?"

"I think this should be a short dinner," Robin said, although it turned out not to be, for the food was exceptional, and both women appreciated fine dining enough that they would never rush it. Besides, they agreed, the buildup was all part of the excitement.

Robin had ordered her favorite dinner, a thick slice of beef filet smeared with pâté and baked in a crisp phyllo crust. The deep pink interior reminded her of the way Charlotte's pussy looked when she spread the lips with her fingers, ready to apply her tongue to that delightful smoothness. The pâté, highly seasoned, was thick and creamy, and she rolled it on her tongue just as she loved to roll Charlotte's clit between her tongue and her lips, coaxing the waves of pleasure out of it. All of the food was sweet and thickly creamy, the slices of baked sweet potato, the pâté, the spinach baked with cream and eggs. Everything she put into her mouth reminded her of Charlotte's secretive flower, which she vowed she would unfold later that evening, to their mutual delight.

Somehow they finished their meals, exciting each other with their descriptions and their fantasies, delivered in low tones accented with blown kisses and low moans of delight. Both women were thoroughly enjoying their erotic discussion so much that their pussies throbbed and they sometimes had to squirm on their chairs in their excitement.

"I can't possibly stay through dessert," Robin said, as the waiter noticed their empty plates and hurried to clear them. She was sure that when she stood up the chair would be wet.

"No dessert?" the waiter smiled at her. "On your birthday, Ms. Smythe, you won't be enjoying your favorite cherries jubilee?" Robin thought for just a moment before nodding her assent. For her, fine food was a turn-on, and the sweetly tart dessert would make the whole evening more complete.

The dessert was made at the table, allowing the women to enjoy the sight of the flambé as they sipped their brandy. When the dishes were set before them and the waiter left, Charlotte made sure that Robin saw her tease a firm, red cherry with her tongue before holding it gently between her teeth and closing her lips around it. Robin closed her eyes for a moment and calmed herself before taking a bite. The ice cream was a soft thickness against her tongue, and the cherry popped between her teeth, releasing a spurt of warm, brandy-rich liquid that she savored as if it were Charlotte's honey.

They could hardly wait to get home, and as much as they had enjoyed their long, luxurious dinner, each could feel her pussy throbbing with want as the front door was opened and they stepped inside. The door was barely closed when they were in each other's arms, their tongues reaching to probe each other, their fingers in each other's hair, pressing closer, kissing deeper.

"I can't stand it any more," Robin whispered, and her expensive coat fell in a heap on the floor. Charlotte shrugged hers off her shoulders, her lips still on Robin's, and they left their coats and shoes where they fell and walked arm-in-arm toward their huge bedroom.

The bed seemed more inviting than it had ever been; the white sheets and the mounds of pillows made them want to stretch out and take each other as quickly as possible. Charlotte sat Robin down on it, and when Robin raised her hands to help with Charlotte's buttons, she was told, "It's your birthday. You just relax and enjoy."

"How can I when my poor pussy's on fire?" Robin asked, squirming on the bedspread to show just how much in need she really was.

"Just think about how good it'll feel when we stoke it a bit more," Charlotte said, and kissed her before standing up straight to take off her clothes.

She did a slow striptease, playing with her shirt as she unbuttoned it, caressing the skin that she exposed as each button was released. When the shirt was opened and hanging loose, she pulled the tails up so that her breasts were lifted with the fabric and framed by the silk. She leaned forward and allowed Robin to lick and suck at them for a little while before she pulled away again. She massaged her breasts with her own fingers, tweaking the nipples and rolling them between her fingertips, tracing the brown aureole with her nails until they were covered with tiny bumps that gave away the height of her excitement. Her breasts glistened with Robin's saliva, her outthrust nipples firm.

Then the shirt was gone, and her fingers sought the waistband of her skirt. Like Robin, she wore no panties, and she teased her lover by flashing glimpses of her light brown pubic hair before finally dropping the skirt entirely. She kept on her stockings and garters, and Robin loved the way they framed her pubis and lapped enticingly at her creamy thighs.

Robin longed to lap there as well, and when Charlotte came close enough, she did. She followed the tops of the stockings with her tongue, licking a circle about them and moving in to slip the tip of her tongue between the tight V of Charlotte's pussy lips. Charlotte moaned softly and stood, trembling very slightly, while the heat and wet of Robin's tongue touched gently at the very tip of her clit. Then she stepped back and said, "Later. Now it's your turn."

She pressed her companion back on the bed and began to undress her as slowly and seductively as she had stripped herself, with as much attention paid to the smooth, dark skin below the fabric. She lingered for a long time on Robin's tits, and when she slipped a hand down to reach below Robin's skirt, she was surprised at how wet that place was. When she removed the skirt, she let her tongue play over the spot, licking the juice away and savoring it before she stood up and reached for the box on the beside dresser.

Robin reached to touch the vibrator; she wanted to feel the rubber, so soft and warm it almost felt like flesh. Charlotte turned it on low, and it buzzed and trembled in her hands.

She used it to massage Robin all over, starting at her throat. Robin could only lie back and revel in the delicious touch of the device. "I always saw them sold this way in magazines," she laughed, as Charlotte rubbed the tip of it around her throat and up and down the back of her neck. "Like they were made just for relaxing a stiff neck. But you know, that does feel pretty good."

"So do you want me to stay up here?" Charlotte teased.

"Not for much longer," Robin smiled. "You know my pussy's just begging for it."

She didn't realize how much she wanted it on her tits until Charlotte worked her way down there. She let it rest ever so gently on the nipples, and the hard brown nubs responded to the vibrating device by becoming firm. "Look how big they are!" Charlotte marveled, and she kept the vibrator on one while she sucked at the other. It seemed to fill her mouth and Robin moaned as she felt her lover's hot, wet tongue tease and tickle her.

Now the vibrator was on her belly, and Robin held her breath as it moved down lower. When it touched the very tip of her slit, she groaned and exhaled hard. She spread her legs, and Charlotte marveled at how good the pink rubber looked against the ruby flesh. She moved it up and down, still on the low setting, just enough to excite and tease. By the way Robin's vaginal lips gleamed with her honey, the teasing wasn't really necessary, but Charlotte kept it up nevertheless, as much for her own excitement as for Robin's.

They were both almost painfully aware of how much their cunts throbbed with desire and the need for orgasm. Robin was so wet the vibrator slipped inside of her effortlessly, and she gasped as she felt the warm rubber part her lips and fill her with its heft and its movement. She could not believe how good it felt, this dildo that buzzed with a life of its own, as Charlotte moved it in and out.

Then Charlotte took it out and replaced it with two of her own fingers. While the vibrator danced on Robin's sex-swollen clit, Charlotte fucked her with her hand, until Robin was gasping and moaning, her hips bucking wildly.

She cried loudly as she came with an intensity that surprised them both. The hot sparks went all through her, leaving her trembling in their wake. When they finally passed through her, seeming to escape right from the tips of her fingers and toes, she was left gasping and limp.

"Better than a pair of fuzzy slippers?" Charlotte smiled.

"The best birthday gift I ever received," Robin gasped.

Her whole body felt bare, every nerve end on edge, ready to receive more pleasure. "But what about you? You have to come too."

"I know," Charlotte said, and she knelt on the bed over Robin's hips. "You think you were hot? My whole body's on fire just watching you."

Her pussy was now above Robin's, and she placed herself so they were touching. Robin adored the feel of Charlotte's hair against hers, the burning heat of her lover. Charlotte moved her hips, gently brushing her cunt against Robin's. To Robin's surprise, her own pussy was just as eager as it had been before. Despite the overwhelming orgasm she had enjoyed, she was hungry for more.

Charlotte took up the rubber vibrator, turned it on, and placed it between them.

It slid smoothly in, shiny and damp from Robin's juices. It rested on both their clits and buzzed with a life of its own, affording pleasure to both of them as they lay together.

To Robin it was a tantalizing motion on her sensitive cunt, and slowly the vibrator brought her near a peak again. For Charlotte, it was the first relief that her swollen pussy had felt that evening, and she almost cried out at the first touch. Unable to help herself, she ground her slit on it, trying to touch every part of her to that rubber lover. As she did, she pressed it deeper into Robin's pussy, exciting them both even more.

It didn't take long before both of them were writhing, grinding on the vibrator, gasping and moaning their pleasure to each other. Charlotte's large breasts brushed against Robin's tits, and she reached up and grabbed them, rubbing the pink nipples on her own hard brown ones. Charlotte nodded with delight, hardly able to speak for the moans that the vibrator was coaxing out of her.

She came first, wildly, pushing her hips into the vibrator and crying out as her pussy throbbed out its relief. Within moments, Robin enjoyed her own orgasm, and they sank into each other's arms with the vibrator still between them. It was some time before Charlotte gained the strength to turn it off and take it out from between them.

They stayed like that for some time, until Charlotte moved over to lie beside her lover and wrap her arms tightly around her. "Happy birthday," she whispered.

"I hope we won't just use my gift once a year," Robin smiled.

"I think the day after a birthday is just as important," Charlotte said, "and we'll have to check it to make sure it works properly. Of course, two days after a birthday, gifts should be used too."

Robin started to get up, but Charlotte hugged her even tighter. "Our clothes are still on the floor," Robin protested, but Charlotte silenced her with a firm kiss, slipped off her stockings and garters, and pulled the crisp sheets up over them.

She reached over to turn off the light, running her fingers softly over the rubber vibrator that lay on the bedside table before she did. "You know," she said to Robin, "there are plenty of things you can do before breakfast. You in or out?"

"What do you think?" Robin smiled, snuggling deeper into Charlotte's arms and closing her eyes. With birthday gifts like that, she thought, maybe getting a year older wasn't so bad after all.

THE REAL ROSE
Susan Anders

*S*he sits hunched over the drafting table with her nose almost touching the blue-print when she hears Ella's voice at the door. Lunch?

Sarah looks up. Sure, why not?

And Ella says noon will be fine, waves, and walks off.

Sarah looks at the blueprint again. Boring. Boring blueprint. Boring job. This job. The other job. Two years after crawling out of a horrible marriage, and what she still has is an unhappy lone-liness. She hates being alone, hates the isolation. She married in the first place to avoid being alone and then regretted it because early in the marriage she came to understand it was a woman she wanted, a woman's arms to hold her, a woman to share her life. She has known only two women, two girls in college, two awkward romances with girls as young as herself, as fearful as herself. Passionate kisses, daring caresses, explorations she now understands were clumsy. There has to be more. She can have more than what she had with those two girls so long ago. But she doesn't know a single woman she might consider as a lover, not one. She knows there are bars in the city where women go to meet women, clubs, organizations devoted to the affairs of women, lesbians. In the city it's only a matter of opening one of those little newspapers available free at the supermarket. I'm a lesbian and I ought to read lesbian newspapers. But it never happens. She's too afraid. She understands she has to turn to a new life to find happiness, but she's too afraid of it. Afraid of what? The unknown, maybe. She's not daring. She's twenty-eight years old, and everything in her life seems to have been predetermined. Her parents chose her schools. Her father was a minor architect, and now she's a minor architect. Her mother introduced her to the man she married, and now that Sarah is divorced, her mother and father are both piqued. She gets divorced and they get piqued. So she lives alone, hardly ever visiting them anymore, her evenings passed with magazines, books, casual women friends she knows would be shocked and revolted if she told them she was a lesbian. Dyke. Queer. The people she met during the short marriage are her ex-husband's friends, and they seem to avoid her. And she avoids them as well because evenings with married men and women only make her feel more lost anyway. These married people talk about their common life, their homes, their children.

In this large architectural firm she's been friendly with Ella, an older woman, almost fifty, a big, pleasant woman with three grown daughters. Not a real friendship—they never see each other outside the office—but sometimes they have lunch together in a restaurant only a few blocks away.

Gritting her teeth at the blueprint, Sarah looks forward to lunch at noon. Better than nothing. Better to eat with someone than to eat alone.

* * *

"I'm starved," Ella says. And then she does her routine with the menu, searching, cogitating, deciding. As she always does, Sarah orders a Julienne salad and coffee. When the waitress walks away, Ella says, "Oh, look, there's someone I know."

And a woman stops at the table, says hello to Ella. They seem to be old friends, but they haven't seen each other in some time. Ella introduces Marcy to Sarah, and when Marcy says she's about to find a table to eat alone, both Ella and Sarah invite her to join them.

The food tastes better when you're with people, Ella says.

Marcy laughs and sits down. She works for a brokerage firm. She's Sarah's age, with a round, attractive face and short dark hair, strong looking, with a certain force that Sarah notices. Appealing. Several times during the meal, Sarah finds herself glancing at Marcy, and when their eyes meet, Marcy holds her gaze a long moment.

Sarah feels a new excitement. What does it mean? Means nothing. Means something. She doesn't know.

Three women talking about the odds and ends of their lives. When lunch is finished, they leave the restaurant together. Since Ella has a dental appointment, she says good-bye on the sidewalk, and so it happens that Sarah and Marcy walk a few blocks alone together as they return to their offices. Sarah learns Marcy is unmarried. As they pass a movie theater where a new film is playing, Sarah says she wants to see that film, but she doesn't like being alone downtown in the evening. She immediately regrets saying that, regrets revealing how ridiculously isolated she is. But Marcy says nothing about that. Instead, Marcy says, "I'm gay, you know."

Stunned, Sarah says, "No, I didn't know it."

"I was hoping you were too."

Marcy looks at her. Sarah feels herself blushing, and says, "Yes, I think I am."

"You think?"

"No, I'm sure of it."

A soft smile from Marcy. "Why don't we see that film together this evening? Unless you're busy."

"No, I'm not busy. I'd love it."

Marcy says all right, she'll drive, and she'll pick Sarah up at her place. She takes Sarah's address and phone number, and they arrange a time. Before they part at the next corner, Marcy shakes Sarah's hand and smiles. "Well, I guess this day didn't turn out so badly after all."

"See you this evening," Sarah says.

At home early in the evening, she's nervous. Did she do the right thing with Marcy? Is she ready for this? She thinks about clothes. What clothes for this evening? She can't make up her mind. She finally decides to dress the same way she dressed during the day, a blouse and skirt and pumps and a raincoat. Same sort of clothes she wore when she and Marcy first met. Conservative. You're too conservative. Yes, I am.

After she bathes, she looks at herself in the mirror. I'm a lesbian. She holds the weight of her breasts in her hands, tweaking the nipples with her thumbs and forefingers. She drops a hand to her belly and slides her fingers into the forest of hair to find her clitoris. Yes, she wants a woman. Memories awaken like flames bursting into life again. The beginnings. The first time she tasted a nipple. The first time she touched someone else's clitoris. The first time she tasted someone else's cunt. Embarrassed by the sexual heat she feels, she turns away from the mirror. Two years without anyone in her bed because she was too afraid, and now that it may happen, she's still afraid.

When Marcy arrives punctually at seven wearing jeans and a sweater, Sarah feels overdressed. I'll change, she says.

But Marcy says no, she looks lovely. "Stay this way for me," Marcy says, an intimacy in her voice that Sarah finds thrilling. She agrees. She'll go dressed as she is. Happy at the way Marcy looks at her. Happy to be looked at.

They leave Sarah's apartment, descend in the elevator, walk to Marcy's car. During the drive downtown, they don't talk much, and after a while Marcy puts her hand on Sarah's and says, "You're nervous."

"Yes," Sarah replies. "I don't know why, but I am."

"It's only a date."

"Yes, I know."

"We're just going to the movies."

Sarah says nothing. She doesn't know what to say. She feels ridiculous, immature, inexperienced. She knows nothing. She doesn't know what she wants. It's easy to imagine herself in bed with Marcy. Exciting. But there her imagination refuses to go on. "I don't know anything," she says finally. "I don't know anything."

Marcy soothes her. "It doesn't matter. Things have a way of working themselves out."

At last they arrive at the theater, and soon, in the darkness, they sit beside each other. For a while, Sarah becomes engrossed in the film. A lovely film about India. Superb photography.

Marcy takes Sarah's hand and holds it, strokes it. Sarah feels nervous again, but also excited by the feel of Marcy's hand caressing hers in the darkness. Fingers intertwined. Marcy's fingers making love to each of Sarah's. Sarah feels herself getting aroused, blood pumping in her vitals, memories of the two girls she has known flooding into her mind. She no longer cares about the film. She adores Marcy's hand.

The film ends anyway, the spell is broken, and they walk out to find Marcy's car.

Marcy says, "Did you like the film?"

"Yes, I loved it," Sarah responds.

"You're very shy."

"I can't help it."

"It doesn't matter," Marcy says finally.

But she doesn't touch Sarah's hand again and Sarah feels very much alone.

When they arrive back at Sarah's apartment building, Marcy accompanies Sarah to the entrance and then says she won't come up. In the shadows near the entrance, she leans forward to kiss Sarah's lips.

"I'll call you," Marcy says.

Sarah turns into the entrance feeling miserable. Her first date with a woman is a complete failure. Catastrophe. She needs a strong drink. Whatever sexual excitement she felt before is now gone. All she wants is to forget everything.

In her apartment, she makes a double Scotch, drinks it, then falls asleep on the living-room sofa with the lights on.

The next morning in the office at her drafting table again. Not long after she starts her work, a small box arrives by special messenger. Sarah opens the box and finds a single red rose inside. A card signed: *M.*

Marcy.

She's thrilled. She feels buoyant all day. She opens the box several times during the day to look at the rose. In the evening, when she's finally home again, she puts the single rose in a small vase and then sets the vase on the coffee table in the living room.

Marcy telephones at seven. Can she come over? Maybe they can have a pizza delivered. Sarah agrees and Marcy offers to bring a bottle of red wine.

She arrives with two bottles of red wine. "I wasn't sure one would be enough," she says.

She kisses Sarah's cheek. A light kiss. Then she steps back and looks at Sarah. This evening they're dressed alike, jeans and sweaters, except that Marcy wears sneakers and Sarah is barefooted. "You look good in jeans," Marcy says.

"Thank you."

"This is one of my workout nights," Marcy says. "But I thought about you and I wanted to be here."

She tells Sarah about the hours each week she spends at an exercise studio. Running in place, using the machines, lifting weights, tension dripping away in her sweat. "I like being strong," she says. She rolls her shoulders like a prize-fighter and they both laugh.

Sarah finds an old Grateful Dead tape and puts it on the stereo. When the pizza arrives, Sarah lights two candles on the dining-room table, and they sit down to eat the pizza and drink the wine. Marcy talks casually about her job, her life. She lives alone, but until three months ago she lived with a woman. "It just didn't work," she says.

And Sarah talks about her failed marriage, her realization that she's a lesbian. "But I don't know anything."

"You already said that."

After dinner, they relax on the sofa in the living room. They have more wine, finish the second bottle. Then Marcy leans over and kisses Sarah's lips.

"I was sorry I didn't come up here last night," she says.

"Me too."

"Don't be too shy."

"I'll try."

Marcy kisses her again, this time a deeper kiss. She takes Sarah in her arms and Sarah huddles against Marcy's shoulder. During the next kiss, Marcy passes her hand over Sarah's breasts through her sweater. Sarah feels a sudden frenzy of desire, her lips melting against Marcy's, her mouth opening to accept Marcy's questing tongue.

Marcy strokes Sarah's face, a gentle caress. "Relax, baby." Her hand slides over Sarah's breasts again. Let's have a look, she whispers. She lifts the sweater, unhooks her bra and lifts that too.

Sarah's breasts tingle in the cool air, her nipples stiff with excitement. Marcy looks at them a long time, just looks, and then she bends her head to take one of the nipples between her lips.

Sarah moans. She holds Marcy's head with her hands. She trembles as she feels Marcy's tongue making love to her nipple.

"I love that," Sarah murmurs.

"You're like a tender flower. Did you like the rose I sent you?" Marcy asks, letting go of the nipple.

"I loved it."

"Let me undress you."

"All right."

She makes Sarah rise. She pulls the sweater over Sarah's head and removes the bra completely. She kisses the tip of each of Sarah's swaying breasts. She unbuckles Sarah's belt and pushes the jeans down to Sarah's feet so Sarah can step out of them. She pulls Sarah's panties down, and Sarah steps out of those too. Sarah blushes when Marcy sniffs at her panties.

"I like your smell," Marcy says. "Smelling a woman is like smelling a flower. The real rose."

"I feel awkward," Sarah says.

"You're not awkward, you're beautiful. Let me look at you. Sit on the sofa and let me look at your cunt."

Sarah trembles as she sits down and opens her legs. She feels terribly lewd. She feels embarrassed as Marcy kneels and pushes her knees wide apart to look at her.

But when she sees the desire in Marcy's eyes, the embarrassment turns into excitement.

"Yes," Sarah says.

Marcy looks up at her and smiles. "Yes?"

"Oh, yes."

Gently Marcy lifts Sarah's legs to her shoulders, and she bends to take Sarah with her mouth.

Sarah cries out, a long moan, knowing she now has her new life.

QUEEN OF THE
BANANA SPLITS
Leslie Gray

J ennifer works at one of the few old-fashioned soda shops still open in San Francisco. There are Formica counters and red leather stools with ornate metal backs. Customers sit two-by-two in the booths, splitting sundaes. The very air in the shop has the fragrance of powdered sugar and when you breathe in, it's like walking into a giant gingerbread house.

When we started dating, I would meet Jennifer outside her store and walk her to her apartment. We never hung out in the shop. She was always ready to leave, and I didn't want to ruin my diet with the free ice cream she would have given me. Jennifer couldn't stand the thought of eating the treats she served. After about a week working there, she explained, none of it looked appetizing.

The owner of the store, an elderly widow who had opened the

shop with her husband years before, left the place to Jennifer. Suddenly she needed assistance. I offered to help out, as much as I could. I'm a free-lance artist, so I worked my hours around when Jennifer needed me.

I became an expert sundae maker. All of the regular customers insisted I fill their orders. I was just as good with a float or a malted, but my special—my forte—were banana splits.

Banana splits are very sexual desserts. There are the bananas, of course, which have their unique, rather easy-to-fantasize-about shape. And then, there are the toppings: whipped cream, chocolate sprinkles, and maraschino cherries, my personal favorite.

The night Jennifer celebrated her first year as owner, we gave out free ice cream all day. That night, once closed, Jennifer lowered the blinds in the windows, turned out all of the lights except the one directly above the counter, and asked if I'd make her a special dessert.

"Would I make you one?" I leered at her. "Or would I make you one?"

She grinned as she stripped and then climbed onto the counter. I balled up my apron and set it behind her head to make her more comfortable. Then I went to work. I peeled the ripest bananas and cut slices of them to place on her nipples and in a line along her belly. I placed one banana inside her cunt, leaving a bit of it protruding like a little cock. Then I went to work with my whipped cream. I make whipped cream fresh, every day, but we also keep cans of the stuff in the refrigerator. I used these because they were fun to aim and squirt, and because Jennifer kept shrieking whenever the cool, sweet foam hit her skin.

I dusted her entire body with chocolate sprinkles and then warmed some chocolate syrup, testing the temperature until it was perfect to dribble onto her naked skin. She moaned at the feel of it, sticky and gooey along her ribs, the base of her belly, that indentation between her collarbones that I love to kiss.

The next touch? Maraschino cherries, of course. I bent to eat the banana from her pussy while she wriggled and begged me to make her come, and then placed a few cherries, stems out, in her lovely honey pot. Hungry for love, I lapped the whipped cream from her breasts, dined on the cut bananas coated with syrup and sprinkles, and moved down again to her pussy, pulling the cherries out with my teeth and devouring each one. She was desperate for release by now—had been waiting during my entire creation—but I wasn't finished.

I lifted her legs in the air and began spooning the still-warm syrup over her cuntlips. After each spoonful, I'd lap her clean—or close to clean—and then I'd spoon another gob of drippy syrup on her. The gooey chocolate made its way between her pussylips to her ass, and she begged me to lick her clean there.

The counter was a soupy mess of ingredients, but we didn't care. I rolled her over, getting her nice and sloppy, and then parted her asscheeks and licked and sucked the chocolate from the opening of her asshole. She was shrieking by now, just wild with pleasure. I slid my hand under her hips and toyed with her clit while I sucked on her asshole.

"More," she whimpered. "More, please...."

I suckled and drank chocolate syrup from her asshole, flicking my tongue between her parted cheeks to catch every drop until finally, shuddering and begging, she came.

Jennifer, my love, was the sweetest dessert I've ever tasted, and I...I continue my reign as the Queen of the Banana Splits.

FAIRY TALE
Bettina Nelson

When I was little, I was a princess every Halloween. My progressive parents tried to persuade me to be something more original. A beatnik. Martha Washington. A cowgirl. I balked. I wrapped a silver scarf around myself, raided my mom's jewelry and makeup. Transformed myself into a creature of angelic beauty, or so I thought. (Pictures reveal that I drew huge circles of rouge on my cheeks and tottered about in heels way too big for my small feet.)

As an adult, each Halloween I find myself searching for something funky to wear to our office party. I work for a weekly paper, and we rent an entire restaurant for our festivities. Most of my coworkers are extremely creative. They have dressed as refrigerators, as pairs of running shoes, as fried eggs with toast. But each Halloween, as I paw through my closet of black suits, I long for a silver scarf, some high heels, and a rouge stick. My princess craving has never left.

When Joy and I hooked up, she thought of me as strictly business. I am that way every day. As page editor of the drama section, my job is fun but difficult. Some story is invariably last-minute. Some picture is always late. I had more freedom when I wrote stories and didn't edit. Now if a deadline isn't made, it's my ass.

Joy seemed happy with my no-nonsense personality. She is a costume designer for movies, and her job allows her to express her creativity constantly. But on our first Halloween as a couple, I surprised her, confessing to her my desire to be a princess.

She didn't laugh at me. She didn't snicker as she looked up and down my 5'11" body, didn't point out that I'm taller than your average prince, that I don't have any of the soft, feminine qualities of the princesses in fairy tales. Instead, she said, "No problem. Leave everything up to me."

On Halloween, in the late afternoon, she drove to my house with a huge garment bag. First she blindfolded me. Then, as I questioned and quizzed, she dressed me. She took the blindfold off to do my hair and makeup, but forced me to close my eyes until the last possible moment, when she needed them open to brush on coats of mascara.

When Joy brought me to the mirror, I was in shock. She had dressed me in a silver, shimmering outfit, made of the same gauzy fabric of my mother's scarf. She had found a dress that suited my flat chest and long torso, and I appeared as light and feminine as I ever had in my dreams. She'd done my hair in ringlets and they fell loosely down my back. From my glittering crown to my sparkling shoes, I was a princess.

Joy left me alone while she dressed. Then came the second surprise of the evening: Joy dressed in the white breeches and velvet jacket of Prince Charming, and, as a couple, we made our way to the office party. Most of my coworkers didn't recognize me out of my normal business-suit attire. Once the thrill of surprise was over, Joy and I made our way to the roof, where we enacted another one of my fantasies: the princess's giving up her maidenhead to the prince.

Joy, who acts in the role of the receiver during much of our lovemaking, was transcendent in her new role. She unfurled her cape and spread it out on the ground to protect me. Then, with me in my finery on the silken lining of her cape, she unsheathed her sword (so to speak) and plundered away. I was careful not to rip the lovely costume, lifting it up for her to gain access. That was the last coherent thought I had, though, because being taken by so handsome a prince left me dizzy and somewhat confused.

Joy cradled my head in her hands as she plunged her cock inside me. She cooed love words at me, calling me her precious gem, her most treasured prize, saying that she'd slay a dragon to capture my heart...but slaying me more with her tool, parting my private hedges and plunging inside for the treasure.

I cried out as she found the rollicking rhythm I like best, the beating of her hips like the beating of my heart, pounding, pounding. Her feverish kisses smeared my lipstick, but I didn't care. Her rough caresses, pawing at the bodice of my breasts, undid the laces, setting my small breasts free for her to kiss. She ravaged my breasts, nipping at them, biting them until I was writhing under her and begging for her to make me come.

That sped her up until she was rocking in and out of my cunt like a wild stallion, using her arms for leverage, gaining momentum with each stroke. I screamed as I came, though my voice was lost into the night, and I'm sure I didn't scare too many of the trick-or-treaters down below.

When I regained my sensibilities, Prince Charming was above me reaching his hand out to me, to help me stand. He steadied me, then shook off his velvet cloak and wrapped it around his most muscular form. As he led me back into the party, he whispered, in a voice so similar to my lovely Joy's, "And they lived happily ever after."

The End.

AMORE
Lucy Artell

I was eighteen when I went to Italy with my parents. It wasn't altogether a dream-like trip for the three of us. We ended up getting on each other's nerves. They were still in the "we can tell you whatever we want" mode and I was in the "no, you cannot" mode. In the end, we spent a lot of time apart, sightseeing on our own.

I met a raven-haired Italian waitress at the café near our hotel. All I knew how to say in Italian was "La Fenicci," which was the name of the hotel, "grazie" (thank you), "per favore" (please), and "San Marco" (the square in Venice). The only English word the waitress knew was "Levi's," which she pronounced, "Leveees."

But she smiled at me in a very seductive way, and somehow we made do with our lack of verbal skills. Made do on the bed in my hotel room, her black uniform on the dresser, my "Leveees" and T-shirt in a heap on the floor. We sat in the bed, stripped completely, her legs over mine, entwined like pretzels. She moaned when I kissed her neck, my favorite part of a woman. She let me kiss her neck for what seemed like hours, lingering on the pulse point, spending much time at the base of it, that sultry spot between her collarbones. She had long, straight dark hair, and she tilted her head way back to let me get at her neck. Her hair tickled my fingers, which were holding onto her back.

I loved her smell. She wore a musky perfume, but she also smelled like the café where she worked. Her skin had the flavor of the coffee that she served, and a bit of the spices that they put in the pasta sauce, and some of the wine, as well. She tasted dark and rich, but I didn't get down to her pussy until I spent a good, long time drinking all of the scent and flavor from the skin of her neck, and arms, and belly.

When she lay back on my bed, her hair spread around her head like a blanket, and I would start at the tips of it, running my fingers through it. Then I would work my way to kissing her eyebrows, which were thick and dark and entirely too sexy for anyone to have been born with. Her eyes were the brown of the coffee she served, and she'd close them so that I could kiss her eyelids. She had a strong nose, which I traced over and over again with my fingers, and she had a slight cleft in her chin which I believed would make her a movie star if she came to America with me.

By the time I made my way down to her breasts, she'd be breathing hard, but it wouldn't make me work any faster. I spent time on her nipples, because they deserved my time. I kissed and licked them, held them between my lips and sucked them to make them stand out. They were browner than mine, like milk choco-late, and small, but her breasts were also small, so they suited her.

I worked my way down her ribs, not missing one, to her belly. She had a little belly, a small swell of a belly, even though she was a thin girl. I liked to cup it in my hands, to kiss all around it, and this made her smile. She wasn't self-conscious about her body the way American girls sometimes are. She seemed pleased with the amount of lust and energy I bestowed on each part of her. But each part of her deserved it. Every inch of her was divine.

Her pussy was covered in a thick mat of silky dark hair that I liked to lick. I pretended to be a cat, giving my cat friend a bath. I lapped at her fur with the flat of my tongue, parting her lips at the same time and tickling her between them. She responded delightfully, grabbing at me, pushing me down, demanding (I could understand the tone, if not the words) that I satisfy her.

I would do nothing less. I would make her come slowly, treating her to the many ways my tongue could bring her pleasure. I taunted her with nips to her pussylips between caressing circles of my tongue. I took her bursting clit between my lips and sucked it gently, flicking my tongue between my lips to tap on it, rap on it, until she could take no more and she exploded with orgasm and more come than any other woman I'd ever been with. She ejaculated in my mouth, and her taste was as pleasing as the perfume of her skin. It was my desire—my duty—to make her come as many times as I could.

We pleasured each other in many positions, turning topsy-turvy on my bed, head-to-tail, bucking against each other like animals. We stole into the square late at night and made love against the base of one of the ancient statues, kissing and fondling in the moonlight.

And, when it was time to part, when, sad though it was, we had to say good-bye in the only way we could, I made love to her a final time, memorizing the lines of her lovely neck. Remembering her taste for eternity. I promised to come back and she promised to visit—at least, I think we did. "Grazie," "por favore," and "San Marco" don't get you very far in long good-byes.

But I did give her my Leveee's, and that seemed to make her happy.

DESIGNATED DRIVER
M. J. Shafer

The four of us had been invited to take Kim out for her birthday to one of the most expensive restaurants in the city. Invited, that is, by Kim. I didn't really mind, since I'd always wanted to see the inside of the domelike trattoria, but I grew less keen on the idea as the evening progressed.

Kim, a ravishing lawyer I've known since high school, ordered champagne and continued to down glass after glass while the rest of us watched her in a sort of dumbstruck awe. Kim is always outspoken, which probably has something to do with her chosen profession, but drunk...she's a nightmare. With her curls high on her head and her blue eyes glistening, she looked like an angel in the reproduction that hung on the wall behind her. But her tongue was purely influenced by the devil, for she proceeded to tell each one of us our shortcomings.

The other three, also drinking, though not as quickly as Kim, were slightly numbed to her harsh words. I, as the designated driver, committed her tirade to memory. The evening was long and unenjoyable. When it was over, I drove my friends home, keeping Kim, well-buckled and passed-out, with me.

In the morning, Kim found herself in my bed. Tied down to my bed. Her bleary eyes must have been startled when she opened them at half-past ten. She was on my satin sheets, on her stomach, completely naked. She turned her head on the pillow as I walked into the room.

"What...?" she started, tensing her arms, trying to get them free from the bindings. That wouldn't work. I'm fairly adept with a knot.

"Your birthday's over, Kim," I said sweetly, "but I didn't get a chance to give you a birthday spanking yesterday."

She closed her eyes and then opened them again, obviously trying to figure out if she were having a dream, or a nightmare. When she couldn't wake herself up, she whispered, "You're not serious."

I showed her the paddle in my hand, brought it very close to her face so she could really see it. "You behaved like a spoiled brat last night, and we had to pay for it. Now, my dear, you're going to pay for it—with your skin."

She swallowed hard and tried to get a sweet, loving expression on her face. She turned her lips up hopefully and said, "But, Jas, you must be joking. You must—"

I gave her the first blow, then, catching both of her asscheeks, leaving a red blushlike print on her pale skin. She was tan elsewhere, but I'd spanked her where her bathing suit covered. She gasped at the sensation and then, glaring at me, demanded that I explain myself.

"You're twenty-eight, now," I said matter-of-factly. "That was one. You have twenty-seven to go."

Now, still tensing her arm muscles, she started to realize I meant business. I gave her two more quick spanks, one on each cheek, to let her know she was right. I wasn't kidding. Then, kneeling on the bed, I continued the spanking, raining blows on her left cheek, then her right, on the backs of her thighs. I paused when I saw the tears on her face. I liked them. She murmured, much more humbly, "What did I do last night?"

"Keep thinking," I said, "It'll all come back to you."

She closed her eyes as I gave her the last of the blows, and she sobbed softly when I'd finished. "Twenty-eight," I said, standing by her, placing one hand on her ass to feel the warmth. She sighed at my touch, and I let my fingers wander down, between her asscheeks, to her pussy, which was (as I'd suspected it would be) dripping wet.

"I was...I was awful last night," Kim confessed, wiping her face on my pillow, "Wasn't I?"

"Slightly unbearable," I agreed, moving to untie her, now, rubbing her wrists and ankles. She stayed in the same position, her ass up. I said, "The others were drunk, too. They won't remember much. But you've known me forever, Kim. The things you said..."

I positioned myself behind her and lifted the paddle again. "One to grow on. Remember?"

She nodded and held herself firmly in place, no longer tied. I made the last one count, and she howled. Then, composing herself, she turned on her side gingerly and looked at me, rubbing her ass with one hand.

"It's been a long time since I was punished like that," she said, her eyes meek, humble.

"Too long," I said, waiting.

She moved, coming into my arms, hugging me. "I've missed being with you, Jas." Her hair was soft against my cheek. I felt my will sliding. I put my arms around her and stroked her back, then lifted her chin and kissed her lips.

"Me, too, Kim," I said, softly. "Me, too."

ASHLEY'S SECRET
Diane Chalk

Ashley had dated Peter for two months before coming to terms with the fact that there was no chemistry between them. There'd been no spark with her and Robert, either. Or the man she'd met on vacation in Paris. Or the boys who had thronged around her in high school, dying to take her out on a date, to the movies, or to the prom.

But Peter had seemed different from the rest. At least, at first. He didn't pressure her, didn't call too often, didn't act demanding about sex or kissing or anything. When they were out, Ashley enjoyed herself, but in the way she enjoyed hanging out with friends. Nothing more...until she met Peter's sister.

Then, suddenly, Ashely's emotions, usually so controlled, so easily kept under wrap, began to play nasty tricks on her. At dinner, with Peter's sister across the way, winking at her, nudging her feet beneath the table, Ashley felt herself blush. Her heart raced. Her mouth was unable to formulate words of pleasant conversation when Peter's mother spoke to her.

Ashley's discomfort was not lost on Gemma. Peter's sister had a sense about things, about people, and she knew Ashley was interested in her from their first glance. Now Gemma was simply making the connection clear, paving the way to Ashley's introduction in the ways of lesbian love. After dinner, when the family moved to the living room for glasses of brandy, Gemma seated herself next to Ashley, and, on the pretext of showing Ashley their family photo album, Gemma moved closer until they were hip to hip.

Ashley saw none of the photos, none of the sweet family ski pictures, happy images captured forever by Kodak. Ashley let Gemma turn the pages, telling stories about the different locations, their vacation to Mammoth, the time in Hawaii when it would not stop raining. Ashley nodded, wondering if it were hot in the room, or if her inner temperature had gone haywire. Gemma understood the way Ashley was feeling, and she kept up her steady monologue of relatives and faraway places, until, sensing that Ashley was on the verge of passing out or freaking out, she suggested they go upstairs, to her old bedroom, where the rest of the albums were kept.

"You don't mind, do you, Peter?" Ashley's voice wavered. He was watching the game with his father, didn't mind at all. Gemma and Ashley walked the stairs in silence and, in silence, undressed the instant the door closed behind them. Ashley wasn't sure what had come over her, but she knew she needed to be in Gemma's arms, and she wasn't going to let herself, her calm rational self, keep this need from being fulfilled.

She tried to speak, to ask Gemma questions, but Gemma shook her head, placed her finger on Ashley's lips, then covered those pretty pink lips with her own mouth, silencing her.

Ashley closed her eyes and let Gemma take over, let Gemma lead her to the bed, covered with a blue flannel blanket. Let herself be spread out on the bed, her legs splayed, her hair falling around her shoulders, but not hiding her breasts. Her nipples were hard. Gemma licked them, kissed them, suckled from them. Ashley cradled Gemma's head in her hands, losing herself in the sensation of being treated warmly, softly, as she'd always fantasized about.

Gemma covered Ashley's body with her own, letting Ashley become used to the passionate feeling of another woman's body. It was right to be doing what they were doing. It was perfect, Ashley assured herself. Nothing—not holding hands with a man, not being kissed by a man—not being fucked by a man, nothing had ever come close to giving her the pleasure that Gemma was with the pressure of her body alone.

Ashley became courageous. She began to stroke Gemma's back, curving her hands into cups over Gemma's hips, then moving lower to stroke her ass. Exploring the dips and curves of her new lover's body was divine. She wanted to explore her forever, lose herself in Gemma's warmth.

They were in a sixty-nine, dripping come juices into each other's mouths, when they heard footsteps in the hall. Gemma tried to cover them with the blanket, but they were too far gone, too busy. There was a knock, and Gemma called out, "Hold on! One sec!" The women scrambled into the clothes, looking disheveled, but dressed, when Peter opened the door and walked in. He leaned against the wall, a smile on his handsome face.

"I knew it," he said to Ashley. "I knew you'd like Gemma...."

Ashley stared at him, her eyes wide.

"I've got a secret of my own that you two can help me with.... I need to introduce Mom and Dad to my lover...Kirk."

THE MODEL
Greta Lipton

She was my model before we dated, recommended by an artist friend who said Eleanor had the look I was after. Jackson was right, Eleanor had exactly the look I was after. The dangerous look. She exuded an air of mystery, of espionage. Her dark eyes were lined with smoke-gray pencil and her black hair had already begun to go a startling silver at the crown. She looked as though she might be any age between twenty-five and forty. She was nineteen.

You've seen models who have that knowing look. They might be vapid, brainless, useless, but they portray a sophistication that other women shell out megadollars to gain. You can't buy that look. It's not available in stores.

Eleanor had it. Perfect for the show I was working on. I had been accepted at a prestigious gallery; they were planning a gala opening. I needed a central piece, something patrons would talk about afterward.

Eleanor, draped with a silk scarf and nothing else, looked over her shoulder at me, then dropped her chin slightly. I took the picture. She lit a cigarette, and instantly the light in the room seemed to change, the glow of the cigarette transforming her features as she inhaled. She was Myrna Loy. She was Rita Hayworth. She was Garbo.

As always, I used black-and-white film. I couldn't wait to get the rolls into my darkroom to develop. I could feel the electricity— her electricity—as I took each shot. I was trembling as I asked her to wait, to make herself comfortable, to put on my silk robe and get herself something to eat while I disappeared into my darkroom.

She smiled, tilting her head. I wished for more time. Every movement she made was art. Every time she blinked, I lost a perfect shot.

When I completed my work, having chosen the shots I would enlarge and frame for my show, I came back into my loft and looked for her. She wasn't in the main living area. She wasn't in the bathroom. I walked down the hall, looking everywhere, even in the closets. Then I heard her call my name. She was sitting outside, on my fire escape, drinking a cup of coffee and smoking another cigarette. I reached for my camera, fascinated by the way she lifted the cup, the way she balanced her two vices so carelessly. But when she looked at me, when those smoky-rimmed eyes looked at me, I set the camera down and joined her on the escape.

She grinned and snuffed out her cigarette. Her smile was somewhat lopsided. A half-smile really. Only the right corner of her mouth went upward. It was a trick, I thought, something she must have practiced in the mirror for effect. As was the next gimmick...

her removal of my red silk robe, her revelation of her naked body on my fire escape, up above the traffic on Fillmore. I shielded her body with my own, wondering what she was doing, what I should do.

"Take me," she said in a low, calm voice. "Right here, right now." She spoke the way forties movie stars spoke: quick, to the point. There was no arguing with her. I placed my hands on her bare shoulders, running my fingers along her skin, down her arms, to her hands. I meant to lead her back inside, to take her to my featherbed, to comfort and sanity. But she shook her head, looked down at my crotch, and gave me her lopsided smile again.

It was time for me to move, anyway, I thought. If the landlord caught us. If other tenants complained. It was time for me to get a bigger place. I pulled out my cock as I rationalized what I was doing: making love to this stunning young model in the hazy late-afternoon sunlight, turning her so that her hands were against the window ledge and her ass was toward me.

I checked with my fingers to see if she were wet enough for me to enter. She was dripping—must have been thinking sweet sinful thoughts while I'd been developing her photos. I plunged the mushroom head of my synthetic cock between her slender legs. I could see her reflection in the window, could watch as she put on a whole new show for me. She kept her eyes half-closed, as if on the verge of sleep or ecstasy. Her ruby lips were parted, and she murmured my name each time I plunged inside her.

"Oh, Karen, oh, Karen, oh…." In a singsong way, almost teasing, but driving me wild with the caress of her voice. She moved one hand from the windowsill and stroked her own breasts, pinched her nipples between her thumb and forefingers. She reacted to her own touch even more than she did to mine, opening her mouth wider and calling my name even louder.

I'll have to move out, I decided. I will…but it doesn't matter.

Only this matters. Fucking her, plunging my cock inside her, rocking deep inside her, making all those fake expressions flicker across her heavenly face. She was a model of perfection, an actress. I knew it. I knew this was a show, that each gesture, each deep inhalation was a performance for me. Knew that if the window hadn't been closed, if I hadn't been able to watch her reflection, her face would have been impassive, immobile. Nothing there at all.

I'm a photographer. I know the difference between life and between art. And I know that sometimes, sometimes it doesn't matter.

CLICHÉS
Maura Finley

The moon was full and bright. It shone down on us like a great golden ball. It hung suspended in the night sky, its wise face beaming down on all the sleeping creatures below.

We weren't sleeping, though, my lover and I. Instead, we'd stolen into the moonlit garden, where the light spilled down upon us. Eliza's eyes were like limpid pools beneath that celestial light. Her hair was lush and dark as a raven's wing. I kissed her parted lips and tasted her honeyed breath. Nothing could have been sweeter in this world...or the next.

Her heart beat loud enough that I could feel it reverberating in my own breast. It seemed to keep the beat for the gilded moonlight, which played melodies in Eliza's ebony hair.

I held my breath as she took my hand and placed it on her heaving alabaster breasts. She whispered to me. I leaned forward to hear her, brushing my lips against her cheek. We were so close together that my breath stirred her hair. She said, "I want you. I want you now. More than I've ever wanted anyone before."

I felt myself responding. My panties were soaked in the center. My thighs felt weak and watery, as unstable as if I were on a boat, that gentle rocking in the silken waves.

Eliza said, "Take me! Take me now."

I lifted her skirt, revealing her shapely ankles, her slender calves, her long, lean legs. She turned around, offering me the prize of her perfect ass. I tucked the hem of her skirt into the waistband and pulled down her panties. Her skin shone in the moonlight. Her pale, milky white skin. I bent down on my knees behind her, parted the perfect globes of her asscheeks, and revealed the rosebud of her asshole.

I kissed her there and she moaned with excitement, desperate with longing for me to continue. "Please, Cath," she murmured. "Please do me, right here, in front of God, and everyone."

I stood and revealed my cock. I placed the head of it against her rear entrance. I pushed gently, just gently, but she screamed in pain and ecstasy as I did. Suddenly I sensed another presence nearby. It was our neighbor, Lara, come to see if everything was all right.

"Fine." I felt myself blush. What a position to be caught in!

"Well," Lara said, hesitating, "as long as you're okay…"

Eliza was bent forward, her head down, but she called out, "Come join us, Lara. You can take up position behind Cathy. That is…if you're packing."

"Never leave home without it," Lara said, removing her coat and revealing her nakedness. She moved behind me quickly, while I continued rocking my member in and out of my sweet Eliza's ass.

"Same way?" Lara whispered to me, pressing the head of her cock against my asshole. I tensed, then relaxed as she began to slide it in. "Of course," I said softly, though I wanted to be screaming as loud as Eliza had. "It's only fair."

"What's good for the goose…" Lara replied, getting into the groove that I set with my body, turning me into a sexual sandwich. We became a solid fucking machine, me banging away at my one true love's ass, Lara filling me completely with her eight inches of molded rubber. I told Eliza to be quieter, that if she kept up the noise we'd have even more neighbors joining us in our backyard.

"If you don't be careful," I warned her, "this will turn into some de Sade fiasco." But then she was coming, and there just is no quieting her when she comes. And then, as Lara continued to work her magic inside me, I was coming, as well.

Finally the three of us collapsed on our lawn, dirty, wicked, and spent, preparing for the rejuvenation when we'd finish each other up with our tongues and our cunts. Lara and I decided to go to work first on Eliza, with me taking the front and Lara taking the rear. We worked through each of our orgasms this way….

Which only goes to prove the old saying: "Two heads are better than one." And three heads? A fucking dream come true.

THE AD
Alison Tyler

STOP! DON'T LOOK ANY FURTHER! THIS STUNNING, 28 YEAR-OLD BROWN-EYED GIRL WILL FULFILL ALL OF YOUR WILDEST FANTASIES. I'M SEARCHING FOR A MODEL-TYPE, PREFERABLY BLONDE, 21 TO 30, WHO ENJOYS DIRTY DANC-ING, MOTORCYCLE RIDES, AND STAYING OUT ALL NIGHT LONG. PUT AN END TO YOUR DREAMING, CALL EXTENSION #400.

SBIF SEARCHING FOR SPANK MISTRESS TO TAKE CARE OF MY NAUGHTY DESIRES. YOUNG LADY WITH EVIL THOUGHTS NEEDS THOROUGH CHASTISING. DO YOU HAVE THE HEAVY HAND TO MAKE ME BURN? CALL EXTENSION #606.

XXX MEANS BEWARE! ONLY THE VERY BRAVE SHOULD ATTEMPT A DATE WITH THIS DOMINANT TIGRESS. DON'T LET MY FEMININE LOOKS FOOL YOU, WITHIN THIS BLONDE-BOMB-SHELL PACKAGE LURKS THE SOUL OF A TRUE DOMINA. I LONG TO RULE YOUR WORLD. CALL EXTENSION #666, IF YOU DARE.

It was the morning after her twenty-second birthday, and Veronica Matthews had decided to change her life. She sat at her dining room table with the latest issue of L.A.'s underground Wild Side, scanning the Women Seeking Women column in the "Personals" section. With one long, red fingernail she followed the tiny print paragraphs. The first selections didn't interest her; they were a little too bold. But as she read the ad at the top of the second column, she felt that familiar stirring a few inches below her delicately indented navel.

PRINCESS, I KNOW YOU'RE OUT THERE, AND I AM GOING
TO FIND YOU. TALL, SLENDER, GREEN-EYED BRUNETTE,
EARLY 40'S, SEEKS PETITE SEX KITTEN, UNDER 25, TO
PAMPER AND PLAY WITH. WE COULD HAVE A GOOD TIME
TOGETHER, COULDN'T WE? NO SMOKERS, DRUG USERS, OR
BUTCH-GIRLS NEED APPLY. (BOTTOMS ONLY, PLEASE.)
YOUR NEW MISTRESS AWAITS YOUR CALL. EXTENSION #453.

"My new mistress..." Veronica said aloud, echoing the advertisement. That one had possibilities. Definite possibilities.

She smiled to herself, imagining it, deciding that she was in dire need of some pampering, and that she might very well be a sex kitten if given the opportunity. The last part sounded intriguing, as well, even if she didn't truly understand the meaning of "bottoms only." (She could guess, though, and the X-rated mental picture further excited her.)

Veronica took a sip of her lukewarm coffee, leaving a crimson kiss on the lip of the white ceramic mug, and then returned to the paper. Nothing, nothing, nothing. Oh...

GORGEOUS, FIRE-HAIRED PROFESSIONAL WITH MIDNIGHT
EYES AND AN EVIL TONGUE WOULD LIKE TO TASTE THE
FORBIDDEN FRUIT. ISO...

She paused. What did ISO mean? Then she checked the information box on the side of the page: I seek only.

...I SEEK ONLY A YOUNGER, VGL...

Again she had to look up the abbreviation: very good looking.

...VERY GOOD LOOKING FRIEND TO HELP ME WARM THESE
COLD WINTER NIGHTS. ARE YOU THE ONE? I PROMISE YOU
WON'T BE DISAPPOINTED. EXTENSION #720.

Well, maybe not. That one was a bit too poetic, especially for

L.A. which rarely had cold nights. Veronica glanced out the window, at the morning sunlight filtering through the branches of the Jacaranda tree. As she watched, a few sad pale purple flowers dropped onto her balcony, adding to the autumn carpet of faded blooms already in place. She stared a moment longer, then went back to the ads in the paper, hoping that she might discover the perfect one.

```
NEVER THOUGHT I'D BE WRITING THIS...
TOO BEAUTIFUL FOR WORDS...
MADONNA LOOK-A-LIKE...
A BOD TO LAUNCH A THOUSAND SHIPS...
LIPSTICK LESBIAN LOOKING FOR SAME...
```

Veronica read for a minute, unimpressed by the ones that simply stated desired appearances, ages, weights, and measurements, and unsure of the ads that were filled with sexual jargon, odd codes, or lesbian lingo.

Then, finally, she found it.

```
DOES HE SATISFY YOU? IS SOMETHING MISSING? MAYBE YOU
DON'T NEED A MAN AT ALL—MAYBE YOU NEED ME. I KNOW
I NEED YOU. I'M 29, HAVE DARK CURLY HAIR, PALE SKIN,
AND BLUE EYES. I LIKE MUSIC, DANCING, AND LATE NIGHT
CONVERSATIONS. YOU SHOULD JUST BE YOU. EXTENSION
#669.
```

Yes. She got up from the glass dining room table and walked into her bedroom to use the cordless phone on the nightstand. The phone was hidden beneath a dirty pair of Rick's striped cotton boxers, and Veronica lifted them off with two fingers, a disgusted frown marring her comely features. She dropped the underpants in a heap on the beige-carpeted floor and reached for the phone, the ad's extension number already memorized. But before dialing, she caught a glimpse of herself in the mirror across the room, and she went to sit at her antique dressing table, wanting a closer look.

Her short hair was silvery blonde, bleached by the sun (with only a little bit of help from Giselle at Très Belle beauty salon). She wore it combed straight back from her forehead, and the soft tresses fell cleanly to the bottoms of her earlobes. Her gray eyes reflected the colors in her clothes. Today, she had on a white skirt and a long-sleeved lavender blouse and her eyes glittered in shifting shades of purple and blue.

Veronica stared hard at her mirrored image, wishing this identical twin could answer the questions that raced through her mind. Wishing she had a real twin to confide in, to share her problems with.

Did she have the nerve to call? Could she get away with it?

She bit her rose-slicked bottom lip, pausing to admire how sweet that made her look, naive and innocent. Virginal. Then, heart racing, she walked back to the phone and dialed the number before she could talk herself out of it.

The recorded message made her tremble, a thrilling combination of fear and desire, similar to the feeling she'd had before bungee jumping with her brothers the previous summer, a feeling surmounted only by the actual free fall. The woman's deep voice had traces of a Southern accent, possibly Texan, and was both mellow and reassuring, like a cool beer on a hot day. The woman said…

"Thank you for calling, darling, I know it took a lot of nerve. I'd like to meet you, talk with you, find out what you need and whether it's something I can give. You've taken the first difficult step by choosing to call. Now's the test. Leave me your name and number, and tell me when I can call you back. I assure discretion. Don't be afraid."

Because the voice hadn't given an identity, Veronica decided not to give her own real name. She prepared herself quickly during the beep, and then (remembering advice from her high school speech teacher) smiled as she said, "My name's Nica. I'm twenty-two, engaged, and confused. I'd like to meet you…as soon as possible." She left her phone number, and the instruction to call between five and seven P.M., when she'd be home from school, but Rick would still be at the law office. Then she cleared her throat and ended with the words, "I'm ready."

Was she?

Her heart still raced even after she hung up; she could hear the sound of it in her ears, beating, like ten thousand soldiers marching. (One, two, three. four. One, two, three, four.)

What had she done?

She looked at the digital clock on the bedside table, saw that was time to get ready for school, but couldn't command the energy. Not yet. Momentarily weak, she sat down on the edge of the bed and lowered her head into her hands. There was no going back now, no erasing the message, no returning to her "real" world. Not ever again.

What would Rick say?

Now she placed one hand over her breast, feeling the rapid rhythm of her heartbeat, the raggedness of it startling to her. With her other hand, she pulled at the hem of her skirt, worrying the edge of the white silk. Underneath, she had on sheer stockings and gray silk garters, garments that she liked but Rick thought overly flamboyant. ("Why not just get the nylons?" was his attitude. "That other stuff all seems too tricky.") *Rick…*

What did it matter now? It was too late to take it back.

Slowly, she slid the smooth fabric up to her knees, at the same time imagining another woman's hands on her thighs, another woman's fingertips taking over from her own. Coming to an impromptu decision, she shifted her hips and pulled her panties down to her ankles, slipping them all the way off in a quick gesture, and settling back against the bed. She still had on the shiny pearl garters, and she liked the feel of them against her otherwise naked legs and ass. The mild bondage sensation appealed to her fantasies.

Her fingers were almost too knowledgeable, deftly playing between the cleanly shaven lips of her pussy, working endless circles upon circles that took her to the edge of climax in only a few rotations. She had the briefest flicker of a thought—Would it be like this with another woman? She wondered if she would reach the pinnacle as quickly. Or would it be drawn out, taking her much longer, the lingering embrace, the lingering caress of a woman's tongue, the desperate need rising inside her, burning inside her. Raging inside her.

The myriad thoughts blossomed into a full-fledged fantasy, one that would have made Rick cringe if she'd ever had the nerve to tell him, because, like most of her fantasies, it involved another woman. Veronica was on her back in a snowdrift, completely naked in the cotton-like fluffs of snow. There was no cold to the scenario, no chill to her skin, only the white clouds caressing her. She made snow angels, and as she slowly spread her legs, she realized how wet she was, her satiny honey coating her inner thighs, sticky as she slid her legs together and then apart.

Then a change, shifting, blurring, as fantasies tend to, and she was now on a beach, a pale pink towel beneath her, hot white sand warming her skin, heating her skin, even through the velvety fabric. The heat was as benign as the cold of the snow had been— erotic in its simplicity. There were the sun and the sand and the smell of the ocean, so close that the fingers of waves reached out to dampen the edge of her towel.

It was not a different scene, but a scent wafting over her that alerted her to the arrival of a woman. This stranger, beautiful (with pale skin and dark hair) settled down on the ocean side of her towel and wrapped Veronica in her arms. And then the towel disappeared entirely, and the women were embracing directly on the sand, as comforting as the banks of fantasy snow had been.

Veronica was vaguely aware of the waves pounding, the sun so hot above, the movement of their bodies tracing lazy circles in the sand beneath them. Aware, as if having an out-of-body experience, looking down on herself from above. They were moving, turning their bodies to form a sixty-nine, and the woman began telling her what to do—her voice, with a slightly aggressive edge to it, working to pull Veronica back into herself.

"Harder, darling," the woman said, "Faster, now."

Veronica plunged her tongue between the woman's pussy lips to find the treasure of her clit and suckled it. She felt as if she'd split open a shimmering sea shell to find the waiting pearl inside. Precious and perfectly round, she bathed it with her tongue, knew instinctively how to touch it, tease it, tickle it with her lips and with the warm heat of her mouth.

Following her lover's orders, Nica worked hard, circling, lapping at the woman's fragrant pussy. There was something in this that reminded her of drinking expensive champagne, the intoxicating effect it had upon her. She was nearly coming from the scent of the woman alone, from the heady perfume of her dream lover's cunt. (Something she'd never tasted, never smelled, in her real life.)

"Very good, sweetheart," the woman crooned in a soft, Southern accent. "Lick harder, now...that's it, baby doll."

Spurred on by her fantasy lover's praise, Veronica used her fingers to spread the woman's netherlips, and she lapped and licked like a kitten, echoing the woman's ministrations of her own pussy. She explored with her fingers, thrusting one, then two, within the hollow of her lover's sex. She used one hand to capture her own short hair in a ponytail at the back of her neck so that she could see what she was doing, watch as she devoured her lover's pussy. It was this image, this flash picture, that brought her to a shuddering, golden-hued climax.

After a moment of fairly heavy breathing, she sat up and found herself staring at a picture of Rick that she'd taken at his parents' vacation home in the mountains the winter before. Rick was making a snowball, preparing to throw it at her, and his face was rigidly serious with the effort of having fun. Even with his blond good looks, skier's tan, and pale blue eyes, he looked severe, driven.

Veronica shook her head. Rick just couldn't do it for her. Perhaps he had guessed, and maybe that was why he had given up trying.

She collapsed back on the bed and shut her eyes again, the early morning light coloring her closed lids in shades of blues and reds and golds like a summer sunset painted by Turner. She closed her eyes more tightly and the colors grew blacker, darker. The need was in her again, the urge rising, and she swallowed hard and recalled that voice on the other end of the phone line. Southern and cooling, soothing in its cadence, in the rise and fall of each word. It had been like a melody, a dream.

Her fingers dipped back between the slightly swollen lips of her pussy, finding the sweet wetness there, and she arched her hips toward an invisible lover and imagined the woman's tongue probing her, searching for the contractions that soon followed. Probing and violating. Making the most perfect circles around her little jewel. Oh, she was almost there...

Please...

What did she honestly want? Was it only one night of passion, a one-night reality to replace her endless fantasies?

No.

Was it an absence, the absence of Rick? Of his endless requirements, rules, and regulations that she never seemed to be able to follow or complete to his satisfaction?

No.

It was simply about the need, the desire, dark and powerful, that had taken over her life, her every waking moment. It had even taken over her dreams.

This is the first dream...

I am alone in my bed—in our bed—waiting for Rick to finish up in the bathroom and join me. It seems as if he's taking a long time, much longer than usual, but I don't mind. The longer he takes, the more believable it will be to him that I have fallen asleep.

The door opens and I shut my eyes, easily mimicking the gentle rise and fall of my breathing, faking sleep like a little kid fakes being sick to get out of a test at school. A weight on the edge of the bed lets me know that he's sat down, then a soft tug at the blankets, pulling them away from my body, revealing my nightgown-clad form. I keep my eyes closed tightly, ignoring him, until I sense the difference, until I sense that this weight on the edge of the bed is not my fiancé, that the hands removing my nightie are not Rick's hands.

Not male hands at all.

I peek out from beneath my lashes without fully making the commitment of opening my eyes. And I see her. She's beautiful, as all dream lovers should be, with dark hair that curls down past her shoulders, and pale skin. Her cherry-red lips are full and her eyes are a clear, calm blue.

I know that she feels me stir, know that she knows my game, but she doesn't say a word, and I don't either. I simply let her continue, unbuttoning my purple silk nightgown, freeing me of my panties, stroking my gold-burnished skin with her fingertips and sighing as if she's just uncovered a precious gift.

"Lovely," she says—the first thing she says. "You are too lovely, darling. But then, I knew you would be." As if I am her dream lover, as if I am here to fulfill her fantasies, instead of the other way around.

"Turn over," she orders, her voice suddenly stern. "Roll onto your tummy for me, darling."

I do so without thinking, without questioning her reasons. I do it only because she has asked, as I feel I might do anything she asked. When I am on my stomach, she sits at my side and waits, as if she's observing me, drinking me in. Then I feel her hands again, caressing me everywhere: my shoulder blades, my ribs, my lower back, my thighs, my calves…then up again, my inner thighs, my pussy (just brushing me here), and then she uses both hands to spread the cheeks of my ass and she starts to touch me there.

"No…" more of a plea than an order. "No, please," I say. "Anything else, but not there." Too embarrassed. Too scared. (What if it felt good? What if…)

"Yes, darling," she insists, though her finger has stopped in place, no more rotations. "This is where I want to play."

I tense up, my entire body becoming one tight wire. "No," I say again, "I can't." I look over my shoulder at her as I say it, the same plea in my eyes, and she nods her head and gets up from the bed.

"Your choice," she says. "Your fantasy."

And in a blink, she's gone.

ROMANTIC ENCOUNTERS
Lindsay Welsh

"**P**ackage for Miss Geddes. Is that you, ma'am?"

Linda signed for the box and closed the door. She had welcomed the interruption, which had broken up a particularly frustrating and unproductive session at her typewriter. The characters weren't turning out the way she wanted, and working at making Jason into a real person was difficult. When she saw the Coats Publishing logo on the return address, though, it immediately became more than just a diversion; she was positively giddy with anticipation.

The excitement was so strong that Linda didn't know what to do. Her first instinct was to tear the package apart and get at the treasure within as fast as she could. Her desire to prolong this enjoyable moment for as long as possible won out, though. She used a pair of scissors to slowly cut through the tape at the ends, and she took the lid off the box gently, as if the pages inside might break.

She gasped when she saw them. She had had her articles published in the newspaper before, but that was nothing like seeing her words actually typeset into real printing. Except for the increased length of the pages and the lack of binding, it looked exactly as it would when it was finally printed.

Her fingers leafed through the pages, and sentences sprang up which she remembered writing. Yet here they were on paper, looking like someone else's work—but it was hers, hers! She was in print!

Of course the pages were just galley proofs, to be corrected and edited once more before they were finally made into the finished book. It would mean several days' work for Linda, but she didn't mind at all. She knew that the excitement of reading her own story in book form would keep her going through every last sentence.

She put the pile of printed sheets on her desk and began to leaf through them. It had been two months since she had met with Julie Gray and signed the contract, and several of the passages seemed new again. It felt like years since she had committed the words to paper.

One thing that struck her, as she continued to read, was how much more interesting Megan was than Brian. He came through very lifelike, very real; his conversation was believable, his personality intact. Still, even though she had created him, Linda couldn't imagine what Megan saw in him. The thought of longing for those muscular arms didn't appeal to her at all.

Megan! Now, there was a character she could identify with. The woman was earthy and sensual. Linda didn't really know why, but she did know with unerring certainty that she'd always found women more intriguing than men. Even though she didn't exist, Megan was no different.

As she read, Linda began to notice a tightening between her

legs. It happened often when she thought about other women. She never dared to fully explore these feelings; sometimes she wondered if she really was lusting after women, and sometimes she dismissed it and thought that she was making too much of it; in any case, she was almost afraid of what she might find out about herself.

It wasn't that Linda was upset at the thought; instead, she didn't want to go off in a direction she couldn't continue with. She didn't know any lesbian women and had no way of meeting them. If she really did want other women, it would have to remain a fantasy, and so she tried to tell herself that it wasn't that way at all. For now, she was content to think about other women and to let the thought of them turn her on. From that point, at least, she could control the situation and make sure that her needs didn't go unmet.

Linda moved her hand almost unconsciously to the crotch of her jeans. The fabric felt hot where it met her skin, and she imagined that it was wet as well. She rubbed herself through her clothes and shivered when she was able to push against her pussylips with the thick seam of her pants.

She found herself doing that a lot and always ending up the same way by making herself come. It happened almost every time she stopped to think about women—really think about them. About their full lips and their hair and the soft curves of their body. The hard lines of a man could be impressive under the right circumstances; she loved to look at artistically photographed nudes and admire the play of shadows under clearly defined muscles or the way light reflected off masculine skin in a completely different way from women. But it was the female nudes that took her beyond mere light and shadow and into flights of fancy that ended inevitably in an orgasm.

Linda tried to concentrate on *Sweet Desire*—no, that's not right, she told herself, they've renamed it *Obsessions*. She liked that. It sounded so much hornier, even if Megan and Brian's love scenes weren't as explicit as she expected many readers would have liked. Linda preferred any love scenes to be down and dirty, even if they were heterosexual; when she read about sex or watched a movie, Linda wanted hard-core or nothing. Soft-core movies, with sex either hinted at or kept off camera, frustrated her so much that she refused to watch them—she wanted the real thing. Sometimes she could hardly believe how raunchy she would like to write those scenes, especially when she was concentrating on Megan.

Her cunt was now throbbing, demanding attention, and she knew that she wouldn't be able to get a thing done until she took care of it. I certainly seem to do this a lot, she told herself as she walked down to her bedroom, but it feels so good!

The bedroom was small but neat, the bed inviting under its thick comforter. On the dresser was a small television that contained a videocassette player built in under the screen. She didn't even need to slip a tape inside; as always, it sat waiting and ready for her.

She switched on the set and pushed the Play button. This was a compilation tape, made up of a number of different scenes, that she'd ordered from a mail-order company. It was by far her favorite—not every scene, but select ones throughout the tape that she knew movement by movement from watching over and over.

The familiar music came through the speakers, along with the gasps and moans. Why does all porno-tape music sound the same? she wondered. Are there albums of "Music to Fuck By" that they all use, and who records them, anyway? —She didn't particularly care for this scene. The guy was huge, she admitted, and the woman's gorgeous tits bounced up and down as he rammed his cock into her again and again. The only reason she liked it was because it was her signal that her favorite scene was the next one up on the tape.

Linda hit that lovely Fast-Forward button and had to smile. Sex looked so silly speeded up! At breakneck speed, the camera panned all around the couple, the male actor's testicles bouncing like Ping-Pong balls against the woman's ass while his buttocks moved like a jackhammer. But then his come spurted out at the speed of light, and when the scene dissolved out she returned it to normal play. She didn't want to miss a second of this, and her eyes never left the screen as she slid open the drawer of the bedside table and took out a long, white plastic vibrator. She slipped her jeans easily, without her attention once being diverted from the action.

The scene opened on two gorgeous women who were inexplicably sitting on a bed, fully clothed, talking to each other. Both of them had elaborately teased hair, and the blonde was playing idly with one of her curls. The black-haired woman was smiling seductively. The dialogue was so bad that Linda had never really listened to all of it; but then, she didn't watch this tape for the talking, anyway.

Without warning, the two women suddenly decided that they wanted each other. They undressed quickly, leaving on their high-heeled black shoes. Their lips met, and they spent a long time kissing each other and moaning as if they already had tongues on their clits. Linda waited for one of her favorite moments, when a close-up shot showed them parting. A tiny string of saliva stretched between their lips for just a second, holding them together. Seeing that made her hot, and she turned on the vibrator to its lowest setting and used it to tease the sensitive skin on her upper thighs. The whole scene was a long one, and from watching it countless times, she could orchestrate her own movements to theirs. They were teasing, and so was she.

The blonde woman now knelt on the bed while the black-haired woman sucked on her tits. They stuck straight out and had obviously been augmented by a skillful plastic surgeon, but Linda didn't care. The idea of being there and having her lips on those luscious nipples turned her on more than she ever thought anything could.

They changed positions and now the blonde woman's mouth was filled with a perfectly formed breast, while the black-haired woman tilted her head back and moaned, "Take it in, take it in, yes, yes!" Linda's hand was on her own ample tit, stroking the large nipple through her shirt, and she longed to feel a hot mouth on it.

The video had obviously been made for masculine tastes; Linda always wondered why men who became disgusted or even violent at the thought of male homosexuality were inevitably turned on by lesbians. The uncomfortable shoes left on and their almost-overdone femininity targeted a male audience, but the sex itself turned Linda on and made her desire them. How much different were real lesbians? she wondered. Was the sex even better? She longed to find out.

She turned the dial on the vibrator to a higher setting when the blonde woman stretched out on the bed and opened her thighs to reveal pussyhair that was considerably darker than the golden hair on her head. Linda pushed the vibrator against her own cuntlips as the camera zoomed in. The woman pulled herself apart with her fingers, exposing the delicious rise of her clit and the shadowy depths of her vagina. The flesh was shiny with juice.

The dark-haired woman bent down and applied her tongue, and Linda shivered with delight. This was what she loved best about this scene. In so many videos, the women weren't really lesbians; they were just working at making a film, and it showed. Those were the movies where cunnilingus consisted of a few quick laps across closed pussylips and much circling of the pubic area with just the very tip of the tongue. Linda would watch these, too, but their lack of enthusiasm made for a less fulfilling orgasm.

These two women obviously enjoyed what they were doing very much. Linda's passion flared as she watched the woman push her tongue in deep and stay inside those swollen pussylips as she moved it back and forth. It wiggled the clitoris, spread the lips apart, and Linda could see the gleam of pussy nectar on the woman's cheeks and chin. She was right inside her lover, and the blonde's moans sounded real as her cunt was licked so expertly.

"Eat her out!" Linda whispered, as she spread her own pussylips with her fingers so that the vibrator could buzz against the most sensitive part of her slit. "Fuck her with your tongue!"

The woman obediently did as Linda instructed. Her tongue flashed in and out of that shadowy space, and Linda looked closely to see another of her favorite moments. When the woman pulled back, Linda could actually see the thick juice on her tongue and see how a bit of it stretched out between tongue and cunt. Linda shivered and pushed the vibrator on her clit. Her hips rocked, savoring each trembling chill.

The women changed position again, and now they were laying beside each other in a sixty-nine. Linda angled the tip of the vibrator so that it was right inside her cuntlips, buzzing against her clit. She loved sixty-nine! Each woman's desire built to a peak as her clit was licked increased her own passion. It would build and build, each tantalizing the other more, until it exploded into a full-blown, pussy-feeding frenzy.

They were going at each other wildly now. Linda loved the way the blonde woman stuck her tongue out and shook her head back and forth to rub on swollen cuntlips. The dark-haired woman was madly lapping the whole length of that soaked pussy. Linda's hole was so wet that the vibrator slipped effortlessly over her skin, lubricated with her own luscious juices.

"Fuck her, fuck her, you bitch," Linda whispered. She held the vibrator tight against her now and wished it was someone's head she was holding as the woman licked her clit. "You slut, eat that pussy! Come on, give her head!"

Linda was so close that she didn't even move the vibrator around. She now held it hard, right on her clit, letting the buzzing motion stimulate her. With one finger, she spun the dial to its highest setting and moaned as the pressure increased. Her fingers were cramped from holding it so tightly. She lifted her hips off the bed and her face contorted with the huge buildup within her belly. This was going to be a good one.

The women on the screen couldn't hold still, either. Both of them were writhing and bucking, trying to increase the pressure of tongue against clit. They were crazy women now, moaning and licking. They had been acting before, but this was obviously for real now. It was easy to see that both were close to coming and desperate for the relief and the high it would bring.

The blonde woman came first. The camera caught all of it. Now Linda, her huge clit about to burst, held her breath for the moment she had been waiting for. The blonde continued to lick the dark pussy until her lover was moaning and crying that she was about to come. As the dark-haired woman began to tremble, the blonde woman lapped several times and then pulled back as the camera moved in.

The hard, engorged pussylips were shiny with saliva and female juice. As Linda watched eagerly, those lips shuddered and trembled by themselves in orgasm. A large gob of hot cunt juice spurted out and trickled down. It was an amazing sight. At that moment, Linda let go. She moaned out loud herself and bucked her hips again and again, convulsively, as wave after wave of orgasm went through her. It seemed she would never stop coming. It was a long time before she took the vibrator out from between her legs and turned the dial to stop its buzzing.

The movie went to another scene, this of a woman sucking a

cock while another one was pushed into her pussy. Linda sighed, for it reminded her that she had to go back and attempt to breathe some life into the character of Jason and finalize the galley proofs that gushed so over Brian. Now if only it were Megan and Ramona, or Patricia, or Barbara, maybe she would find some enthusiasm. Or Julie…but Linda had to laugh out loud for thinking of that name. As if! A romance editor who wasn't turned on by flexed biceps and a deep masculine voice whispering her name? It would be too good to be true, Linda said to herself as she pulled up her jeans, put the vibrator away, and reset the tape machine for the next time that particular scene would come in handy. Too good to be true, but she had to admit that it certainly would be nice if it were.

VULCAN MINDBLOWER
Mary Jo Vaughn

I'm not even sure if that's the right name for it. Maybe you know. Maybe you've had one. Those iced pink drinks served in martini glasses at Jezebelle's on 13th Street. They're mean, they are. They'll blow you away.

I'm not a lightweight. Don't even let that thought enter your head. I can do tequila body shots all night long. But the mind-blowers, they're different. They sneak the fuck up on you when you're not looking, when you're not thinking much except "Mmmm…that was good. I'll have another."

I was in that sort of a state when Mira found me. I was leaning up against the cool, wood bar of Jezebelle's, my face flushed, my dark hair pulled high off my neck and captured there with a sterling silver clip. I had on a black turtleneck that I'd just freed from storage and it smelled a bit like the sachet I'd tucked into the box: faded roses and baby powder. A comfort smell.

Mira glided up behind me. I didn't notice her until I saw her reflection in the blue-tinted mirror behind the bar. She said, "Buy you the next?"

I didn't turn toward her, I simply steeled myself and met her eyes in the mirror. She looked clear and crisp, her short white-blonde hair slicked back, her gray-green eyes razor sharp, even in the dim light of the bar.

"You bet." I nodded, feeling her hand snake down the back of my loose 501s. She was checking to see if I had panties on. I didn't.

The bartender replaced my dead drink with a new one, and Mira turned sideways and watched me down it. When I'd finished, she grabbed my hand and led me down the dark hallway to the ladies' room.

"You smell like sex," she said under her breath as she pulled me along.

"Roses and baby powder," I corrected her, taking a whiff of my sweater.

She pulled me after her into the ladies' room and locked the door behind us.

"And sex," she said again, pulling the turtleneck over my head, propping me up against the sink while she pulled my jeans down, leaving them on me.

The sink was cold against my naked ass, but her hands were warm as they spread my cuntlips. Her mouth was hot as she pressed it against me. I liked the feel of the metal ball that rides her tongue as she tickled my clit with it. Warm mouth and cool silver combined can start a fire within me. Mira knows that well.

I held onto the edge of the sink, kicked off my shoes, and waited for her to pull my jeans all the way off. Then, balancing most of my weight on the sink, I wrapped my slender legs around her, capturing her to me, capturing her face to my cunt. If she wanted to play, we'd play my way, drunk though I was.

I loved the feeling of that silver ball rolling back and forth over my clit, then icing my insides as she used her tongue like a cock and probed me deeper. Mira knows what to do. Yes, she does.

There are two mirrors in Jezebelle's ladies' room. I stared in the glass across the way to watch my face as I came. I moved again, so I was standing, and I placed my hands on the back of Mira's shaved neck and jammed her hard against me, rolling her with the vibrations that swelled inside me and cascaded over. I bounced back and forth, slamming my ass against the rim of the sink and then forward, into her face. She punished me for the intensity of my movements by digging that silver ball right into my clit, spiraling me into a violent world of pain and pleasure and pain and pleasure...and pain.

"Hurts so good, doesn't it?" She grinned at me when she stood up, wiping her mouth on the back of her hand.

"It always does when you ride the helm," I agreed, staring into her clear eyes and waiting.

"I miss you," she said next, working hard to get that hurt look to her face that doesn't belong on it. So far as I can tell, Mira doesn't feel any real emotions. And after dating her for four years and being the one to instigate the recent breakup, I should know.

"Miss me," I said as I left her alone in the bathroom. I poked my head in for one last dig. "But thanks for the climax. It was great."

DEBUT
Sasha Johnson

My lover, a director-to-be, staged a fabulous film on Saturday. Screenwriter/director/producer/ caterer (providing pizza and beer for all), she generously cast me as the star of her semi-autobiographical video.

I played her.

This taxed my already quite limited acting abilities to the max. Conveying a drop-dead redhead with Mediterranean blue eyes is difficult enough for a brown-on-brown girl, anyhow. But after three beers on an empty stomach (which might not fell your average movie star, but knocks this featherweight down for the count) I sprouted a full-grown Hollywood ego. Soon our guests/costars began to wonder who died and made me Sean Young.

It's not an experience I'm proud of, and one I remember only vaguely (thankfully).

What I do remember is watching Cassandra shoo our company out the front door, saying in her hushed, unhurried tone, "That's a wrap for today. We'll finish up next weekend."

Then I remember her stalking, seriously stalking over to me, her calm face changing completely as she made her way to my side. "You"—she began, sticking a finger in my face—"You need to deal with yourself."

I was puzzled and drunk, and I shrugged and said, "What do you mean?"

"Bossing people around...what gives? Your job was to help me out. Becoming a prima donna is not in your contract."

I relaxed on our sofa and opened another bottle, feeling no pain. She ended that, taking the Corona out of my hand and sitting down next to me.

"If you act spoiled, I will treat you like a spoiled child," she said, more to herself than to me. I gave her another one of my puzzled puppy-dog looks, and was surprised even more as she pulled me over her lap and lifted my silver-spangled dress.

"This is not a game," she hissed, pulling my lace panties down my thighs. "You ruined a serious day of filming."

I felt the smack of her hand on my naked ass before I truly realized what was going on. Then, in the whining tone she despises —I should have known better—I said, "But we goof around in front of the camera all the time." (This is true. We film dinner parties, park picnics, ourselves in bed...everything.)

"This is my senior project," she yelled, punctuating each word with another blow to my naked ass, making me squirm and try to get away. She held me firmly in place. "I need this film to be good," she said, more softly now, almost lost beneath the resounding smacks of her hand punishing my ass. I looked at our reflection in the mirror across the room. My bum was a deep cherry red. By the look on Cassandra's face, it was going to be magenta before she finished. I decided to do some apologizing. Quickly.

"Really," I slurred, trying to push up so I could talk to her. A firm hand pressed me back on the sofa. "I was just messing around."

Her hand moved lower to heat the backs of my thighs. I howled and squirmed more, but she would not let up.

"I'll be good next week," I said next. "I promise." She didn't stop.

My mind raced with possible explanations for my behavior. When I realized that I couldn't come up with anything acceptable, I stilled myself and accepted her wrath. I'd earned it.

Finally, when a stream of tears had covered my cheeks, Cassie shoved me off her lap and glared down at me.

"At least we got one good take." She sounded more like herself. Calm. Easy.

I pulled up my panties and straightened my dress. "What do you mean," I asked, much quieter now, completely cowed. She pointed in the direction of her camera, still on the tripod, still running. I felt my face go pale.

"We'll start with that next weekend," she said. "I'm sure the crew will be thrilled."

I stared at my hands, and in a low, humble voice, I said, "Cassie, I'm sorry."

She sat on the floor at my side and took me in her arms, as she always does when I've gone through a punishment session. "I know you are," she said. "It's over now. And we'll keep that tape for a reminder...."

Then she led me into the bedroom, where our second camera is set up on permanent display, and we made another, different kind of movie.

WHOLE
Kinde Moore

She fucked my ass last night. It's not the first time we've done it anally, but it's the first time I liked it. More than that. It's the first time I asked her to do it, begged her to do it.

"Please, Libby, please…"

We fuck raw. We fuck like animals. Hard, heavy, the sweat-sheen gleaming on our bodies. We fit together like pieces of a puzzle, two strikingly similar bodies, long, lean, muscular. When I look at our reflection in the mirror, sometimes it's like seeing double. Often when we're out, people ask if we're sisters.

Now, there's a twisted thought.

When we fuck, Libby puts the mirror right next to the bed so that we can watch. She likes to watch. It's one of her favorite things. She says, "See, that's you. That's the way you look when I'm inside you."

I stare at my reflection, seeing but not seeing. Falling into myself, into the hot gold glow of my brown eyes, the parted-helpless look of my lips. I look hungry when we fuck. I look overwhelmed.

Last night, though, was different.

She said, "Touch yourself. Find that clit of yours and stroke it."

Fingers wet, clumsy, finding the hard nub of tingling flesh and rubbing, rubbing, rubbing.

She said, "Watch while you come. Watch your face change."

I wasn't close to coming. I was on fire. My skin burned. I wanted something more. I tugged at my clit, rubbed it hard with my middle finger, knowing I'd be sore the next day, but not caring. I looked into my eyes, as she wanted me to do. Then I looked into her eyes and I said, "Please, Libby, please...."

"Please what?" Her cock was stroking me inside, pushing against the walls of my cunt, touching me in all the places that usually work to get me off but weren't working last night. "Please what?"

"Put it in my ass." It was difficult for me to say, and I looked down at the bed when the words were out of my mouth. She reached forward, cupped my chin in her hand, and forced my head up.

"Look at yourself," she demanded.

I did.

"Now say it again."

I bit my bottom lip, not wanting to obey. I kept my fingers going in those endless rotations that only I know how to make. I said, "Please, Libby, please..." and then my voice got hoarse and lowered in pitch. "Please put it in my ass."

"Put what in your ass?"

My head wanted to go down again. My eyes wanted to focus on the bed, on the pillows, on anything but my reflection. She wouldn't let me.

"Put your cock in my ass," I said in a rush, to get it out all at once.

"Why?"

She pulled it from my cunt and moved away as she asked. Being emptied of her was a horrifying sensation. I needed her touch. I needed her body against mine.

"I want"—I started, unsure—"I want to feel it."

"You want it to hurt a little, don't you?" She knew she was on the right track. Her cock was already wet with my cuntjuices. She parted the cheeks of my ass and pressed the head of it against my hole.

"You want to feel it deep inside you," she continued, answering her own questions.

I nodded, keeping my eyes on hers in the mirror as she bucked her hips forward and drove the thing home.

And I liked it. I liked the fullness of it. The weight of it inside me. It was different from the other times, when she's taken me by force. It was a partnership. I moved back on her and used my body with hers and relaxed against hers.

Sometimes, when I stare at my reflection, I look overwhelmed. Last night was different. Last night I looked satiated. I looked complete.

I looked whole.

SWEET
Mablyn Cohen

When she comes, she says, "Oh, Jesus. Oh, Jesus. Oh, sweet Jesus, here I come."

Something about that. Something about the way her voice breaks, the way her cheeks flush, the way her breathing speeds up until I can almost see her heart beating in that beautiful chest of hers. Something about the way she comes makes me come.

I wait for it. I rein in my own raging orgasm until I see the change in her and that's what releases me. That's what makes my own climax burst through from my core, racking my body with spasm after spasm. I come more quietly than she does. I am contained. My eyes glow, my lips part, but no sounds issue forth. I let her do all the talking for me.

We are the reverse outside the bedroom (or kitchen, living room, bathroom, car...). In the real world, I am the one who does the talking. I order her food. I choose her clothing. I design the world in which we live. In my leather jacket and faded jeans, I surround her young, nubile form. She, clad in a whisper-thin dress, wearing her hair up with becoming ringlets framing her cameo face—she is mine. Her skin is made fragrant by perfume of my choosing. She would never think to speak without a nod from me, without permission granted.

When we are in public, that is.

But in private, I swim in the sound of her voice. I glide on the melody of her orgasms. I wait and watch the change of her face, the way her smile grows wider into almost a grimace. The way her fever breaks through the surface of her skin to paint her cheeks in shades of blush not sold by cosmetic companies. If they could, they would. If they could package the blush on my lover's cheeks, could make a rouge called "Climax," they would make money hand over fist. But no one could capture it. The flush that creeps along her jaw line, that bursts, like a primrose in bloom on each cheek, that darkens the hollows beneath her eyes and shades her eyelids in the color of the early morning sky… That is not for sale.

My own sweet girl is a canvas painted with the rainbow palette of our lovemaking. She is my canvas, and I am the master artist. Though I don't know what it is that my brush tickles to make her come so. I don't know which of our encounters will bring forth screams of pleasure from her lips. I try each time to make it magical, and succeed only once or twice in ten sessions.

But those mystic times are worth it. And I wait for them. And I watch the change as it creeps over her, steals over her, re-creates her. Her lips pull back from her teeth and her voice, softly at first, says, "Oh!" And I swallow hard and still myself on top of her and wait to hear it again. But she won't continue if I don't continue, so I rock forward, pressing into her, filling her, and she rewards me, "Oh, sweet…" And I stop again and wait, and she stops again and waits, and I rock forward and fill her and her voice grows louder and she wraps her thighs around me pulling me down.

"Oh, sweet Jesus! Oh…"

And together, together, we are transported.

THE ODD WOMEN
Rachel Perez

F rankie notices the girl as soon as she enters the elevator. The two of them are alone together, Frankie just returning from a boring lunch with a pair of LaSalle Street attorneys, and now here is this interesting girl riding up with her in the elevator. More a woman than a girl, maybe twenty-four or twenty-five, a chunky brunette with big breasts under a tight sweater, and a manner of looking at Frankie that says they have something in common. Recognition. Whenever it happens this way, unexpectedly, Frankie is always thrilled because it means there are so many women out there unknown to her who might be available. She does have Valerie, but Valerie is domestic and this is foreign—an unknown girl—and unknown girls are always exciting.

Frankie starts the conversation, mentioning something about the weather, and then about the building and the air conditioning and how sometimes it's too warm in the office, all the while her eyes taking in the girl's tight sweater, the big breasts, wondering what the nipples are like. "Aren't you warm in that sweater?"

The girl gives her a wry smile. "No, it's not too heavy." But the breasts are heavy. Oh my, yes. Frankie can tell the girl is wearing a bra, full support for those lovely tits.

They talk some more, Frankie learning the girl is visiting a dentist on her floor and, as they step out of the elevator, Frankie makes a joke about how awful it is to have a frozen anesthetized mouth after a visit to the dentist.

"Oh, I'm just having a cleaning," the girl says.

"I'm due for one myself," Frankie says. "But I've been so busy in court, there's no time."

"You're a lawyer?" A look that says the girl is impressed.

"That's right."

They have now stopped in front of Frankie's office, the girl hesitating a moment before she says, "Gee, I could use a lawyer, I'm having so much trouble with my landlord."

Frankie chuckles. "Well, here I am. But you've got that dental appointment now, don't you? Maybe we could meet for a drink later on."

"Sure, I'd love that."

"There's a place called Ricky's just around the corner. How about four o'clock?"

So easy. Before they say good-by, Frankie learns that the girl is a nurse and her name is Marcia. Which makes Frankie more excited than ever, because the one thing she knows for certain is that nurses can be hot.

Ricky's is crowded, the usual late-afternoon gaggle of executive types pretending to foster business connections. Frankie takes a seat at the long bar, orders a whiskey sour, and waits. Promptly at five minutes past four, Marcia arrives and sits down next to her with a smile. "Well, I'm here."

Frankie asks her what she's drinking and then buys her a daiquiri. "I haven't been in here in ages," Frankie says.

Marcia chuckles and leans closer. "Listen, I just want to be sure we're on the same track."

"What track is that?"

"Do you read *Gay News*?"

"I do sometimes."

"I'm just trying to make sure about you. Anyway, I'm living with someone, and I want you to know that."

"So am I."

Marcia laughs again and says her lover is out of town. "She's in Los Angeles until next Tuesday."

"And mine's right at home."

Marcia raises her glass. "Well, here's to home sweet home."

"And to us."

"Sure, why not?"

Frankie feels happy as she gazes at the front of Marcia's sweater. "Do you mind if I say something dirty?"

Marcia giggles. "Hurry up and tell me."

"I'd like to get you in a corner and fuck you silly."

Marcia flushes and giggles again. "Come on, there's no one at my place, so why are we sitting here?"

Why indeed? They kiss in the taxi, Marcia leaning against Frankie to accept a tender kiss on her cheek, both afraid to do more because the cabdriver keeps talking about the traffic, the government, the holes in the streets. When they finally arrive in front of the building where Marcia lives, they hurry out of the taxi and into the cluttered apartment. More kissing as soon as the door is closed. Now Frankie can get a hand on Marcia's breasts, feeling the curves, the weight of them. Marcia moans as she sucks on Frankie's probing tongue. Frankie drops her hand down to get it under Marcia's skirt, between her thighs, and into the wet crotch of her pantyhose. "Oh, Jesus, I'm hot," Marcia says. Frankie kisses her and rubs her cunt through her pantyhose at the same time, keeps rubbing until Marcia groans against her mouth and comes. After that they kiss some more, sweaty frenzied kissing in the hallway just inside the front door of the apartment. Marcia has her turn with Frankie, her hand sliding under Frankie's gray wool skirt to clutch at Frankie's cunt, squeeze the lips and jerk her fingers against her clit and coax her. "Come on, baby." And Frankie shudders, humping her cunt at Marcia's hand, both of them awash with sweat and juice and the frenzy of a new fuck.

They finally disentangle themselves, but they walk into the bedroom with their arms around each other's waists. Marcia apologizes for the mess in the bedroom, the clothes and underwear draped over the chairs and doorknobs. "I wasn't expecting company. Don't look."

"You're the only thing I'm looking at."

Marcia gives her a coquettish glance as she starts undressing. "I sure didn't think anything interesting would happen to me today. Not on the way to the dentist, anyhow."

Frankie has her jacket off, her fingers unbuttoning her blouse as she watches Marcia pull her sweater over her head. And there they are, Marcia's luscious breasts packed into that simple white bra like a pair of melons waiting to be tasted. Marcia knows her own assets, and in a moment she has the bra unhooked and pulled away from her body to show herself.

"That's better," Marcia says. She laughs as she holds her big breasts with her hands. "I saw you looking at these in the elevator when we first met. You were looking, weren't you?"

"Yes, I was."

"Eating up my tits with your eyes." Frankie has to have them, and she stops undressing and walks over to get her face between the two lovely breasts. She takes one of the fat nipples in her mouth, sucking at it, whipping it with her tongue as Marcia groans with pleasure. Then Marcia pulls Frankie's head up and they kiss again, Marcia's naked breasts pushing against Frankie's blouse. They press against each other, their breasts and bellies rubbing, Frankie's knee sliding up between Marcia's thighs to massage her crotch.

Marcia giggles. "Hey, let's get our clothes off while there's a bed here."

When they separate, Marcia quickly drops her skirt. As she bends over to retrieve it, her breasts swing from side to side like a pair of white honeydews. Now all she wears is the sheer black pantyhose with a lace panty, her solid legs and thighs gleaming through the nylon, a generous dark bush visible through the lace in the crotch. With a coy look at Frankie, she walks over to the dressing table, picks up a hairbrush, and starts brushing her hair.

"You're slow," Marcia says.

"I'm busy looking at you."

"I could lose ten pounds, but every time I try, I gain it back."

"Never mind, you're perfect."

"You're not so bad yourself, but I wish I could see more."

But instead of waiting for Frankie to undress, Marcia now puts down the hairbrush and peels off her pantyhose. Since she has her back partly turned toward Frankie, it's her ass that Frankie fixes her eyes on, Marcia's luscious full buttocks with a cleft so deep Frankie has an urge to bury her face in it.

Naked, Marcia climbs onto the bed and lies on her side facing Frankie. Her rosy skin catches the light of the lamp on the night table. She has a thick pubic bush, a mass of dark curled hair at the joining of her thighs. As if to tease Frankie, she keeps her legs closed to hide her cunt.

Frankie finishes undressing while Marcia watches her with bright eyes. All Frankie can think about is Marcia's breasts, those lovely brown nipples. She hungers to have Marcia's breasts in her mouth.

When Frankie is naked, Marcia says, "You look great, like a runner. Do you do any of that?"

Frankie nods, proud of her athletic body. "I run when I can, usually on weekends." She's happy that Marcia likes her body. Sometimes she thinks that Valerie takes it for granted. Frankie is convinced Valerie is a great narcissist, always loving her own body more than someone else's.

Now Frankie climbs onto the bed and she moves forward to take Marcia in her arms. They kiss, their mouths fusing, their tongues wagging against each other.

Marcia moans. "I really like you."

"And I like you, too."

"You know, sometimes you meet someone, and it just doesn't work. This is working, isn't it?"

"Yes, it is." They kiss again. Frankie slides a hand down to Marcia's cunt to explore her thicket of pubic hair. Marcia opens her legs, making herself available, her thick-lipped pussy dripping on Frankie's probing fingers. A smell of woman-heat fills Frankie's nostrils, making her mind whirl with excitement. She rubs her open palm over Marcia's hairy cunt, thrilled by the wet feel of it. Then she parts the lush lips and slowly pushes two fingers inside the opening. Marcia groans as Frankie takes her, her elastic canal gripping Frankie's fingers as Frankie begins a slow stroking in and out of her vagina. When Frankie uses another finger to tickle Marcia's anus, Marcia cries out and starts coming immediately. "Oh, God, yes, do it!"

Frankie's pleasure lies in watching her come. Marcia's face glistens with sweat. Her mouth hangs open, her eyes are closed. As

Frankie's fingers continue stroking in and out of her vagina, Marcia makes whimpering sounds in her throat and sometimes bites her lower lip. She begs for more, hunching at Frankie's hand. Frankie makes her open her legs wide, and then she begins a hard fucking with her fingers that makes Marcia cry out with pleasure. Frankie delights in making Marcia come again and again. Her hand wet with Marcia's juices, Frankie urges her on. "Don't stop, sweet. Keep coming." Marcia tosses on the bed, her ass heaving, her sopping cunt slamming against Frankie's invading fingers. At the end, she rolls over on her back with her knees in the air while Frankie kneels in front of her, driving her fingers in and out like a battering ram.

When Marcia comes down, she groans. "Oh, Jesus, you're good."

Her fingers out of Marcia's vagina but still stroking her thighs, Frankie chuckles. "No, it's not me, it's you." And then she slides her fingers down farther to touch the puckered ring of Marcia's anus.

Marcia smiles and pulls her knees up again. "You could be a nurse. Nurses like to get their fingers everywhere."

Frankie blushes and pulls her fingers away, but Marcia laughs as she tugs Frankie's hand back to her ass. "No, go on, I like it. I can come that way. But slide up a little so I can touch you. Do it to me in both holes."

Both holes. The words make Frankie quiver. She's always inhibited by assplay, but she finds it exciting because it's nasty. She hardly ever does it with Valerie, even if sometimes she thinks that Valerie wants it. Some things you don't do with the person closest to you. With Marcia there is no need to wonder whether she wants it; it's obvious she does. After lubricating her fingers in Marcia's cunt, Frankie finds she can easily slide two fingers inside Marcia's anus. The chunky brunette groans as she takes the fingers, and then she wants something in her cunt and Frankie uses her thumb there.

"Oh, that's great," Marcia says with a gasp.

"I'm afraid I'll hurt you."

Marcia giggles. "Don't worry about that. I'm a nurse. I know what I'm doing."

Meanwhile Marcia has managed to get a hand between Frankie's thighs, and her fingers are now hooked inside Frankie's wet cunt, holding onto Frankie as Frankie starts fucking Marcia with her hand. Frankie's excitement is intense. Marcia pushes her fingers deep inside Frankie's cunt and groans as Frankie's fingers move in both openings. Frankie loves getting dirty like this with a new girl. The fact that Marcia is a nurse excites her. She keeps her fingers moving slowly, driving her thumb inside Marcia's cunt to the last knuckle each time she pushes her hand forward. Marcia starts coming and it seems endless, her body shaking, the cries coming out of her throat as Frankie keeps her hand moving. At the end, Frankie bends over to take one of Marcia's fat nipples in her mouth. She sucks and bites the nipple, the biting making Marcia come again.

"Oh, hell, don't stop!" Marcia says, grabbing Frankie's wrist as Frankie is about to pull her fingers out.

Frankie is amused. "Are you sure?"

"Just a little more."

So Frankie gives Marcia what she wants, a little more in both openings, at the same time humping her cunt at Marcia's hand. Marcia says she loves assfucking, and she never gets enough of it. Frankie's cunt is hot and dripping, her clit swollen. She comes suddenly, jerking her pussy at Marcia's fingers, feeling her juices running everywhere.

They kiss after that, Marcia's ass gripping Frankie's fingers as Frankie slowly pulls them out of both openings. Marcia giggles and says Frankie is as good as her lover the way she does her ass. Frankie is a bit embarrassed talking about it, but she likes looking at Marcia's luscious ass when Marcia rolls over onto her belly.

After that Frankie excuses herself and she goes to the bathroom still excited by the sex, her hands trembling as she washes them. She uses a towel to wipe her cunt and the insides of her thighs, and then she studies her face in the mirror, her flushed cheeks. She always looks good after sex. And this is about as good as she has ever looked.

BOYS' NIGHT OUT
Red Jordan Arobateau

"I seized the girl. And I communed
with devils and angels!
Forcibly she hugs me. She would,
because I understand her pain,
and feel her tears!
Power rushes thru me!
I kick & punch and stomp at the gates
—until the walls fell!"

Club Venus was full to capacity—500
lesbians. Who dance, talk, drink—
or are shy.

The three butches sat, talked.

Mack says: "The last time I had a girlfriend, or whatever it's
called, the bitch couldn't take my cock, said it hurt too much.
Claims: 'I'm a lesbian! Dykes don't get fucked like that!'" Mack
minced, flipped his hand effeminately like a fag, squealed in a
high voice. "So, I sez, 'Bitch, spread your legs, let me ride your cunt
with mine.'" And pats the front of his fly, in illustration. "Well,
the sorry bitch couldn't hold her legs apart wide enough; so I roll
out of bed, stand up, lean against the wall, pound my fist against
the wall & sez: 'Bitch, get down on your knees. You're gonna suck
me off.' So after two minutes her tongue gives out, so the bitch had
to give me a hand job and it was OK."

Club Venus was so crowded on Saturday night, by 10, that the three were hidden behind women; couldn't see anywhere more than a few feet. Women packed everywhere.

"I bet there's women I've had in this bar. I'll go down to Miami and meet women from here, and go up to New York and meet women from here & Miami and Hawaii. —The same ones. I used to travel when I was dealing drugs—before I squared up. Each city you go in, there's a bar. One bar for lesbians, if they're lucky. And all the broads go there. If they come in from out of town, they go there. —It's a small world. A very small, tiny world, and everybody knows each other. And I know 'em all.

"I'd rather buy a bitch than have a girlfriend."

Mack was packin'. Bulge down his left trouser leg, 8" long and thick. Rusty's eyes fell to examine it a few times—when Mack's head was turned to look at a passing girl. The butch wore a man's suit & tie. Rusty was envious; doubts crept across her mind. "Maybe I should start packing my dick out to the clubs, too. Jesus, what good is it to tell a girl, 'Baby, I'm packin', I'll give all my sweet love to you,' and they look down at your crotch, and nothing. 'Uh, uh, baby, I mean, I'm carrying it—in my jacket pocket, or something.'"

And Frankie, the big dyke in the raincoat sat silent. She saw it and was embarrassed.

Deepening frown on Mack's face. Hunches over the bar, watches faces of glamorous women on the other side. Rusty, the redheaded boygirl was passing time, waiting for the go-go dancer. Frankie was morose.

Colored lights flash on them, mixing with sound.

"I use escort services in New York. It's a bill and a bill tip for the girl. The first bill just gets her to your hotel room—she'll sit there and look at you. That's it. The 2nd bill is for her. It's her action. I CALL UP, I CAN'T EVEN GET A GIRL HERE!"

Mack yells over the din, as a new music track plays. "Finally found this one, they tell me it's $275. And women never call, they say. I've met some dogs at the escort services in New York. Some bow-wows. Take a look at some of those dogs. Not broads, dogs. And think I ought to go buy stock in pet food. Ha!"

Mack's weather-darkened face was mild, did not reflect much anger—not to match the intensity of his words. It was a lifelong anger—a hurt, or whatever. It was ingrained into him, and he was accustomed to it. Some dykes have no peace inside them. Mack was one of them.

Tinkle of ice cubes in glass. Bottle against lip. Pouring the amber substance of forgetfulness.

A go-go dancer was preparing to climb up onstage.

Bartenders move like robots speeded up at a turn of electricity; fast, fast, pour drinks, take orders, ring up change in the cash register.

A single file of women entered at the door, paid their $5 admission, while others exited by a second door behind the dance floor.

The bartender took new orders, wiped up after the old, & dunked their used glasses in the soapy water.

Pace moved fast at the Venus Club.

Mack eyed the files of girls as they moved in as if on a conveyer belt, to stand, pose, & show; lesbian models. They all looked. Frankie, Rusty, and the girls themselves.

"Don't get me wrong. I don't do it all the time. Just after breaking up a relationship—to help get over her.

"I call up the escort services: 'Do you do women?' 'NO!' they sez and hang up. NO! In New York they do, I do it all the time; and Miami & Hawaii.

"San Francisco is supposed to be the gay capital of the world, & I can't get a bitch!"

"I'll ask her for you," the butch with red hair slicked behind her ears says to Frankie, who slouches, broad shouldered, in a raincoat. They're talking about going somewhere together—to see a girl.

Mack had a binder on, tits flattened out, and he wore it in bed. Was muscular, from lifting sacks as a landscaper—90, 100 pounds. And he lifted weights off season.

Stocky, he passed easily as a man.

Very male in build and style of dress and manner. It was just the extra liquidity in his eyes—more than a man—that you could tell he was a female.

But you had to search very carefully for these signs to read him, and if Mack caught an intruder, he'd turn savage. Look them back, eyes snap half-shut into narrow slits of anger. Stare at the intruder while he mentally located his knife—in the waistband of the trousers; his gun, in the breast pocket of the jacket; and wonder why the fuck you were staring so hard at him.

Ready to fight. To take it as a challenge.

"I been burnt by so many bitches. Ain't thinkin' about another bitch." Mack growled in response to a question Frankie had asked.

"They ain't women, they bitches!" Mack snaps. "Nasty stuff comes out of their cunts, and worse nasty stuff comes out of their minds! They're nasty, self-centered, jealous, backbiting, gossipy, and you can't trust them any further than you can throw them.

"I'd rather just fuck a bitch from the escort service. I always do this when I get over a relationship. I have them in New York, in Hawaii, in Miami. But here, it's dead. And Reno, too. That's why I went to Reno—for sex services, and can't get any."

Music pounded & lights flashed. Girls posed, and the big heavy-set butch tried to agree, tho she found it difficult:

"The straight people don't really want us. They don't want our money. We're more trouble than it's worth to them. Dykes have got to learn to cater to each other, and take care of our own people!

"THEY DON'T EVEN WANT MY FUCKIN' MONEY!"
Mack howls.

"That's one thing I like about New York, they got a saying:
'Money is green. It spends.' "

Frankie was one of the Warlords of the bar. —An odd success.
She had survived thru times of trouble.

Expensive slacks, wool blend, masculine, and a shirt with cuff
links and a sweater whose fiber blended into the fabric of the
trousers.

And now she was broken. —Trembling inside, tho her stoic
face, layered with extra flab, didn't show it. She'd listen to the
two talk back & forth at each other over the tavern din.

"So many lesbians—they're not letting 'em in the door. Whenever the line stops moving it means the house is full to capacity—
that's 500 women. When I was young, you'd be lucky to see 60 in
one room."

"I been gay all my life," Rusty muses.

Mack turns, stares at Rusty, then at Frankie. "I ain't thinking
about none of these dykes. I don't even see them. I just live my life.
If they ain't paying my bills or they ain't laying in my bed, I got
no use for them."

Frankie hunches her big shoulders in the raincoat. Light brown
hair short, light eyes. 500 women, and she wasn't getting
acquainted with none of them & been to Club Venus now for
months.

To the three butches, the club held 500 strangers. A few faces
recognized. Frankie was over age 50, and Rusty would hit that
age soon. Some of the old-timers look at the young girls, but the
young ones don't want them. Pretty, smooth faces; they must look
into the mirror of their souls when they see an older, creased-
face dyke—the young are afraid, because they know someday—not
far, it will be them, old, on a bar stool needing somebody, not

getting sex, or companionship, or whatever, to make life worth living—and their lives ain't so great now.

Cute girl, blue jeans rolled up. Derby hat, red lipstick, a beauty mark, & earrings, is on the stage. Some women in dresses that show cleavage, others in leather jackets, stand looking up at her.

Tall & short. Women of all sizes and colors, who've come from the surrounding Bay Area, mix thru each other; & their voices combat the music in a din.

Listless, Frankie surveys the crowd.

Women—both popular and those dying on the vine.

Venus Club on a Saturday night.

Rusty wore jeans and a black leather jacket. Boots; rough. A street butch who'd made it out of the street and worked most of her life, but never achieved the financial security of her friend Frankie. Drew pale white fingers thru her hair so it stood up like a red crest. She, too, was musing. Looked down into the tunnel of last drops of the soft drink in her glass. Wondering about access to females. Frankie had complained about something, and Mack responded: "I don't care if she's straight, bi, or what, just as long as she's a bitch. I'm not looking for a relationship, not now. I just got over one. I'm fed up."

So all the big problem in Lesbian Life, despite all the fertility of being woman—it was difficult to get joy because women didn't want to share cunt with each other. "Women don't take lovers, they take hostages," Mack quoted, like a lesbian sage. "They don't give you the time of day & got no use for you unless you marry them."

Problems like finding women who are willing.

It was like pushing against an inexorable wall that wouldn't give way.

Rusty wondered when the walls would fall. Seemed like she'd been fighting all her life, and it still wasn't EZ.

Mack was a person who every day looked into the window of

life, saw what was there and wanted to vomit at what he saw.

The aloneness, the anger, the trouble seething there, & few joys.

"This world is such a fucked-up place, I can't deal with it unless I'm high."

Mack holds up a glass of vodka in stubby fingers browned by the sun. "This bartender's trying to kill me. This is a shot of vodka? She don't know what a shot is!"

"It's a double."

"It's a triple!" He held up the clear liquid in its glass. How many girls had this dyke had when drunk? It blurred the boundaries and soothed their fears.

Golden webs of liquor. Did it so they would accept a stranger in their arms.

Drawn in by an alcoholic web.

When the women awoke mornings, saw the he-she they'd made love with that night, many changed their minds about the deal, put on their clothes, left, and Mack never saw them again.

An arm reached around Rusty to get to the crowded bar. 'Touch me baby. I love it,' the redhead dyke thinks. 'Squeeze me a little harder. Yeah. Yeah.'

Music pounds. The go-go dancer warms up on her platform. Rusty's mind heats in a fantasy of a beautiful female.

So many nights she'd lain down with one hand spread across her chest, between the nipples of both tits, to touch each one; while the other hand moved in her cunt, wet, over and over her clit, jerking herself off.

And then fantasy flowed into fact, into figure—of a woman who was available. Rosa, the Mexican. To suck her tits for a while, a long while. And put fingers in her cunt, two, three, then four, then her thumb, too, folded over into a fist & pound her steady, hard, & make the woman holler and claw her back in ecstasy.

Thought of a lesbian, & wished Rosa was one. Her naked body. One hour of work, sweat, & pleasure in Rosa's bed.

"Rosa is dirty-minded," Rusty tells Frankie. "Wait till you meet her. She gets on all fours, and wiggles her ass, and I stick it to her with my dick."

Rusty's getting hot in her crotch, damp in her blue jeans. Sees Rosa in her mind's eye, spread legs sit, rear end on the mattress, using her red-nailpolished fingers to spread open her pussylips & demand Rusty crawl to her naked and lick it. Lick her clit till she gets off good.

But Rosa ain't a full lesbian.

"It's not you, Mack," Frankie says. "It's not you, I know you're still hurting. But it's never you. It's them."

"The bitch couldn't think enough of me to wait 5 more minutes." They didn't think of him. Seldom thought enough of Mack.

"'I'm not going to meet you,' she says. Stand me up. It's just like a woman," Mack fumes. "That's why they're women. I'll be damned if I lose sleep over a bitch standing me up again. I want to tear you apart limb by limb and see your blood, bitch!" Mack hollers.

"She can spread her legs. That's all she can do for me. All the nice words, that don't mean shit!

"I met her, go out with her, and she spends my time and money—if I'm fool enough to spend any money on her & not know if I'm gonna get laid for my money.

"She can give me her pussy—that's the best thing she can do for me....

"Let me fuck her." Mack growls. His tie and shirt look nice, jacket & pants match. For all appearances to the world, Mack is a man. A man with a cunt under his boxer shorts.

Mack liked to fuck his women with a strap-on dick and cum doing it.

"Only thing she can do is lay down & spread it, baby. Pussy, baby. I had a broad make me hot on the phone, but wouldn't do it in bed. I had a broad give me a used car. Fine. Keep the car, baby. Save your sweet talk. Just give me the cunt."

Frankie remained silent.

"Bitch, I'll tear you apart limb by limb and make you bleed in your pussy!" Mack repeats, pounds a fist into the palm of his hand.

Then Mack wipes a rough, calloused hand over his face, looks at Frankie, who sits there, too quiet; raincoat, satiny man's shirt, a gold watch—man's; chubby fingers wrapped around her drink. "Pardon me, I'm a creep, so anything goes," Mack says low, apologetically.

Tan face, dark hair; the most masculine of the three. "I'll pull her hair out by the roots! If you pull out clumps of her hair, the scalp comes out, too!" Frankie looks away. "You can give a bitch a concussion like that. —NAW, DON'T LOOK AWAY FROM ME LIKE THAT, FRANKIE! I NEVER DONE IT! I SWEAR! Me, I'm all talk! I saw that in jail! Then both girls get sent down to solitary."

Music pounds. The dance floor is a sea of writhing bodies.

"I know a black girl, a stud, she set her bitch on fire. A black bitch. Burnt her up. I met her in the pen. She's still locked up. Serving a lot of time. —No, not for burning the wench up!" Mack answers Rusty's question. "No, but for the sale of drugs. No. It ain't worth space in the penitentiary for burning up a bitch—don't you know that?

"I spent a year in the penitentiary to save a bitch... because her record was clean. I did it to save her reputation. She was going to become something one day. I ain't shit. I been locked up before. So I took the rap," Mack says.

"It's mostly niggers & spics in jail, didja know that? All the white cons are in Washington, D.C. They run the White House and the Pentagon. They run the whole U.S. Government.

"Yeah. So I spent a year in jail to save a bitch.

"They need to take those babes and slaughter them. Slaughter them! Do what that man did to them up in Alaska. Get a machine gun and shoot them all! Ought to cut their legs off so they can't run after no more butches anymore.

"I hate these bimbos! I hate them! Skinny wenches! Blondes!

"Kill them with a chain saw!

"I'm 35. Yeah. You don't believe me?

"I'm more jaded than you. —I know you're older, but I've lived in more cities, been thru more bad women, I bet.... It makes you jaded." Mack says.

"I'll take escort services anytime."

"You're gonna undress her and know she's yours for 1 hour," Rusty agrees.

"If I can't get one on my own merits, then I'll be by myself," Frankie says gruffly.

Dark bar, music notes; lights from the spotlight fixtures in the ceiling probe the stage where the go-go dancer performs.

Thoughts inside Frankie's head wail.... She wants out...out of the inner turmoil.

Sighs. Her big chest heaves, and for a moment the raincoat stretches too tight over her broad back.

Now it must be said that most of the lesbians in Club Venus thought only of paying for sex in an erotic fantasy they might use with their partner during lovemaking. —A scene worked out between them in advance, maybe with props—fishnet stockings, short leather skirts, and push-up bras.

And certainly not use this service. Not even their fantasy, with the same desperation that Rusty or Mack had.

So it was atypical behavior—lifestyles of characters on the edge.

Mack felt really ugly. That he was supermasculine. That he didn't fit in the gay world—or the straight.

Night, and no woman on his arm. So he struts around in a circle between the bar stool and Rusty, who alternately stands & sits in her jeans & black leather jacket, handsome & butch, but recognizably a female. —And Frankie, big, handsome, but who has turned to flab. Frankie sits and leans against the polished wood bar & half-listens. Mack looks nice—for a man, not a dyke. And having a woman on his arm always soothes Mack. He is more like a Lamb than a Lion. Mack could even get down on his knees and beg a woman's forgiveness.

Lights flash at the bar across rows of amber-colored liquor bottles. Some heads tip up from the crowd to gaze at the go-go dancer on her elevated platform, scantily clad in a G-string. She works, pumping her hips; sweat glistens on her body under silver & blue party lights. There'll be a second dancer soon, and a third. And the butches watch them peel off their clothes with hungry hearts.

Mack watches the nude go-go dancer thrust her hips in and out above the audience of women who can't touch her. "That's why men kill women!" Mack growls.

Rusty's freckled face is solemn. Swipe of her hand slicks red hair back behind her ears.

"I ask her, 'Do you fist?'—Meaning, do you fist with your lovers? 'Have you before?' She says, 'Oh, yes, I like it, too.' And she ain't never had more than 3 fingers inside her. Don't even know if they can & never done it before, stupid bitches!" Mack creased her pants leg between a stubby finger & thumb, one foot up on the barstool rung. "So when I go in there and try fisting the bitch, I'm tearing her pussy & she's drunk & bleeding & accuses me of brutality the next morning—because that night she's drunk & wants to fist & ain't never did it & says I ripped her cunt.

"I ought to snuff a bitch; it's less problems afterward.

"I hate pain. When I felt my leg break, it was excruciating. The worst motherfucking pain; worse than the cramps."

Frankie winces. Her pale eyes shift from Mack into visions of the interior of her past. Nancy had wanted to fill her, too. And so she had felt their whole cock down deep in her cunt, filling it, and Nancy loving her, kissing her face, loving her way down deep inside her hot pussy.

Nancy in her big, pretty-patterned dress. She was an ample woman, and wore it down to her ankles.

Mack remembered pain searing in her. They had pulled his head back & broke his nose, so it hurt. Still a woman's body in a man's suit. More delicate. And his leg snapped. And was that pain greater than the pain caused by the girl who had caused it in the beginning? Betraying Mack, and then the drug bust comes down, and so the man-woman had to protect the one he loves.

It was still early evening—not quite 11 P.M. on the busiest night of the week.

This was time between lovers. And Rusty was so lonesome.

So this time—of killing—was held off in abeyance.

Women, one by one sent to Rusty like drops of water over the years, or a handful of crumbs fate tossed to keep her alive....

Dark bar, purple cast with yellow streaks of lights; a moving line of women in the door, & out the exit. One by one, or two by two.

"Goddamn escort service!—Don't take women! Shit! In New York they have a saying, 'Money spends.' They'll take your money; they don't care. Out here in California, they don't know what the hell is going on."

So in reality, that, too, is how Rusty and Frankie, both butches, felt; tho not with equal intensity.

That they were locked out from women. Denied female companions.

Rejection from lesbians was worse—worse than shades of a fierce straight society's rejection.

'Women. I'd like them to suffer over me, like I've suffered over them.' Rusty thought. Mack's hurt was also bringing the hurt in her to the surface.

"Well…what do you like a bitch to do for you?" Mack growled finally, after a time had passed & the music din & voices had engulfed the trio in waves. "If you don't mind me asking, that is. Some people don't like to talk about it."

"Suck me off." Rusty shrugs in her black leather jacket. Silver buckles and studs stand out like armor in the crowd. "Let me fuck her with my fingers, or my fist. Yuh know. Fuck her in the ass. Make her suck my cock —yuh know & work it so it makes me cum. —If I feel perverted."

Three butches on their night out.

Mack & Rusty feeling so low they fantasized killing women, and Frankie just wanted to die.

"This society created a sociopath. I didn't create myself," Mack was saying. She had come from a destroyed childhood. "As an adult I kept trying and trying! I tried to work & got fired, and nobody wanted me once they found out my sex. I tried to be a success. Job after job failed. So I start dealing drugs. Nearly got killed. Saw my partners die, my woman's career go down the drain…. So I went to the pen. And I got out and bought my landscaping business & I got a house out of the deal too, before the drugs went sour…. So life hit me below the belt, but it paid off, too, so I've always had a taste of money, and so I always have a woman, somehow, some way."

Mack drinks hard. Hard liquor for a hard life. Frankie nurses a beer, so pretty soon, in the middle, Rusty is the only sober one. & Frankie blubbers her tale of woe over the music din: "Why? Am I that bad?" Hat on her head like she was going to leave, but changed her mind. Coat stretched over broad shoulders, and pants tight at the crotch, and wet from alcohol sweat, and from getting hot watching the go-go dancer wiggle & fuck air under gold & purple lights. Red-faced from the drinks, and Rusty half-expects Frankie to get down on her knees and cry. "WHY! Am I that bad that she'd sleep with a man before she'd sleep with me?

"She's an airline stewardess, so she's off in some foreign country, and lonely, and she says how long she was out of the United States, and how lonely she was & he kept after her, so she broke down and did, and hated herself after & had got pregnant and had to have an abortion & still feels guilty, and the night before she left she could have let me love her. I dated her for weeks—about 4 times. She could have with me. I begged her to. I took her out to nice places. I bought her stuff. WHY?"

And the redhead shifts, blue-jeaned butt on the bar stool, uncomfortable. Can envision her pal down on her knees in the airline stewardess's bedroom begging for a chance, just a few hours together in a private transaction between two females that would result in no harm, just relief; and the woman says, "NO."

Frankie shakes her head, plays with her chubby fingers. And Rusty tries to talk Frankie up out of the blues. They're both old-timers, and Frankie has money in the bank—Rusty don't—but it's Frankie who's sobbing, and it's a ridiculous, heartrending sight. A dyke with too much fat on her body and too much heart, and not enough balls...or not enough of a hard edge...a hard edge....

Frankie calms down. Then, in a while, bends her head over to be near Rusty and simply whispers over the music, over the chatter, "You don't know, Rusty, I'm at the edge.... I'm just at the edge.... At the end of my rope."

And then Rusty's telling her about Rosa because she trusts Frankie, but says it quietly, because she don't want to share this with Mack seated at her left, because Rusty don't quite trust him.

And, simultaneously, has to battle with her own thoughts. —Of aloneness, since she and Judy split up, but also amazed…. 'Three women in 5 years. That's all she's had. All this time. And when we were young, she was a Butch of the World. She wasn't shy or afraid like she's become.'

"I feel like such a fool," Frankie's saying.

And Rusty watches the go-go dancer, remembers her own parade of lesbian lovers. 'I don't want to hurt them. —I wanted to love them. I wanted to do everything for them, but they took my love in disgust.'

And Rusty is angry about the women & mad about what the airline stewardess has done to Frankie, and mad about what life has done to Mack & pissed about her own need, her wet cunt on a bar stool, the ache in her loins, the hunger in her tits. —Her real need of female companionship that Saturday Night—on a Butches' Night Out.

Frankie's brown-blonde hair is coiffed neatly. —She has the money to get it done professionally, wears her best clothes—and here she is lonely again.

Thinks about the one-night stands. If the woman would just fill her sexually as well; but they just take Frankie for a big bulldagger, old & experienced, and want her to just exclusively take them like a man, on top & do all the work, and give little in return, which by now Frankie was used to doing, reverting to what she'd done in her teens, with most of the pickups—those lucky bright spots in the cold endless chain of lonely nights and ground-out cigarette butts on the floor of lesbian clubs.

As she'd done most of the straight and half-gay and lezzie pickups; done what women expect a butch to do.

But she remains calm, the sob gone out of her voice, and answers Mack, leaning across Rusty: "Seems like our femaleness is always working against us."

"We get too emotional," Rusty agrees. Knows it's true.

"Women get too attached," Mack mutters. "Lesbians don't get lovers, they take a hostage. By the second date, they bring their suitcase over & are ready to move in with you."

The trio sits, stares across the bar at the women who talk & laugh and stare back.

"Only way to keep a bitch is on a chain. Had one I kept on a chain—she liked it. Don't get me wrong, guys. She came to me with the chain in her hand."

"I had one; first time we fucked, she stops in the middle: 'Oh, could you tie me up?' It was years ago, and I wasn't ready for it.

"'Well, I don't got nothing to tie you up with,' I tell her.

"'Well, I've got a clothesline outside in my car.'" Ha. So anyway, the bitch is on the chain. I come home one day, the chain is snapped."

"She must have tried to run away."

"No, no, man, she's there. She shows me the end of the chain. She's mad because I didn't have it really bolted into the bed. 'Why, if you love me so much like you say you do, would you let me run away? A two-year-old could pull this chain loose.'"

Rusty laughs. Frankie shrugs her shoulders.

"I got another girl, her last lover was a sadomasochist. And she was a dumb fuck and didn't know what the hell she was doing. She had the girl tied up by her wrists in restraints to the ceiling. No care had been made for her comfort. It wasn't padded wrist bands, just wires or something, so it slowly cut off the circulation, and the woman was afraid to drive her to the hospital. See, they like me, 'cause I've learned how to do it right."

"Sometimes I get so—it's just a feeling, but what I do to a woman…" Mack made a fist. "When I do it, she's begging me to stop. 'Please! Please!' Begging for her life. And they love it. It's sexual. I didn't realize that. What I was doing, because I was mad.

But the girls like it…. I was doing sadomasochism all my life, but I just didn't have a name for it back then.

"Shit! Escort service don't do females. Ain't that a bitch!" Mack's weather-beaten face took on a dreamy look. —He gazed into space. "They describe their girls, and you have a chance to tell them what you like. And so I'm dialing the phone, thinking: 'Which one of their fabulous babes do I want? I come into town all self-confident. Sit up in my motel room. Two hours later, I'm a deflated balloon. Dial straight out of the yellow pages in the phone book. None of 'em do women. And I got a wallet full of fifty-dollar bills. Enough to choke a bitch to death."

"See that bartender?" Rusty interjects. Both butches turn to look. "She femmes it up real good. See her, those earrings, and that low-cut shirt?"

"Yeah."

"Well, wait and see her on her day off. She's a big dyke, in pants and motorcycle boots. —She just femmes it up to get tips from the ladies."

"Then she's not the one for you." Mack says gruffly. "I'll take a bitch, and you know what I'll do with her."

And Frankie sat. Felt softhearted.

Finally, Frankie leans her head over by Rusty's shoulder, on her right side, and asks, "Will they…do me?" Thinking about her female anatomy under her gray trousers.

Beside them on Rusty's other side, Mack leans on the bar; strap-on bulges his trousers, square body with a rugged handsomeness; hand beating time to the music; Mack hadn't heard.

"Rosa will," Rusty whispers back at Frankie. "Only problem, man, I haven't got the money for her myself."

"It's OK, Rusty. You're doing me a favor. I'll pay for it."

"You're gonna buy me a girl?" Rusty asks Frankie.

"How much is a girl over there?" Frankie wants to know.

"One hundred dollars."

And Rusty swells with anticipation. 'Damn, Frankie is gonna buy me Rosa! WOW! I'll be glad to see her! God damn! I hope she'll be glad to see me! Shit!' And her blue-jeaned figure springs alive inside, pink tongue licks over her lips. A fantasy girl cum alive! A session with ecstasy!

Frankie wondered listlessly what kind of house it was; she'd been to them before—a few incidents scattered down the long lesbian path of her life. Hard-core, in a dangerous neighborhood, with hookers strung out on drugs? Or just a few ladies working out of their apartment that Rusty happened to know? A crime-syndicate place—Big Time, or what? And in the sad condition of her feelings, Frankie really didn't care.

Music jammed. The go-go dancer kicked up her legs. The crowed of lesbians swayed and made a noise of its own. Over this came Frankie's low, even voice. —Even Rusty wasn't supposed to know she liked it—to be fucked sometimes like a broad, with a femme's cock up inside her, strapped around her waist; like Nancy had done; or more, her sweet fingers pushing into Frankie's butch wetness, while she sucked on Frankie's big tits, and her moaning—as her femme brought her over the threshold, cumming.

Frankie leaned over to Rusty so their heads, blonde & red, touched, and whispered, "Will she do everything?"

"Of course."

Thinks: how it was bad in the old days with the straight women who were inexperienced; & even lesbians who assumed a butch's whole pleasure was to give them pleasure, who lay back on Frankie's satin sheets in their filmy nightgowns, tits poked out to be sucked, warm cunt spread. And a butch had to do all the work, to suck clit with her mouth, and stroke her vagina with her fingers—while keeping her own clothes on. The girls who wanted only to be pleasured—and claimed they couldn't go down because they had to save that act for someone they loved—not Frankie. And really didn't care if they did nothing for her. —So she rode them, & squeezed them tight, as her breath came hoarse, fast, hard… And then she'd drive out of there next morning, over the red-brick cobblestones of the old inner city back to work, back to her dreams of a real woman, a real home.

Mack's eyes darted like snakes. A society that didn't take him into consideration gave her unlimited license.

The door to the Club Venus spilled forth its new arrivals. — Hope continued on in a file of girls past the door checker, each going into her wallet or purse to pay the cover charge. In the file of girls thru the long evening, eventually Rusty knew several well enough to speak. And then, seizing a chance, Mack waded into the sea of women and came back with a girl in tow.

Rusty takes the opportunity while he's gone to discuss with Frankie, because she don't want Mack to hear about the House— because she don't want nobody rough with Rosa.

Then the two came back, and Mack has her girl leaned up against the bar and is stroking her neck, gentle as a lamb.

Lights spot-lit the go-go dancer. And Mack tries all the sweet talk she knows. And presses the girl slowly into her hard cock. "—I look pretty good in a strap-on, remember? That's what you told me last time." Tan, hard muscles. Binder on to strap down his tits & T-shirt over, hiding his chest. —A perfect muscle-bound female body with a 8" cock sticking out from fluffy brown pubic hair & a leather harness.

The girl laughs and lets Mack lick her neck. She wears a black leather jacket, black pants, and chains. She is an Outlaw.

Mack's hands are brown & flash with the glitter of rings. He holds them up in the air to demonstrate. They move fast. Mack makes a circle with the index finger & thumb of his left hand & then inserts 2 fingers of his right hand into the circle; pushes it in

& out in the age-old symbol of fucking. And says, "I'll do anything you want. You tell me to drive it, I'll drive it. Tell me to stop and lick your pussy, I'll lick your pussy."

The girl smiles, eyes drop to watch Mack's hands move in front of his flat chest in the suit jacket; then back up to his face a moment, in amusement; then she turns to survey the crowd of women who dance in front of them.

"OK," the girl says, simply. "But don't go bragging about it, Mack. I don't want anybody think I'm giving it away to everybody."

The girl went off to dance & be with the party she came with. And she and Mack had a rendezvous for when the club closed.

"You know her a long time?" Frankie asked, after the girl left.

"Yeah."

"She looks nice."

"She's OK."

"How old is she? She looks young."

"Nineteen. She's got a fake ID. She looks older. She's been around a lot."

"There's marks on her."

"Yeah, but take a good look at 'em when she comes back. —Those are old marks. I didn't give them to her.... She likes me 'cause we're both jaded." Mack adds. "Last time we went to bed together, I fucked her till she was sore. She couldn't get enough. And I whipped her with a cat-o'-nine-tails. She likes whipping. There was blood all over my sheets. When I have a woman, they call me up 4 days later and they're still limping," Mack said roughly. "I'm worse on them than a man. 'Cause I can keep it hard. Ha!" Laughs and threw a dark look because he hated not being a man.

Rusty felt rage oozing out of Mack's being into a kind of rainbow-colored truce. The girl. She would ease his savage frenzy. He shifted in his suit, a being half-woman, half-man. Man in self—female in genitals.

Face tipped up into smile from a frown.

"IT'S MY TURN NOW!" Frankie said loudly. "You guys have done all these things with these women! You've had all these women! Now it's my turn for a woman!"

"It's OK, pal!" Rusty reached out, a black-leather-jacketed arm went around Frankie's shoulders. She could feel the strong mass stir beneath.

Most dykes are very frustrated if they are single. Or even when married. They don't get what they want. When they do get sex, it's not the sex they want, it's not the way they want it.

Only 10 percent of women who go to the bars get somebody to take home that night.

Say a dyke is going to the bar to pick somebody up to have sex; only a handful really do this—the lucky few.

So, many nights were spent up in a lesbian meeting place, just to have to go home and jerk herself off.

It was true for all of the trio. —Separate, in their private agony.

Most of the time couldn't get a prostitute.

Nothing.

Mostly then, it was about loneliness. It wasn't about Party Girls hired for Pleasure. Not about One Night Stands, nor Scoring with the Babes. Not even Savoir Faire—handsome, debonair, satin shirt & tight-fitting slacks, trim figure, fancy car & the girl goes crazy over you, and gets naked and lies back for you.

This happened, sure; but mostly it wasn't romantic images, or hard erotic conquests. —It was about loneliness.

The bar, purple streaks of gold light, gyrating dancers on the floor, individuals posed. Couples entwined. Groups in a circle, laughing & sharing among themselves.

"These homosexuals and their problems. —I ought to know, I'm one," Frankie mused, after the departing figure of Mack, who stomps off, arm around this girl.

A dyke they didn't know sat down on Mack's vacated bar stool. The crowd pressed in on them as their circle had narrowed down to two.

Although she had tried in previous nights gone by, Frankie didn't feel courage enough to go up to any pretty femmes and get told NO. So she clung by her butt to the bar stool, as a kind of haven. Just too defeated to take a risk.

Rusty retreated into the music.

Fantasized an erotic love scene & aroused herself.

High up on the pedestal, out of reach, the go-go dancer performed.

Fantasized, until the last vestige was drummed out of her, by the sight of all the women who are so hard to get & the sexual rhythm of the music.

Watched the go-go dancer.

Thought: 'Just love me, honey. Run your hands all over my body, lick my clit until I feel so good.' And shifted her blue-jeaned rump on the bar stool, flexed her strong shoulders and arms.

THE KEY
Alison Tyler

Whenas in silks my Julia goes,
Then, then, methinks, how sweetly flows
The liquefaction of her clothes.

Next, when I cast mine eyes and see
That brave vibration each way free,
Oh how that glittering taketh me!

—Robert Herrick

Julia knocks, as a courtesy, but comes in before I can call out to her. She stands in the doorway for a moment, looking at me, and then she walks to the desk and sits in the padded swivel-chair next to mine.

"What'cha working on?"

"Just editing."

"I brought you something."

Coffee, as always. This time it's a double espresso. On Tuesday it was a latté with extra foam. Julia chooses different flavors and styles every time she sees me. She says that my life is too boring, that I play it too close to the lines in my Filofax. She likes to keep me off guard.

"And something else, too," she says, doubly surprising me by pulling a small box out of her pocket, the secret pocket on the inside of her faded leather jacket. She places the box on the edge of my desk and then taps it with her short, manicured fingernails.

"What is it?"

"You'll have to see for yourself, won't you, love?"

I smile at her and turn in my chair to study the fine bones of her face, the smooth brow and golden-brown eyes that change when she looks at me, soften somehow. She puts her hands on the sides of my chair and rotates the whole thing, turning it on the wheels and pulling both me and the chair closer to her. Every movement is graceful, unconscious, feline. She does difficult things without thinking twice. I have a hard time getting my jacket on without the shoulder pads bunching up on me.

Julia continues to slide the chair forward until our legs are touching. I smile, then stop—I suddenly sense that she has something serious to tell me.

"Twice a week isn't enough anymore," she says quietly. "I think about you all the time, Sonja."

She moves her hands to my legs, just above my knees, resting them there on my gray flannel slacks, setting her hands on me as a precursor, an appetizer, of what is to come. I sigh at her touch, knowing that she's right...this is no longer a fling. I miss her so much when we are apart, the warmth of her, scent of her.

"It's not my birthday," I say, half-teasing, attempting to lighten the mood. We're so close now that my breath stirs the wayward lock of hair that always falls over her forehead. "It's not Christmas. Or even Valentine's day."

"Just a present..." she flashes me her unique smile, imperfect only because of one slightly chipped front tooth—that flaw makes me love her more—"...just because I wanted to."

Again, she taps the thin, flat box for emphasis, then pushes it along my desk until it rests against my coffee cup. She takes my right hand and turns it up so that she can kiss my palm, kiss my life lines, my love lines, tracing her tongue along those delicate, near-dainty wrinkles worn well into my palm, the map that tells a future I'm not sure I want to know.

Am I ready for it?

"Should I open it now…or after?"

"After," she grins, dipping and swirling her tongue around each one of my unpolished fingernails. "After."

When she leaves, I look at the present again. It's wrapped in red foil and tied with a tiny satin ribbon. I stroke the shiny paper and glossy black ribbon. Then I slip the box into the top drawer of my desk, turn off my computer, and get ready to go home.

As I grab my trench coat from the rack, I imagine the mystery gift. Until I open it, I can dream of the contents nestled safely within the box.

What if it held the key to freedom, I wonder. Wouldn't that be nice? Wouldn't that be magic?

"You're gonna watch me," she says, "Watch me eat your pussy, lick the cherry juices off your inner lips, slide my tongue inside your cunt…deep inside you there, where you're all warm and secret and safe. Baby, I want you to watch."

I take a deep breath, a ragged breath, listening to Julia on the other end of the phone line while rubbing myself on the edge of my chair. I wish I could talk back to her, but I'm suddenly shy, blushing like a teenager, even though I'm the older one in this relationship. I open my lips to speak, but the words won't come out of my mouth—I can't even formulate them in my mind.

"I'm gonna fuck you," she says, and I moan, thrilling at the urgency in her voice, the borderline desperation. "Gonna fuck my working girl, my good girl."

I sigh again and realize, as the phone shakes in my hand, that I'm trembling.

"I'll bend you over your desk, lift up your skirt— you'll wear a skirt for me, won't you, darling? Not one of your power suits."

"Uh huh." There, that's something, "Yes, Jules, I will."

"I'll lift it up, exposing you, your legs, thighs, ass, your beautiful, creamy white ass."

And then? Then? Oh, please tell me, please talk to me. I want to record your voice in my head to play back at night, when I'm in bed next to her, when I'm awake and alive and on the verge of...

"I'm gonna fuck you, baby, hard and fast, just like you want it, just like you need it, fuck your sweet slippery pussy until you scream. I'll thrust into you and make you come over and over again. You are my princess, Sonja, and I want to take care of you. You are my bad girl, Sonja, and I want to make sure that you understand that. And when I do, you'll be so loud for me, you will scream and moan and sob...and everyone's gonna know."

Everyone. Everyone's gonna know. What will they say? What can they possibly say?

"Did you hear about Sonja? She had a lover in her office, just last Tuesday. You must have seen her, younger, butch, rugged. You must have noticed her bringing coffee twice a week, as if she worked at Dante's Café. As if. She closes the door and stays in there with her, for much too long, much longer than it takes to get a buck seventy five out of your purse."

"But Sonja? I don't believe it. She's a good girl, a good girl. And she seems so, well...boring. Not to be cruel, or anything, but she is sort of mousy. You know?"

"That's only because of the way she dresses. She shouldn't wear so much gray, someone should take pity and tell her."

Pause and laughter. Two toilets flush.

"Well, maybe gray is sexy to some women. It sounds as if she's getting more than you are, Meredith."

"You should talk, Joyce. You're more of a slut than she is."

Giggling, then, "Bitch."

"Do you think her girlfriend knows? Shouldn't someone tell her? To save the poor soul some pain."

"'Poor soul'? I don't think that dyke can feel pain. Didn't you see her at the Christmas party? The way she bossed Sonja around. She's a bad dream, a nightmare. A Neanderthal."

More wild laughter partially drowned out by running water.

Then: "That's a great color lipstick on you."

"Thanks, it's new. Russet Moon. Chanel."

The bathroom door whooshes open and then closes, and I put my feet back down on the blue tile floor and smile to myself—though, honestly, shouldn't I be crying?

Julia knocks as a courtesy, but comes in before I can call out to her. Still, what would I say? "Enter, lover," the way she talks. "Come and fuck me against the wall. Tear off my clothes, my good work shoes, my Jones New York blazer, my one hundred and eighty-nine dollar Ann Taylor dress. Fuck me like a locomotive, let me feel… anything, let me feel anything again. I'm so tired of being boring, gray, mousy, dead. I want to live again, Julia, in your kiss, in your embrace, in your fire."

"Sonja, my lovely lady, you look delicious." She seems to drink me in with her eyes, lifting up her black wayfarer sunglasses to get a better look. She brushes the mahogany curls away from my forehead and kisses me there first, chastely, sweetly, and then she undoes the top button of my red silk shirt and presses two fingers in the indent there, to feel my pulse, my life line, love line.

"This color suits you, darling. It makes you look like a firecracker."

"Really? You think so?"

"Mm hmm." She undoes the rest of my buttons, "It looks wonderful on you, but truly, I think it will look much better on the floor."

I laugh—can't help it—and she unfastens the clasp of my black lace bra.

"And this," she says, helping me slip it off, "is incredibly sexy."

"I know. Much better than the old-maid things I usually wear."

She gets down on her knees in front of me, and slowly begins stroking my body, along my shoulders, across my naked breasts, and down my belly.

"Did you buy it for me?"

"No, not really."

She pauses and looks up at my face, misunderstanding, thinking that I'm seeing someone else. Her eyes cloud with worry, with jealousy, but when I smile, reassuring her—"I bought it for myself"—she immediately continues where she left off, kneeling on the floor between my legs and cupping my breasts tenderly.

"I don't know why I wore those others for so long. I've always wanted to dress like this."

"You were scared of what you might unleash," she murmurs against my warm flesh. "You were afraid you'd like it."

Then there's silence again as she kisses the valley between my breasts and down the flat curve of my stomach to the waistband of my skirt. Silence that hangs in the air around us—richly colored like a woven tapestry, it's filled with thoughts and dreams and fantasies...all of which are about to come true.

"You wore this for me, though, didn't you?"

"Yes," I sigh, and she motions for me to stand and then bends me over my desk, slowly lifting up the back panel of my floral skirt and exposing me from behind. She strokes me through my sheer nylons and then carefully peels them down my legs, helping me step out of my shoes and stockings.

"You are exquisite," she whispers, "Such a vision. I can't wait to be taste you...."

They were wrong, those catty women in the bathroom. Julia has long been my admirer, my sweetheart, my obscene caller. She has kissed me and touched me, and we have indulged in "petting" like two high school kids, but never, not until this moment, have we actually made love.

She slips one hand under the elastic of my naughty lace panties, black ones to match the bra, and then pulls them down to my ankles and leaves them there, capturing me. I feel her hot breath on the inside of my thighs before her tongue begins the journey upward, parting my nether lips and diving inside me where I am so ready for her, so willing. My thighs are damp with my honey, and Julia flicks and licks her tongue in circles, catching each drop, making sweet hungry noises as she devours me.

I grip the edge of my desk with both hands, digging my nails into the carved wood border. I bite my bottom lip to keep from crying out, and I wonder, belatedly, if she locked the door. But does it matter?

"Gonna make you scream, Sonja," she says, soft and low, without moving her mouth from me. Her voice resonates within my pussy, vibrating amazingly inside me.

"Gonna make you cry...and everyone will know, darling. Everyone."

God, it feels so good, her tongue and now her fingers, probing, opening me, teasing my clit with just the tip of her tongue and then moving away, pinching it between two fingers, the sensations building, the need rising. I want her cock there—I know she's packing—I want her filling me, fixing me, making me whole. Yet somehow, though she doesn't say it, I know that she wants me to come first, that she won't stop until I come, won't fuck me until I come.

"No more secrets, darling, no more pretending."

She presses two fingers into my pussy and then uses her thumb to part the cheeks of my ass and violate me there, exposing, exploring. I feel weak, find myself suddenly grateful for the support of my desk—"Gonna make you scream, Sonja,"—I hear my moans as if they belong to someone else, some other woman's voice, some other woman's body being played so well, so masterfully, being stroked and suckled and teased and (deep breath)...fucked, oh, thank you, God, fucked as she stands and thrusts her cock inside me, impaling me, making the head of it dance within the tight walls of my cunt.

"Squeeze me," she orders, and I do, helplessly contracting on her, coming from the very first dull thrust inside me. Her cock throbs inside me, rocks back and forth as she pulls out to the tip and then slams right back in.

"Squeeze..." she says again, wrapping one hand in my long brown hair and pulling my head back so that she can kiss my lips, kiss me softly while she fucks me fast, forcefully—just how she said, just how I need it.

"That's right, baby, keep it steady now"—as if she's talking to a pony, steady pace, keep the rhythm. I buck against her, loving the feel of her open jeans on my naked thighs, her cool leather vest on my hot skin.

I moan louder, knowing that I'll be heard, but not caring, not giving any thought to the repercussions, calling her name out, "Oh, my God, Oh, Julia! Yes, please, yes!" as I come on her, move with her, hit the stride and keep it, sliding up and down on her powerful cock, riding it, then moving away at her signal and getting down on my knees in front of her and licking my own come from the toy, lapping at the sweet drops that coat my lips—ignoring the pounding at my door.

* * *

Afterward, we're warm and sticky, naked and sweaty, collapsed on the floor of my office with our clothes piled behind us for pillows. I lean up on one side to kiss her, to kiss her open mouth and taste myself there, to let her taste herself on my lips. I know that I can talk to her now, that something has changed inside me. Know that next time I will say, "Julia, I need your cock. Please, baby, please let me suck it, let me drink from your cunt, devour you. I am so hungry…" Say anything I want, anything at all.

"Did you open your gift yet?" she asks softly, stroking my hair away from my face, staring directly into my eyes.

"No. I was…saving it." Imagining something like this, not as good as this, but the same freedom of it, the key that would unlock this door and let loose my soul.

But now, I realize the truth, that I don't need a key. Or really, that I had the key the whole time, and only lacked the courage to turn it.

JOINING THE CLUB

Lisa Pacheco

I'm sure you've heard of the Mile-High Club. Personally, I never saw the point. What's so cool about having sex in one of those miniature bathrooms? I wondered. Slammed against the mirror with your legs spread wide, trying to avoid plunging one foot in the neon-blue toilet water while keeping your ass out of the sink. I like comfort. I like plenty of room. I like to make noise.

But on our recent flight from New York to San Francisco, Samantha and I found ourselves in a new predicament. We fell asleep, my head resting lightly on her shoulder, her arm wrapped firmly around my body. And, once asleep, I began to dream.

Have you ever had a sex dream so real that you were certain the person you dreamed about must have shared it with you? This one was like that—an image of us from recent memory. Raw. Outta control. It was a vision of Sam fucking me on the hood of my car, my legs hooked over her shoulders. Staring down at me in the dimly lit parking garage, that greedy look filling her gray-green eyes, whisper-hissing, "Like that? You like it like that?" with each forward thrust.

"Yeah…"

"Oh, I know you do, my hungry one. I know all about you."

I stirred on the plane, feeling the flushed, embarrassed heat in my cheeks, the wetness between my legs from just a dream. Then I looked at her. Her eyes were open, watching me.

"You're beautiful when you sleep," she said

I smiled, then told her about my dream. She leaned back in the seat and said, "I wish we were somewhere we could turn that into a reality." I checked my watch. We had three more hours of flight time.

"Do you want to…?" she asked finally, motioning toward the rear of the plane. Suddenly I understood the whole concept of doing it on a plane. I unbuckled my seat belt and walked back to the lavatories. She followed.

When you hear people bragging about their indoctrination into the Mile-High Club, they don't usually mention the amazing difficulty it can be to get two people into one bathroom. We are both full-grown adults, and airplane restrooms were built for munchkins. Despite the close quarters, Sam pushed me into the lavatory, followed me in, and shut the door behind us.

In a flash, I was up on the rim of the sink, back against the mirror, legs splayed—forgetting all about my previous misgivings. I hiked my black skirt as high as it would go and slid my cream-colored panties to the side. Sam was ready, pressing forward, cock plunging inside me.

And that's when the turbulence hit. The little red warning light flashed, commanding us to return to our seats. The pilot's manly drone insisted that our belts be buckled. Sam kept right on going.

It was like taking a ride on the top of a washing machine—the motion of the plane, the delicious friction of her body against mine. Disregard everything I said about the tiny compartment, about the foul blue water, about the sink. My breath caught in my throat, my hands gripped the edge of the steely counter for leverage. My mind was consumed entirely with want.

There was a knock on the door. "You have to return to your seat...."

"I'm not feeling well," I hissed, my voice heavy and dark with urgency.

"Oh." She left it alone, not wanting to get involved.

"Ohhhh..." I murmured, echoing her. "That's right. Yeah, that's right."

Sam grabbed the back of my hair, lifting my face upward for a kiss. We tried, but missed, as the plane bucked suddenly and we were thrown against each other. Now I was pressed against her, her hands cradling my ass, plunging me up and down on her rod. The red light continued to flash. The captain continued to speak over the intercom, describing exactly what was causing the pockets of rocking air. Didn't matter. Nothing mattered except the way it felt to be in Sam's embrace, the way the motion of the plane worked with the motion of our bodies.

Samantha turned in a tight circle, so that her back was now against the rim of the sink and I was still in her arms. I could see my reflection in the mirror. My blue eyes glowed in the fluorescent light. My cheeks were rose-tinted, fever-flushed. My teeth bit hard into my lower lip, smearing what lipstick I still had on.

"Now," Sam said.

"Now." I breathed a harsh sigh of release, relief, as we came together. The vibrations worked to set me off, those, and the last wild jerks of the plane caught in a violent burst of air. Then, as the turbulence lessened, slowed, and the air become calm...so did I.

Sam set me gently down on the floor. She slid the door open cautiously and then slipped out quickly and closed the door. I relatched it, cleaned up, and then joined her back at our seats. No one saw. But the flight attendant came to my side after a moment, handing me an extra airsick bag, saying with caution, "Just in case…"

SYNTHETIC SEX
Tori White

We live in the age of technology. I can call up my friends anywhere in the world and hold a face-to-face conversation via videophone. I can log onto my computer and communicate with beings all over the universe, my words translated instantly into any and every language. If I decide I want children, there's a sperm bank in town that delivers. Now, that's what I call service. I could conduct my entire life without ever leaving my cubicle—no human contact necessary.

And for pleasure, for sexual fulfillment, I can charge up my solar-powered vibrator, relax on the flotation bed, and cruise to an inner beat.

Somehow, somewhere along the line I lost my sense of touch, of being held and caressed, stroked and loved. That feeling of safety, locked in a slick and sweaty embrace that requires two consenting adults. So tonight I log onto the computer using my code name, "Elijah," one who comes and goes as she pleases. I think for a minute, feeling the calm wash over me.

"Hey, all of you cats and kitties," I type. "You out there? Yeah, I'm talking to you. The moon is full, though I know not many of your pads have windows. Those wall-sized video screens make the real outdoors pale in comparison. But, if you've got one, if you live in one of the older buildings, why don't ya peek out of your window and check out that moon. It's amazing, golden yellow, ripe like a hothouse papaya.

"Y'know, I'm lonesome tonight. Like that Elvis song. Does anyone out there remember Elvis? He's one of the old-timers, from the days when music still had lyrics, before the New Age 'songs' of today. I know, I know, our music soothes the troubled mind, eases our biorhythms and all that. But I need words tonight, 'cause I'm so lonesome tonight, and I miss you tonight. Can you all hear me singing on your screens? Can you see the tears on my face, crystal drops that well up in my hazel eyes before spilling over, rolling down my cheeks to fall like rain on my keyboard.

"No? How soon we grow accustomed to the here and now. And even with our advanced life spans, with our newly accessed mental powers, yesterdays just seem to slip away, like shadows in an empty room.

"I'm melancholy tonight, my friends. I've got my antique lava lamp on, and my black light filtering onto wild acid-rock posters. But something's missing. Something's lost, and I can't remember what. Maybe it's only that moon outside, pulling on me like she pulls the tides. Technology can't change that.

"You know what I really want? I want to feel skin on skin. I don't want to watch animated fucking on a screen. I don't want to have sex with my virtual-reality headset. I want a woman to appear in my bedroom, like Athena in a shower of golden light. I can see her in my mind—not so much her body, but the way that she feels. We fall into each other's arms and twirl around the room. We dance to the music of a lost era, something hard and low. We rock to the beat, to the shattering beat that invades our souls and shakes our minds to pieces. I let down my long red hair. When I dance, my curls swirl around me in a curtain of fire.

"I know I'll get into trouble for saying all this, but, hell, it's over for me. So, until they come to get me, I'll keep on writing. Writing about that beat. Can you feel it...slowly at first and then, ohhh, so sweet as the guitar picks it up, joins the lickin' of the drums, and then the singer, whispering at first, but building, growing. It's so good, it's like coming.

"And my lover, my dream lover, dancing with me, holding me as we rock and rock and rock. And then suddenly, we're not dancing anymore; we're moving together in that ancient ritual. I feel her inside me, throbbing. The heat from her burns as she thrusts into me. I move with her, rocking my hips in a way they've never moved before, swiveling, spiraling, contracting, keeping with her, keeping that beat—that nasty beat that underlies every rock-'n'-roll song ever written.

"We're naked and sweaty and still standing up. She grabs me and lifts me. Now I wrap my legs around her. She carries me to a wall and holds me against it so that she can drive into me. Hard. Real hard. Harder and faster with that beat running through us, tying us together, tying us to every human being who ever made love—I'm not talking synthetic sex—but hard-core, one on one until there's nothing left.

"I hear them at the door. People. I don't have much time.

"She kisses me on the lips just as I start to come, she kisses me softly as she pounds into me. The contrast is amazing. It's unreal. Kissing so gently, licking each other's lips, twisting our tongues in delicate circles while our bodies move like overwound machines, faster and faster until we come together—explosions, fireworks, multicolored lights.

"And, oh, I'm dying, I want it so bad. I'm...I am Elijah. I come and go as I please. And it was so nice to talk to you all. So much fun while it lasted.

"Error. Error. Error. Error. Error."

THREESOME
Aarona Griffin

I nstead of leading out into a room as the woman in the tunnel had promised, the right turn took Leda into a wide hall. Directly across from her—and across a small sea of women milling about—were two doors that said Restroom on them. Leda thought for a moment. There was something near the restrooms that the woman had told her about. Was it the Viewing Room room? Her head swam. The whole damn place seemed suddenly not to fit; she couldn't get her bearings, not even where the front door of the club was situated from here, and she couldn't recall the specifics of what the Victorian woman had said.

"Shit," she swore aloud. Exasperated, Leda turned right and moved through the loose crowd. On her left was an elevator and a group of women waiting for it. The light above the door flashed on and the doors opened. A few females—some in wet bathing suits or wrapped in towels, and some just plain wet and naked or semi-naked, breasts bare and hair slicked back away from a variety of beautiful faces—disembarked from the elevator.

"C'mon, let's get something to eat," a white woman in a light blue towel wrapped only around her narrow hips, said to a few others beside her.

Leda watched them go off to her left, heading toward the archway that opened into a room on the opposite end of the hall, back past the restrooms. She considered following them as she made a quick search of the faces in the hall for the one burned in her mind from the Viewing Room. But before she could decide, the group in front of the elevators moved in a mass through the open doors and Leda was being pushed in by more women from behind. She found herself on board, doors closing; the packed-in group descended.

A dark-haired, petite woman on Leda's right glanced over at her, checking out Leda's attire. Leda watched her looking, the woman's gaze eventually making its way up to Leda's amused face. The woman smiled a little and nodded.

"Nice vest," she said.

"Thanks," Leda returned, glancing down at the woman's attire. With a start, she realized she was standing next to an almost buck-naked gorgeous female, naked except for a slick black G-string that sat high on her slim hips, small, tight buns exposed, legs smoothly shaved and bare except for heavy black boots that went just below her knees, her upper body covered only in a black shorty tank top made out of a very, very, open-weave, lightweight net fabric. The woman's perky tits peeked through, as tan as the rest of her.

"You've got guts," Leda said with a smile. The woman laughed a sparkly laugh, her slightly slanted, very long-lashed eyes creasing with pleasure.

"That's a nice way of putting it," she said. "My girlfriend just calls me a tease."

"Lucky woman," Leda offered.

On the woman's other side, a woman with a pretty face on which sat a slightly turned-up nose leaned over to see who she was talking to. Her face, framed by shiny gold hair, was curious, shy. Leda smiled and waved a little. The woman smiled back, blushed, moved back out of Leda's view, and giggled to the woman next to Leda. Leda smiled openly and chuckled, amused at their youthful goofiness.

"This is not my girlfriend," the dark-haired woman next to her said, rolling her eyes and smiling as she pointed to her blushing, still-giggling friend. Leda nodded her understanding, preoccupied with thinking about the three of them getting naked together; what this petite beauty would like done to her, or to do; what she was into, or would be willing to try. But cute and femme wasn't really what Leda was into tonight. Still, the thought lingered in her head: removing the young woman's net shirt and kissing those incredible tits. Leda's own nipples throbbed behind the soft leather that held them.

She sighed just as the elevator doors opened. Everyone moved out, fanning off in different directions. The shy woman looked back over her shoulder, still smiling, and waved a little good-bye to Leda. Her friend in the G-string and net shirt who had been beside Leda slapped her playfully on the shoulder as if to tell her to stop being such a pain. But Leda didn't mind the flirt. She took a breath and shook her head, feeling hot in her jeans, smoldering even. But she hadn't brought anything else to walk around in, since of course she was just going to watch.

So, you don't have to walk around in anything! a voice in her head countered. Just that cute girly G-string you chose!

Oh, yeah, right, like I'm really going to do that, she said back. Yeah, right, sure.

Instead, she focused on the crowd milling about and the absolutely stunning scenery: real palm trees, high ceiling painted like a midnight blue sky with shiny stars all across it, blinking, the lighting soft like moonlight, but as bright as a full-moon night. Dripping wet women were everywhere and the sound of water rushing, splashing, and Caribbean-style music moved around Leda. The smell of food was here, too, though Leda couldn't quite tell what kind of food was cooking. She scanned the scene and noticed a few cabanas, one larger than the others with tables outside. Closer to where she stood, a very tan topless woman in just a grass skirt and arm bracelets was standing at a fruit stand laden with exotic fruits and plastic cups of fruit salad. It was a popular place.

Women sat at little round wooden tables placed around the stand, eating and feeding each other fruit. One couple passed fruit to each other with kisses, mouths lingering with each bite as they sat side-by-side at the corner of a table. During one fruit-passing kiss, Leda watched them linger and one of the women—who was tall, with a strong squarish jaw and short bleached hair—moved in closer to her partner, her mouth working the kiss, hands reaching for her partner's pink tits, which were bare. She caressed them, then moved back up to the woman's smooth cheek as they kissed furiously. The other woman—also somewhat tall, her head shaved and tattooed with an intricate design on one side, ears pierced all the way up with thick silver hoops—ended the kiss and smiled languidly, the ring in her nose catching the light, striking dark eyes heavy with passion. She reached for the bleached-haired woman's chair, pulling it in as close as it would go as the woman stood up to allow it, face intense on her lover's mouth throughout the exchange.

Obediently she sat back down, hands remaining on her partner's naked thigh. Leda watched the two of them feed each other for another moment, then Leda turned and moved into the crowd a way, but glanced back. She noticed from this angle that the two women wore only towels around their waists and Leda smiled as she watched the white-haired woman trying mischievously to get her hands up under the other woman's towel, moving up her thighs playfully as her partner pretended to bat her hands away. The tension between them was riveting. Leda's own cunt ached, trapped as it was in her too-stifling black jeans.

Quickly, and in a huff of frustration, she turned and moved further into the huge warehouse-sized space, searching for the woman she'd seen from the Viewing Room. No way she'd still be where Leda had last seen her; it felt as though hours had passed since then. But no trace of her here. Leda's eyes wandered up the incredibly high walls and saw a huge waterfall on the far end to her left, tumbling down over a high ledge of rocks and down, down, into the wide constructed river. At the top of the ledge where the water shot out over the rocks, a naked woman stood perched to one side. She stepped to the edge, balanced herself with her arms, lowered them, concentrating still, then pushed off in a swan dive, hitting the water with hardly a ripple.

Leda was impressed. She joined in as women all along the "bank" of the river hooted and clapped. Many women, she noticed, were paired up, or in a group already. She strolled down the walkway by the riverside, watching the women swimming or lying on the strip of sandy shore. There was also a strip of island in the middle of the wide river. The sound of exotic birds and wind in the trees mixed with the Caribbean-flavored dance music that pumped through the Jungle Room and Leda closed her eyes for a minute, appreciating the lush soundtrack that transformed this place—along with the incredible scenery—into an exotic island of sexual fantasy.

Leda took a long breath and opened her eyes, distracted by a crowd of women's voices whooping and hollering from across the river. Her eyes were drawn to the island in the middle of the river where a bonfire circled by large stones was in full flame. Huge multicolored spotlights were focused on the strip of island and they were moving now, like searchlights. Women of all types and sizes were dancing and moving, performing for those on the shore. Some wore grass skirts and bathing suits and moved together in an impersonation of a Hawaiian sort of dance; some just wore grass skirts and nothing else, also trying to follow along with the first group. Others wore only men's boxers or a G-string, with their hair—short, long, or in-between—slicked back, faces shining. One butch woman danced with another butch and their packed dildos—not so packed anymore in their loose boxer shorts— bounced and danced right along with them, making their boxers pooch out, the tips of the dildos appearing, then disappearing.

Leda laughed out loud and shook her head as the two women danced and raised their beers in a whoop and holler of celebratory enthusiasm. Their cheer was infectious and pretty soon all the women on the island were dancing and whooping and raising their beers or various other drinks in a toast, too. It was like an all-female Carnivale without the distraction of ogling men.

"Yay, women!" Leda whooped, swept up in the growing tide of revelry. Someone next to her added, "Amen, sister!"

Leda turned, smiling, and met the wide, pretty smile of a dread-locked African-American woman dressed in a striking skirt and bathing suit–type top of eye-catching multicolored fabrics. She was sipping a large fruity drink and bobbing with the rhythm of the music.

"Ain't that the truth!" she said, sort of to Leda.

"Definitely!" Leda replied. The woman looked her over briefly.

"You need a drink," she asked after a moment. "Can I buy you one?"

Leda was tempted, but reminded herself that if she stuck around much longer, she might not find the woman she'd come in for, not for the rest of the night probably. The thought panicked her some in an odd way, since of course she didn't even know the woman she was pining after. She felt like Cinderella at the ball: Hurry before the clock strikes midnight and you're sent back to your old self, old world, old stuck place! There was just something so seductive about the woman she'd seen through the window. In some strange way the attraction was incredibly intense, as though she'd known the woman a long, long time; just hadn't been able to get close to her before, intimately. But tonight there was a possibility. Tonight, everything was possible. Leda just couldn't give up yet. First she had to finish her search.

"Thanks so much for the offer, I'd love to hang with you a while. But I'm looking for someone," Leda explained. The woman smiled and nodded as she continued to bob to the music. Her body was beautiful, breasts crisscrossed with the colorful cloth, ample hips moving with the music.

"I hope you find her," the woman said, raising her drink in a toast to Leda. "Have fun. Come back if you don't find her." She smiled.

"Thanks, I will," Leda said, and the woman moved on down the path that ran along the river.

I'll definitely be back if that happens, Leda thought to herself.

Reggae music followed her back to the elevators, which opened before she had a chance to touch the up arrow button. Another crowd of women in various states of undress moved out of the elevator, some already caught up in the reggae beat. Leda slipped into the elevator as the last woman disembarked. A couple of other women got on with her and she hit the up button, taking the calm moment to check out her hair, teeth, face, in the shiny metal panel that housed the elevator buttons. She also watched the two women making out madly behind her. One wore a collar and the other woman was holding it tight as she pressed against her, kissing her furiously and deeply. The sound of her leather pants as she moved caught Leda's attention and she felt a shiver of disappointment that she'd never put aside enough money to buy some of her own, luxury that they were.

But oh, so worth it.

When the elevator doors opened, she was back in the hallway. Leda got off and looked both ways. A brighter light was coming from the room to her right at the end of the hall so she turned that way, remembering that the light seemed pretty bright in the room she had been watching from the Viewing Room. She moved quickly down the dim hallway, past the bathrooms where a line was forming, hoping that at last she'd be in the right place at the right time tonight.

Leda walked through the archway and entered a large room, the one she recognized from the Viewing Room! It was much brighter in this room than in the passage from which she'd just emerged and Leda squinted, waiting a minute for her eyes to adjust.

After a moment, she checked out the wall where the windows were, behind which she knew other women watched the goings-on in this room. By the way the lights were set up, all you could see were mirrors mostly, or the effects of mirrors. If you didn't know they were there, you might miss the fact that this was a room to be watched in.

I definitely wouldn't want to do anything in here, Leda thought, stepping up and onto a low platform to move out of the way as women filed past her. But then who had actually been watching in the Viewing Room other than her? It was hard to tell. And besides, more people were showing up by the minute; it might be full of women up there by now. Leda squinted up, trying to see the Viewing Room through the mirrored glass.

Suddenly she felt someone's gaze on her. She looked out of

the corner of her eye, for some reason too shy to turn around and look. Her body tingled and her mouth went dry. She forced herself at least to turn her head a little to get a better view out of the corner of her eye.

And there she was. And close by: the soft butch she had seen from the Viewing Room.

The woman seemed to be watching Leda before Leda had a chance to do it first. Leda smiled inside, but out of nervousness, didn't smile outwardly, keeping a carefully cool exterior, trying not to show that she had noticed the woman's gaze. She tried doggedly to stay relaxed, but her hand went up and ran itself nervously through her spiky hair, seemingly of its own accord. The music pumped through this room, too, but the lighting was brighter than even the other main room she'd been in, obviously for better viewing. Still, the lighting wasn't harsh, some dramatic accents to it coming mostly from colored lights and hurricane lamps, and spotlights illuminating equipment and certain scene areas of the playroom.

Leda tried to turn nonchalantly toward the woman whose eyes she could feel on her body so intensely even from this distance. Stay cool, calm, she thought, don't do anything stupid. But as she turned and took a few steps as if she were just casually moving a little further into the room, she found herself accidentally stepping right into the beam of a bright white spotlight, looking straight into it and temporarily blinded by the hot light. Leda raised her hand to shield her eyes, then turned away from the blaze, blinking, making a disgusted face as the cameras of her eyes played back the image again and again.

Oh, that was very very very cool, she commented disgustedly to herself, her pulse racing now, feeling just like the awkward novice she'd been when she'd first stepped into the world of women, sex, and SM play years ago. It was like some terrible embarrassing flashback.

She groaned.

But as the image of the lights dissipated, she worked up the guts to turn back and look. The spot where the woman had been standing was empty; she was gone.

"Shit," Leda mumbled under her breath.

Suddenly all the white spotlights in the room started to roam, making big sweeping circles like a police helicopter as the music changed into a pounding dance tune with a wailing female vocalist. Leda noticed as she glanced around that she was standing in a scene space (hence, the spotlight). A wooden wall just behind her was equipped with heavy hooks all the way up at different heights, chains hanging from the ceiling, which was low here, the area constructed like a sort of cage with metal barrel-shaped doors that were swung wide open. Leda pulled on one and saw that they would meet in the center with a metal rod that slid into a little cylinder to secure them. In the same scene area was a black leather vault-style horse, heavily padded, and a large wooden step stool.

A world of possibilities, Leda thought, a fire in her eyes and streaking through her overheated body. She could feel the wetness of the fabric of her underwear that clung to her mound, the heat most intense between her legs.

"Lots of possibilities in this room," a sexy tenor voice said from behind her, making her jump a little.

Leda turned and there before her was the object of her desire, the one woman she knew could make her do things she really shouldn't.

But, oh, man, she wanted to.

"That's just what I was thinking," Leda said, the sides of her mouth creeping up into a slight smile, the surprise still on her face, blue eyes sparkling at the brown ones eyeing her coolly, but with great interest and friendly enough.

Wow. Wow, wow, wow! Leda thought stupidly, struck dumb for the moment and uncertain how to proceed.

The soft tan of the woman's skin and the obvious strength of her toned arms; the way she stood so confidently and seductively in her body; her legs which were actually much longer up close, incredibly shaped; her thick dark hair which had been pulled back loosely in a low ponytail, away from a beautiful face—all of this served only to absolutely transfix Leda where she stood, unable to move or speak, much less breathe.

The overwhelming shyness that Leda hated so much threatened to wipe out any attempt at boldness. She noted this internally with disgust, but couldn't change it for the moment. There was something about this woman, as though she'd been wanting her for a lifetime. Luckily, all was not lost.

"Would you be interested in joining me in trying out some of this great equipment?" the woman asked. "My name is Michelle, but I go by Mikki or Mik most of the time."

Leda almost choked with excitement, still feeling self-conscious but more confident by the minute. Mikki was eyeing her with great approval and a hunger in her eyes that seemed to match what Leda felt. Leda suddenly realized that her composure was beginning to loosen, that the words take me! were probably actually visible to the eye in big flashing letters across her whole nervous face.

"Leda," she answered, "my name is Leda. And yes, oh, yes, I would love to."

She tried to sound casual about the whole thing, but she could hear her own voice too sincere, too emphatic, and she couldn't take her eyes away from Mikki's. It was like falling into a deep chocolate sea and she was high already from the sugar rush.

Yes, I would love to give you my body and my passion and drink madly from your mouth and take you and open you and open wide for you and scream for you and be your dog, oh mama mama mama...

Leda felt relief that the only empaths she knew of only showed up on Star Trek and she blushed at her own thoughts, her obvious ravenous hunger, so starved as she was for what turned her on.

"Great, what are you into?" Mikki asked intimately, moving in closer.

Leda felt suddenly overwhelmed by everything she'd just seen and heard and this woman in front of her, and she moved in as if pushed by a tidal wave of passion, almost against Mikki's hot body, no words for the desire she felt, just action. She boldly slipped one hand around and held one of Mikki's leather-clad asscheeks, turning her a little until Leda could see the hankies in the pocket of Mikki's obviously custom-made pants. They fit like a glove on her firm ass.

"Sixty-nine is good..." Leda said in agreement, speaking to Mikki's butt and flipping through the tails of colored hankies with her fingertip: robin's egg blue, gray...

"...but I don't know you well enough for that yet," Leda continued. "A good beating by a strong but caring hand with a little torture and a lot of challenge is my taste. Yeah. Do you switch with the fisting or just top?"

Leda took a breath and looked back up, slowly, travelling over the impossible perfection of Mikki's thighs, ass, waist, small but ample tits, smooth round shoulders covered with creamy brown flesh, soft neck, beautiful high-cheekboned face. The face was smiling and a laugh was escaping through that incredible open mouth.

"Well, great!" Mikki laughed. "We must be meant for each other, destined to meet!" Her laugh was mellow and friendly, but there was serious passion in those eyes. She didn't pull away either. "Like I've been waiting all night for you to get here or something," she added.

Leda's gaze matched Mik's intensity and suddenly there wasn't room for any thoughts of Chrys or other considerations that had appeared before her as she'd first wrapped her arm around this new woman. There was just Mik, and their bodies together: tits, hips, thighs almost touching, and the rippled subtle flexing of the muscles in Mik's arms as she looked down slightly to gaze at the parted lips of Leda's mouth.

"Yeah," Leda whispered, definitely feeling an odd familiarity and uncharacteristic boldness.

"What about kissing?" Mikki asked in a quiet voice, her breath touching Leda's cheek as she spoke.

"Kissing is good," Leda whispered back. "Before we play, though, are you negative?"

"I am," Mik confirmed. "You?"

"Yep."

"No lies," the woman insisted.

"No lies," Leda agreed.

"And kisses are good?"

"Can be very very good," Leda replied.

The two women were now close against each other. Leda felt the rest of the club fade away. And to her surprise, without further ado, Mik leaned down into a deep kiss that seemed electrified with the energy between them, transferring back and forth in a frantic current and waking up every cell in Leda's body. Mikki's hands found Leda's hips and held them, but only tentatively, not overly intimate or aggressive, the passion escaping instead in their kiss, bonding them.

Leda's tongue found Mik's and they battled hungrily for command, Mik ultimately winning and orchestrating the ending of the kiss with the control of a good leader, top, commander…lover.

"Mmh," Leda said through a fog of passion, eyes lingering on Mikki's lips. "You taste good. And you won."

"Right back at you. Yeah, I did. You consent to it?" Mik whispered hoarsely, studying Leda's face, her eyes a wash of hunger, too, but smoldering, not wild untamed flames like Leda's.

Leda realized she meant for playing together, that whoever won control of the kiss won control of the scene…or maybe the night, if she was lucky. Leda wished she'd known, but liked it, too, that she didn't—and lost.

"Yeah," Leda answered thoughtfully. "For Round One. Do you switch for anything?"

"Not much," Mikki said honestly. "But you never know."

Her knee had found its way, subtly, up between Leda's legs, ever so slightly parting them, the ball of her booted foot still resting on the ground. Leda was delighted: someone more aggressive than herself! Although she often would get shy in groups, Leda wasn't, in general, especially once she got to know someone. In fact, when faced with another similarly strong character, she usually bristled and faced off with the person, not actually meaning to, just instinctively.

But tonight she fed on this woman's aggressiveness, glad for it and shocked by her own passive behavior when faced with someone maybe even more strong-willed than herself. There was something about Mik that turned her upside down, lowered her guard. It had been ages since she'd bottomed but she was surprised to see she hadn't lost the feel of it, the behavior and hunger for it.

"You like sex with your pain and torture?" Mik asked, obvious hope in her voice.

Leda smiled, pleased with Mik's upfront communication style and courage.

"I do," she said. "You practice safe sex?"

"I don't like it, but I do," she replied. "You?"

"Yeah, don't like it either, though."

"Then safe sex it is."

"Cool," Leda agreed.

"Do you like to get fucked by a woman who's just gotta have you?" Mik asked fearlessly, smiling.

Leda's cunt ached at the sound of the words and it answered for her with a throbbing beat she wondered if Mik could feel with her leg still up gently between Leda's thighs.

"Oh yeah," she said, running her hands over the outside of Mik's arms, admiring them, envisioning their strength when in use.

She looked up. "And I pack a mean fuck myself," she offered. "You up to the competition?"

Ah, there she is, Leda thought. The cocky butch inside her stood up to face off with Mik for a moment.

Mikki laughed her great amused laugh again. There wasn't a hint of anything but pleasure and amusement in it.

"I'm up for the possibility and challenge if you trust me to lead this one first...to, well, satisfaction."

Leda felt stupid for admitting it to herself and with a complete stranger, but she could feel it in everything about this woman that she could trust her, would trust her, maybe with her life if they committed to play that hard.

Well, maybe.

But definitely something special, and something that woke up a place in Leda that had no problem being the collar bearer.

"I don't know why, but I do trust you," Leda said. She felt a whimper of desire in her throat, the clothes on her body suddenly overwhelmingly constraining.

"Shall we start here and make our way up to the padded room for further testing?" Mikki asked, still gathering information but with a great deal of taste and flair—and sexiness, Leda noted. Practiced. Almost slick.

"You come here often?" Leda asked, leaning back, checking her out. "You know everything about this club?"

Mikki looked surprised, then chuckled. "Not too often, but yeah, I know the place. Never had an experience like this, though; I'm usually playing early on in the night, but like I said, guess I was waiting for you."

Her eyes sparkled and she seemed as surprised and dumbfounded as Leda. "Have you been here before?"

"No, my first time," Leda answered honestly. "But I learn fast. And I've been to other play parties."

Mikki nodded.

"Didn't think I've seen you here before. What other places do you like to frequent?"

"Oh, I haven't been...out...for a long time. I mean out to the sex clubs. I'm, well, really out of practice, you might say. Almost...," she considered the right wording, "...virginal." Leda said this a little shyly, surprised at her own honesty.

"You don't seem it," Mik said brightly, leaning in toward her, her eyes studying Leda's face.

"Well, almost virginal." Leda's eyes twinkled with mischief. "Uh huh," Mik pressed.

Leda was having fun with their banter. She loved it, in fact.

"You wanna show me the, uh, ropes here tonight since I'm such a, well, you know?"

"Oh, I do," Mik answered almost earnestly, no smile on her face now.

Leda's body hummed. "Well, now we've both said 'I do,'" she whispered, smiling. "So I guess we're, like, committed." Leda paused for a moment, feeling her body in this space, connecting with this woman. "Okay, I submit to you, Mikki," she said with finality. "To...satisfaction."

She couldn't believe she was saying this, how right and natural it felt to say such dramatic, but absolutely true words. Her life with Chrys felt far away, disconnected, and what opened up inside her like a bulb in the spring after a long cold season was a shedding of her usual control as the aggressor, the caretaker, the controller, the negotiator, the compromiser. This was something else, somehow truer than what she'd been doing for way, way, too long.

Leda watched Mik's face light up as she spoke the words of submission to her.

"And if you rip off my clothes, I won't beg you to stop either," Leda whispered like a challenge, leaning in toward Mik's ear to say it, her breath lingering.

"Oh, man, you make me wanna do it all at once, nice and nasty and cruel and kind," Mik hoarsely whispered back. She couldn't help but grasp Leda's hips hard, then move her hands around and grip Leda's ass in both strong palms, moving her hips in against Leda's and pulling her in.

Leda smiled and her breathing got a little ragged. She chuckled with pleasure down deep in her throat and pretended to resist.

"No, oh please, no, stop..." Then the chuckle escaped and she blurted out, "Oh fuck! where have you been all my life, woman?" Leda realized with horror that she asked this only half jokingly, but they both broke into all-out laughter. Leda couldn't help herself, though, pact or no pact, she had to have another one, couldn't wait suddenly. They had contracted, in a way, and she'd submitted to the passive role. But without thinking, Leda pushed in and took a kiss from Mik's surprised mouth without asking, interrupting their laughter. Those muscular arms wrapped around her then, Leda feeling the heat and pulse of Mikki's active body; active, hard... yeah...hard...really hard.

Leda was totally and completely shocked to feel a hard-on under Mik's pants and almost hooted and laughed out loud at how she'd picked a kindred packer; amazed even more at how hungry her body was for just such a pleasure, even without the promise of a switch. She was glad her own toys were in her bag tonight. In fact, if Leda hadn't been sober, she was sure she'd have jumped right into Mik's arms and wrapped her legs right around those strong gorgeous hips.

Leda didn't want to relinquish it, but somehow Mik took it without question—the control of the kiss—and ended it before Leda would have liked.

"What have you got on under those jeans?" Mik asked.

This caught Leda a little by surprise as she embarrassedly remembered what she was wearing.

"Um, you know, underwear...well, a thong sort of thang actually..."

Leda grimaced at her babbling and at her Victoria's Secret ultra-femme possibly-humiliatingly-so underwear choice. Really, she hadn't dressed thinking of actually playing. Well, mostly not.

But Mikki smiled, apparently not noticing her babbling, and actually seeming perfectly pleased with Leda's response.

"Oooo, girly lingerie, mmm, I love it. You're a surprise a minute! I like that."

Leda watched the smile fade and the commander slip in. An attendant passed by. "'Scuse me," Mik called out. The attendant turned, looked at Mik, and came back.

"Yeah, babe," the woman said in a friendly voice from behind a leather cat mask. Leda couldn't hear what Mik was saying to the woman, but she saw money change hands. The attendant turned and moved quickly away, her body language saying that she was definitely on a mission.

Mik turned back to her.

"So I don't think I'd wanna rip off your nice jeans, but there's definitely too much clothing between us. I'll take it from here if you don't mind," Mik told her, rather than asked. She commanded Leda gently and surely. To Leda, it felt completely natural and she slipped into the scene with absolute commitment and anticipation, surprised, but too caught up to be amazed.

"Yes, Mik," she said.

Mik smiled, a wicked and mischievous glint in her eyes, and obvious pleasure. She nodded her approval.

"Good girl," she said. "Let's begin."

Mik undid the ties on Leda's vest, her body moving with the beat of the trancelike music that filled the place as she undressed Leda. Rather than undoing the ties and slipping the vest up over Leda's head, Mik lingered, running her thumbs over Leda's hard buds and tweaking them lightly, squeezing her tits, and teasing Leda, who had been instructed to keep her hands at her sides. Then Mik pulled the cord completely out of the vest with a long tug, and the vest fell open, exposing Leda's chest, belly, waist. "Take it off," Mik told her.

Leda removed the vest and stood naked from the waist up.

"Off with the boots."

Leda squatted down and attended to her boots, setting them aside.

"Good girl. Well done—so far." Mik's eyes were playful, the edge of her mouth just barely turned up in a suggestion of a smile.

Leda blushed at the pride and pleasure she felt, how much she liked the approving words; pleasing Mik. She felt free with her body and her desires as she hadn't felt for years. It was like a rebirth into the sensation of her passion; into the ultimate exchange between two passionately attracted women.

Passionately attracted—that was the key. A key that had been missing in her life for how long now? The feel of it here, so strong, almost brought tears to her eyes, the intensity of it—but not quite.

Mik was in front of Leda, opening the zipper of Leda's jeans, slipping her strong hand inside just a little way, feeling Leda's heat, the muscles in her arms flexing and rippling as she maneuvered.

"Mmmmm, so hot, Leda, so wet. I think I'll have to teach you some control, girl. Yeah, a little control."

And with that she removed her hand and pulled Leda's jeans down hard, all at once, exposing her thong-covered mound. Leda stepped obediently out of her pants as Mik instructed. Mik set the pants aside with the vest and swung the horse into the center of the stage area—the middle of the cage if the doors were swung shut. At this moment, they were not. Mik moved the wide rectangular step stool in front of the horse, then glanced around.

Leda glanced around, too, suddenly remembering what room they were in; that she hadn't left the Viewing Room playroom.

Oh, Lord, she swore silently, don't let anyone I know be watching tonight... But the thought passed right out of her mind at the harsh sound of Mik's voice.

"I didn't give you permission to avert your eyes!" Mik barked.

Leda quickly looked back at her, attempting to stand taller, proud but quite naked except for her thong. She wanted to reach back and tug it out of the crack of her ass, but knew better. Mikki seemed to read her mind, but Leda had actually unconsciously moved her hand toward doing the deed, then stopped as she remembered her place.

"Bet those sexy fucking panties are driving you crazy, way up between your ass where they shouldn't be...." Mik smiled. "Bet you wish I would let you give them a good yank...."

The smile was wicked and wonderful and made Leda's cunt swell, which only worsened the panty situation.

"Yes," Leda said a little too emphatically.

"Yes, ma'am, when you answer."

"Yes, ma'am," Leda corrected obediently.

"Since we're strangers," Mik told her, "and it's our first time together…" Mik felt the throbbing of her sex as she envisioned fucking Leda. "…I'll let you choose the safe word this time. I prefer to have one, I hope you do."

"Yes, ma'am," Leda answered, thinking. "Justice."

"Justice. Okay, justice it is. You can prove there exists such a thing; I highly doubt it. I can't wait to test-drive you, see how far you go before you use it." She smiled her cruel smile again. "Approach the horse, Leda."

Leda moved forward and stood in front of the horse, facing it, as Mik stepped aside. Just then the attendant returned with a large black bag in hand. Out of the corner of her eye, Leda watched Mik take it from the woman. She thanked her and barely missed a beat, swinging the bag up onto the horse in front of Leda.

"I have a test or two for you, my slave, before I enter your body and fill you up and let you fly out into oblivion. First you take what I give you here, with these."

Mik opened her bag and withdrew three different whips: a cat, a rather soft-looking short whip, and a large, heavy-looking, beautifully crafted, thick long-tailed whip.

"But first I'll have to secure you because you might not stay still for me and that wouldn't do." She pulled out narrow shackles and chains with clips, which she secured to four hooks on the horse.

Just the words of what Mik was going to do to her melted Leda where she stood. Every inch of her was seduced into absolute submission. The sound of the metal clips as they closed around the hooks made her whimper just barely audibly. Mikki adjusted the height of the horse to a satisfactory level, then instructed Leda to lean over. She did. Mik took her wrists, shackled them, and secured each to a short chain that had been added to the hooks. Then, from behind, with her heavy boots she parted Leda's legs to a satisfactory width apart, shackled them, and secured each to chains that met at either side of the base of the horse.

"Tug," Mik said.

Leda tugged at each binding. They didn't give, and the length of the chain didn't allow any play so her legs were forced to remain open. The cool leather of the horse chilled Leda's skin as she bent over it, her tits squished in against it, resting there. Then Mik's hand reached into the crack of her ass and graciously pulled the thong free.

"Thank you, ma'am," Leda said sincerely.

"Yes, you learn fast. You will thank me for everything I give you. After each gift I give you. Understand?"

"Yes, ma'am."

And with that she pulled Leda's panties down around her ankles and left them there. Leda was appalled, feeling the rush of embarrassment at standing there with her panties down around her ankles, especially such froofy ones as these. She swallowed hard, hoping her pride would stay put.

The sound of a whip behind her caught her attention. The huge playroom was warm, especially their little area, and smelled of incense and sex. Leda listened as the music changed, one song melting into the next, following the bass beat. A single scream broke through the tapestry of the music like punctuation and the music carried it away. Leda shivered, but not with cold. Here she was: naked, bottoming to a strong-armed, obviously skilled top she didn't know. What if she had wussed out over the years; what if she couldn't take what turned her on anymore?

Take it, girl, she told herself, you can do it. Go with it, ride it, ride with her, connect with it. You haven't forgotten how to take it, all the way.

And then there was a strong hand rubbing Leda's back, kneading her muscles briefly, relaxing her; then caressing her sides, her ass, pushing through under her arms to grasp her tits and squeeze them gently, knead them, excite them. They continued up her back to her neck, where Leda's head hung down over the horse as she leaned over it. Mik's hands grabbed a handful of Leda's hair and pulled Leda's head back gently but with purpose. Lips caressed her right ear.

"I know you can take it," Mikki whispered passionately, straight into her soul. "Make me proud; show me your strength."

Leda felt a rush of adrenaline, everything melting into a desire to please, to be pleased. And as she relaxed into Mik's words—head returning to its original spot, looking out at the wall behind the horse, torso bent over, arms braced against the padded leather, wrists shackled to the heavy hooks—she could feel the floor beneath her, feet firm on parted, shackled legs, as steady as the whispered words.

And just as she slipped into a quieter place, guard down for just a moment, Mikki moved back away from her, and the whipping began. Light, rhythmic thwacks, lightly at first, with the soft-tailed shorter whip landed as an introduction against Leda's bare back. The music was a perfect rhythm for accompaniment and Mik was alive with the beat of the scene, her arm strong, body full of energy, completely tuned in to Leda and to the rhythm between them.

Behind Leda, Mik smiled, her eyes blazing with a mixture of sadistic pleasure and excitement as she discovered the landscape of Leda's naked body with the whip, landing here, there, watching for a reaction to each new spot, laying the foundation as they warmed up together.

"I will tell you when to thank me and I will expect you to, each and every time I say so, understood?"

Mik spoke to Leda as she continued the light whipping, slowly increasing the intensity, the tempo.

"Yes, ma'am," Leda answered, feeling her skin light up with each contact, the wetness of her cunt, the heat, even with her legs wide.

Mikki could see it, too, the silky wetness of Leda's sex between her open legs, asscheeks presented to her for her pleasure. She used it as a gauge, carefully watching the muscles of Leda's body and her ass, her cunt, watching all of it as the intensity of the whipping increased.

Leda breathed into it, anticipating each point of contact landing with purpose on her back, thwack! against her shoulders, ass, thighs, and back up to begin again. Leda's body was alive with concentration and sensation.

The softness of the short whip was replaced by a harder, stinging connection as the intensity of the blows increased, coming faster, more edgy. Leda wanted to turn and look at her delicious tormentor, but couldn't. Instead, she envisioned those arms in her mind, muscles flexed as Mik raised the whip in preparation, her whole body behind each blow. Leda could feel the electricity between them, the concentration. But most of all now she could feel the pain as Mik carefully orchestrated the scene to the next level.

Yes! Leda wanted to cry out, unable to contain herself. Oh, God, yes! Her voice pushed at her chest, her throat, wanting to release itself into the humid warm air of the playroom. But it wasn't allowed. She hadn't been given permission even to speak. Leda breathed carefully: control, control, she repeated silently to herself.

But then Mikki gave her a gift, just as she said we would. There was a brief pause, then Mik commanded: "Thank me! Thank me loud so I can hear you. I'll count for you."

"One!" Mik cried out, and Leda felt the first blow from the long, heavy-gauge whip as it smacked into her ass.

"Thank you!" she cried out almost automatically, her entire body flushing with pleasure and pain and determination. The tails were not wide, but thick and mean—the way she liked them best.

"Two!" Mik said as the whip flew into the air, then came straight down onto Leda's upper back.

"Thank you!" she cried again, feeling her skin burn with the whip's bite. Mik's arms were indeed strong, and Leda braced herself, wanting to take it, to please her, to prove herself not only to Mikki, but to herself.

Breathe, breathe…, Leda reminded herself.

"Three!" Mik hollered.

"Thank you," she half grunted.

"I can't hear you, speak up!" Mik told her loudly. "Four!"

"Thank you!" Leda hollered. "Ahh shiiit!"

"Just thank you, slave, that's all I want to hear from you!" came the command.

Mik and Leda continued this way, in a steady rhythm of pain, up to twenty-three, twenty-four…. And on the twenty-fifth blow, Leda let out a curse and a holler and gripped the horse, her legs unsteady beneath her, breathing hard, sweat stinging her eyes and flying off the tips of her spiky hair as she momentarily shook her head as if to shake off the pressurized pain that burned on her skin.

"Good girl," Mik said with great care and kindness as she stopped the whipping, approaching Leda from behind and kissing her angry skin, the light welts that stood up in a fury. She inspected her work: no skin broken, just a little tormented.

"Good girl," Mikki said over and over, lightly stroking Leda's waist with one hand, then down over her reddened ass, flat soft palm against it, then slipping down further between Leda's shaky legs from behind, palm against the heat of Leda's pussy, fingers lightly stroking her hard clit, playing in the wetness of Leda's swollen lips as they opened to Mik's touch.

"Oh, yes, oh, please, please," Leda breathed, unable to remain silent, her body on fire, the incredible rush of pleasure temporarily obliterating the rage of her skin, the echoing pain. Sweat stung the angry places on her back and ass, on her thighs. But all of it disappeared at the touch of Mikki's fingers on her sex, her clit hardening and straining for the woman's touch. Leda's empty cunt throbbed with longing she hadn't felt in what seemed a lifetime.

"Do you wanna be fucked?" Mik asked her in a husky voice. "Or should I make you wait?"

A desperate groan was all Leda could offer, unable to see or think behind the veil of her hunger, lost in the sweet wickedness of pain and heady pleasure.

"Maybe I should pin your tits and mask you, make you wait...."

How cruel you are, Leda thought, almost smiling. She didn't know Mik well enough to know if the woman really would make her wait or not, and the not knowing was the worst—and best— of all.

"Please," Leda begged as Mik continued to stroke her sex, her clit, but not fast enough or hard enough. And still Leda remained empty, aching with need, on the edge of being downright irritable.

"What do you want?" Mik asked in a hoarse, excited voice, watching Leda squirm. "Ask me nicely."

"Please, ma'am, please fuck me, please..." She could hardly catch her breath. "Touch me harder."

"Oooo, you didn't say please on that second one," Mik countered. "Hmmm."

"Please!" Leda begged, trying doggedly to press her cunt against Mikki's too-gentle hand. But the hand moved with her, making her beg, remaining lightly against her, with just the hint, the suggestion of contact.

Behind Leda, Mik smiled, feeling the incredible wetness of Leda's swollen, ready cunt. "But you're not allowed to come yet," Mik admonished. "Too soon. Uh uh."

Leda groaned loudly, a whimper mixed in with it, pulling at the chains that held her hands, frustrated, unable to do anything about this last word, this denial of release.

"Thank me for the discipline, for my skilled training of you," Mik directed.

Leda couldn't do that. No way. She couldn't thank Mik for denying her, not after bringing her to such a wild state of hunger, her clit feeling every breeze that passed between her spread and shackled legs. Leda remained defiantly silent.

"Thank me," Mik said again, an order this time.

Leda was enraged, almost out of control at the audacity of this woman's denial of her basic needs after Leda had taken her pain so well. She teetered at the edge of losing her temper, of forgetting her place and falling into the flames that entranced her, provoked her, controlled her.

But she didn't. Leda wasn't quite that gone yet.

This she realized as the braided cat-o'-nine-tails cruelly met the already raw skin of her ass when the required words did not obediently emerge from her mouth as ordered.

"Thank you!" Leda cried out, the words bursting from her lips, surprised into submission and obedience.

"Again!" Mik ordered as the cat whipped through the air and down again on the other cheek like jagged teeth biting into her tender flesh.

"Thank you!" Leda hollered again, sweat dripping down her face, the pain intense, stars flashing before her unfocused eyes.

"One more gift to you for your insolence," Mik said.

The cat crashed down across Leda's ass once more and this time Leda screamed out her thanks with enthusiasm, and desperation, the cry of a wild animal cornered by a predator, caught.

"Thank you!"

The sound blasted from her throat with emphatic force, the blow sending spikes of pain exploding outward like fireworks from her center and out her limbs, exploding her alive. Blood pounded through Leda's veins and in her head, blocking out the music, this place, the crowd, everything, her life force travelling at light speed through her entire body, only to be magnetized into a single point at the apex of her thighs, filling her clit to bursting.

"Good girl," Mik offered flatly. "Next time I trust you'll follow orders. Am I right?"

"Yes, ma'am," Leda answered automatically, her breathing ragged, vision cloudy with the distraction of her throbbing clit.

Mik approached Leda once again, but this time she dropped the whips into her bag as she passed it, moving around to the opposite side of the horse. She studied Leda, looking hard at her, gauging her next move, assessing the situation, determining if maybe she had been too hard on her new pet. But it was apparent that Leda was getting off on the whole orchestration, even though the obviousness of this was temporarily lost in an entertaining rage of indignation.

Mik smiled approvingly, her face beaming with enjoyment at the frustration she was causing, the pleasure of her power to control, to choose to cause either pain or pleasure at will.

"You take it well," she said gently to Leda.

Leda leaned heavily against the horse, head hanging down, the sweat on her chest gleaming as it pooled slightly between her cleavage, dripping onto and slippery against the leather of the horse beneath her. Droplets of sweat fell in a slow rhythm off the tips of Leda's soft, spiky hair as she breathed, lost in her body's sensations and the rush of willing herself to go the distance with this woman; to give it all up to her.

As the throbbing in her cunt subsided a little and the flaming skin of her buttcheeks began to cool, Leda found she could focus on her surroundings again. She lifted her head, which felt heavy.

There in front of her eyes was smooth naked olive skin above leather pants, the top button open seductively at the waist, the muscles of Mik's naked stomach easily visible beneath her skin, the indentation of her navel beckoning Leda's tongue—but too far away to reach. Leda raised her head higher, her eyes taking in the shapely curves of Mikki's waist, firm chest—not too small, but not large—sloping slightly down and up again at the tips, soft brown-pink nipples hard at attention. Mik's arms rested at her sides, the veins sticking out on her right bicep and forearm, even in a relaxed state, from the effort of her attentions. Leda's eyes travelled up again to smooth, round, muscular shoulders, then rested again on Mikki's inviting chest and lingered there, hungry for a taste.

Mikki watched Leda's hungry, appreciative eyes. She stepped closer, leaning forward and down slightly to line up one of her tits with Leda's mouth.

Out of her mind with passion, Leda opened her mouth at the first touch of Mik's nipple against the flesh of her lips and sucked in the hard bud, running her tongue around the soft skin and flicking the tip again and again, sucking and loving it. It felt to Leda as though a lifetime had passed since she'd been with another woman. Only this moment existed, the taste and texture of Mikki's sweet tit in her mouth, the after-effects of the woman's ministrations still lingering on Leda's marked flesh. Leda moaned with pleasure, forgetting her tied wrists that kept her restrained as she instinctively tried to reach up, to hold and stroke Mik's body. Finding the restraints denying her access, she sucked harder in frustration, the passion growing once again to an overwhelming pitch.

"Good girl," Mik whispered to her intimately, "no biting now. Yeah, like that. Mmm. Good."

Leda looked up at Mik's face then and saw the excitement in her eyes as Leda sucked and teased her hard nipple. Then Mik slipped gently out of Leda's mouth and moved the other tit to Leda's lips, running it against them first, not allowing her to have it yet, feeling the smoothness of Leda's mouth.

Leda opened wider, waiting, gauging, then closed suddenly on the hard bud as it passed, catching it and sucking it hard, licking the smooth surface around it. Desperately wishing for freedom of motion, Leda nonetheless obediently took what she was given, believing her longing for more to be well hidden. But with every taste of Mik's flesh, the heat between her legs became almost unbearably insistent and Leda, sensing the danger of this growing tide of frustration, had to gather all her strength, fight like a warrior against the urge to bite and cause pain to her tormentor, her goddess, the one who both denied and fed her.

On the receiving end, Mik watched Leda battle for control, then smiled slightly, closing her eyes, enjoying the sensations, blocking out the ones she would not allow until later. "Mmmm, yes, very good," she praised.

After a moment, Mik slid her breast out of Leda's warm moist mouth, then leaned in and kissed her deeply. They sought out each other's tongues and played with them as if they were clits, hard-ons, the key to the climax. Both women breathed heavily, completely, into each other and the music dancing around them, the scene—contact. The spotlights swirled around the play space, moving over them repeatedly as the beat fed them.

Mik took Leda's face in her hands as they kissed, leaning in against the horse, on the opposite side, grinding in just a little against it, feeling the dildo in her pants push back against her, anticipating the moment when there would be no horse between them, no leather containing her; just the force of her body, her muscles, the thrust of her hips opening the sweet passageway into Leda's hot body.

"Mmmm yes," she moaned into Leda's open mouth as she

ended the kiss. "Shall we move on?" she whispered hoarsely.
Leda looked into her eyes. How could she do it, deny her like
this, and herself? Was Leda the only one crazy with wanting?
Suddenly Leda was struck with consideration of a potentially serious problem: Maybe Mik didn't feel the same way Leda did, about
the fucking part. Maybe the tease was going to be everything and
enough for her. It didn't really appear that way, but...shit!

Maybe it's the Great Spirit of Chastity and Monogamy talking,
her head said loudly.

Oh shut UP! she angrily told the nagging voice, silently but with
great force. Don't even try and take me there.

And to her surprise, her head was silent.

Beyond it, the music blasted into another tune that turned sort
of dreamy, otherworldly, seductive. The spotlights stood still, but
tiny lights flashed and whirled from a myriad of slowly turning
disco-type balls and light fixtures that hung from the somewhat
high ceilings beyond the low-ceilinged area of their particular
play space. Leda temporarily floated out of her body and away
with the entrancing music.

When she returned after a moment, her eyes refocusing, Mikki
was removing the chains that secured Leda's wrists to the horse,
then unhooked the clips at her ankles. Leda stood up straight,
stretching her stiff back, feeling the ache of her skin. Without
thinking, she started to undo the buckles of the shackles on her
wrists; now that the chains no longer held her, of course she
wouldn't need these.

"Oh, hell no," Mik said, grabbing her wrist with great force.
"Don't even think about removing these, ever. My job. And I say
they stay on."

She resecured the buckle, turning Leda back around to the
horse, pushing her hard against it. Then she came in close, up
behind Leda, placing her entire body—naked torso and leather-

clad hips—up against Leda's naked backside. Mik's firm tits teased against Leda's back as she pressed in against her, hips and packed woman-cock pumping seductively against Leda's bare, welted ass.

"Damn, you look good enough to take right now and I do so want to. Mmm...shit...," she whispered.

Mik lost herself momentarily in the nasty hunger that could easily bring things to a quick finish if she let it. She moaned into Leda's short dark hair. There was nothing she liked more than to fuck a good hot woman who wanted her bad, like Leda did. And the energy between the two of them was beyond anything she'd experienced, by far. Anticipation pushed at Mik's control, her mind filling with ideas of how Leda would be with Mikki inside her, deep inside her and rockin' and rollin' as only two women can, as long as they want it, until they've both had enough. Would she scream? Would she swear and cry out? Would she call out Mik's name and beg her for more, open wider for her?

Christ, it was tempting.

"But...," Mik said aloud, unable to stop the rhythm of her hips as they continued to pump with the bass heavy, slow-ridin' R&B beat blasting through the playroom and finding its way into their scene.

Beneath her, Leda held her breath, eyes closed as every part of her concentrated on the meeting places of their bodies; the two moving together, her body opening to Mikki's thrusts, the hardness of the packed dildo now so obviously apparent against Leda's bare sensitive ass and thighs.

She wanted it so bad, she couldn't believe it. The sensation of aching and hunger was unlike anything Leda had ever experienced. Though Chrys had been nice enough to try to fuck Leda with a strap-on once or twice, it didn't work. Chrys giggled and was obviously uncomfortable.

Leda realized at that incredible moment of high-pitched passion that she had given up a lot to be with Chrys. She couldn't remember the last time she had been taken to the edge, blasted out of her skin with a little cruelty; overtaken and controlled by the friction and motion and thrust of an able woman. No one had ever really taken her, not where she ached to go, beyond all control and with a wicked hunger.

Not the way that she was sure that Mikki could...would. She was taking her there already. Spellbound. That's how Leda felt: spellbound with anticipation, curiosity...and hope. She groaned with excitement and frustration as Mik pumped against her through the animal skin, wanting so bad, trying somehow to will Mik's tool free of the leather that held it captive; the leather that rubbed against Leda with the heat of Mik's incredibly warm and alive body behind it, the electric energy of her humming right into Leda as she ran her hands down and up Leda's sides, sliding them over Leda's arms as Leda braced herself against the horse. Mik's tits against her back felt delicious, firm and soft and moist with sweat. Leda tried harder, with all her might, her mind, to will the fabric between them to melt away like a miracle, obliterate the only barrier between the thrust of Mik's incredible thighs and hips, and Leda's heated cunt.

Please give it to me, she wanted to beg, please fuck me, take me, blast me wide open. But she knew better now. Disobedience, though it had its place, was not the route to pleasure here.

Mik kissed Leda's neck, bit it playfully but with a sting of purpose, almost breaking the skin. Leda drew in her breath, shutting her eyes tight. Mikki changed sides, sucking hard on her soft skin almost to pain, stopping just before Leda felt the need to holler. She breathed hard, her heart beating through her entire body, barely drowned out by the music and Mik's mesmerizing voice as she continued.

"I'm going to take you on your hands and knees, my slave, take you hard and wild and with nasty intentions—the same as yours—with no mercy." Mik's breath was ragged, her words heavy with passion. "I wanna hear you scream, Leda. I wanna hear you beg me for more. And I won't let you come, not until I say so."

She paused to bite the top of Leda's shoulder, then kiss it. Pain, then sweetness... Mik smiled to herself, a knowing smiling that seemed to say aloud that tonight, yes tonight she would get what she wanted, exactly what she wanted. She spoke in an intense, breathy whisper into Leda's ear, a word or two tumbling out full force in a sort of gravelly moan every now and then, the dam pressing against Mik's control, too.

"Then I'll flip you over, girl, tie you up in the sling and slip my lubed and hungry fist into your hole and fill you up to bursting; fuck you until you can't stand it, until I feel gracious enough to work your clit into a frenzy. And then, when I'm good and ready, and you can't hold it anymore, maybe I'll let you come, explode your body with pleasure. Maybe. If I feel like it. If you're real good."

Mik's voice got progressively more husky and intense as she described her plans to Leda, punctuating with hungry kisses, bites, taking Leda's hair in her hands and pulling her head to the left to get a better patch of her neck and suck it again like a creature of the night. Leda half wondered if Mik really wanted to sink those teeth into her soft neck, Mik's passion was so intense as if for blood, meeting Leda's passion breath for breath. Leda melted, panting under the rain of Mik's erotic words in her ear, her tough affections, telling Leda what was in store—her so-tasteful way, Leda noted, of offering the chance to use the safe word if any of the above went beyond her zone, her agreement.

Yes, was all she heard in her mind, yes yes, all of it, everything you've got...

Mikki was quiet for a moment, letting her words sink in. Her hands explored Leda's body as she leaned in against her from behind, her hands slinking around Leda's waist, around to her pelvis, strong hands pressing in a diamond shape around Leda's mound, the very tops of her thighs, around her pubic hair, as if framing the object of her desire. Contact, of course, would be denied until Mikki decided otherwise.

Leda held her breath for a moment, feeling Mik's fingers so close, so close to her clit, to the moist opening of her sex. She would have done almost anything to get that touch, to win that caress tonight, Leda realized. She knew that the trust and openness she felt toward this woman seemed ridiculous and naive on the one hand. But on the other hand, it made perfect sense because she felt as though she had known Mik for years, a sense of intense familiarity and almost joyousness at connecting—more like reconnecting—with her; as though they'd known each other all their lives, just as Mikki had said.

"Shall we proceed?" Mik asked suddenly in a voice full of anticipation, bringing Leda back to the moment. Leda wanted to tell her everything, share everything.

"Yes, yes, please, yes, ma'am," Leda stuttered, the words tumbling over themselves as she fumbled with her words, trying to form the right phrase, flustered. Oh God fucking heavenly shit yes yes and yes! she really wanted to holler. Instead, she said it all with her eyes as Mik turned her around. Face-to-face, Mik smiled in return, her eyes mirroring Leda's sentiments exactly.

"Then let us move on," she said.

Surprising Leda completely, Mik moved forward and grabbed Leda around the legs, catching her off balance and forcing her to lean over Mik's shoulder like a cavewoman's prize after a good hunt.

"Come on, girl, I get to take you now, you're all mine!" she playfully roared into the room, ending with a laugh of delight as the thrill and the rush of the night washed over her.

Lying across Mik's shoulders, Leda had to hang her shackled

hands down Mik's back and they bounced as Mik moved away from the table. A few of the wild leather dykes in the room had responded to Mik's roar with replies of their own: "Shit yeah!" and "Hell yes, mama!" and "Go for it!" and "Watch out, girl!" and wolf whistles in support of what was about to take place.

But before Leda could get in a position to raise her head and check out who was in the room, Mik was laying her down on her back in the black leather sling that connected to the ceiling with heavy-duty silver chains, each wrapped around the other in a pattern of bondage and discipline that would hold Leda's naked body in a firm grip. In a flash, Mik had Leda's wrist shackles apart, then each attached to the chains at the top on either side of Leda's head. She did the same with Leda's ankles—still-smarting ankles—and secured them to the chains at the other end which faced the large room. The scene continued.

"Want me?" Mik asked, her face bright with excitement as she leaned in from the side, running her smooth hands over Leda's vulnerable body, lightly with her fingernails over Leda's round tits, tense belly, a tease of a stroke over Leda's sex, up her sensitive thighs as Leda's legs opened wider from just the suggestion.

"You better want me because you're going to have me, all of me, as much as I want to give you because you're a slut, you know it. Sex-starved, want it all. Don't you, Leda? Don't you want it all?" Mik teased, playing her with words, taunting Leda.

"Yes," was all Leda could answer, her body on fire, responding to Mik's words, to the curve and swell of Mik's naked torso, the beautiful cheekbones of her face, strong shoulders, firm tits with hard buds that Leda fucking ached to suck again, to suck and bite and flick with her tongue. And those hands, those strong hands that were slipping on black rubber gloves with gauntlets now. Leda groaned, imagining what those gloved hands might do to her, and yes, fucking yes, she wanted it all!

"I was gonna fuck you with my hard dyke dick, Leda, but I think you need more than I've got to give you, faster than my hips could pump into your incredibly beautiful cunt that needs the very best, mmm hmm." Her voice was intense, low, almost a whisper, as she slathered lube all over her right gloved hand and wrist.

"I'm gonna take you now, Leda, fill you up completely because that's what I wanna do, I just have to do it now. See what you do to me? See what you make me do?"

Leda was breathing in ragged excited breaths, her head spinning from the wild pumping of her heart in her chest as she lay with her body open wide for all the women to see. She could see them watching, could even hear one dyke say quietly, but insistently, "Fuck her, yeah, she needs a good fuck, you can see she's a bratty one..."

"You stay with me now, Leda girl, only with me..." Leda's mind reconnected with Mik's voice as Mik leaned in between Leda's open legs, eyes riveted on Leda's face, keeping Leda with her. Leda clutched the chains with her hands. Mik slipped two fingers into Leda's open cunt; they slipped in easily and Leda's eyes closed for a moment as she felt Mik enter her body, clutching Mik's fingers with her still-capable muscles.

"Oh God," she whispered, "yes..."

Mik let Leda speak, slipping a third finger into her forgiving cunt, slowly pumping into Leda's body that seemed to feed itself to her, as if each were feeding the other in the exchange. As Mik began slowly to fuck her, Leda breathed hard, feeling the sweat pooling along her back. The smell of sex surrounded them, the sweet smell of fresh lube mixing with her own juices and Mik's sweating body close to hers at last, leaning in with her shoulder as she slid a fourth finger into Leda's willing body.

"Yeah, oh yeah, I can take it, give it to me, Mik, give me what you've got...," Leda whispered hoarsely, insistently, not a command, but an impassioned plea, dare, hope. Leda's clit was pounding with the pressure of a much-needed climax, aching to move toward it with the sure touch of Mik's tongue, of her touch on Leda's clit. Leda moved her hips hard into Mik's hand that was slowly sliding in and out of her pussy, seducing her open, open...

"Oh yes, oh fuck me, oohhh yeah...," Leda groaned as Mik squeezed more lube into her now barely exposed palm, four fingers inside Leda already, covering her thumb and all the rest with a thick coat of lube. And as soon as that was done, Mik looked up at Leda's face and their eyes met. Ready? Mik's eyes asked. Oh please, Leda's answered. And with a long, strong, slippery thrust, Mik's thumb tucking in tight as she felt Leda's muscles relax, inviting her in, she slid her fist into Leda's cunt, filling it completely.

"Oh, yeah, oh fuck yeah, aahhhh...," Leda moaned, lost in a waterfall of pleasure and sensation that thrilled through her body. She wanted to cry, to scream, to howl with the incredible pleasure that was like a smorgasbord of food and drink after an eternity lost in the desert somewhere. But her words barely escaped her mouth, so controlled had she become. She took Mik's fist and held it, warmed it, welcomed it into the deepest recesses of her hot, tight hole.

Mik began slowly to pump her fist into Leda's cunt, leaning in to listen to Leda's words, feeling the woman's need for a release of sound. Just then the music segued into a new song and for some reason Mik noticed it: "Wicked," by an artist whose name she couldn't recall at the moment. She loved the song. The lyrics slithered through the room and into Mik's ears.

"I wanna be in her while you're in me, and then the three of us will truly see the light...ooohhh wicked, that's how I feel tonight..."

Mik's face lit up, her eyebrows rising, and she turned her head, still pumping into Leda's sweet body, her own cunt slick with excitement, pressing her clit against the firm flesh of the dildo in her jeans as she worked her fist deep in Leda's body. With her head, she motioned for a woman watching nearby to come forward. The woman nodded and approached her.

"Grab the vibrator that's in my bag there, would you mind?" she asked in a whisper. The woman kneeled down and withdrew the vibrator, then looked up as Mik whispered something else to her. The woman smiled—at least that's all Leda saw when she looked down to try and see what was going on: a woman in a neat blue cop suit, hair slicked back away from a strong, attractive face beneath the cop cap, a smile creeping across it now, a mischievous one. The best kind, Leda thought.

The woman disappeared from Leda's view again, then reappeared at Leda's side. Caught off guard, Leda self-consciously saw herself as she must appear from the woman's view: laid out buck naked, tits jiggling as the black leather sling rocked with their sex, her hands gripping the chains as if for dear life, knees rudely wide and accepting all of Mik's strong, sweet fist, breathing hard, hair wild, certain her face was flushed and exposing...

But Mik was moving faster now and Leda was shiny with sweat, completely at Mik's mercy, out of control and unable to stop the moans and groans and small cries that escaped from her lips as her body was filled and pumping with the pleasure of Mik's strong arm and fist. It didn't matter who was joining the party at that moment; Leda could hardly see through the crimson pleasure that draped across her view, blocking out events around her. She felt isolated in her own intense sensation, her body a vehicle in flames, Mik's ministrations creating a vacuum that sucked her deeper and deeper still into their trancelike sex. The blood in her veins blasted through her body, crashing through at double speed, every drop making its way to her swelling cunt and engorged clit as it pounded out a path toward ecstasy.

The cop held a magic wand in one black leather– gloved hand. Leda had watched her lean in and had tried to hear what Mik had said to her just a minute ago, but was unsuccessful. The woman didn't say a word now, but switched on the vibrator with a whir of the little motor. Leda didn't notice: She and Mik were connected like one life form, connected by fist to cunt, eye to eye, rockin' and rollin' together as Mik's body rippled with the workings of the muscles in her shoulders, chest, arms, biceps tight, triceps flexing.... Leda had watched Mik's incredible body from the beginning and now the image hung in her mind as she closed her eyes under the tidal wave of sensation. She could see Mik even with her eyes closed, connected by heat and desire, by their minds....

"... so go on and light your cigarette, but only after the feelin' is gone...cuz me I guarantee I can make you last 'til dawn, yeah that long...ooohhh wicked, that's how I feel tonight...," the singer sang.

The music found its way into Leda's mind, too, and she smiled slightly, the appropriateness of the lyric almost too perfect. But any thoughts other than the pleasure and desperation she felt as her body was worked into a frenzy quickly passed, dissipated in the moist heat around the three women. The pounding beat of the music mixed with the rhythm of Mik's fist as it thrust and fucked Leda again and again.

Mik's eyes were like lasers on Leda's face as she worked the woman; Leda could feel her watching and, with great effort, raised the heavy lids of her eyes that were filled with a million intense pleasures, wanting to watch Mik fucking her, to see the wild rush of their sex in her eyes. And she did—saw everything as their eyes met. Leda gripped the chains tighter. Mik quickened the pace, pumping faster as she watched Leda's belly tighten, the woman's eyes glaze over, the muscles of her cunt flickering with zaps of electrical pleasure that lit around Mik's fist as Leda's cunt muscles tightened their hold.

But even this deep into it, Leda could still feel the embarrassment of her position, and doggedly she tried not to make a lot of noise, feeling keenly aware of the need for control, here in a public place, with a woman she hardly knew beside her. But the pressure of this wanting, this aching for release—for a fucking wild, raucous, unbridled release—was more than she could handle. It had been too long and too long a night, teased and played like a puppet right into this woman's able hands....

So when the cop ever so unobtrusively slipped the round head of the vibrator down onto Leda's throbbing clit, Leda lost control completely and cried out with a deep groan that rose to a wail, and then to words: "Yes, oh fuck!" The vibrator summoned all the blood in Leda's body to the one fine point at the tip of her clit. The throbbing of her cunt around Mik's hand as the woman fucked her madly grew and expanded, one pressure front building over another. The vibrator hummed and seduced her pleasure until the force inside Leda became desperate, beyond desperate, a massive balloon inside her blowing up to inhuman proportions, trying to force its way out through the one point on the swollen tip of her throbbing clit.

Leda couldn't feel the metal then as the chains that she gripped dug into her soft hands, knuckles turning white as she shut her eyes tight and threw her head back, holding her breath as the pressure broke out in a million crashing pieces, blasting through her and out out out with a wailing cry and scream and holler of sweet release—out through her open mouth and into the wooden dungeon. She arched into the hands of the two women and bucked again and again as her clit exploded, her cunt gripping Mik's fist in a death grip of orgasm, clamping and releasing over and over, then pushing, forcing, rocketing it out from her pounding body.

"Ohhhh, God, yes, aaaahhhhhhhh…!" she screamed. But the cop kept the vibrator at its home base, electrifying Leda's clit in a continuous wave until the pleasure turned almost to pain, so extended was Leda's clit, her entire body an intricate highway of rushing blood and electrified nerve endings.

"No, please, no more, stop, ah shiiiit!" she said hoarsely.

Leda bucked again and again, breathing hard, arching her naked body, narrow rib cage rising and falling, nipples hard buds on tits thrust high into the air, lungs filling again, then holding as she gritted her teeth against the barrage, her body tensed in response to the continuous now over-stimulation. She couldn't breath for the overwhelming sensation. And as the experience peeked—and she was sure she'd have to scream to make it stop since she was powerless to do so any other way—like a drowning person, Leda made a decision just to let go, to fall into the powerlessness rather than try to escape it. She wasn't altogether sure she had any other choice at this point.

But the change in attitude caused a change in her body. Like a miracle, her clit seemed to recede, step back and take a breather beneath its hood; still feeling the vibration but cloaked from it. But really her clit was just reloading, gathering up the blazing tips of nerves from all corners of her sweating, shining body and building the pressure once again.

Leda concentrated, tried to resist but barely able to pull in enough air to stop the spinning in her head. She opened her eyes and met those of the uniformed woman head-on. The cop looked out at Leda from under her low-slung cap and dark eyebrows. A wicked smile curled the corners of the woman's thin-lipped mouth. Her eyes were light gray with intense points of black in the middle, rimmed with a thin line of black that made them appear incredibly light, almost colorless; strange.

A weird open place you could fall into, Leda thought, sweat stinging her eyes as she blinked, suddenly feeling the impact of this stranger's stare, harsh and ravenous; eyes that would not accept a bargain, a deal, a plea, to be sure. Leda suddenly wished she could pull her legs closed against this woman, feeling too exposed for those eyes. Her discomfort began to grow, but still the hum of the vibrator continued, pulling her attention back to the point of contact. Though she tried, Leda could not coerce her clit away from its hungry journey back to the vibrator's touch—to the woman's touch, then, too, and who knew what else.

Was this what Mik wanted to do with her? Hand her off to someone else? Maybe this wasn't such a good idea after all, Leda thought.

"No, stop," Leda whispered to the woman, for the first time that night almost imploring in her tone of voice, on the edge of using the safe word just to stop this uncomfortable game. It must have been apparent, because Mik's familiar intimate tones filled her world then.

"Don't worry, Leda girl," Mik was whispering into Leda's ear, having approached from the side, fist no longer sunk deep in Leda's body, and now leaning in, running her long fingers through Leda's short wild hair. She kissed Leda's forehead with incredibly soft, firm, warm lips, moving behind Leda to the back of the sling. Leda sighed, immediately slipping back into the trance of Mik's voice and passion, unable to find the track her thoughts had been following only seconds before.

"She has strict orders, this one," Mik said in her husky whisper. "Only my hands on you, that's the rule. She only has one job and I told her to stay on you, not to give in, no matter how you begged. You see, I'm in charge here, don't worry my slave. Just relax, relax into the pleasure." Her tongue slowly ran a path over the curve of Leda's ear, arousing Leda with her hot breath.

"I know it's there, coming around again; let it come, I can see it coming, see the flush just under your skin. Your tits are so hard, slave, your hungry muscles seeking out that touch, you know it's true. You want it, don't you?" Mikki asked.

Leda didn't respond. Mik waited.

"Talk to me, Leda, tell me you do, want it," Mik said, entwining her fingers in Leda's brown locks and giving them a tug. Leda sucked in her breath.

"Open your eyes and tell me you want it, you want more, whatever I have to give you. Tell me you want everything I want to give you," Mik commanded now, though her voice never rose a decibel, just increased in intensity.

"Yes, yes, I want it," Leda almost whimpered, a fly in the web, the same web, again; over and over. She just wasn't learning, she knew it. But there was something that lured her to this woman's game, beyond what she wanted and into what she didn't even know she wanted, until after.

Oh, but she did want it.

"I do want you, what you have to give me," Leda admitted out loud, her breath ragged, body still tense but slowly melting into the sound of Mik's seductive words, body humming like the sound of the vibrator still on her clit.

"Good. And, oh, I do have something for you. And I just know you can go further than this. I have faith in you, Leda girl. Faith."

Mikki's hands slid over Leda's face then, the woman standing, still, at the crown of Leda's head, an ungloved finger on her left hand sliding across Leda's open mouth, outlining her lips. And Leda was hungry again, the familiar sound of Mik's voice blocking out the outside attendant busy at her clit, creating safety in an atmosphere of danger, her body willing in Mik's able hands. She felt drugged by her own desire and the energy that their scene brought to the room; a connection with this woman that she had never felt with anyone before.

She sighed and shivered as Mik ran her open palms down over Leda's tits, running light circles over the hard tips. The gentleness was exquisitely unbearable and Leda squirmed under Mik's touch. Then the hands were travelling down to Leda's tense belly, Mikki's beautiful torso and tits momentarily bending down over her captive, almost close enough for Leda to nip at, or flick her tongue out for a taste. But before she could consider either, the hands doubled back with a vengeance, fingernails dragging an "I still mean business" path back up across Leda's belly and up to her chest where fingers squeezed and twisted her nipples painfully.

Leda groaned, though she really wanted to scream out her pain. She did not, but she could not control her instinct to pull her body back away from the pain, wonderful as it was. A sudden slap, meant more to get her attention than to cause real pain, reminded Leda of who was in charge.

"Stay still," Mik commanded, "don't move until I tell you to." And then the hands were gone, leaving her tits throbbing in their wake, her clit humming with the vibrator's insistent contact, though it moved over her mound every now and then, and down over her wet open lips, then back to its target.

Leda's eyes darted, following Mik as the woman moved around the sling at a slow pace. Mik leaned down and momentarily disappeared; Leda knew the play bag was there, but what Mik was doing in it remained unknown to her. Leda's ears strained to distinguish any clues as to what was going on below her rudely open legs. The soft flesh of her thighs left her exposed, feet still held captive by the sling, and she blushed profusely as her eyes travelled down to the light brown hair on her mound which was now half covered by the large white head of a vibrator, actually an extension of the pale hand with neatly trimmed nails which gripped it. Caught off guard, Leda moaned as the woman moved the head of the vibrator over her sex, calling her back, hitting a spot that sparked her entire body back to life.

"Oh, shit," she whimpered, not wanting to respond to this woman, but only to Mik. But she couldn't help it, her hot sweaty ass seemed to lift off the leather sling of its own accord. Out of the corner of her eye, she saw the cop smile. Like a tangible blow, Leda felt the humiliation blast into her and she hated it, hated the woman. But still the pleasure continued at her clit, commanding her body and too much of her mind. She tried to breathe through it, but it was too much. The cop's hand teased her, moving the vibrator over and around her now attentive clit. Again, her hips rose of their own accord and Leda moaned.

The moan quickly turned into a cry of surprise as Leda felt a pressure against her ass. Her eyes flew open, afraid the cop had overstepped her bounds. But it wasn't the cop. She turned to see that Mik stood tall between her legs, obviously on a step of some sort because the wickedly long dick that hung between her strong naked thighs was dressed with a shining condom and poised at Leda's exposed asshole, ready to make its way into her world.

And before Leda could take another breath or tense up, Mik slid the head of the long dildo into Leda's relaxed ass, plunging the tool in with one long steady thrust of her hips. And in a flash, Mik's hips were flush against Leda's asscheeks, hands holding onto Leda's legs as they hung, parted, on either side of her.

Leda cried out then. Swore and screamed into the room as her ass was filled to the bursting point with Mik's long, hard rod. The vibrator continued its dance. Leda opened her eyes and looked out through a haze at Mik standing, face wild with desire, between her open legs, face intensely concentrated on the tool plunging into Leda's pink asshole. And like a volcano kept simmering for way too long, Mik was explosive with her passion. After two brief, but kind, slower, easier thrusts, Leda tried hard to keep her eyes open to watch Mik's incredible body as it finally got what it wanted. But far too quickly, the rhythmic thrusting increased in speed, Mik plunging into Leda's open body harder and harder with each re-entry. Mik leaned into Leda, holding both of Leda's ankles in her strong grip, her face a wild display of hunger, intention, and lust.

Leda was on fire, her ass was on fire, her clit, too. Her body pounded as the women both took her hungrily, feeding her own ravenous appetite as they ate her alive. The electricity of their sex fried Leda's body as she climbed again toward climax, eyes threatening to close. But she didn't want to miss this. Mik was incredible, her skin shining with sweat and the muscles in her stomach rippling as she thrust and pulled out, thrust and pulled out, faster and faster now. The contact of the base of the dildo against Mik's female form was a vision that filled Leda's imagi-nation. Her mouth watered just thinking about Mikki's pussy beneath the hard dyke cock that blasted away inside her ass, crash-ing the passion into her faster and faster now.

Mik grunted and growled as the pressure of her approaching orgasm shimmered over her flushed skin, pressing against her control. Leda couldn't help it then, but closed her eyes as the vibrator doggedly began to coax an orgasm from her pulsing clit, a million points of sensation flaming to life inside her. Mik fucked her in the ass, launching into her again and again like a rocket, slamming into Leda's forgiving flesh, boring her out like a hot metal rod, taking all of her in its wake. And as Mik plunged deeply, Leda raised her hips and gave herself to Mik, and to the cop's insistent command of the vibrator that opened the tiny doorway that Leda's orgasm now blasted through, all valves open for the floodwaters this time, no holding back.

Leda screamed into the room, thrashing her throat with her

animal cries. At the sound of Leda's orgasm, Mik blew, too, pumping madly into the woman and crying out in a guttural cry of release, "Yes! Yes! Fuck, oh, uhn!" Mik groaned and forced her strong hips in tight against Leda, thrusting the tool in just as deep as it would go with tiny thrusts just to get it in a little more, if possible, her clit flush against Leda's ass.

Leda felt her orgasm take hold deep in her gut, felt it grip her very soul and fill it with a rush of energy that expanded out and away, at last, soaring and bursting out through the tip of her clit and this time, this time she took Mik with her, the sound of their voices echoing off the walls.

Mik, Leda, and the cop—whose name turned out to be Bobbie—sat at a small round table in the jungle eating exotic fruit salad from clear plastic cups.

"God, I'd swear I'm stoned, this shit tastes so fucking good!" Leda said in amazement, keeping her voice low but enthusiastic. She sat wrapped in a big white towel, one edge tucked into the wrap to keep it closed.

Mik looked at her: Leda's face was flushed a soft pink from the night's events and a cool dip she'd taken in the river as Mik had sat on the shore, legs leather-clad once again, but dangling her bare feet in the cool water while she talked with Bobbie, who crouched, fully clothed, beside her. Mik liked the look of Leda's hair like this: slicked back away from her face and glistening under the lights.

"You really look different without your hair all spiked out," Mik noted out loud.

Leda looked at her. She didn't know what to say to Mik's comment and "oh" didn't even seem like a fair choice. So she didn't say anything. But their eyes met and stayed that way for a long minute.

Bobbie the cop tossed her own empty fruit cup into a waste-basket nearby and ran her tongue over her lips. The woman was still in full cop regalia, which got her plenty of attention from interested bottoms that seemed to be sort of passing by in a pretty regular pattern or hovering like flies over an especially sweet find.

"Well, ladies," Bobbie said, pushing up from her chair where she had been sitting next to Mik, "the night is still young and I have yet to find me a woman worthy of me taking off my uniform."

Both Leda and Mik broke their gaze and craned their necks to look up at Bobbie with indignant looks on their faces.

"Thought that would get your attention!" A wry smile creased her usually reserved face. "But, hey, no offense intended. You know this was a...special situation." She winked at them. Mik leaned back in her chair, then reached out and swatted Bobbie's butt as she moved slowly by.

"Oh, you go get your fillies, Bobbie. Don't you dare let all that sexy uniform and preparation go to waste!" Mik grinned at her friend. "And thanks for the favor; I owe you one." Both women grinned then.

"Yes, you do. I'll talk to you soon, Mik," Bobbie added through her smile. "Pleasure meeting you, Leda. We'll have to explore this further sometime."

Leda couldn't see Bobbie's eyes behind her sunglasses, which had yet to leave the woman's face, but she nodded her head in response, smiling. Sure, what the hell, Leda thought good-naturedly.

Bobbie moved off into the milling crowd of half-naked and naked women. Reggae strains seemed to feed her movements as she moved away from Leda and Mik toward the river's edge, danc-ing a little as she went. A small crowd of naked dancers on the island in the middle of the river started a round of whoops that moved like a wave through the crowd across from the island, along the shore, to the women seated at the small umbrellaed tables and those hiding in the foliage, doin' the nasty or making out or just hiding out together. The waterfall continued its endless cascade. And what a night it was.

Leda sighed, putting aside her empty cup and leaning in on her elbows. Mik leaned in, too. Leda smiled at her.

"Thanks," she said, "for a really incredible night."

"My pleasure," Mik replied. "You're fun to play with, bold. You really trusted me and you hardly know me. Pretty awesome."

"I know, damn, that's the weirdest thing!" Leda agreed. "I don't know what it is, but there's something. I just..."

Leda looked up, words not forming into complete sentences. And there was Mikki, long dark wavy hair down at last, loose and beautiful around her glorious face, creamy olive skin and high cheekbones, brown eyes bright with intelligence and a continuous sparkle of mischief. Without thinking, Leda leaned in on a rush of passion and kissed Mik's soft mouth, her eyes closing as Mik kissed her back. It was like a connection of pure matter; you couldn't see it, but it was there, tangible between them as they lingered in the connection.

The kiss ended. They opened their eyes and looked at each other.

"Mmm," Leda said.

Mik pooched out her lips a little and nodded her agreement, eyes resting on where her mouth had just been. Leda pulled her gaze away and panned the jungle room, trying to get herself together.

"It's pretty late," Leda said with regret.

"Got somewhere you have to be?" Mik asked, sitting back in her chair, opening her legs noticeably. She'd unpacked her leathers, that is, stowed the dildo in her play bag, leaving her pants fitting a bit looser. Now all Leda could think about was Mik's bare snatch under the thin layer of leather. Leda knew it was close to 5:00 A.M. because the club had called one more hour to closing: there was no alcohol served after 2:00 A.M., but the club stayed open until 6:00 A.M. for playing, swimming, eating, or drinking non-alcoholic beverages.

Leda considered Mik's question.

"Well, yes and no. I've been babysitting tonight," she said with a grin.

"Oh," Mik answered, almost a question, understanding appearing on her face. Then she added mischievously, "And was I a good baby?"

"Oh, man, the best," Leda said emphatically, smiling. "I think my discipline was lax, though."

"Mmm. Then maybe I'll see you here again sometime for another shot; sometime soon," Mik said, "real soon."

"Yeah," Leda answered, "definitely." What else could she say? She meant it, wanted it. Everything was changing tonight, opening up possibilities she hadn't considered for years that made her blood pump with passion and enthusiasm. She felt revived after a long, long sleep.

There was a pause as the two women sat side by side, not wanting the night to end, but both a little unsure of how to proceed.

"You're one helluva good lover," Leda said, wanting to make sure Mik knew just what a great night this had been, how grateful she was for it.

"Thank you," Mik said. "I do my best. Nice woman to make lo...um, play with," Mik added, her brows furrowing for a moment, then her face returning to a smile. "Well," she said, rising from her chair. "C'mon then, I'll go help you change, then walk you to your car." She winked at the offer to help Leda change.

"Aren't you leaving yet?" Leda asked.

"Yeah, soon, why? You need a ride home? A place to stay for the night maybe? A place to move into, someone to spend the rest of your life with?" She smiled that open smile that just seemed to glow with charm and chuckled at herself. "I got a place with room to spare, at least for one more anyway."

"Damn, Mikki, you are hard to resist. And I don't really want to resist, but I...I got a few things to figure out first. Can I hold on to that offer and get back to you on it? Maybe call you?"

Mik's business card appeared between her fingers like a magician's trick. "Call me anytime. I'm not in the phone book, so hang on tight to this. No phone at your place?" she asked.

"No, not really," Leda answered, embarrassed, looking down for a moment. When she looked back up she said, "But I promise, if you really want me to, that I will give this one some good hard thought."

"Agreed," Mik smiled seriously. "Take your time. But don't forget lonely ol' me here at the sex camp for girls pining away for my perfect partner. If you know what I mean."

"Oh, I do, I do," Leda said, smiling.

Mik leaned in and kissed Leda on the cheek. "I'll be thinking of you," Mik said. Leda wanted to reach out and hold that beautiful face in her hands and kiss it for hours. But she had other obligations that she cared about as well. And some hard decisions to make. She sat there, head close to Mik's after the kiss.

"Well, c'mon then," Mik said, reaching for Leda's hand. "Let's get you dressed and outta here."

The two women rose from their chairs, tossed their garbage in the can. Leda didn't take Mik's hand, but stood equal beside her, not willing to play the femme. Mik smiled and nodded. Together they headed toward the archway back to the elevators, talking easily, shoulders almost touching as they moved through the crowd to the changing room.

EULOGY FOR A BUTCH
Chea Villanueva

W e called our group La Macha. There were three of us, and we were all butches. Franky Aguilar was the oldest, then Denise Cruz (who we called "Dennie"), and me—Jamie Delos Reyes, I was the youngest. All three of us were Filipino and good-looking in that gangster sort of a way, with our black hair slicked back DA style, tan skin, and mysterious deep brown eyes. We were always together and always had a lot of pretty women hanging on us. The girls all thought Franky was cool, had a nice smile, broad shoulders, and strong arms. Dennie had a good sense of humor and made the ladies laugh. And me—I was the smooth talker. Dennie always said I could corrupt a saint, and Franky said I could charm the panties off a virgin. What mattered was we were all polite, and the women loved us for it.

But Franky was definitely the dresser. In my memories of Franky, I can still see her wearing those expensive Italian suits, and the silk shirts she had especially made. She was older, wiser, and her style of dressing was a big plus with the ladies. Franky was our role model, and Dennie and I would spend hours trying to get the right stance and practicing Franky's half-smile while lowering our eyelids into this sleepy kind of a way look. It must have worked 'cause the women all thought it was sexy. We got our wink down, too. Franky didn't talk much, but she said the right wink was important in picking up women. One wink from Franky would make a girl blush and send her slipping off the bar stool.

Yeah, Franky loved the women, and they all loved her. When she died, every woman she had ever been with came to her funeral —even the ones she had hurt. Franky was good to her women, but she couldn't stay faithful. No matter how much she told you she loved you, somebody would always come around and turn her head. Next thing you know, Franky and her girl would be break-ing up, and off she'd go with the new one. It would last until the next girl came around. Each girl thought she'd be the one to settle Franky down. There was one girl, though....

It was the year before Franky died. She must have been forty-seven and just diagnosed with breast cancer. Franky tried to make a joke out of it by saying she didn't need any tits. She didn't want them anyway, and butches shouldn't have to put up with them. "Tits were for femmes, and for butches to play with," she'd say. But underneath it all, I knew Franky was scared. We kept her secret between the three of us until Nora came around....

One Friday night, we were hanging in our favorite bar. It used to be called Rusty's and was owned by a straight couple until this older Filipina woman bought it, and then it became The Hideout. We liked Mahogany, too, which was around the corner, but that was a classier place and the place to be on a Saturday night when the rented limos would pull up and the women would be decked out in semiformal to formal clothes. It was like a prom night, except we were all dykes. Mahogany was primarily a Black lesbian club, and the most beautiful women in the city hung out there. The Hideout, our regular bar, was kind of a neighborhood place. It had a cozy roadhouse type of a feeling to it, with a few tables in dark corners, a jukebox, a small dance floor wedged between the bar and the tables, and a back room with a pool table. It was the place to be when the night shift let out. There was a military base close by, and the Navy girls would show up from shore leave still in their uniforms, and once in a while an off-duty dyke cop, but that was a rare thing because they were really in the closet. The Hideout had it all—the strippers and hookers, sanitation workers, and the nurses. You could tell who wasn't working that night 'cause, depending if you were butch or femme, they'd be the ones wearing regular suits or dresses.

So one night this pretty Filipina came in. We found out from Billy the bartender that her name was Nora, she was thirty-seven, had been in the U.S. for about a year, and was new to our bar scene. Nora was a critical-care nurse and worked the four-to-midnight shift. There wasn't much to do after her shift, so she kind of wandered in off the street after hearing rumors that "the place in the back alley on Camac Street was a lezzie bar."

I'll never forget how Franky went crazy when she saw her. She was on a date with her girl, Barbara; but when Nora came through the door, Franky thought up every excuse to take Barbara home. I remember her telling me, "You take Barbara in the back room and teach her to shoot pool. I gotta check out this chick at the bar." Franky was so out of control about her passion for Nora that her girlfriend noticed and ended up walking out on her. For the rest of the night, Franky was free to do what she wanted; but what nobody seemed to notice was that Dennie had managed to get all of Nora's attention and the two of them were now engaged in a slow grind on the dance floor. I was kicking myself because I wanted Nora, too. The three of us never dated white women, had gone out only with the Black and Puerto Rican ones, but none of us had ever seen a femme from our own culture in the bars. I just didn't know how to act.

When she first came in, she sat at the bar, her white uniform hidden under a long raincoat. She kept her back to us, and I didn't notice how sexy she was until she brushed her hair off her shoulder. I guess it was the movement of her hand, graceful and seductive at the same time, and the way she moved her head, first to the right and then to the left. She sighed—tired, I guessed. And when she unbuttoned her coat, I could see the uniform was tight around her breasts. They were small, but shapely, and I wanted to run my hand down her open cleavage and grab what I wanted to be mine. Any other time, I would have made a fast move; but like I said, she was a femme Filipina, and the thought of it stunned me.

Franky, being twenty-one years older than me, was a little bolder and tried a couple of times to cut in on their dancing, but Dennie and Nora were oblivious to her advances. I couldn't believe little baby-faced Dennie, who looked more like a teenage boy, had scored this gorgeous older woman. Frankie was more upset than I was. She wanted to go home right away. "Let's get the fuck out of here!"

I wanted to stay because we still had about two hours before the bar closed, but I knew this thing with Dennie and Nora could take all night, and if Franky left, I'd have to ride the last train home by myself. I was a little drunk and didn't want to be a lone target for the butch bashers, so I left with Franky.

* * *

Dennie came home a little after seven the next morning. Franky and I woke up, having slept in the living room all night. It was a custom in our house to wait up until everyone was in and safe; unless you had a steady girl and it was assumed you'd spend the weekend at her place. With three butches in the house, there wasn't too much room for privacy.

Dennie tried to slip past the sofa where Franky was lying and got caught up in one of Franky's bear hugs. "Where you think you're going? Sit down—I wanna talk to you."

Dennie tried to get away from Franky's steel grip. "Aw, lemme alone Franky, I just wanna go to sleep. I'm tired."

"You're not going anywhere till you look me in the eye and tell me you got laid last night!"

I stayed out of it when Franky picked up Dennie and sat her squarely on the couch. I had to admit, I wanted to know, too.

"So did you get laid last night, or what?"

Dennie looked Franky in the eye and shook her head. She knew it was useless to try to talk us into leaving her alone. If it involved sex and girls, we wanted to know all about it. "No. I didn't get laid. I took her home, and she kissed me on the cheek."

"Oh, so you didn't have sex with her. So how come it took you all night to come home?" Franky wasn't giving up yet.

"Well, we stayed until the bar closed, and then we went to the Savoy for breakfast and talked for a while, and then I took the train with her to her place. She lives really far away, Franky, like almost out of the city."

Franky was mad. "You could have called me! What if you were killed somewhere? What were you doing riding home with this chick you don't even know, and she didn't even invite you to stay? She's probably one of those spoiled bitches that you're never going to see again!"

Now Dennie was yelling. "I don't know what you're so upset

about. You're always the first one to volunteer to walk a lady home! I remember when you first met Barbara, you rode home with her in a cab and then took the train home by yourself. Did I get upset? No. And I am gonna see her again. She's a nice girl, Franky. I got her phone number, and I'm goin' out with her next week!" I could tell Dennie was so happy now, she forgot all about their argument. Franky turned her back and started out of the room, Dennie following her. "So where you going, Franky? Let's all go out for breakfast." Franky stomped up the stairs to the bathroom. "I'm going to take a shower and go out and get my hair cut!" She slammed the door behind her.

Dennie looked confused and hurt at the same time. "What's the matter with her?"

I followed Franky's lead up the stairs. "I don't know. I'm going upstairs and back to bed."

The rest of the week breezed by, and Friday night we went back to The Hideout. It was always the same. The butches vying for the femmes' attentions. And of course the femmes were all over us, especially on Franky. We carried on as usual until a few of the older butches stopped by our table and congratulated Dennie on "scoring Nora," and the femmes complimented her on her new suit. I had to admit, Dennie was more dressed up than Franky that night.

By 12:15, Dennie was nervous. She kept adjusting her tie, and every five minutes, she'd ask me what time it was. The atmosphere was getting tense, and every time Dennie mentioned Nora's name, Franky would go off and talk with an old friend.

At 12:30, Nora finally came through the door, and all eyes were on Dennie, who rushed to meet her.

The next couple of weeks were just as tense at our house. Anytime Dennie talked about Nora, Franky would change the subject or find an excuse to leave the room. Dennie's feelings were hurt. She wanted Franky's approval and Nora's acceptance into our small circle of family. Finally, Franky called a house meeting. She was moving out, she said, "'cause I need some privacy and you kids are drivin' me nuts. Besides, I might meet a nice girl like Dennie did and settle down." She looked Dennie in the eye when she said it and tried to look casual, but I'd known Franky for a long time and noticed the tightness of her jaw and the glare in her eyes. What's going on? I thought. And then I remembered the look that passed between Franky and Nora. The flush of color in Nora's cheeks and the look of excitement in Franky's eyes the first few moments of their meeting. I realized that Franky saw Dennie as her competitor, with Nora as the prize, and Dennie had won. For the first time, I worried what was to become of their friendship. Of all our friendships? I met Dennie through the bars, but Franky and I had always been friends from our first handshake at the printing plant when I was just a sixteen- year-old printer's apprentice and Franky was already in her late thirties. That was 1967, just ten years ago, and I remembered every little detail like it was yesterday.

Franky finally moved out a few days later. Dennie had spent the night at Nora's, and I was left to follow Franky from room to room, checking and rechecking that she didn't leave anything behind. I told her if she left anything, I'd be glad to bring it by. She said she didn't need any help and put her few belongings in a couple of army duffel bags. "You wait, kid, we're going to have some wild parties in my new place." She said she was tired of being the "father figure," and Dennie and I were old enough to be on our own, but we'd always be a family, and we'd still hang out in the bars together. As I watched Franky walk away, my intuition told me things would never be the same again.

* * *

It took us a few weeks to get adjusted to Franky not being there. Dennie blamed it all on Franky's illness, and I didn't have the heart to tell her it was Nora. I was still hanging out with her, but Dennie and Franky hardly crossed paths. When they did, if Nora and Dennie were together, Franky was always in a hurry to meet her date or catch up with some other friend. The lies went over Dennie's head, but it was all too obvious at least to me, that there was some kind of psychic erotic foreplay going on between Franky and Nora.

It was New Year's Eve and Billy from The Hideout had her annual party. Everybody was dancing in the living room, and I guess Dennie had gone off to the bathroom. I went to get another beer and found Franky and Nora alone in the kitchen. The lights were off, and Franky had her backed up against the refrigerator trying to kiss her, and Nora wasn't putting up too much of a fuss. I was in shock. The three of us had made a pact that we'd never steal each other's girls. I left the room as quietly as I came in and went to find Dennie. After all, she was my friend, my roommate, and Nora was her girlfriend, and she had the right to know what was going on.

Everybody was mad at me for telling Dennie. Billy told me it was none of my business, but Dennie was one of my best friends, and if some butch was making out with my girl behind my back, Dennie wouldna' pretended she didn't see anything.

Franky denied everything, and Nora asked Dennie to please take her home. Dennie was angry, and I could see she was really trying to hold back the tears. "I'll deal with you later Franky Aguilar!" And she shoved her way through the small crowd that gathered on the porch ready for a fight.

I put my coat on and made ready to leave, too, but Franky caught up with me halfway through the door. She made a move to grab me, and I pushed her away. "That was really fucked up,

Franky. I knew you had a crush on Nora, but I never thought you'd act on it. Can't you see Dennie's in love with her?"

She yelled back, "You're the one who's fucked up! Why'd you have to tell Dennie that shit? It was only a little kiss, and Nora wanted it. Besides, Nora's never been in love with Dennie. It's me she wants, and now you ruined it!" Franky was drunk and getting dangerous. She jabbed her fingers into my shoulder.

I knew there was no way to avoid the fight that was coming. "C'mon, Franky, you think you're so tough. Let's go down the street and duke it out!"

We found a vacant lot halfway down the block. Franky took off her tie and jacket as I rolled up my sleeves preparing to fight with the best friend I ever had. I felt like Dennie did; like crying, but I knew there was no turning back. If I could erase that whole evening from my mind, I would have done so gladly. Franky's fist connected with my jaw, and I punched her in the stomach. She hit me in the eye, and I went for her nose. We pounded each other for a few minutes, both thinking it was crazy. We were losing our friendship over a woman who would never share the past that we did, and never share the same loyalty that Franky and I had for each other. We realized it, and we realized the bond that held us together as butches was too strong to end that night. I wasn't angry anymore, and neither was Franky. We had fought out our aggressions, and there wasn't anything left to fight over.

For the first time in months Franky and I spent the night together at her place. Me on the couch, and her on the floor.

Dennie and Nora never made it as a couple, and they broke up soon after the party. It was a long time before Franky and Dennie spoke again. Dennie met a Puerto Rican girl named Cecelia, and after a respectable amount of time, Franky started seeing Nora.

What Franky never counted on was that Nora was a typical Filipina. There's an old saying in our culture that Filipinos marry for life, and Nora wasn't any different. Franky bought her candy, perfume, and courted her for months before Nora agreed to sleep with her. And even then, Franky told me, they slept in the same bed, Nora with her nightgown on and Franky in her underwear, and they never did make love. "Wow!" I thought. "Franky must really be changing," when she told me it would be too disrespectful to touch Nora before they were even going together. Franky still had a girl on the side, and she was very careful not to cross paths with her when she was with Nora. Before you know it, Franky stopped going to the bars, and she and Nora were living together. I was the best man at their wedding 'cause Dennie was still mad.

That last year for Franky was rough. I'd go over their house once a week for fried fish and adobo. Then it dwindled down to every couple of weeks. Franky finally had her mastectomy, but the cancer had spread to her lymph nodes and she started chemotherapy, which caused her to lose weight and lose her hair at the same time. She was always tired, but still managed to smile, and she and Nora seemed so happy together. And me—I was a wreck. I was losing one of my oldest and best friends. Dennie had a new girl, Franky was dying before my eyes, and I was still single with no one to hold me at night. I was scared I'd lose my two best friends and end up like the old bulldaggers sitting drunk at the bar. The ones Franky always warned me about.

Dennie and I were still roommates, and I was careful not to mention Franky's or Nora's names in the house. One night I was going to see them when Dennie stopped me in the hallway. "Hey, when you see Franky, tell her I said hi." I was surprised.

I didn't know if Dennie knew that Franky wasn't going to live much longer, but it was time. "Yeah," I said, "I'll do that. It's time, Dennie."

Nora blushed and looked away when I told them what Dennie said. Franky averted her eyes, and her shoulders slumped as though she had the weight of the world upon them. There was silence until Nora laid her hand gently on Franky's and said, "It's time, Franky."

Franky turned her head. The tears were beginning to show and I knew she was thinking about the day, eleven years ago, when her, Dennie, and I formed La Macha.

"Yeah, you're right, baby. Look, Jamie, tell Dennie not to be a stranger around here."

That night Nora walked me to the door. "Please tell Dennie I'm sorry for any hurt I caused her, and tell her to bring her new girl for dinner next week."

I mumbled something like "It's time," and we both knew those words had a double meaning.

Franky died at home a few weeks later. That old dyke had never let a man touch her, and she left it in her will that in death her body would be handled only by the women she loved. It was part of our culture to have your loved ones spend the last night with you, and Nora, Dennie, and I held hands with Franky and guided her through those last steps of her life. Franky said she had never felt such love, and they were to be the last words she ever said.

At her funeral, Franky had only the best of butches and the most loving of femmes carry her body to its final place. She was buried as she lived—surrounded by the people and lifestyle she loved, which is the best tribute anyone could ever give to a friend.

DAMASK ROSES
Angelica Dillon

When I have money, I will buy her flowers. She likes country roses, the kind that have rich, full blooms, petals fading in various hues. Sometimes she picks them from a garden in one of the upper-class neighborhoods, late at night, when nobody is watching.

When I have money, I will take her to expensive hotels. I will rent the penthouse suite and order room service for her. Anything she wants. I will hire a masseuse to ease all the kinks from her muscles, to rub her body with almond oil until her skin has the golden shine of an ancient Egyptian goddess.

She doesn't ask me for anything, not anything like this. She simply smiles at me when she gets home from her job at the grocery store, sets her feet on our coffee table, and thanks me sweetly when I bring her a glass of cheap red wine.

Sometimes we make love on the living-room floor with the curtains open so that moonlight fills the empty space. Her hair is a shade of pale red, almost pinkish, like a tiger-striped kitty's. When the moonlight hits it, her hair seems woven with golden threads.

When I have money, she will wear gold. I will buy her strand upon strand, and she will stand before the mirror, naked, save for those expensive knots of gold around her white throat. I will spread her on a bed filled with goose down and make love to her while she wears those shining strands. They will sparkle in the tears that fill my eyes when I come. They will blend into her skin until it seems that she herself is woven of those magic threads.

She doesn't ask me for jewelry. She sits with her feet on our wobbly coffee table, and she closes her eyes. I've worked all day, too, but I have more energy. I sink to my knees on the floor and I take her feet in my lap and I rub gently, lovingly, with my thumbs along the balls of her feet, in the curves of her arches, cupping her heels in my hands. She sighs, with her eyes still closed, and she says, "Oh, love, that feels good."

Next I run her a bath. I light candles on the ledge of the window and on the counter. When I have money, I will pour bottles of champagne to fill her tub. The bubbles will refresh her and they will make the secret, special place between her legs tingle and tickle. She'll squirm as the bubbles find their way inside her, and she'll laugh at me and touch my lips with her fingers.

When I dry her off, I will lick the champagne from the nape of her neck. I will lie her down on a snow-white bath towel, and I will lap every drop of champagne from the valley of her stomach, from the lips of her sweetness, tonguing in between those lips to taste her own liquid, her own treasure.

She says she's fine with the cheap wine I can afford. She smiles at me when she sees the candles all around the tub, the candlelight hiding the crack in our mirror, the places in the wall where the tiles have fallen. She says she doesn't mind that we don't have money, that we can't travel to faraway places, that we are still paying off school loans and car loans.

Sometimes, late at night, I sneak out of our bed and I drive to the neighborhood where the houses are big. Sometimes, I park my car and walk along the sidewalks that line the park-sized lawns. I know it's bad but I pick flowers from the gardens—flowers that I can never afford—and I hurry to my car and drive home so that she'll have roses by the bed when she wakes up. I want her to breathe in deeply in the morning and smell the rich, haunting fragrance of the roses that she adores.

At dawn, she stirs in my arms and she inhales and she smiles, still half-asleep. She curls herself around me for warmth, finding my lips and kissing me until I am dizzy with want. I return her kisses. I part her lips with my own and play dancing games with her tongue. I kiss her cheeks and her eyelids and her earlobes. I make love to her face with my lips, leaving no part forgotten. She smiles as she falls back asleep. She presses her mouth to mine and whispers, "Thank you."

And when I have money, she'll have roses all the time.